P9-CQM-565

Murther &
Walking Spirits

Also by Robertson Davies

Murther &
Walking Spirits

ROBERTSON
DAVIES

VIKING

VIKING
Published by the Penguin Group
Viking Penguin, a division of Penguin Books USA Inc.,
375 Hudson Street, New York, New York 10014, U.S.A.
Penguin Books Ltd, 27 Wrights Lane, London W8 5TZ, England
Penguin Books Australia Ltd, Ringwood, Victoria, Australia
Penguin Books Canada Ltd, 10 Alcorn Avenue, Suite 300,
Toronto, Ontario, Canada M4V 3B2
Penguin Books (N.Z.) Ltd, 182–190 Wairau Road,
Auckland 10, New Zealand

Penguin Books Ltd, Registered Offices:
Harmondsworth, Middlesex, England

First Viking Edition
Published in 1991 by Viking Penguin,
a division of Penguin Books USA Inc.

Copyright © Robertson Davies, 1991
All rights reserved

A signed first American edition of this book has been privately
published by The Franklin Library.

Publisher's Note
This is a work of fiction. Names, characters, places, and incidents either are
the product of the author's imagination or are used fictitiously, and any
resemblance to actual persons, living or dead, events, or locales is entirely
coincidental.

Originally published in Canada by McClelland & Stewart Inc.

LIBRARY OF CONGRESS CATALOGING IN PUBLICATION DATA
Davies, Robertson.
Murther & walking spirits: a novel/by Robertson Davies.
p. cm.
ISBN 0-670-84189-7
I. Title. II. Title: Murther and walking spirits.
PR9199.3.D3M87 1991
813'.54—dc20 91-29844

Printed in the United States of America
Set in Bembo

Without limiting the rights under copyright reserved above, no part of this
publication may be reproduced, stored in or introduced into a retrieval system,
or transmitted, in any form or by any means (electronic, mechanical,
photocopying, recording or otherwise), without the prior written permission
of both the copyright owner and the above publisher of this book.

For Brenda

Printers finde by experience that one Murther is worth two Monsters, and at least three Walking Spirits. For the consequence of Murther is hanging, with which the Rabble is wonderfully delighted. But where Murthers and Walking Spirits meet, there is no other Narrative can come near it.

(Samuel Butler: 1612–80)

Contents

I

Roughly Translated

I WAS NEVER so amazed in my life as when the Sniffer drew his concealed weapon from its case and struck me to the ground, stone dead.

How did I know that I was dead? As it seemed to me, I recovered consciousness in an instant after the blow, and heard the Sniffer saying, in a quavering voice: "He's dead! My God, I've killed him!" My wife was kneeling by my side, feeling my pulse, her ear to my heart; she said, with what I thought was remarkable self-possession in the circumstances, "Yes, you've killed him."

(2)

W HERE WAS I? I was surveying the scene at close range but I was not in the body that lay on the floor. My body, looking as I had never seen it in my life. Had I really been such a big man? Not a huge man, not a

3

giant, but six feet and rather heavy? So it seemed, for there I lay, in my not-very-well-pressed summer suit, a contrast to my wife and the Sniffer, who were both naked, as they had leapt from the bed – my bed – in which I had surprised them.

A cliché of human experience, but a novelty for me: husband finds wife in bed with lover, lover leaps up, discloses concealed weapon and strikes husband a severe blow – much too severe, it now appears – on the temple, and husband falls dead at his feet. My astonishment, as I have said, was greater than anything I had ever experienced before, and I had no room for indignation. Why on earth had he done it? And was it true that he could not undo it, as both he and I devoutly wished?

The Sniffer was losing his nerve, had shrunk back toward the bed and was sitting on it, weeping hysterically.

"Oh shut up," said my wife, fiercely. "We've no time for that. Be quiet and let me think."

"Oh my God!" the Sniffer wailed. "Poor old Gil! I never meant it. I didn't! I couldn't! What's going to happen? What will they do to me?"

"If they catch you, they'll probably hang you," said my wife, "so stop that noise and do exactly what I say. First of all, get some clothes on. No – wait! First wipe that damned thing on a tissue and then put it back in its case. There's blood on it. Then get dressed, and go home, and take care nobody sees you. You have five minutes, and then I'm going to phone the police. Hurry up!"

"The police!" His fright was so farcical that I laughed, and realized that they could not hear me. The Sniffer was wholly unmanned.

No so my wife. She was manly and decisive and I admired her self-command. "Of course the police," she said. "A man has been murdered. Right? It must be reported immediately. Right? Have you worked on a newspaper and you don't know that? Do what I say, and be quick about it."

Had these two been lovers? What tenderness was to be felt now? The only sign my wife gave that her nerves were shaken was that she had returned to her old trick of interposing that interrogative clincher "Right?" into her conversation. I thought I had broken her of that, but in this moment of crisis she reverted to type. She had never been what I call a good writer. No serious regard for language.

Moaning and snuffling, the Sniffer began to pull on his clothes; his foolishly elegant clothes, of which his newspaper colleagues made such unceasing fun. But he did as he was told. His first act was to use a tissue to wipe the ugly metal cosh that had sprung from inside his beautiful walking-stick. The handle of the stick, when it was unscrewed, was also the handle of the cosh, and now he screwed it back into its hiding-place. How proud he had been of that nasty weapon, against which I had warned him countless times. People who carry weapons are certain at some time to use them, I had said. But he thought the thing dashing, and a sign of his dangerous masculinity, his macho ostentation. He had paid a lot of money for it in a famous London shop. Better than a sword-stick, he said. But why did he want either a sword-stick or a bludgeon? Now he knew the good sense of what I had told him. Miserable little wretch! A murderer. My murderer.

I was angry still but I could not help laughing. Why had he struck me? I suppose it was because when I found the two *in flagrante* I spoke jocosely, angry though I was.

"My God, Esme, *not* the Sniffer?" I said.

And in his fury, fed, I suppose, by sexual excitement, he fetched out his weapon and clouted me.

He dressed, but did not look fully his accustomed smart self. He crept around my body, that almost blocked the door, and went into the living-room of our apartment, heading straight for the drinks cupboard. He took out a bottle of cognac.

"No," said my wife, who had followed him. "Remember? 'Never touches a drop till after the show.'" She laughed but he did not. The old joke, which he had used so often about so many actors who were given to the bottle, could not raise a smile when it was turned on himself. He put the bottle back. "Wipe the neck where you've touched it," said my wife. "The police will be looking for dabs."

Dabs! Fingerprints. What a command she had of detective-story lingo. I was full of admiration for her coolness. He turned at the door, plainly asking for a kiss. But she was not now in the kissing vein. "Hurry up," she said, "and take care not to be seen."

He went, as smart a murderer as you could hope to meet in a day's march, though his face was tense with pain. But then, who notices when they meet a theatre critic whose face is tense with pain? It is one of the marks of the profession.

(3)

T HE MOMENT HE was gone my wife, still as naked as the breeze, set about tidying up the bed. She put it to rights, then she hopped into it and made an impression of single occupancy. Next, some tidying in the bedroom and two glasses rinsed and dried in the bathroom. Then a quick but careful examination of the floor; she fetched a carpet-sweeper and swept the rug. She dampened a face-cloth very slightly and wiped all the surfaces that the Sniffer might have touched. Oh, but she was a methodical woman!

I watched her with admiration and a strong charge of erotic feeling. A naked woman may be enticing when she lies on the bed, ready for love, but how much more beautiful she is when she is at work. The muscles of her back and legs moved so elegantly as she plied the sweeper! The fine curve of her neck as she searched for dabs! What made her so lovely at this moment? Excitement? Danger? Crime? For she had been witness to a murder, and might well be thought an accessory.

Now, the telephone. "Police?" she said; "a man has been

murdered. My husband. Please come at once," and she gave our address. Not a bad actress. For the first time her voice betrayed emotion. But there was no emotion when she had been assured that the police would come. Quicker than I would have thought possible she wiped off her make-up, which had been somewhat smudged in her raptures with the Sniffer, put on a nightgown and a dressing-gown, combed her hair – and then mussed it in what I suppose she thought was an appropriate disarray. Then she sat down at her desk – her desk, for she was going to prepare a story – to wait for the police to ring at the door of the apartment building.

　　She did not have to wait long.

(4)

Of COURSE YOU want details. Who are these people?

　　The Sniffer, to begin with. His name is Randal Allard Going, and he insists that you get it right – Allard Going – because it is a distinguished name, as names go in Canada. One of his great-great-great-grandfathers – Sir Alured Going – had been a Governor in our part of the world in the colonial days, and there is a memorial tablet to him in the old church at Niagara-on-the-Lake which proclaims his virtues in the regretful prose of his time: "His Character was too Great to be described, and yet too Good to be concealed . . . truly Humble without Affectation, Grave without Moroseness, Cheerfull without Levity . . ." and much more in the same encomiastic style. But the history books have little to say about Sir Alured, and the likelihood is that he was simply one of those nonentities who were sent by the Motherland to her colonies because he needed a job and was not influential enough to be given one at home. But in the Canada of his day he was a big toad in an obscure puddle and was well able to hold his own in that group of early settlers of good family whom the Sniffer likes to refer to as "the squirearchy," and whose passing he regrets and wishes to perpetuate in himself.

He assumes what he believes to be a distinguished air, his manners are a little too elaborate for his place in the modern world, and he dresses formally and indeed ostenta-tiously, for although he is a young man – thirty-two, I believe – he always carries a walking-stick. In keeping with his pretension, he feels that he needs a weapon always about him, and the stick, which conceals in its length the cosh with which he struck me down, is his constant companion. He is not physically a large man – rather a squirt, indeed – but he thinks of himself as a d'Artagnan. He would have preferred a sword-stick but, as he explains to the very few people to whom he confides his secret, the cosh is more appropriate to our time where mugging is not unknown, even in godly Toronto.

One cannot dismiss Allard Going as a fop or a fool, because, in spite of his eccentricities, he is quite a capable journalist and does his work as a theatre critic pretty well, though not as well as I, his editor, would like. I did not appoint him to his position on *The Colonial Advocate*, the newspaper (the very good newspaper) on which I serve as Entertainment Editor; I inherited him from my predecessor. I have not myself been more than three years in my job – or what was my job before the Sniffer retired me permanently.

The Sniffer's nickname, which he hates, is a newspaper joke. He writes criticism of modern plays in which it is his delight to detect "influences," and his way of introducing such influences as put-downs for new writers is to say – too often, but I have not been able to break him of the trick – "Do we sniff an influence from Pinter (or Ayckbourn, or Ionesco, or even Chekov) in this latest work of Mr. Whoever-it-is?" Whoever, that's to say, the Sniffer wants to reduce to his lowest common denominator. The Sniffer is certain that nobody who writes a play, especially a first play, in Canada can be original in any important sense; he must be leaning upon, and dipping into, the work of some playwright of established fame, most often an Englishman. The Sniffer is one of the vanishing breed of Canadians for whom England is still The Great Good Place.

Of course his colleagues on the *Advocate*, who are a facetious lot, as journalists tend to be, call him the Sniffer, and the boys in the Sports department have gone farther, and hint darkly that he really is a sniffer, and gets his sexual fulfilment by sniffing the bicycle saddles of teen-age girls. This is especially galling to the Sniffer, who fancies himself as a Byronic ladies' man, and indeed is one, as his success with my wife makes clear.

He is not popular, although because of his ability he must be tolerated. Twice the wags at the Press Club have nominated him for their annual award as Asshole of the Year, but in the final election he has always been nosed out by some superior claimant, from the world of politics. He is not popular, I shall say, among men. With women it is another matter.

My wife, the latest conquest of the Sniffer, is far too good for him, and until I came upon them in bed I refused to believe the rumours which kind friends were careful should reach my ears.

My wife is also employed by the *Advocate*, though not in my department; she is in Features, and is high among our most popular columnists. She writes about women's affairs, in the broadest sense, and does so with discretion and conviction. She is not a snorting feminist, though she is firm in her determination to get for women anything to which they have a right, or even a less certain claim. She urges greater political action upon her sisters, she champions the right to abortion, she is particularly good in the realm of compassion, that powerful journalistic emollient, and is strong in her defence of beaten wives, incestuously tormented children, and bag ladies in their bewildering variety. In all of these things I support her and admire her zeal, though her prose gets on my nerves.

Her name is Esme Baron. She was christened Edna, a

name of some biblical resonance, but as a schoolgirl she took
against it, and told her parents firmly that she was going to be
Esme; she knew that it was originally a man's name, but
possibly in an early manifestation of her enthusiasm for the
female cause she claimed it for herself; if anyone wanted to
think she was a man, they were free to do so. She advanced
rapidly as a journalist, and at the time of my murder she was
making some progress as a broadcaster. If not precisely a
beautiful woman – but who can be precise about beauty – she
undoubtedly had a beautiful figure, and an attractive, serious
face. She had in a high degree the power to make you think,
when she was talking to you, that she considered you the
most significant person in the world, and she was able to
project this invaluable trait into her broadcasting; hundreds
of thousands of listeners were convinced that she was talking
to them, and them alone. With this rare gift, was it strange
that she should be thinking about a career chiefly in broadcasting, and was drawn to the Sniffer, who seemed to have
influence in that sphere? Even so she had been drawn to me,
when it looked as though I could further her career as a
journalist. If that sounds unkind, I do not mean it. I loved
Esme very much, and if she did not love me quite as much, or
without some measure of calculation, I am certainly not the
first man to find himself in that position.

    I do not propose, however, to excuse her for her betrayal
of me. She could have told me she was tired of our marriage,
and I suppose something might have been done about that.
She might even have told me that she preferred Allard Going,
and after I had recovered from laughter and incredulity, I
suppose we might even have done something about *that*, as
well. If she had wanted a fling with the Sniffer, I suppose I
could have put up with it, for a while. Perhaps she was not
perfectly sure that the Sniffer could deliver the goods she
wanted, and would have brought up the matter with me at a
later time, when his influence was made clear, and his price
made clear, as well. I don't think for a moment that he wanted
to marry her; his image of himself demanded a succession of

conquests, not anything permanent. An artist (and he included himself in that category, for if criticism is not an art, what is it?) must be free.

I suppose all this sounds second-rate and tacky, but it was not our fate to live on a higher moral level in the world in which we found ourselves. That I should be killed, however – that put the affair in a different and lurid light.

(5)

ND I, the murdered man? My name is – was – still is, I suppose, Connor Gilmartin, and I am the Entertainment Editor of the *Advocate*. Thus Allard Going is one of my staff; I suppose I should call him a colleague, because it is not my way to lean too heavily on the writers who work under my direction; I recognize their right to a good deal of freedom in their work, and my directions are given more as suggestions than as orders, though there are times when I disagree totally with what they say, and the way they say it. It is woefully hard to find good, or even merely literate, writers, and they laugh at me when I say that sloppy, go-as-you-please writing carries less authority than decent prose. You must remember our public, they say. And indeed that is what I do, and I think the public is fully able to deal with the best they can produce. Patronizing the public, and assuming that it hangs, breathless, upon what it reads in the papers, is almost the worst of journalistic sins.

My parish, as Hugh McWearie calls it, includes not only the writers about theatre, ballet, opera and films, as well as music, and painting, and architecture, and of course the book editor and his reviewers, but also some odds and ends – the stamp columnist, the astrology columnist, and the religion columnist. I even have a place under my umbrella for our restaurant critic, known in our trade as Madam Greedygut.

They ought to be in Features, where Esme is, but in some ways our paper is ill-organized. McWearie, who writes about religion, is, I suppose, my best friend, which many people find strange, for McWearie, a stern Scot, is not on first acquaintance a particularly attractive fellow. I like to go to his office now and then to smoke a pipe, for Hugh is an unrepentant smoker. Anti-tobacco zealots, of whom my wife is one, have persuaded the General Manager to outlaw smoking in all the public and general rooms of the building, but he did not go quite so far as to say that people might not smoke in private offices. I do not smoke in my own office, for Esme says I must set an example, but I sneak off to Hugh when I want tobacco and good conversation.

Is that enough about me, for the present? As I wait in my apartment, observing my wife, who has no awareness of how near I am, I am amazed to see her go to a locked drawer in her desk, take out a package of cigarettes and light one. She smokes near a window, and carefully blows the smoke outside. She must be more shaken than she admits, or she would never revert to an old habit. She used to be a two-package-a-day woman, in the time when smoking was part of her persona as a woman of the world, and an angel of public compassion.

(6)

T HE POLICE COME. They are commendably prompt in answer to her call. No need, surely, to describe the scene that follows. A doctor examines me, and measures, and makes careful notes. Detectives measure, and examine, and make careful notes. A constable with a stenographic machine takes down my wife's statement. She is a little uncertain about the time of my murder; she loses a few minutes somewhere and who is to know but I? Understandably she cannot be too explicit, for she now permits them to see that she is shaken and distressed – more so than I have observed since my sudden taking-off. They remove my body, and I discover that I am in no way tied to it; indeed, I feel no impulse to follow them, for I know what nasty things they are going to do with it, and where they are going to store it until they have found out all they can from it. I prefer to stay with Esme, because I want to see what she will do in this unusual situation.

To my astonishment, I have begun to feel hungry, but this familiar sensation abates as soon as the police have wrapped my body in a winding-sheet of coarse cotton and carried it away. I recall having been told by a biologist that the digestive process continues for something like forty-five minutes after death, and clearly the carcass that is lugged to the waiting truck is still busy at its work.

(How do medical people know this particular piece of *post mortem* information? My friend told me that it had been established as long ago as 1887, when two curious French physiologists, Regnard and Loye, examined the bodies of two decapitated French criminals in the cart in which they were lugged away from the guillotine. One thinks of Regnard and Loye, hacking and peeping in the jolting cart, as the horses dragged them toward the murderers' graveyard. What devotion to science!)

When my body is taken away, my hunger goes with it. My gut and I have bid farewell forever. But my powers of observation are at a peak.

My wife's performance for the police filled me with admiration. What an actress was lost to the stage when she chose journalism. Perhaps if her television career develops as she wishes, that brilliance may not be wholly lost.

She displayed a refined dramatic sense, not sobbing or giving way to hysteria, but like a woman of strong character who finds herself in a trying position and is determined to meet it with courage. She would not embarrass the young constable who took her statement, but from time to time she hesitated, and I could see how deeply he felt for her.

She told her story briefly and well, for she had been rehearsing it before the police came. Lying in bed, with some of her work as a crusading journalist spread about her, she had heard sounds from the little balcony outside the bedroom window. Before she could investigate a man pushed aside the long, sliding window which was also the door to the balcony. He was surprised to find her in bed. He menaced her with a weapon he held – a cudgel of some sort – and warned her not to cry out. No, he had no identifiable accent. At that instant I had come into the room from the adjacent sitting-room and rushed at the man, who struck me a forcible blow and then escaped through the window as I fell to the floor. No, she could not describe him except as a man of perhaps thirty years of age, dressed in a T-shirt and jeans. He was dark and was either unshaven or had a scrubby beard. (A man, I thought, like ten thousand other men.) She had rushed to my aid, but I was dead. Yes, she had felt for a heartbeat, a pulse, but there was none. She had then called the police.

The other policemen were trying to discover how a man had reached a balcony seventeen storeys above the ground; he must have come from a nearby apartment, climbing from one balcony to another, dangerous though that was, but he had left no marks.

As a man who had, for a few years, served his time as a theatre and film critic, I was delighted with Esme's performance and her subtle management of the scene. One or two of the cops, I sensed, found her irresistible, and hated to leave. Was this the woman I thought I knew as my wife? How fully does one ever know anybody?

When the police have gone, I watch as Esme helps herself to a stiff drink, returns to bed and, as she is not yet sleepy, reads some reports on the frequency of wife-beating in the city of Toronto, but I do not think she takes in much of what she reads. After an hour or so she falls asleep, and in time a film of bee's wing coloration forms on her full lower lip.

(7)

J UST WHAT OF Randal Allard Going? To my delight it was easy to remove myself to his apartment. I did not fly, or float; I simply wished to be with my murderer, and behold! I was. I found him in what I suppose I may call a pretty pickle. He had tried to steady his nerves with a lot of whisky, but had only made himself sick, and had vomited with extraordinary force until he could vomit no more, and now lay in his bed, weeping. Not presentable, dramatic weeping. No: racking sobs, as though he could not get enough oxygen.

I was not touched by his distress. This fellow had killed me, and I saw no reason to forgive him. No, indeed. I decided that, in so far as my unaccustomed condition would permit, I would hound him down, and revenge myself upon him in any way I found possible. What that way would be I had still to find out, but my determination was total.

(8)

M Y FUNERAL RITES were a comedy beyond even my expectation. Newspapers are very good to their own, and my murder was a front-page story. A smudge, said to be a picture of me, was well displayed. I was popular, I found to my astonishment. My colleagues regarded me as a first-rate journalist. (Well, that was true.) A fine career had been brutally interrupted. (Would my subsequent career have been fine? And what might the word fine imply, in the circumstances? But obituaries do not quibble about such things.) I was married to Esme Baron, the well-known and widely admired columnist on feminist affairs, a friend of the poor and afflicted, a writer of moderate but firm opinions. We had no children. (It was not said that Esme had refused to have any, though the obituarist, who was obviously my friend McWearie, knew it.) All of this was sober and pretty well factual. It was the funeral which moved into the realm of comedy and even of fantasy.

It was a church affair. Esme and McWearie had a fine row about that, for Esme had no use for churches, but McWearie had insisted that I was a Believer – a word he loved and used somewhat immoderately – and must be buried like one. So, to a small Anglican church adjacent to the crematorium my carcass was conveyed and there I drew a full house of my newspaper associates who showed themselves, like most journalists, men of strong emotions. Newspaper people like to be thought of by the public as tough, hardened creatures, made cynical by the procession of crime, political duplicity and public shenanigans that passes continually under their gaze. My experience is that, apart from policemen, they are the most sentimental people you will meet anywhere. And so at my funeral they sat in rows of weeping men and grim-faced women (for in our day there has been a reversal which makes it perfectly all right for a man to give way to feeling, whereas women must show no such weakness) as the parson read the ancient burial service and read it, I thought as a former theatre critic, pretty well, though I could have given him a few pointers about emphasis and the value of pauses.

I suppose it is not astonishing that one should be moved by one's own funeral, but I had not expected one tribute Hugh McWearie had prepared for me. He had been put in charge of the funeral, on behalf of the paper. Who else, as a special friend of mine, and the Religion Man of the *Advocate*? Esme had been satisfied to leave the details of the affair to him, though he consulted her, as a matter of form, about everything. The paper had not been mean. There was a handsomely printed Order of Service and I was stirred to find that the only hymn was a favourite of mine, and of Hugh's. It was Bunyan's hymn, from *Pilgrim's Progress*, and Hugh had insisted on Bunyan's own words and not the watered-down modern version. My colleagues were not great singers, but they did their best, and I rejoiced to hear the final verse:

> *Hobgoblin nor foul fiend*
> > *Can daunt his spirit;*
> *He knows he at the end*
> > *Shall life inherit.*

I rejoiced, though I think I would have trembled if I could have known how prophetic the words were.

I took the hymn as a splendid compliment.

> *His first avowed intent*
> > *To be a pilgrim.*

Yes, I suppose now that I no longer had to pretend to a Canadian modesty, which can sometimes sink to a Gee Whiz, Aw Shucks simpletonism, the hymn told of what I had meant in my life, whenever I could collect my thoughts together enough to discover a meaning. I had wanted some self-recognition, as a path to – to what? In what path had I been a pilgrim? Was I now to find out?

The hymn gave nobility to the service. Farce was provided by the Publisher of the *Advocate*, who spoke the eulogy. He did not know me; I suppose I had shaken hands with him half a dozen times at newspaper functions. But he had been assured by the Editor-in-Chief and also by the General Manager that he ought to make an appearance and a strong statement on this occasion, because of late there had been two or three assaults on newspaper men – cameras broken, some shoving, one punch on a sensitive newsnose – and here we had a murder. It is part of the received wisdom of the press that newspaper men, like priests and pregnant women, should be immune from violence, however much they may be thought to provoke it, and somehow the idea had taken hold among the great ones of the *Advocate* that my profession had something to do with my murder. The killer was not a frightened, probably doped, hoodlum; he was surely some outraged poet or affronted actor who had sought revenge for being sorely wronged in the entertainment pages of the paper. There must be a stop to such enormities, and the Publisher, as the principal figure in the hierarchy of the paper – not to speak of the moneybags – was the man to speak out for the profession.

The Publisher, however, was no speaker. He was a finan-cier of the backroom type, a small, stone-bald, unremarkable man whose money commanded great power. The eulogy had been written for him by the Editor-in-Chief, who had col-laborated with the General Manager on the purple paragraph which spoke of the iniquity of killing a newspaper man. Surely this was an attack on freedom of speech, and on that much touted and widely misunderstood windegg, the free-dom of the press? In the fuss that had followed my death, Esme's statement to the police that the man had been sur-prised and frightened, and had pretty clearly been a robber and not a vengeful artist, had been forgotten.

The eulogy was typed for the Publisher in large print, but he made a bad job of reading it. There was a paragraph, surely written by McWearie, that spoke of my intellectual interests, which had lent distinction to the Entertainment section. This was handsome, for the paper had the traditional journalistic fear of scholarship as being over the heads of its readers. But as I was dead, a whiff of scholarship could do no harm, so long as it did not give my successor dangerous ideas. The eulogist spoke of my concern with metaphysics, which was also described as scholarly. Nobody but McWearie knew that I cared a damn about metaphysics, or that I was no more than a bewildered amateur in that murky realm. But McWearie had, with the kindest intentions, put the best face on the long conversations, descending often to undignified wrangles, which I had had with him in his office. McWearie deserved to be called a metaphysician, for he had given the best of his life to such speculation, and he was my tutor, and not, as the eulogy suggested, an equal in those talks. I was grateful to Hugh for his kind words, and was even persuaded that I had been a little more intelligent than I had supposed. I have always thought of myself as an unappeasably curious, but not particularly bright, fellow in my concern with things of the spirit.

It was in McWearie's paragraph that our Publisher came to grief. There were words he did not know, and had not asked his secretary to look up for him. He had sought no guidance about pronunciation. I could tell from his struggles that he had not even troubled to look over the eulogy until the time came for him to read it. So he emerged as the clown of the funeral, and even people from the sports and advertising departments, who were certainly not themselves metaphysicians, stopped weeping or looking grim, and could hardly control their laughter as he struggled and fumbled through what was supposed to be an expression of his personal estimate of a valued employee.

Thus my funeral might well have ended as a farce, if Esme had not redeemed it by a fine stroke – or what seemed to everybody present except myself to be a touching gesture. Touching is the proper word, for as the parson spoke the committal, she stepped out of her pew and laid a gently caressing hand on the coffin, above where my face might be presumed to be, and then returned to her seat with finely controlled emotion. A flash! An alert photographer had captured the moment for tomorrow's *Advocate*. *Widow's Farewell*.

It was at this moment that I heard my mother gasp. She and my father had been self-possessed and dignified; they had not smiled at the Publisher's performance. But Esme's bit of theatre was almost more than they could endure. Poor dears, I thought, they are beginning to look old. I had not noticed it before. And certainly they had never "taken" to Esme, though relations between them were civil. They were the saddest, and least demonstrative, people at my funeral.

There was a muted humming of machinery, and my coffin moved slowly toward the doors beyond which presumably lay the furnace, or the antechamber to the furnace, and the Publisher, nudged by the General Manager, took Esme's arm and led her out of the chapel.

Am I cynical about this final farewell by a grieving wife? I suppose, as in so many situations in life, I was both right and wrong. She had loved me once, I am sure, but she had never been greatly demonstrative, and certainly not in public. She walked firmly, gracefully, solemnly out of the chapel on the arm of the Publisher – not easily managed, for he was much shorter than she was – without a glance at the spot where, in the third row of seats, Randal Allard Going was making an ass of himself.

He had broken down and was sobbing noisily. Two women colleagues assisted, and indeed almost manhandled, him toward the door. One of them had to recover and press upon him his famous walking-stick, without which he was never seen in public. The murder weapon, and now he could never be rid of it.

I was laughing uncontrollably as I joined the procession, right behind him, so that I should not miss a snivel or a tear. I was a free spirit, free to go wherever I wished. I did not want to go with my body beyond the crematory doors. This scene from life's unceasing comedy was too good to be missed.

(9)

Now THAT THE excitement of the funeral and the inquest is over, I have time to take stock of myself and my situation. Immediately a philosophical, or metaphysical or perhaps merely physiological question arises: what self am I talking about? And why do I speak of "having time"? My sense of time has gone; day and night are one to me; there are periods – long, so far as I can judge – of which I have no awareness. I have no substance. I have looked in vain in the mirrors in my apartment for my reflection, and there is none. I have no physical appetites but I have keenly experienced emotions; no hunger, no drowsiness, but a mounting anger tempered with hilarity as I watch the misery of my murderer.

I have not yet tested my powers, for I am still a green hand at this business of death, and I have no clear idea of what my powers may be. Can I haunt Going? I have never given any consideration to the matter of haunting before, and what I recollect from ghost stories does not especially appeal to me. To be a crude spectre, appearing in doorways or discovered squatting by the fireside when people enter rooms, is out of the question for such a spirit as I. My intended prey lives in an apartment, and has no fireside; I shall certainly not make a fool of myself squatting by his thermostat. No, no; the conventional ghost business is not for me.

Of course there have been ghosts in the Henry James manner, ghosts who assert themselves as influences or invasions of the mind; ghosts who are seen only when the observer is in a state where certainty about what is seen is out of the question. I might try that, or perhaps I should say more discreetly that I may hope for that. I do not feel that I can be definite about what I shall do. Oh, for an hour's talk with Hugh McWearie!

McWearie would know, or at least he would have some opinion backed up by his learning in such matters. Hugh is an odd duck, a man who had been ordained in his youth as a Presbyterian minister; he had assumed that solemnity to please his parents, but he could not endure it and defected to be a journalist commenting on religious matters, and devoting himself to the study of metaphysics. But even as a metaphysician he was out of step with his contemporaries. He simply would not consent to be of his time; Hugh was a pre-Kant man, and to him the fact that an idea was three hundred or three thousand years old did not in the least invalidate it. In such things, he would say, there is no question of progress forward; the journey is always inward, where time is measured by a different clock. But as the inward journey is necessarily taken alone, how much credence may we give to what is said by those who undertake it? Is it wholly personal, or is some part at least of general validity?

"My answer to that," he had once said during one of our collogues in his office, when I put the question to him, "has to be a qualified Yes, conditioned by a prudential No. These matters require what I think of as the Shakespearean cast of thought. That is to say, a fine credulity about everything, kept in check by a lively scepticism about everything."

"That doesn't get you anywhere," I said.

"Oh, but it does. It keeps you constantly alert to every possibility. It is a little understood aspect of the Golden Mean. You were speculating about the afterlife. You can believe anything you like, with a good chance that you're wrong, because nobody knows anything about it."

"Yes, but what about these 'after-death experiences' that are so much discussed nowadays? People who have been pronounced dead, and who have been brought back to life by electric shock or something of the sort, and who report that they stood outside themselves and saw and heard the doctors working over their supposedly dead bodies? There are too many of those to be dismissed."

"Ah, yes – well – but they are never absent from the body for more than a few minutes. Suppose the electric shock doesn't work, and they don't return?"

"Lots of them have said they didn't want to return. They were well pleased to be wherever they were and dismayed by the idea of returning to all the trivialities and petty burdens of life."

"They returned, all the same, or you wouldn't know what they said. What about those that don't return? What do you suppose happens to them?"

"Nobody knows."

"Quite a few people have thought they knew. Orientals of all kinds have been eloquent on the subject, and believe me it isn't any simple Christian Heaven they postulate. One of their great notions is that after death comes a waiting period before rebirth. A lot of them are very great on rebirth."

"Reincarnation?"

"In a sophisticated sense. You scramble up and down on the great ladder of Nature, and when you've made it as far as Man you can be Man in wide variety – pig-man, dog-man, monkey-man, as you struggle toward Buddhahood. That's the great aim, you see, and it carries great privileges. The Lord Buddha, before he came to earth for the last time in human form, took pains to make sure that he was born at the right time, into the right nation, into a suitable family, with a worthy woman to be his mother. He took no chances. Pernickety, for a god, wouldn't you say?"

"I thought you were scornful of accepting Eastern religious ideas into Western religious thought?"

"Cautious, yes: scornful, no. I don't believe in trying to turn Westerners into Easterners. People who have failed at Christianity aren't likely to make great Buddhists. You can't neglect the demands of geography and race in determining what people can seriously believe. But you don't have to; Swedenborg was quite definite about a waiting-period after death, and he was as Western as they come."

"I don't know anything about Swedenborg."

"You and too many others. A great man, but not an easy man. A fine scientist, who then became what people call a mystic, because he talked about what couldn't be seen or proven, but could be speculated on by a man with the right sort of intelligence. Himself, in fact. If you don't know anything about Swedenborg, I presume you've heard of William Blake? Yes? Well. You don't have to look insulted; I can't count on anybody knowing anything in these bad days. And I suppose you've read all the poems, and skipped the Prophetic Books."

"My professor said they would not be required reading."

"Aye, too difficult for tiny minds. Remarkable stuff. Like struggling in porridge, which nourishes you richly as you drown. Well, anyhow, Swedenborg, and I expect Blake, would both have found a lot to make them nod their wigs in the descriptions of the Bardo."

"The Bardo?"

"That's the Tibetan term. State of being, roughly. It would frighten you out of your wits, some of it. The Encounter With The Eight Wrathful Ones, for instance. Rather like walking naked through a very long car-wash. Darkness, terrifying noise, and all the while you are slapped, spanked, squirted on from above and below and mauled and insulted until at last you emerge into the light, cleansed and humbled and ready for rebirth in whatever form you now merit."

"I'll skip the Bardo," I said.

"If you can. Anyhow, I doubt if it would be the same for you as for a Tibetan monk. You're a Celt, like myself. If there is a waiting-period for us after we peg out, I rather hope it will include some encounters with Arawn, or Brigit, or Arianrhod, or Gwen of the Three Breasts."

"All goddesses?"

"I'd rather take my chances with a goddess than with the Eight Wrathful Ones. What reason have we to suppose that Ultimate Reality isn't feminine?"

"We were both brought up with a prejudice in favour of a masculine God."

"That's one of the reasons why I hung up my gown and fled from the pulpit. These male gods – damn them – all law-givers and judges. All eternally right. No chance there for the Shakespearean cast of thought. No, no, my lad; it is the Eternal Feminine that leads us aloft, as Goethe very finely said at the end of his eighty years."

"Oh God, Goethe. I thought you'd get to him."

"Yes, Goethe. Worth a regiment of your theologians."

It was hopeless to argue with Hugh. The Celtic spirit raged in him, when his pipe was drawing well. If he had a god – a male god – it was certainly Ogma, the Celtic god of eloquence. To the Celts speech, not silence, was golden.

With such a man argument was futile, for he had a fine command of irrelevance and irrationality, and out of it, I must say, came a splendid wildness of theological speculation, where all beliefs had their own validity, to say nothing of their own absurdity. It was refreshing to be reminded that one's range of intellect was so trivial, in the face of great mysteries.

(10)

WHERE ARE THE great mysteries? I appear to be stranded in a state of nothingness, in which no hints reach me of anything to come. Feelings I certainly have. Emotions, perhaps I should say. I feel a humorous relish for what I can still observe of the world from which I have been untimely ripped. Esme has already written a couple of good articles telling her readers how she copes with bereavement, and I know that now she is thinking about enlarging on this theme, and writing a how-to book for widows. What do I feel about that? My affection for Esme is not precisely waning, but it is changing, and her brisk opportunism is beginning to grate. As for Allard Going, though it amuses me to see how miserable he is, and to follow the tortuous arguments by which he attempts to convince himself that he is not really a murderer, but an ill-used toy of circumstances, I despise him, hate him, and am determined, if I can manage it, to do him some notable harm.

He has robbed me, in the most grievous way. He has robbed me of a possible thirty years of life. I never, while living, thought of my life expectancy in quite this possessive fashion. But now I am obsessed by thoughts of Hugh McWearie's admonitory picture.

It hangs over his desk, and at the top it is plainly labelled

Degrés des Âges. I gather that it was a picture familiar enough
in simple homes in France, but not often seen in the New
World.

It is a picture, a print, of the journey of life. Over a
curved bridge marches Mankind, male and female. At the
bottom of the bridge, on the left, two infants lie in a cradle,
heavily swaddled and smiling in carefree innocence. Up the
curve of the bridge marches Childhood, Youth, Maturity and
then – as the curve begins its descent – the marching couples
portray Decay, Old Age, and at last arrive at a couple lying in
bed in their hundredth year, again like infants, but now
hideously wrinkled and toothless, labelled *Âge d'imbécilité.*
Right back to their beginning, indeed, but without that
hopeful journey ahead.

To judge by the dress of these people I should date the
picture, or chart, at about 1830; they are depicted in gaudy
colours, for this was an example of the art of the people, not a
sophisticated composition. The possible fate of the travellers
is also represented; a conventional Christian Heaven, pre-
sided over by a smiling, embracing, bearded Creator, awaits
the good, and for the bad lies a Hell with horned and tailed
tormentors; these two possibilities are labelled *Jugement
Universel.* I suppose this thing was intended for simple people
to hang over the bed, side by side perhaps with a Plenary
Absolution, for which they had laid down good money.

I used to amuse myself by placing my colleagues on the
Advocate according to their time of life, and speculating which
of the two opposed fates awaited them. Hugh deplored such
facetiousness.

"It's verra crude," he would say, "but not without merit
for all of that. Look at it and think about it seriously, if you
have a serious bone in your reprobate body."

"But I do," I would say. "Look – there's the Sniffer, and
see how gallantly he is arming that handsome woman at his
side. No doubt about it, he's in *L'Âge viril.*"

"Aye, aye. And who's the woman with him? Not his
wife, of course. Undoubtedly somebody else's wife. A fine,

sonsy lass. Perhaps she's really the wife of the man on the next grade, labelled *L'Âge de maturité*. Quite a decent figure of a man, wouldn't you say? What did you tell me your age was, Gil?"

"Forty-four," said I.

"Ah, well – *L'Âge de maturité* right enough. He looks a bit simple for maturity, though that may just be the crudeness of the drawing. A bit self-satisfied, I would say myself."

"That's because you belong in the next rank," said I. "*L'Âge de discrétion*. It makes you sour about anybody behind you."

He never commented on that, and now I know that he was trying to hint to me that the Sniffer was seen rather too often with Esme. He took her with him to a lot of the plays he attended professionally. My work did not give me as many evenings for the theatre as I should have liked. I never paid much attention to their evenings together.

A bit simple, I see now. A bit self-satisfied.

And now, beyond question, I had been hustled out of life before my time. The Sniffer had robbed me of a possible thirty or forty years. Without being one of those rapturous creatures who declare that they love life, I certainly enjoyed it deeply, if perhaps a little dully, and did not want to miss a day of what I felt to be my due. Fool! That was my life and my marriage, which Going – and I suppose Esme cannot be wholly exempted from complicity – had invaded cynically and trivially.

Fool! And because I now see myself to have acted like a fool, I do not hate Going any the less. More, indeed.

(11)

HUGH AND I often talked about marriage, and I teased him about his single state.

"If a man aspires to the condition of a philosopher, and I do that, with proper humility," he said, "he knows that philosophers are either unmarried, or their wives are slaves or tyrants. I could not reduce any woman to slavery, because that would be unworthy of an enlightened man, and I certainly have no wish to live with a tyrant. We exist in a time that is supposed to be cynical about marriage. Popular prophets predict that it cannot last long as a social institution. But I respect marriage too much to trifle with it. Also, I fear my own Woman, who would probably betray me."

"What woman are you talking about?" said I. "Have you been hiding some Highland beauty from us, Hugh? Tell all. Who is this mistress you hint at?"

"No, no; you don't understand. Listen to me. Every marriage involves not two, but four people. There are the two that are seen before the altar, or the city clerk, or whoever links them, but they are attended invisibly by two others, and those invisible ones may prove very soon to be of equal or even greater importance. There is the Woman who is concealed in the Man, and there is the Man who is concealed in the Woman. That's the marriage quaternity, and anybody who fails to understand it must be very simple, or bound for trouble."

"Is this some of your Oriental philosophy?"

"The farthest thing from it. It's not fanciful, it's physiological. Even you must know that every man contains a fair number of female genes, and every woman has her masculine genes in some proportion or other – probably quite substantial. Is it fanciful to think that those genes, those numerically fewer but not necessarily inferior elements, never assert themselves?"

"Oh, come on Hugh! You're pushing it too far!"

"I'm doing nothing of the sort. You're a man of some discernment. Do you have no hours when you find yourself unexpectedly intuitive or forbearing with Esme, or maybe in a quarrel you become a wee bit hysterical and bitchy - which is the negative aspect of that same wisdom and mercy? And Esme, now – consider her substantial career. Do you honestly think she has never had to call on powers that carried her over a rough patch, and gave her strength to bear what she thought she might not be able to endure? Or – I don't want to intrude on your marriage – but are there never times when she seems simply coarse and domineering? Think, man, and think clearly. If your marriage has not made you aware of those other people who live with you and Esme – with you and in you – you're asking me to think it's a far more primitive affair than I am ready to believe."

"What did you mean by saying you feared your own Woman?"

"I have a disposition toward tenderness within me that could make me a slave, if the condition favoured that. Or it might make me a snarling, ugly devil, whose home was a hell. That's what feminine feeling does in a man, when it goes sour. I've never met a woman who would have me whom I felt I could trust in the same house and the same bed with my own Woman."

"You make marriage sound even more difficult than the popular marriage counsellors."

"Of course it's difficult, you gowk! Too many people trust to love, which is the worst of guides. Marriage is no game for simpletons. Love's just the joker in the pack."

(12)

Is THERE ANY point in remembering these talks with Hugh now? Yes, there is, though it is uncomfortable to recall how lightly I took them, simply as amusements to refresh me during my work of reading endless copy written by critics and commentators, most of whom seemed to me to be wide of their mark.

I remember so much. Indeed I remember with greater clarity than when I was alive. I remember now something that Hugh McWearie once dredged up from his apparently inexhaustible reading about matters of the spirit, and of the life after death. In the *Bhagavad Gita*, said he, it was firmly stated that after death one attains the state that one was thinking about at the moment of death, and so it behoved a man to be careful of what he thought of as he died. As usual, he was diffuse and sometimes incoherent on that point. He talked about Famous Last Words.

"Which was that English statesman who is said to have died exclaiming, 'My country! How I leave my country!' Was it Pitt? Or was it Burke? But somebody else reports that he said, 'I think I could eat one of Bellamy's veal pies.' What was his fate? A splendid brooding over the history of England, or an eternity of veal pie? If there is anything in what the B.G. says, it behoves us to be very careful what we say or even think in our last moments."

What I had said at *my* last moment was an astonished, derisive question to my wife: "My God, Esme, *not* the Sniffer?" Nothing much there. But an instant beforehand I had been settling a problem incidental to my newspaper work; we were shortly to have a large and important Film Festival in Toronto, and our best film critic had left a month ago to take a job in some university where he was to give courses in film work. (God help them, those wretched students; he knew little enough about anything but the emotions that fuelled his work as a critic.) Who was to write about the most important films that would appear? The Sniffer wanted to do it. He had told me so rather offensively, as if reminding a forgetful child of some obvious obligation. And just as I took that fatal step into my bedroom I had decided that I would have to do what the Sniffer wanted, not because I had any particular faith in his ideas about films, but because there seemed to be no better way of meeting the difficulty. But I was determined to see those films myself.

It was an editor's problem. I had been made head of the Entertainment section of the *Advocate* because I was a good critic. Good, that is to say, from the reader's point of view because what I wrote was much appreciated. It was the old error of management: take a man out of a job he does well, and make him a boss, for which he has little liking or ability. The theatrical forms of entertainment have always been my great delight and recreation, and I write about them with gusto. Theatre, yes; opera, most decidedly; even television had its place in my affections. But for films I had a special affection, though not for the reasons that possess the majority of critics; I did not care much for technicalities of film-making, though I knew a good deal about them; I never treated film actors as real actors, because their work does not allow of the full range of the actor's art and they are the creatures of the director and his technicians; I was gentle in my dealings with the writers, for I knew how little those poor wretches amounted to in the film world. But for a handful of truly great directors I had a warm-hearted admiration; they were artists, working in an especially recalcitrant medium, and when they succeeded they brought me great dreams. Dreams, not of a crass reality, a thin-spirited comedy, a blockhead's notion of tragedy, but of the stuff that lies just beyond the observable, everyday world, that world of the daily news and the club gossip. Dreams in which something significant is told, not in bold Civil Service narrative, but in a puzzle of ambiguity and omission.

When I went into a movie house to see something made by one of these great men, I felt that the half-darkness, the tunnel-like auditorium, spoke of that world of phantasmagoria and dream grotto of which I was aware as a part of my own life, which I could touch only in dreams or waking reverie. But film could open the door to it, for me; film therefore had a place in my life that I had never tried to define,

for fear that too much definition might injure the fabric of the
dreams.

So of course I wanted to attend myself and write the
reviews of these great films, retrieved from splendid archives,
which were to be so much a feature of this Festival. Ah, but as
an editor I had to play fair. I could not grab all the best jobs for
myself, as the loss of my film critic strongly tempted me to do
in this case. The Sniffer must have his way, damn him!

But I shall be there. Yes, I shall be there. A favourite
quotation of my father's rises in my memory –

> *My soul, sit thou a patient looker-on;*
> *Judge not the play – something-something –*
> *Something-something – every day*
> *Speaks a new scene – and so forth –*

I can't recall it exactly, but beyond doubt I shall be a patient
looker-on.

Suppose McWearie was right. Or rather, suppose the
Bhagavad Gita is right. Is my eternity to be unending movies,
sitting beside the Sniffer, as he sniffs for influences?

That would be Hell indeed, or at least a Purgatory worse
than any McWearie had ever described. An eternity of
watching dearly loved movies, at the side of a man who, in
my opinion, had a shallow, self-serving, nincompoop's attitude toward them? My murderer, furthermore. Can it be?
Have I deserved this?

In the true sense of the word, I have been roughly
translated, without the complicity of a normal death, into
another sort of existence. Can I face what awaits me? What
choice have I? An unauthorized translation has always been a
shady sort of narrative.

II

Cain Raised

THE FILM FESTIVAL was prepared for film zealots of all kinds, and was to occupy them for a full week. New films from all over the world were to be shown, and prizes and awards and assessments were offered to tempt the best and challenge the most aspiring. A somewhat unusual feature was to be a showing of historic films, notable films that few people had seen, and films that had been, for one reason or another, suppressed. Great film archives had been ransacked, and persuaded to allow precious reels to leave their vaults; guarantees of safety had been exacted by the Moscow School of Cinema, by the Cinématique Française, by the Reichsfilmarchiv of Berlin, to ensure that their perishable nitrate-based prints should be cherished as they deserved. The organizers of the Festival assured the public that it was the most extraordinary assemblage of hitherto forgotten or neglected films – each one a masterpiece, deserving of breathless scrutiny by those who regarded the film as the great art form of the twentieth century – that had ever been put together. A large and costly program had been prepared for the Festival as a whole, but the most space and the most exultant prose had been reserved for these reclaimed jewels.

This was the part of the Festival that excited the Sniffer, for surely it would be rich in influences and forgotten injustices and anticipations of film techniques that had been attributed to the wrong people; he would gleefully right such wrongs.

The grand opening, which I attended as the shadow of Going, was what one might expect. It took place in a large, enclosed space in one of our best hotels, which could not be called a room, because it had no focus, no centre of interest; nor was it a hall, because it had no architectural concentration to point an audience in any single direction. It was simply a huge, carpeted area, windowless and in no way associated with either nature or art, and its multitude of electric lights could not wholly dispel its cavern-like quality. It was approached through a long tunnel-corridor, hung with modern tapestries, from which masses of yarns hung out at intervals, as if a bull had gored them and their entrails were bursting forth. Otherwise the great space was entered by almost invisible doors, through which waiters and waitresses came and went, bearing trays of jewel-like edibles, the work of artificers whose days were passed in preparing these destructible beauties. Although air was intruded and removed from it mechanically, the space smelled of many such earlier functions; a compound of food and ladies' scents.

The Lieutenant-Governor of Ontario was patron of the Festival, and as he was the patron of many ambitious and deserving ventures it was not expected that he should show much knowledge of what was happening, but that he should shed the light of his countenance upon it and appear as host of this party, which our provincial government gave in its honour. He did so, with a fine demonstration of viceregal goodwill, greeting people he hardly knew, or did not know at all, with the warmth appropriate to his office. He himself was resolutely democratic, but his hovering uniformed aides, and the splendour that attended his appearance, made it clear that he was indeed a grandee, though of course one who owed his place to the approval of the people – which meant, in effect, the government in office. A curious grandee, surely, for though he bore the democratic stamp of approval he was primarily the representative of the Queen. The provincial premier was not present because he had to be two hundred miles away, warming up the voters in an important by-election, but his wife came, gracious in the highest degree but also unaffectedly democratic. Ontario wines, and especially Ontario champagne, flowed without stint, and were consumed in quantity befitting the occasion. They too were democratic – quite without affectation of superiority. The guests in the room were in evening dress, and those who possessed the Order of Canada wore their enamelled marks of distinction with pride tempered by democratic *bonhomie*, as though to say, "I wear this because I have been awarded it, but I am very much aware that there are many here more worthy of such meritorious ornaments than my humble self."

It was, indeed, one of those Canadian occasions where the vestiges of a monarchical system of government vie with the determination to prove that everybody is, when all is said, exactly like everybody else. These disquiets are inseparable from a country which is, in effect, a socialist monarchy, and is resolved to make it work – and, to an astonishing degree, achieves its aim; for though an egalitarian system appeals to the head, monarchy is enthroned in the heart.

It is not in human nature to set aside all ideas of rank. The Lieutenant-Governor and his lady shouldered the task of mixing these ingredients into a fine, eager assembly of film enthusiasts, but their best efforts could not fully mingle the Socially Prominent, the Very Rich, and the Intelligentsia into a smooth broth. Here and there the Socially Prominent and the Very Rich were united in couples who glowed with a special radiance of certainty, but there were bigwigs and moneybags whose eyes moved restlessly as they felt that they should blend, but did not quite know how to do it. As for the

Intelligentsia, they were chiefly critics, and it was they who stayed closest to the bars, and sometimes looked at the others with what might have been interpreted as scorn. The aristocracy of intellect admits nothing of democracy.

Going felt no uncertainty. He was, after all, socially prominent as a descendant of one of the old families, wearing about him the glory of Sir Alured, that long-dead colonial official. Although not himself rich he had rich connections, and they were Old Money, not latecomers to affluence. He was unquestionably, and indeed clamorously, intelligent, for had not the country's foremost newspaper invited him to instruct its readers as to what was, and what was not, worthy of their attention? Although he wore no Order, he had his walking-stick, which was in itself a mark of distinction, and all but a few of those present knew that it was his critical sceptre, and would certainly not have been left in the *garderobe*. All of this was made manifest in his evening clothes, which were from a first-rate tailor, and fitted him elegantly.

He was the only critic to wear a dinner jacket. The others scorned such frivolities, and wore everything from messy turtlenecks and corduroys to tweed jackets and flannel slacks; the woman from a large populist paper wore a rather dirty pullover with loud roundabout stripes, which did nothing for her figure (a lost cause) but was irrelevant because of her critical status, and the rancorous distaste with which she regarded just about everything.

Thus I was present at the Gala Opening, though I was invisible and cost the government nothing, as eating and drinking were no longer within my range. But I was able to watch Going in his glory. Indeed, I had no choice in the matter. As McWearie had said, and as I now recalled with dismay, I was less of a free spirit than I had thought and was now tied to Going, for how long I could not tell.

Indeed, my sense of time was changing rapidly. Time, as we are so frequently assured, and as we so frequently forget, is a relative concept. But if I was tied to Going, in what degree was he tied to me?

(2)

Is THE HORROR of Death the loneliness I feel so overwhelmingly as I wait – wait – wait with a decreasing sense of time as the living world knows it, and an expanding sense of the *pleroma* that enfolds me? I frequent the world of men, but there is no creature of my own kind anywhere, to whom I may speak, or from whom I can hope for counsel or sympathy. Is this a time of probation, or can it be that this is what I shall know for – I dare not imagine for how long? Whatever the answer I must do what I am impelled to do, and now I must go to the movies with my murderer.

(3)

It IS A MORNING session, and by Going's watch it is five minutes to eleven when I go with him into the theatre where the special, precious old prints are to be shown. Several movie houses are engaged for the Festival, and this is the least important as it is assumed that these films of historic interest will draw the smallest audiences. How desolate a film house is at this time of day! It is lighted just enough for the audience to find seats, and the dimness compels a silence and subdues the people who are spread about and fill perhaps a third of the house. There is the half-sanctified air of a funeral parlour about it, and it stinks of children, feet and old popcorn. The walls are painted a shade which would once have been called *vieux rose*. Has it a modern name other than dirty pink? At one end, as one descends a gentle slope, is what looks like a stage, but is not, although it has skimpy velvet curtains inside what would be a proscenium if there were any scene for it to enclose. Movie houses feel an impulsion to imitate theatres, feebly and unconvincingly, just as manufacturers of automobiles cannot rid themselves of the ghosts of elegant nineteenth-century carriages. As Going entered this dismal place a few other critics looked at him, but did not nod or smile. This was not ill-will but professional custom; surgeons do not shake hands with each other in the operating theatre.

The film to be shown was *The Spirit of '76*. It had been produced in the U.S. in 1917 by one Robert Goldstein, who for his pains received ten years' imprisonment under the Espionage Code. The reason? The film was rowdily anti-British, and had the bad luck to appear just as the United States entered the First Great War as Britain's ally. It was suppressed and it was a great coup for the Festival to have unearthed a print. Would it cause outrage now? Most unlikely.

As it was a silent film a woman took her place at a piano in front of the screen, removed her rings and laid them carefully at the side of the keyboard, crunched up a handkerchief and put it on the top of the rings, and, as the first shadows appeared, began to play, and played without a stop until the film came to an end. She was skilled at her job, and ranged through every emotion – from grave to gay, from lively to severe – without ever seeming to change gears. She had an historic sense, and played nothing written later than 1917. She also had a sense of congruity and her moments of sentiment, when she played "Hearts and Flowers," were the sentiment of 1917, offered without irony or comment. Her style was lush – musically unchaste – and she dashed off arpeggios like confetti. In her peculiar realm, she was an artist of no trivial achievement, as must have been many of the women who, in the Old Red Sandstone Period of film, did what she was doing now.

I dwell on her achievement although I was aware of it only fitfully. For almost from the beginning, as I saw grainy images of actors rigged out in a rough approximation of late-eighteenth-century dress gesticulating and moving their lips soundlessly, in some overheated drama of their own, I was aware that I was seeing something else. Seeing, yes and hearing, for my film – *my private film* – was accompanied by orchestral music of great subtlety and modern in manner; my images were clear and convincing; my actors – if that is what they were – spoke aloud. I did not immediately or easily understand them; for, though their language was English, it seemed to be American English of the period of the American Revolution, and it was spoken in a tune and with an accent unfamiliar to me. Mine was an astonishing film, and if I had seen it during my days of life, I would have been delighted with it. But now it frightened me.

Was this what Going was watching? From time to time he scribbled notes on a pad on his knee, and so far as I could read them they had no connection with my film. None whatever. What I was watching was life, strange life, but life without a doubt, and I could enter into it only with difficulty, but with the sense that what I saw was of deep importance to me.

(4)

WHAT I SAW was New York, as it was in 1775. Or was it 1774? I could not be sure. But there it was; John Street, a street of respectable but not affluent houses where lived, so far as I could make out, middle-class families – shopkeepers, lawyers, physicians and the like – and in the one to which my attention was directed, a soldier. There he was, confident and trim, in the uniform of an officer of a British regiment, coming down the three nicely holystoned steps of his dwelling into the sunshine. As he walked down the street, civilian neighbours greeted him. *Good morning, Major Gage. A fine day, Major.* His progress was

stately, not marching but with soldierly bearing, a man proud
in his profession. From his own windows a little girl waved,
and he gave her a smart salute, which was plainly a joke
between father and daughter. To the others who greeted him
his acknowledgement was not quite a salute, but a lifting of
his gloved hand to the foremost horn of his three-cornered
hat, correctly pointing over the left eye. A popular man. A
good neighbour. A credit to the neighbourhood.

Then there was an indication – do film people call it a
wipe? – of passing time, and the music gave a strong hint of
changed circumstances, of poorer weather, of autumn,
indeed, and there was the Major coming down his steps
again. His look was sterner, as well it might be, for running
toward him was a crowd of street boys, shouting *Bloody-back!*
Tory bloody-back! and as they ran past him one of them turned
and hurled a dirty sod which left a stain on the back of his red
coat. The child in the window disappeared, plainly frightened; the Major gave no sign of discomfiture, but walked on
proudly, and this time there was something of the military
march in his step.

The scene changes again, and this time it is inside the
Major's house, where he and his family are at table for their
evening meal. It is a good meal and there are two black
servants – not slaves, but in some ill-specified area of
indenture – to put it on the table. With some trepidation the
little girl, who is the second of the three children, asks her
father about the insult of the morning. *Nothing whatever, my*
dear. It don't signify. Ragamuffins from the poorer quarter, who have
been listening to foolish talk from malcontents. A soldier's daughter
must know that her father will not be popular with rogues, who fear
the law and the army. It is not for a soldier to heed such riff-raff. If he
meets them again let them beware of the cane which is part of his
uniform.

Major Gage talks to his wife later, when they are tucked
up in their pretty four-poster; he admits under questioning
that perhaps the clod of dirt signifies a little more than he
would say to Elizabeth. He has the imperturbable confidence

of an Englishman and a soldier. Is he not an officer in one of the seventeen regiments Britain keeps in her American Colonies, for their defence against the French, and the Spanish, and the privateers and smugglers? To say nothing of the Indians. And are not these ruffians under pretty sharp control? If he meets the street boys again he will dust their jackets.

Mrs. Gage is not so confident. She is not English. She was Anna Vermuelen before she met and fell deeply in love with the Major, and her Old New York Dutch blood sometimes runs a little coldly in her veins when she talks with her Dutch gossips over the morning coffee, for they hear things the British seem not to hear, or at any rate to heed. Downstairs in the parlour there is a fine print of King George III, splendidly uniformed and supremely confident, and the children respect it almost as a holy image, but Anna knows from her un-British cronies that there are rumours that the King is concerned about what his ministers are doing in the American Colonies, and that there is a substantial pro-American faction in London, and even in Parliament, which urges that the grievances of the Colonies be heard.

Of course many of the grievances are all my eye and Betty Martin (Anna has picked up this soldiers' phrase from her husband and likes to use it to show how thoroughly British she has become) and were stirred up by rogues like the notorious smuggler John Hancock and that untrustworthy lawyer Sam Adams. But there are other grievances that are not so easily set aside.

(5)

THERE IS NOT much open talk of these grievances or what ill-will they are causing among the New York people the Gages know, until one Sunday morning when the Reverend Cephas Willoughby speaks of them from the pulpit of Trinity Church, which is the foremost English church in New York. The Gages have a pew and on Sunday mornings they make quite a procession as they go there; the two older children, Roger and Elizabeth, walk first, trying to move as their dancing master instructs, erect yet easy, and with a somewhat duck-like placing of the feet; after them come the Major and his handsome wife, a splendid pair whose deportment is a joy to those who are connoisseurs of such matters; then come the two black women, Emmeline and Chloe, the latter carrying baby Hannah – she is three – in a handsome Turkey shawl; and bringing up the rear the footman, porter and odd-job man James, in a good brown coat (formerly the Major's) and carrying all the prayer-books. When they reach the portico of Trinity they greet any friends in subdued, Sunday tones, before they go to their pew, a box-like affair in which they can enjoy some privacy, and are to be seen with ease only by the clergyman when he mounts his pulpit. There are many of these boxes, and they command a respectable yearly rental; poorer folk sit further back in the church, in free seats. The church is eminently respectable, eminently English, emi-nently Tory, and the service it offers is bland and the music excellent. But today the parson is anything but bland.

He takes his text from Jude, the sixteenth verse: *These are murmurers, complainers, walking after their own lusts; and their mouth speaketh great swelling words, having men's persons in admira-tion because of advantage.* The Reverend Cephas Willoughby makes no bones about the modern exemplars of this wicked-ness; they are Bostonians, almost to a man. And Boston is a high-stomached city. Their pretensions are noble, but their trade is treachery. Some among them are well-known smug-glers, whose wealth lifts them above easy criticism; some are lawyers who would twist the law to their own advantage. They are the filthy dreamers who despise dominion and speak evil of dignities. They would rouse the good people of the American Colonies against the King and the King's laws – yes, and the King's taxes, which have repeatedly been shown to be just imposts, meant to pay the cost of protecting the Colonies against many enemies. *These speak evil of things which they know not – or rather, which they pretend they know not; but what they know naturally* – which is to say from the impulses of their own dark and greedy hearts – *they know as brute beasts, in those things they corrupt themselves* – and would corrupt those whose ignorance disposes them to such corruption.

As a preacher, the Reverend Cephas Willoughby labours under a weight of scholarship which sometimes rests heavily on his parishioners; he has been known to harangue them for two long hours, measured by the sand-glass which stands upon his pulpit, on some obscure point of doctrine. But today he is brief and vehement and his flock are all ears. Can Mr. Willoughby truly be speaking of what, from the pulpit, should surely be unspeakable, so long as it can be kept in the realm of whispered confidence and familiar gossip? Indeed that is what Mr. Willoughby is doing. The Church intervening in politics? Is it proper?

Having made it plain that he intends to talk about the revolutionary discontent that everybody fears, but which has so far not appeared openly in New York, Mr. Willoughby takes a deep and indignant breath as he settles to his task.

What lies behind these murmurings, which are now growing to the pitch of clamourings? Rebellion? Certainly. But rebellion must have a cause, and its cause is not complaint against taxes, and the cost of England's standing army of seventeen regiments in the American Colonies. It is not the popular cry of *No Taxation Without Representation*. It is not the cost of maintaining the various colonial governors, for without them who would mediate between our own elected representatives and our King in London? These are the matters the murmurers and complainers talk of so impudently and contentiously, but the real cause lies deeper.

It lies in the heart of man, where many evil things have their abode and where for a time they may prevail, when the Prince of Darkness gains a supremacy. It was in the heart of Cain that the Evil Prince found a foothold, when Cain rebelled and struck down his worthy brother Abel. And was not Cain abundant in excuses, saying *Am I my brother's keeper? Do not these wicked men who seek to mislead us say the same? Am I to give my help in Britain's wars with France and Spain? What are they to me? Am I not sufficient unto myself?* Dearly beloved, it is not the murmurers and complainers who speak from their own hearts in their tempestuous words. It is the voice of Cain, and through Cain, the Dark Angel himself. It is the Dark Angel who in our America would set brother against brother, and subject against King.

Dearly beloved, I speak a terrible truth unto you: *Cain is raised in our midst!* Cain is raised, and until Cain is laid again we shall know no peace, in this land which our God has so richly framed for peace. Cain is raised, I say to you! *Cain is raised!*

The sermon was a great subject of talk at Sunday dinner tables, and not only among Mr. Willoughby's own parishioners. News of it spread through New York so rapidly that by Sunday evening Presbyterians and Lutherans, yes, even Quakers, were thinking of Cain. For it was better to blame Cain, who was not known in New York, than to blame Patrick Henry, who was, and who had said for anyone to hear that Caesar had his Brutus, and Charles I his Cromwell, and that George III might learn from their example. True, King George was in London, and Patrick Henry was in Virginia, and something must be attributed to the professional loud mouth of the lawyer, but such talk was evil and an incitement to simple folk who did not understand statesmanship. The spectre of Cain seemed to enclose and explain so many things that were whispered of at the coffee meetings. Good wives like Anna were not expected to understand them, but they understood Cain, or thought they did.

"Mamma, what is a bloody-back?" asks Elizabeth when her father is not in the room.

"It is a wicked name for a soldier, my darling, because of his red coat."

"They call them lobsters, and red herrings, too," said Roger.

"You must not heed them. They will be glad to see the red coat when the Indians come. As they may at any minute, if you do not go to your beds at once."

But Roger knows that "bloody-back" means also the soldier who is strapped to the triangle made of four halberds, and flogged for some misdemeanour. Twenty lashes is common; three hundred lashes had been heard of, laid on by a stout drummer. Before the offender is released a pail of brine from the cookhouse is thrown over his bleeding back, to cleanse and heal the cuts. A first-rate soldier, apt for promotion, bears no marks of the cat-o'-nine-tails, but a ruffian, fit for nothing but the lowest service, might have a back that was as rough and furrowed as a farmer's field. The brutality of this punishment is turned against the soldiers by the colonists, whose own choice of correction is tarring and feathering.

As I watch this, I understand that the film-makers, whoever they may be, are taking their acknowledged liberty of compressing the action of months and years into a few scenes. But now actions appear that have a date. Here is the Boston Massacre, as long ago as 1770, but the bitterness has grown with time; the British had fired into an unarmed mob – which they should not have done, but which armed men with nervous officers have done since the invention of fire-arms, and will do again – and although the damage was slight, and only five people were killed, one was the egregious Crispus Attucks, and their funeral was a great occasion of rebellious feeling. Indeed, the British captain was tried for murder, and acquitted, for many people had the uneasy feeling that they might behave no better, if they were in the accused man's shoes. But feeling in Boston is very bad, and it is there, in 1775, that real fighting breaks out.

(6)

Before the Major marched off to fight at Breed's Hill (which should have been Bunker Hill if William Prescott had not chosen the other one, a choice which the voice of popular history has since reversed) he enjoyed one night of especial pleasure, the sort of pleasure he truly relished. For, although he was an excellent family man and did his family duty with satisfaction, the Major liked nothing better than an evening among his fellow officers, where there was plenty to eat and drink, plenty of the kind of conversation that most refreshed him, and often some entertainment of the sort that military men most enjoy.

It is thus I see him the night before his regiment leaves New York for Boston; he goes to the King's Arms in Maiden Lane where, in an upper room, more than fifty fellow officers are gathered for a supper of oysters, lobsters, clams, roast beef (of course), roast mutton, and such trifles as hare and pigeon pie, and turkey, with everything that such dishes demand in the way of garnish, to be washed down with claret, iced hock, Madeira and port, which were probably smuggled, though the officers do not care to hear about it.

It is a great evening, given particular savour by the thought that at last British troops will be getting some serious work, and will undoubtedly vanquish the American greenhorns. They will not hurt them more than may be necessary, but certainly they will show the rebels that high-stomached Boston is no match for men raised on true British beef and beer. Just as they had shown the French at Quebec. They remember the song of that time:

> *With lantern jaw and croaking gut*
> *See how the starveling Frenchmen strut*
> *   And call us English dogs.*
> *But we shall show those braggart foes*

> *That beef and beer give heavier blows*
> *Than soup and roasted frogs.*

They had shown the Mounseers who was who and what was what, and it had cost Old England many millions of pounds to do it. And for what? To protect ungrateful Boston and let the Redskins know the true rulers of America. Let them pay their score, and stop their plagued whining about Stamp Tax, and Sugar Tax. What is the Stamp Tax? An ingenious fellow has worked out that it costs the two million Americans about a penny apiece each month. Can safety come cheaper? This is the tenor of the talk of these happy officers, and they play their familiar tunes over and over without ever tiring of them.

The Major sits at the head of the table, for though his seniority might have been questioned, his name is Gage, and in some mystical way he seems to figure as the Commander-in-Chief. At the other end of the table – Mr. Vice to his Mr. President – sits Major Featherstone, a much decorated officer and a wit in the military understanding of the term.

Toasts are drunk, with less formality than if it had been a fully regimental occasion. It is Gage's privilege to propose the loyal toast: "His Majesty King George the Third," and bumpers are emptied. To Featherstone falls the honour of proposing the toast to Queen Charlotte, which would not have been the case if the officers had been in the mess. No lady's name must be mentioned in the mess. But here the Queen's name is woven by Featherstone into a rhapsody to Woman, or, as he says frequently, The Sex. Without The Sex man's life is but vain, his valour without an inspiration, his hours of ease without sweetness. Without The Sex Mars's sword is unavailing, and Apollo's lyre unstrung. He gives them The Sex. And the officers drink to The Sex with loud acclaim; a retired Colonel, who is not going to Boston on the morrow, falls under his chair from the weight of his emotion, and has to be picked up by a couple of waiters.

A great evening! Oh, a memorable evening, and when

everything has been eaten and there is still much to be drunk, some entertainment has been promised. Ensign Larkin is present; although his rank is inferior to that of the other guests his voice is indispensable. It is a very high tenor, a male alto, and he is an adept at florid ornamentation. Furthermore, he is a dab at the spinet and a good spinet stands at one end of the room. It is the object of many excellent jokes, for above the keyboard it is inscribed *Harris of Boston*, and it is both paradoxical and very proper that it should supply music for those who will shortly show Boston who is who and what is what.

Larkin, who is a pretty youth, sings as prettily as he looks and, although the officers do not know it, I the onlooker know that when he sings the popular air "Anacreon in Heaven" the tune is the one which will later become famous as "The Star-Spangled Banner." But this evening it is only one of many favourites, not as rapturously received as "When forc'd from dear Hebe to go," the verses of which Larkin ornaments so richly that the tune is almost wholly obscured. The pathos of the final line –

If Hebe approves of my lay
Go poets and envy my song

– brings tears to the eyes of several scarred veterans who, like so many men of war, are touched to the heart by the songs of peace.

But Featherstone and the gifted Larkin have a surprise for the company, and as they are settling to an evening of drinking and singing – several attempts have been made to lure Larkin into "Rule, Britannia" – the door opens and an extraordinary figure appears: a raw-boned gandershanks of a boy with one foot bare and the other thrust into a decayed soldier's boot, his breeches out at the seat, so that a tail of his red shirt hangs almost to the ground, wearing a tricorne hat with the flaps unbuttoned, but with a huge bunch of ribbon stuck to it, like a cockade. At his side dangles a monstrous sabre that clanks upon the ground; he carries a rifle that cannot be identified, but which might have been meant to shoot squirrels, with an immensely elongated barrel and a bayonet made from a rusted scythe. He leers slowly at the company, taking them all in with a looby stare, before he spits a good half-pint of tobacco juice on the floor, allowing some of it to dribble down his chin.

"Aw, here ye be, sirries," he cries, in a raucous version of the Colonial accent. "I wuz expectin' ye to Bahston, but ye never come yit. We're a-waitin' fur ye, to be sure. But so's I found ye, I'll sing ye a little song."

By now he has made his way up the room, where he salutes farcically toward Major Gage, and then goes on to the spinet. Larkin strikes up a tune, unfamiliar to most of the officers, and with words that they have never heard.

> *Me and feyther went to camp*
> *Along 'ith Captain Goodin'*
> *And there we seen the men and boys*
> *As thick as hasty puddin'.*

And here the scarecrow breaks into a clownish dance –

> *Yankee Doodle, kep it up*
> *Yankee Doodle Dandy,*
> *Mind the music, mind the step*
> *And with the girls be handy*

Several verses follow, some of them so scurrilous that a few of the officers wonder if they should laugh, concluding –

> *In Bahston was a shoal o' men*
> *A-diggin' graves they told me*
> *So 'tarnal long, so 'tarnal deep*
> *They 'tended they should hold me.*

Then, in clod-hopping retreat –

> *It skeert me so I hooked it off,*
> *Nor stopped as I remember,*
> *Nor turned about till I got home*
> *Locked up in mother's chamber.*

By this time the officers have mastered the chorus, and "Yankee Doodle" is sung again and again, as the actor – a junior
officer who had gained some reputation as a comic country-
man in regimental theatricals – goes through a drill of arms,
in which he drops his sword, tumbles over his shirt-tail, and
at last discharges his absurd gun, from which shoots a mass of
chicken feathers.

Yankee Doodle is the hit of the evening. The officers are
transported. This is the enemy as they think of him. He is
toasted as a mighty fellow, and plied with wine, which he
drinks after he has impaled his quid of tobacco on his bayonet, until he pretends to fall in a stupor.

Anything after this is anticlimax, even the rousing rendi-
tion of "Rule, Britannia," in which Larkin almost destroys
the Boston spinet.

It is not many days later that the British vanquish Yankee
Doodle at Breed's Hill, without heavy losses. But one who
does not survive the battle is Major Gage. So 'tarnal long, so
'tarnal deep, the grave is not all for Yankee Doodle.

Perhaps the Major had been expected to bear too much
responsibility, because of the accident that his name was the
same as that of the British Commander-in-Chief. Such follies do happen, in war and everywhere else; a name is more
important than unimaginative people suppose. But the
Major is dead, and the family in John Street, New York, sees
the face of Cain in its desolating loss.

(7)

IT APPEARS WE are to have an
intermission, for *The Spirit of '76* has come to a rowdy conclusion with George Washington, and the Stars and Stripes, and
a young woman who is probably meant to represent Freedom all tumbled together in a *mélange* which film buffs like
Going greet with excitement as a very early use of this technique. They talk about it in the foyer, where the inevitable
collation has been prepared, and every ticket-holder is entitled to one drink of very thin white wine and one very thin
white sandwich, as long as they last. But these early films are
brief affairs of a few reels, and as soon as the food has been
devoured the audience huddles back into the smelly auditorium to see another retrieved classic about revolution, which
is the theme of the day. It is familiar to many of those present,
for it is the famous *Battleship Potemkin* of 1925, which the
truly knowing ones like Going call *Bronenosets Potemkin*. He
pronounces it slushily in what he believes to be a truly Russian manner.

But what am I to see?

All through the showing of *The Spirit of '76* I had been
peripherally aware of what was on the screen visible to the
audience, while much more powerfully conscious of my own
film, which carried so much more conviction as a true representation of the prelude to the American Revolutionary War.
The old film was about an idea, an historical reconstruction
with a propagandist bias, whereas mine was about ordinary
people who carried a vastly deeper conviction to my understanding. Was I to continue in that vein, or was I to be
whisked off to Eisenstein's powerfully propagandist notion
of the 1905 uprising in the Black Sea fleet, which was famous
for its use of real mobs, for its startling depiction of stone
lions rousing themselves on behalf of the revolutionaries, for
its innovative editing and its splendid music? Apparently not

so, for again I found myself watching and comprehending two films at once, and mine began in the comparative peace of New York.

New York had been cool toward the Revolution in its early manifestations, and it is the lukewarm city of 1776 that I now behold. There were a lot of Dutchmen – British subjects, but still Dutch in the depths of their hearts – in New York then, and many of them were firmly in control of large sums of money. One of these is old Claes van Someren, part lawyer and part banker, and all financier, and it is in his hands that the fortune of Anna Vermuelen Gage is safely lodged. So, when Major Gage has met a soldier's death, it is to him that Anna turns for advice, and his advice is banker's advice: be quiet, be confident and do nothing hastily. Money talks, and Anna has plenty of money in Claes van Someren's careful hands.

Anna is an heiress, and it is upon her fortune that the Major had been able to maintain a manner of living well beyond what a Major's pay would support. By law, of course – that eighteenth-century law which made a wife's property the possession of her husband – everything Anna had was the Major's, but the Major could gain access to it only through old Claes, who was affable in the highest degree, but not very communicative. He had his own ideas about the financial responsibility of English soldiers, and he had put reasonable quarterly sums in the Major's hands without ever giving him a full account of Anna's fortune. Her father, Paulus Vermuelen, had been a close friend of Claes van Someren, and the lawyer had resolved that his ward, who was also his cousin once removed – the Dutch are very strong on the dignity of cousins – should not be despoiled. So the Major, who was a financial innocent and inclined to trust lawyers, had never truly known about the mortgages that were Anna's, or the good farms up the Hudson in Greenbush from which she received substantial rents. Or rather, she did not receive them, for old Claes collected them, and they went into very strong boxes in his place of business, in bags to which her name was attached with strong wire. Not all of these bags, and indeed never quite half of them, ever sweetened the Major's happy life.

Anna was astonished to learn from her old cousin how much money she had, and it is not to her discredit that the knowledge did much to dry her tears. To be a widow is grievous, and Anna loved the Major truly. But between being a rich widow, and being a soldier's wife rawly left, hoping for a pension from the British, there is a great difference. And thus her tears were dried with the finest of cambric handkerchiefs, and old Claes reflected in his lawyer's mind that it is wonderful how money cobbles the broken shoe. He was not a hard old man, but like so many people who handle much money, he was not without cynicism about human emotions.

(8)

THE OUTWARD PATTERN of Anna's daily life does not greatly change. New York is not hot or hasty in its acceptance of the new republic. It is recognized, of course, that a new nation has been born, but there is much doubt as to whether the infant will live. George Washington has been made commander-in-chief of the American forces, and it is known that when he served the British he had been snubbed and overlooked when promotion was possible; the little-minded are certain that this has made him bitter against England, and the more generous are certain that he is above such petty considerations. Nobody denies that he is a man of fine spirit, which cannot be said for all the signers of the famous Declaration, but has he the forces to carry through a war against trained troops? It is whispered that when he beheld some of his forces he was dismayed and said, "Are these the men with whom I am to defend America?" As well he might, for my film allows me to have a look at them.

Compared with the British, who have a marionette-like

regularity and dignity as they drill, and march, and mount guard, these American forces are farcical chawbacons. There has not been time to whip them into a smart army, and it seems unlikely that they would have submitted to such discipline. But they have a spirit of their own, which is more formidable than the British have yet discovered. These farmer boys are deadly shots, and they have a trick of rapid reloading that the British cannot equal. They have fought the Indians, and know methods of what would now be called guerilla fighting which dismay and annoy troops who fight by the book. In pitched battles, such as the defence of New York, the British know exactly what they are doing, and they win. But they are not prepared to deal with a mob who call themselves the Sons of Liberty, and succeed in burning down a large part of the city. In Boston they learn a bitter lesson against firing on mobs. In a melee where the insurgents are not in uniform, how is a British officer to know who is an experienced rabble-rouser and who may be merely an excited citizen, hysterical in the muddle like Crispus Attucks? Let honest folk stay out of mobs and they will come to no hurt.

The Americans too are furious. The sense of fair play that enrages the British against the American irregularity of battle enrages the Americans equally, because General Howe has brought in mercenary Hessian troops – thousands of Germans – to fight against them. When brother turns against brother, is it decent to bring in foreigners from outside the family? The grievance is compounded because these Hessians – not all were Hessians but all were from the German duchies – are splendid fighters, not so lethargic as the British, and their Jäger Corps is the best army in the field. Bringing in foreigners – it is not to be endured, and it adds bitterness to bitterness. It is easy to hate General Howe, who displays haughty British superiority, but he is not feared so much as is von Riedersel, a Brunswicker who is not ashamed to learn from the enemy and quickly trains his men in rapid fire. The Americans are waking up to the fact that this is a real war, and not just a family feud, and that dirty fighting is being met with fighting just as dirty. Both sides are learning that all war is dirty and that the noble deeds on the plains before Troy, about which so many of their officers are well informed, had no reality except in the imagination of Homer. As usual it is the common soldiers, who have never heard of Homer, who know the worst of it.

It is all a muddle, and the women, like Anna, cannot understand why the men have created such a muddle, and cannot find a way out of it. She knows only that there has been destruction in New York city, but that General Howe and his men have it firmly under their control, so far as a city may be controlled where there are so many people who favour the other side. There is trouble about food, but it is not serious for her, because she has money to buy whatever food there is. Claes van Someren is firm in his advice to be quiet, be confident and do nothing hastily, and Anna is careful of what she says, even to trusted Dutch friends, who are just as cautious with her. In time it will blow over.

(9)

I T DOES NOT blow over. The colony of New York, as opposed to the city, has accepted the Declaration of Independence, and it is assumed that all the citizens of the city are waiting eagerly for the day when the British will have to give it up. Roger, who is big enough to do some scouting unnoticed, as boys tend to be, sees the gilded statue of George III in Bowling Green torn down and insulted, and his British heart turns in his breast. His father had heard "Yankee Doodle" sung in derision of the American troops, but Roger hears it everywhere turned into an American patriotic song, with a variety of inflammatory words. Loyal British boys have words of their own, and Anna hears her son singing in the street –

Yankee Doodle came to town
A-riding on his pony;
He stuck a feather in his arse
And called it macaroni.

She beats Roger for singing a dirty song. Or rather, she orders James to beat Roger, and James, who is an old friend of Roger's, conspires with him to accept a noisy but not a painful punishment. But it is undignified and Roger is resentful. His notion of loyal partisanship is already masculine, and he thinks women should keep out of men's affairs. Elizabeth, who has been listening when she should have been at her embroidery, wants to know what macaroni means.

"It means foolishly elegant, like Ensign Larkin," says Anna. She is indignant when, a few weeks later, it is learned that Ensign Larkin has accepted big Yankee money to go over to the rebellious troops, to act as a drill-instructor. There are several such defections, for British pay is not generous.

All of this I see, with an eye cocked now and then at *Battleship Potemkin*, which hammers home the lesson that all rebellions are ill-shaped and bring heavy troubles on those who want no part of them, but cannot get away from them. When Cain is raised, Cain's fury will strike blindly. Roger knows that Loyalist windows - so costly to re-glaze - have been broken in the night by gangs whose blackened faces make them unrecognizable. There is a terrible week when James, the porter and odd-job man, talks too loudly in the tavern about the iniquities of the Americans, who won't fight fair; he does not see the three men in the corner, who lie in wait for him the next day, and lead the gang that tars and feathers him and rides him on a rail through streets where American sympathy is strong. When James manages to crawl home he is in a very bad way, and Anna and the two black women have to nurse him for a fortnight before he is able to take up his duties again.

Tarring and feathering lives now only as a form of

jocose speech, but it was a dreadful and dangerous humiliation. If the hot tar were spread too widely over the victim's
body it might kill him, for his skin could not breathe. The
feathers were a purely decorative indignity, but being
ridden – half naked – on a rail might destroy a man's privates
for any future generative employment, because the rail was
sharp, and those who carried it shook it to bounce the victim
up and down. The tar could be removed with turpentine,
but that could burn if it were too generously applied, so
rubbing with vinegar was the usual treatment, slow and
painful; too generous use of either removing agent left sores
which were slow to heal, despite Anna's generous use of
porter as a balm. For the bruised testicles only compresses
were of any use, and they were not of very much use. The
mob who enjoyed the spectacle hooted and jeered, for what
they saw was a scarecrow, a human chicken, a creature
rejected by his peers, and thus a fine object for Cain's mirth.
But the wretch, when he escaped, would never be fully
himself again. To be scalped by Indians was preferable,
because the flesh from which the topknot had been cut
would heal in time, and in a wig-wearing age it could be
concealed. But the victim of tar and feathers might think
himself lucky to escape with one eye, and a limp, and a
broken spirit.

I was sickened by the scene of James's humiliation, and
tried to close my eyes to it, and found I could not. Whatever
power was showing me this film was determined that I
should see it all.

So much of it was strange in ways that had never entered
my head. So many of these men and women of the eighteenth
century were of low stature, almost to the point of dwarfish-
ness; girls and boys not yet twenty might have no teeth at all,
or mouths filled with rotten snags; among the ordinary folk
tobacco-chewing was the common solace, and their spitting
was indiscriminate and prodigious. Outside Trinity Church
on a Sunday morning the pavement was filthy with quids the
worshippers had spat out before going in to service. It was

through this filth that many of the ladies trailed their long skirts.

I had seen films of the eighteenth century in my lifetime, and I now became conscious how much they depended on ingenious designers of costume; these people wore clothes that looked as if they had been made not by tailors but by upholsterers who had heard tell of the human figure but had never seen one; many of the poor wore outfits of extraordinary antiquity, for square-cut coats were not unknown, leather breeches were common, and even steeple-crown hats that spoke of a century earlier could be seen; as they were of beaver they were virtually indestructible; these heirlooms were far too good to throw away. The well-to-do were dressed expensively, but not elegantly, except for the officers, British and Hessian, whose uniforms were made abroad. Anna, who was a woman of means, had the best, but her gowns were so stiff they could have stood alone, and she never wore fewer than four petticoats, one of which was invariably of the densest flannel and flaming red. But she wore no drawers, in the manner of her time, and this was made plain in a scene which I would have preferred not to see.

She was a woman of principle, but she was a young widow; she had a number of suitors, and of these, two or three aroused in her desires and memories of her married state which she could not always fight down. Captain van der Heyden, for instance, was a Hessian of distinguished address, and a killing moustache. He had visited the house on John Street a few times, with friends Anna had made among the occupying force, and on a particular morning he called alone, and what could Anna do but receive him and regale him with the inevitable coffee and some fine "cookies"; the Dutch word for biscuits was already common in America. The Captain grew bold, and Anna did not receive him as coldly as would have been advisable. So she found herself on a sofa beside the Captain, who talked so winningly that she was off her guard when he put his arm, which had been on the back of the sofa, around her neck, and drew her to him and kissed her so pleasantly that she did not draw back when his other hand slipped beneath her heavy skirts and mounted gently to her knee, and then above her garter until it rested warmly on her naked thigh, and mounted to where no widow should have allowed it to be, but to which this widow offered only the most formal resistance.

A love scene, and nothing to the scenes of naked passion common enough in the movies in the latter part of the twentieth century, so why was I squeamish? Unquestionably because it was a love scene of a sort to which I was unaccustomed, and this overdressed seduction I found both fusty and repellent. In the manner of the day, the Captain wore his hat, and his coat was stiff with braid; Anna wore her widow's cap, and had not brushed all the cookie crumbs from her bosom, which was rising and falling rapidly as she murmured in what I suppose was Dutch. It was a close call, for when matters had gone so far that the conclusion seemed inevitable, Emmeline tapped at the door and asked if she might carry away the coffee cups. The result was therefore what musicians of the day called a disappointed climax. What would the completed seduction have looked like – hat, cap, buckskin breeches, top boots and Anna's heavy eighteenth-century shoes and petticoats like bedclothes all milling away in an attempt at an intimate union? Doubtless it was a passionate moment for Anna and the Captain but for me it was absurd and pitiful. I have the usual dash of voyeurism in my nature, but I was forced to realize that I liked to peep only at cleverly managed scenes directed to suit the taste of films as I knew them. I am – or I must say I was – a man of my time, and I found that time and time's fashions were of first importance in matters that I had foolishly supposed were timeless.

That evening Anna was particularly strict with her children, and was severe with Elizabeth, whom she accused of lolling in her chair – the child had allowed her back to touch the chairback in defiance of polite custom – in a manner which a guest would certainly consider immodest. Other times, other manners. Should I say, other times, other notions of human nature?

(10)

HOW STRANGE THEY looked! How strange the food they ate and the way they ate it, the gentlemen picking their teeth freely in the drawing-room with the same elegance with which they took snuff. How unaccustomed and often repugnant were the smells, for this was not simply a movie and a talkie but also a smellie. Everywhere was the smell of horse, not in itself a bad smell but heavy, and when it mingled with the stench from the drains, down which the maidservants emptied the slops every morning, too insidiously creatural to be ignored, whatever might be done with sprigs of lavender among the linen, and bowls of pot-pourri in the drawing-room. But in New York there was often a relieving breeze from the sea, salty and fishy, to be sure, but a pleasant change from the brown fug of a town where the horse was the common carrier, and voided its dung and its water everywhere.

Did I witness the rise of the famous American sense of humour? I think I did. What the British laughed at ranged from the polished wit of the playhouse and the best authors to heavy jokes of a clumsy, ill-managed obscenity. The Americans seemed to be forging a humour that was a new weapon to their troops. An ironical, wry fun, a dry mockery which did not call for laughter so often as it demanded the crooked smile. They took "Yankee Doodle" and turned it on the British until the lobster-backs were sick of that sportive tune, played on shrieking fifes as the Americans approached, flying the flag they had made out of the elements in George Washington's own armorial bearings – the Stars and Stripes. The Americans laughed at themselves, which the British

were not inclined to do, and which the Hessians simply did
not consider as a possibility. What Yankee wag was it who
recalled the song from *Polly*, the popular ballad opera which
followed *The Beggar's Opera*:

> *Despair leads to battle*
> > *No courage so great;*
> *They must conquer or die*
> > *Who have no retreat;*
> *No retreat, no retreat*
> *We must conquer or die*
> > *Who have no retreat!*

The Americans sang it without ever tiring of it. Never tiring
of the joke, never tiring of the tune. Sang it, moreover, in
tones of whining despair, as if they would gladly have run
away, even when they were advancing briskly. When the
British heard them singing, and laughing, they were puzzled.
This had been called a war of brother against brother, but
how unfamiliar these brothers had become! To allow the
word retreat even to pass the lips of the troops – it was totally
contrary to the disciplines of war. As of course was the
American custom of deserting whenever he felt like returning to his farm. Poor Washington!

New York remained in British hands until late in 1783,
and to the end of his life Roger remembered George Washington's triumphal entrance into the city. City – it was a little
more than twelve thousand people, but it was already a
metropolis.

(11)

IT IS DINNER TIME – four
o'clock – on November 25, 1783. Anna sits at table with her

two older children. Little Hannah is being given soft food in her bedroom, by her black nurse.

"Why did you go to the parade on Broadway?" she asks her son. She is stern, he formal.

"To see General Washington, madam. It was his triumphal entry into the city."

"Not the place for the son of a brave British officer, who died to defend us against such upstarts, I should have supposed."

"But madam, it was like Plutarch. A conqueror entering a capital city. How often does one have a chance to see that?"

"Plutarch wrote of heroes. Of noble men."

"General Washington looked like a hero today."

"A fine hero!"

"How does General Washington look?" asks Elizabeth, somewhat fearful of her mother.

"He is the tallest man I've ever seen. And he had a splendid horse. And such a look! Stern, implacable. He raised his hat now and then to the crowd, when they cheered him, but not a smile did he give."

"He cannot smile," says Anna, who has heard much about the conqueror from her coffee cronies. "His false teeth will not allow it."

"False teeth!" says Elizabeth, incredulous. "Oh Moeder, are you sure?"

"It is well known," says Anna, pleased to have given the conversation the proper Loyalist tone. "They are joined – the tops to the bottoms – at the back, with springs. If he does not keep his jaw firmly shut, they will fly open and you will see the inside of his mouth, which no gentleman ever shows. His teeth are as false as his heart."

"He looked like a conqueror," says Roger, who is sullen. "I should know, madam. I was there."

"He has not conquered me," says Anna.

"He has conquered us all, and we shall have to look to it," says Roger.

"Roger, you are too old for me to tell you to leave the

table, but you must understand that I will hear no more of this adoration of Mr. Washington."

"I'm not adoring him. I'm facing a fact."

(12)

SOME PEOPLE ARE quicker to face facts than others. Anna knows that hundreds of Loyalists have already made their way north, to the Canadas or the British colonies on the northeast coast, or to the warmer islands in the Caribbean. Anna is phlegmatic – stubborn indeed, with the stubbornness born of ample funds. But Anna is not a fool and she listens carefully to the last sermon preached by the Reverend Cephas Willoughby to his flock at Trinity Church.

His text is from the one hundred and thirty-seventh Psalm: *How shall we sing the Lord's song, in a strange land*? For is not this land now strange to us? The songs we know of loyalty and gratitude toward our Motherland may no longer be heard here. Have we not seen the British force withdraw from New York, marching with heads high, in splendid order? And what was the tune the band played, as they marched toward their waiting ships? Was it not "The World turn'd upside down"? Dearly beloved, what a comment was made thereby upon the state in which we now find ourselves. What solemn truth was borne upon our ears by that air, once thought a merry tune, but now heavy with comment upon the present and foreboding for the future?

And much more to the same effect, but in the end what it came down to was that the Reverend Cephas had received hints that his style of pulpit rhetoric was no longer popular in the city which was now the capital of the United States, and that he might be wise to embrace the facts of conquest. Not all of his parishioners were of his way of thinking, for some were won to the rebel cause, and others thought that a judicious acceptance of realities might serve them best in a city where they had been born and hoped to die. There were Loyalists among them, certainly, but they were not easy in their minds. Loyalist windows had been broken, and rude messages had been daubed on Loyalist walls. But the Reverend Cephas was not a man to admit defeat. He had heard a call, and that call came from the northern city of Halifax, still staunch under British rule, where he had been invited to go, and sing the songs of Zion in a more favourable climate. Would he be true to his principles if he refused to heed such a call? Who among his parishioners could imagine such a vain thing? So the Reverend Cephas had packed his bags and he and his wife and children (whom he referred to only as his olive branches) were shortly to take ship, and Trinity would see, and hear, them no more. It was a splendid sermon, and some of his hearers wept. There were a few, infected perhaps with the new-born sense of Yankee humour, who knew that the Reverend Cephas had been intriguing for this call for several months, but they were polite enough to conceal their smiles.

(13)

OTHERS RECEIVED THE message in a more reflective spirit, and Anna was one of them, for during the preceding week she had had a disagreeable talk with Dr. Abraham Shanks, headmaster of the school that Roger attended.

"Have you reflected, Mrs. Gage, that Roger is now almost fifteen, and might well be thought ready to meet the world and find his fortune there?" Dr. Shanks had asked, all smiles.

No, Anna had not thought any such thing. She thought that Roger should have at least another year of schooling, before he sought entry to Harvard College, with a view to equipping himself for a life in the legal profession.

"Then I must be frank, Mrs. Gage. These are troubled times, and I have in my school many boys who are sons of British officers, and I am sorry to say that they are a disruptive influence, and hard words and even open fighting are becoming common. The boys whose parents are supporters of the new government are patient. Oh yes, very patient indeed, but you must know that boys are high-tempered, and such disruptions are not friendly to the spirit of education, which it is my duty to foster. *Absit invidia*, madam, as I am sure you understand, and no rebuke to Roger *ad personam*, but the *amor patriae* of another day must submit to the *tempus edax rerum*. The *ultima ratio regum* resides with our new government, and my own situation must be governed by the *maxim volenti non fit injuria*. So I must, with the uttermost reluctance, I assure you, request that Roger be withdrawn. *Salus populi suprema est lex*, and whatever my personal feelings must be, I am obliged to think of the good of my school. And so, madam – ? "

Thumped with Latin, Anna withdrew, very angry with the schoolmaster. Roger went to school no more.

(14)

ANNA IS VISITING her man of business. This is not old Claes van Someren, but his successor, Diedrick Potter, a small worried man instead of a large phlegmatic one.

"But the Greenbush rents have been collected as usual? There was no default there?"

"Oh, none in the least, madam. The tenants are prompt and good. The money is perfectly safe. But as I say, it is not available to you at present."

"Because this new government has put some sort of stop on it. How can they do that?"

"Not precisely a stop. The money is quite secure, but some arrangements must be made before we can lay hands on it."

"I thought you said it was in your strong-room in your vaults?"

"Oh yes, indeed, the substance is in our vaults, but the spirit is not, so to speak, in our possession. It is in escrow, madam."

"What is this escrow?"

"It is a law term, and it means that the money, though held by us, is not available to you until a future condition has been fulfilled."

"Yes, yes; but *what* future condition?"

"Not to put too fine a point on it, Mrs. Gage, until the present government – the new government of the sovereign state of New York – has determined what damages are owing to the state, and its citizens, by the British who so long occupied the state capital, and who may be held responsible for the damage sustained during the siege and liberation of the city."

"So I have to pay damages because the British lost the war? Who says so?"

Tears came into the little man's eyes. "Oh madam, if only I could tell you! But you have not had to deal with governments, where there are only spokesmen who interpret somebody or something which is never seen, and has indeed only a mystical being. The people I talk to at Federal Hall are so polite, and so ready to listen when I talk of injustice, but so determined in saying that it is not *their* desire, but that of the newly formed state, and that their sole responsibility is to see that the laws are administered equitably. And when I ask to see the statutes, they say that they are still being put in final form, but that they have nevertheless the effect of laws. Oh, madam, need I say that they are every man jack of them Whigs, and we are Tories, and they have us at the pistol's point? When the flag was lowered on the City Hall, was not Cain's flag raised? They talk so smoothly about 'natural justice,' which excuses this spoliation of the defeated. For we *are* defeated, and we must bow to it. When the Royal Arms were torn down at the City Hall, I tell you without shame, Mrs. Gage, I wept! These were our guarantees of order and justice, and what have we now? A parcel of Whigs! Think of what Mr. Willoughby said on Sunday last!"

Think of it indeed. Mr. Willoughby had raged against Federal Hall, but he had not come right out and said that the new government was sequestering the monies of the Loyalists to pay its own debts. Instead he had insisted once more that Cain was raised; he took refuge in Milton and spoke of

> *. . . what the grim wolf with privy paw*
> *Daily devours apace and nothing said*

by which those in the know, like Mr. Diedrick Potter, were well assured he meant the lawyers at Federal Hall, who took what they wanted, and could not be asked to account for it.

"So I have no assurance about when I may get my money?"

"Oh, Mrs. Gage, I wish I could say otherwise, but I fear you may never get it. Every day I expect news that the Greenbush farms have been sequestered. They are garnering every penny piece that can be found among people like ourselves."

"But it is utterly unjust!"

"Mrs. Gage, I am sorry to contradict you, but when it is a question of war, our notions of justice have no application whatever. Just as it was in pagan times, the cry is *Vae victis* – Woe to the vanquished! We are lucky not to be shot or beheaded, I suppose. This new government puts its faith in the treasury and not in the armoury. Very modern, I suppose."

"So I have nothing left?"

"Oh, not quite that, Mrs. Gage. You have never spent

your whole income in any single year since you came into your property, and those residuary funds are in our vaults, and we did not think it necessary to mention them to the taxing men, as they were neither income, nor yet capital, but just – just trifles, shall we say, hardly worth bothering about."

"Thank you, Mr. Potter. And what do these trifles come to, can you tell?"

"They come to six hundred and forty-six guineas, eleven shillings and ninepence, Mrs. Gage. I thought it better to get this money into gold."

"I thought you would be exact. And how may I put hands on this six hundred and forty-six guineas, eleven shillings and ninepence?"

"It would relieve my mind greatly if you would take them out of our vaults as soon as you can, for the tax men are demanding another accounting and if it is not precise – well, *Vae victis* it will be."

"Carry them off with me this instant?"

"You could not do better. Shall I have them made ready? A trusted person will do it in a very short time."

So, while the trusted person is doing it, Anna and Mr. Potter entertain each other very agreeably by abusing the Whigs and the conquerors, and assuring one another that "The World turn'd upside down" is the only tune for the times.

At last the trusted person taps at the door, and enters with a large leather bag. He puts it on Mr. Potter's table and leaves without a word, but perhaps the wrinkles of his coat-tails might be interpreted as a wink. When Anna tries to lift it she finds so much weight in a small bag unwieldy, so Mr. Potter arranges that she shall go home in a coach, and that the trusted person shall carry the duplicitous bag for her.

He does not think it proper to ask for a receipt for the bag. Too much attention to the details of business can be as bad as too little.

(15)

Dinner that afternoon at
the house on John Street is an exciting affair, and the manners
of the dancing-school, and of parental instruction, suffer
because of it.

"Hurrah! When do we set out?" Roger wants to know.

"Not until spring. Christmas has not yet come and we
shall need all the time until Easter to prepare. For we are not
running away, my dears. We are making a considered journey.
We are going to visit your Uncle Gus in Canada. We must
choose what we will take with us, and we must prepare for
hardship. But whatever can be done by care and planning
must be done, and not a word to anyone."

"But people are going all the time, madam. Last week
the Bertrams went to Jamaica, with a mass of things."

"Yes, and when their ship dropped its pilot in the harbour the American revenue people took every trunk and
bale, and the Bertrams will reach Jamaica with nothing but
what they stand up in."

"Parson Willoughby went, and nobody bothered him."

"We don't know that for a certainty. Leaving the harbour is not the same as arriving with all your packages. For
anything we know, the Willoughbys may have been stripped
to the skin before they reached Halifax."

"I should be glad to see that."

"Roger! Let me hear no more of that!"

"Do the servants know?" asks Elizabeth.

"I shall tell them at the proper time, but they are not
coming with us."

"Not even Emmeline?" says Elizabeth, looking very
downcast.

"Canada is not a climate for black people," says Anna.
"And James is almost a cripple now, so he would be a hindrance on our journey."

"A hindrance on our journey," says Elizabeth, reflectively. And then – "So there will be nobody to turn down our beds?"

"What beds?" says Roger. "Do you suppose we shall have beds on this journey? Miss Ninnyhammer!"

"Do not speak to your sister like that, Roger."

"But she is being stupid. This is going to be an adventure. Nobody has beds on an adventure. Lizzie had better wear some of my clothes."

"Oh Roger! Whatever for?" says Elizabeth.

"To protect your virtue, Miss," says Roger. "We shall meet Indians and Whigs and God knows what in the forests. You had better cut your hair, too."

Elizabeth screams.

"Roger, what sort of journey do you think we are undertaking?" says Anna.

"We are escaping. We are fleeing. *Abiit, excessit, evasit, erupit*!" Roger is shouting, flown with the spirit of adventure and with all the masculine zest for Latin – in this case wildly unsuitable to number and gender.

"If we travel in that spirit I doubt if we shall get past Spuyten Duyvil," says Anna. "No, Roger, no. All must be as orderly and as ordinary as it can be made. I have thought carefully. We cannot go by wagon and packhorse. Travellers by land have to pass too many turnpikes and inquisitive people. We must travel on the water."

"Hurrah! I shall paddle!"

"You will not. I shall paddle."

"Have you ever paddled in your life, madam?" says Roger with heavy sarcasm.

"No, but I do not suppose it is beyond me."

"Well, God be praised, I can paddle."

"You may paddle as well. You are a strong boy. I must say now, a strong young man."

Roger is appeased. "Well, I shall carry the pistols," says he. His father's pistols have long been in his envious eye.

"I think I had better carry the pistols, and they will be very well concealed," says Anna.

Elizabeth has been thinking, and not happily.

"Moeder, you spoke of hindrances on the journey," she says now, in a very small voice. "Have you thought at all about Hannah?"

"I have. Hannah shall be your care, Elizabeth."

Elizabeth bursts into tears.

(16)

A CARE HANNAH is certain to be. Poor wretch, not yet quite eleven years old, she suffers dreadfully with her teeth. She can eat only the softest foods, and has not yet been promoted to the adults' table because of her unpleasing habit of chewing whatever juice she can from her meat, and placing the grey, unswallowed lumps on the side of her plate. Because she eats so little, her growth is stunted and she looks like a child of six, and a poor child at that. Because of her misery she has already a marked kyphosis, which Anna will not hear called a hunched back; it will vanish, she is sure, once Hannah has been delivered from the grief of her teeth. But when will that be? Dentists are few in New York, but Hannah has been taken to one of them, whose resort was to make room for her incoming teeth by screwing out a few of her baby teeth with an instrument called a pelican, as Hannah screamed with a force extraordinary in so small a creature. Hannah is a living, breathing toothache and it seems that nothing can be done for her. In addition to her teeth, and probably because of them, she suffers from what the physician calls catarrh of the ears, and a noisome yellow mess leaks out onto the bandages that the devoted Emmeline changes every day. Hannah seems marked for deafness, and is already a child whom Anna finds it difficult to love. Elizabeth, who has a tender heart, pities her, but Hannah does not respond well to pity. She is hateful, and pulls Elizabeth's beautiful auburn hair and screams against the fate that has made her ugly and a little bundle of pain.

Roger calls her Little Nuisance, and Elizabeth is sharp with him about this, although in everything else she worships her daring, healthy, handsome brother.

No doubt about it, Hannah will be a care.

(17)

W HAT I NEXT SEE in the formal, elegant parlour of the house on John Street appears so farcical that I wonder if the director of this film – whoever he may be – is having a joke with me. For I still accept it as a film. What else can I do?

There is Anna, that woman of impeccable propriety of manner, kneeling on the *chaise longue* and in her hands she holds a wooden paddle with which she strikes to right and left at imaginary water.

"No, madam, no! First the stroke, long and free, and at the end the J-shaped turn. But not too much! You will have us into the river bank if you do it like that! Let me show you again. See – like this – long and easy and not too fast, then the J just as you come to the end of your reach. Again. Better but not good yet. Again."

Roger is teaching his mother to paddle a canoe, and like many boys given authority over an adult, he is apt to be tyrannous. Anna is puffing from the unaccustomed effort, and her legs are growing numb from kneeling. But Roger assures her that she must kneel; there will be no sitting in the canoe; there must be hours, and hours, and hours of kneeling, and there is nothing for it but to accustom herself to the position, and the effort, and what she feels to be the indignity.

Elizabeth, meanwhile, is lying face downward on a stool, which supports her stomach but leaves the rest of her body free. As if galvanized, she strikes out with arms and legs, like a frog.

"Oh, Roger! Please! I can't do any more!"

"But you must, Miss."

"I shall swoon! I know I shall!"

"If you swoon in the water, Lizzie, you will drown. And Hannah will drown. Now listen carefully; if the canoe oversets, you are to seize Hannah by the hair, kick off your shoes, and swim for shore. And be sure you keep Hannah's head above the water."

"I don't think I shall be able to keep my own head above the water."

"That doesn't signify. The water won't hurt your face, Miss Baby."

"But I shall get it into my mouth. And it will be dirty."

"Very likely. But you are a soldier's daughter, as Mama tells you every day, and you must be brave, and resolute, and save Hannah."

"Oh Roger! Do you think we shall overturn?"

"Nothing more likely. A canoe is a delicate craft."

"I shall never learn."

"It's learn or drown, Lizzie. If the current is very swift you would be best to catch hold of the canoe, and I shall save you after I have saved Mama. And Hannah, of course. Though by the time I have managed that the canoe will have drifted far below us, so don't expect a miracle."

"I shall drown!"

"Not if you learn to swim. You must harden your muscles. A great strong girl like you! For shame, Miss!"

Tears from Elizabeth. Remonstrances from Anna. But they are women of their time, and must submit to male tyranny in such matters as this. Every night the parlour becomes a gymnasium, with Roger as its implacable master. He is enjoying himself immensely, as a tyrant in an indisputably worthy cause.

Roger does not have it all his own way. The Gage house has so far escaped looting by the ruffians who are despoiling Loyalist dwellings wherever they can. The Federal authorities are regretful, but their excuse is the familiar one: their watchmen are few and overworked and cannot be everywhere at once, and any question of setting a guard on John Street is absurd. Nor is the zeal for protecting the Tories as strong as perhaps it might be. This is where Anna asserts herself.

The servants are sent out every week with parcels of silver, which they take to goldsmiths' shops that are not too scrupulous and will buy valuables which they suspect have been looted without making enquiries. But the servants are not good hagglers, and so Anna, in clothes she has borrowed from the maids, and without powder in her hair, goes to shops as far as possible from John Street, and does most of her own selling. Paulus Vermuelen's daughter discovers unexpected powers of rapacity in herself, and gets as much as she can. She speaks an English heavily salted with Dutch, and passes as a woman of the people – the sort of people who are looting – and she takes a miser's delight in a good deal. She even laughs with the merchants, and says nasty things about the Loyalists, and is pleased with her duplicity. Anna has determined to survive, and not to survive empty-handed; if the canoe sinks, she will sink a wealthy woman.

She works at a petticoat, made with many pockets, in which her guineas, her shillings, and even pence if need be, will be stowed away. She practises walking in this garment, which is of many pounds weight, distributed as evenly as she can arrange it. Anna, who has always been devout, knows well that Despair is a mortal sin, and now she knows that it is a luxury, as well. She has seen Loyalist friends, not so tough-minded as herself, set out on a journey to another land, weeping at their misfortunes, without ever having done anything of a practical nature to lessen those misfortunes. She will have nothing to do with Despair. She prays every night for a good deliverance from the journey that lies before her, but she knows that God helps those who help themselves, and she will not fail God in this duty to herself and her children. As she sees her handsome house grow barer with each sale of silver, damask hangings and anything else that will fetch money, she is not downcast. She is resolute. She wishes she could sell the furniture as well, but it cannot be got out of the house without attracting notice. The furniture – some of it very good of its kind – must be sacrificed. Only the picture of King George III, which has acquired a talismanic value, must go with her, even though it must be disframed, and rolled into a bundle of clothing.

So, as Easter approaches, and the great day of escape comes near, she reduces everything she can take to British North America to bundles that weigh, in all, about one hundred and fifty pounds, which Roger assures her the canoe can carry.

(18)

T HE CANOE. They see it on the morning of Easter Sunday, as the first light of dawn is breaking. Roger has seen it, of course. For weeks he has been searching, haggling, talking with fishermen and half-breeds who know about canoes, and he has bought what seems best, a cedar-sided canoe of about seventeen feet in length. He was not ridiculously overcharged. He would have preferred birchbark, as being more sporting and in keeping with his new-found character as an adventurer, but he has been warned that such craft are not for beginners and women, and that they demand constant skilled attention to their easily punctured skins. Roger thinks he has been crafty, pretending that he is looking for a canoe for a friend, but the men at Burling Slip, at the end of John Street, are not stupid, and they know that the Gages are making a run for it. The convinced

Americans do not care; the fewer Loyalists in New York, the better for everybody; some of the men are friendly and give good advice.

Indeed, two or three of these men are at the slip when the Gages approach, with James pushing their bundles in a wheelbarrow. They seem to emerge from the darkness, and silently help to stow the bundles in the canoe, as it is plain Roger has no idea how best to do it. All that remains now is to set out.

James is in tears. Anna thinks he is weeping at losing her, and that is so, but not quite as she supposes. He is weeping for himself. Like many an old servant James has become virtually a child in his master's house; his master is dead, and now he is losing his mother. What does the future hold for him? A hanger-on at a tavern, sprinkling the white sand over the floor? The night before the journey Anna gathered the servants in the now desolated drawing-room, to read prayers, ask for the prayers of Emmeline and Chloe, who promised them from full hearts, and gave out three little purses of twenty guineas each. They were overwhelmed, for the gift is munificent, but Anna was determined not to be mean. James now kisses Anna's hand, which he has never done before in his life, and tries to help the plainly dressed woman, a most improbable boy – Elizabeth in breeches – and the child into the canoe.

Anna, although she has toiled to learn to paddle in the drawing-room school, has never been in a canoe in her life, and she is very clumsy as she takes her place in the bow. Kneeling is not easy, for her fourth petticoat is heavy with money – perhaps twenty-five pounds weight in gold, for the original six hundred guineas is now nearer nine hundred – and the canoe rocks perilously. If the men had not steadied it, she would have been in the water. She rests her buttocks on the bow thwart. Now the timorous Hannah must somehow be put in the canoe. Hannah shrieks; Roger angrily tells her to hold her noise. Elizabeth must get aboard and, though she is lighter than her mother, she is not so courageous, and makes a sad mess of it, but she takes Hannah. Roger steps into the stern, lightly and expertly, for he has been practising for weeks, and the men hand paddles to him and to Anna. They are square-ended paddles – what are called voyageur paddles – and there is nothing to be done now but to venture out into the East River. The water seems perilously high on the gunwale. Roger gives the word and the men, who have not spoken until now, give a muted cheer, and the Gages set out for Canada.

Must I be witness to their fearful misery for – who can say what journey? Their progress is pitifully clumsy, and if they manage to keep afloat for a hundred yards in the water it will be a miracle. But the film-maker, whoever he is, spares me that agony, and there is a film dissolve, and when next I see them they have reached the Hudson River, and are on their way. Anna is doing better than before, and Roger has acquired some skill as a steersman.

So off they go, and I can only judge how long they are on the Hudson by the changing foliage of the trees and the increased strength of the sun, as they pass Pollock's Wharf, and the Albany Basin, and Rhinelander's Dock and creep along as close to the shore as they can, for the great river is a mile and a half in width, and the current is against them. They must ascend the Hudson for something like a hundred and fifty miles. But the canoe travels faster than might have been expected, and as Anna gains in skill, and Elizabeth and Hannah learn that they must not move – no, not an inch – their spirits lighten, and after a few days they are filled with a sense of adventure, though the women are still frightened. But when have adventure and a fear of danger been far apart?

(*19*)

I F I HAD BEEN asked to invent their progress during my lifetime, when I did a little romancing in hopes of becoming an author rather than a newspaper man, I would certainly have resorted to the usual cheap goods of the romantic novel. Elizabeth, wandering too far on land at one of their evening stops, would have encountered a group of ruffians who would have tormented her and threatened to rape her, thwarted at the last minute by the brave Roger, brandishing the Major's pistols. There would undoubtedly have been an encounter with Indians, alarming figures with painted faces. Could I have omitted a few Quakers, speaking quaintly and being shrewd about changing a golden guinea? Certainly I should have included a meeting with a band of strolling players, who would have enlivened the evening around the campfire with choice passages from the popular plays of the period.

> *My name is Norval; on the Grampian hills*
> *My father feeds his flocks; a frugal swain,*
> *Whose constant cares were to increase his store,*
> *And keep his only son, myself, at home.*

Perhaps one of the actresses would have introduced the virgin Roger to the pleasures of sex; such a scene always goes down well with lecherous readers. Certainly Anna would have been despoiled of many, or all, of those golden guineas.

The film shows me that it was not at all like that. Their adventures were of a less romantic order, but none the less exhausting. After a few attempts to stop the night at inns in the settlements along the river, they gave up all hope of that, for the inns were filthy, their food disgusting and their beds thick with bugs. Thereafter they asked leave of farmers to sleep under haystacks, and such leave was usually granted without much cordiality. Not bedbugs, but fleas came of the haystacks. An entire day was spent on land, the Gages stripped to the skin – Roger far apart, so that his eyes might not be blasted by the sight of naked female flesh – as they searched their clothes for the insects, and held them over a pot of burning brimstone, which they bought of a farmer's wife, who also gave them bags of pennyroyal to wear, to check

further infestation. They bought food of the farmers and
though it was rough it was not nauseous. They met with little
outright incivility, for most of the farmers did not greatly care
if Tories left the new country, and some were Tory sympa-
thizers who had no intention of leaving their homes, but
would give a helping hand to those who were doing so.
Money, as Anna had discovered, was the great emollient and
would often moderate the fervour of a rancorous Yankee
Doodle who was uncivil until he saw it, bit the coin and
decided that it was good. They were not beggars, though
they came very near to looking like beggars.

None of them were used to unremitting physical work,
and it was soon clear that they could not travel from dawn till
dusk. They must rest at midday; food must be prepared, or
bought. Anna was used to a certain amount of wine every
day; she now had to put up with rum, and Roger insisted that
he too must have rum, and had too much until his mother
rationed him strictly, after he had come near to capsizing the
canoe. They all washed as much as they could, but that was
not enough, and they began to look like gypsies, sunburned
and grubby. Because they were always in the open air, they
did not smell very much. They itched and, to Anna's dismay,
they scratched.

They attracted no unwelcome attention, for they were
simply part of the river traffic. There were canoes of a bolder
design than their own, ends out of the water in turn, as they
seemed to bound over the waves. Skiffs and dories, and craft
to which it would be hard to give a name, were everywhere.
There were even a few small vessels under sail, towing light-
ers in their wake. When they came near a substantial settlement, scows were busy with cargo. Now and then a raft made
stately progress down the strongest pull of the current, and
on these were little tents where the raftsmen lounged when
they were not busy with the sweeps that guided them; usually these had a small fire aboard, for rough cooking. The
Hudson was the best and easiest path for traffic up and down
the big state, and in the press of business a canoe was of no

consequence, even when it was labouring under the guidance
of two poorly skilled paddlers. But they made progress, and
after their early misadventures with inns, they sought a creek
each night, and found a quiet place for their encampment, if
so important a word might be used for their overnight rest.

They could not always avoid notice where they stopped,
and once they had to lay up for five days, as Anna had been
bitten by insects, or suffered some misadventure they could
not identify, and her fever was too bad to allow her to travel.
They had no medicine with them except what was needed for
Hannah, and Anna refused to be dosed with laudanum,
which Roger supposed was a cure-all. A woman, obviously
mad, who said that her name was Tabitha Drinker, offered
them the shelter of her cabin, but as it was too filthy to be
endured, they had to extricate themselves from her hospitality as best they could, and endure her scoldings. Snotty
Tories! Too good for a decent Christian, were they? But on
the whole they went undisturbed.

The further north they travelled, the less they suffered
contempt for being Tories. Revolution is a city flower; it does
not flourish in the country. Thus they travelled roughly, but
free of molestation.

Other unforeseen interventions of nature slowed them.
Elizabeth, who was fourteen, underwent the onset of her
menarche when they had been four weeks on the journey. She
had no idea what was happening; neither her mother nor
Emmeline had thought to inform her; it might have been
supposed at that time that two years might pass before this
event. But perhaps the swimming lessons in the parlour had
given her a push forward, or it might have been some deep
protest against wearing boy's clothes; she was in a panic and
wept uncontrollably. At last Anna found out what was
wrong, and the party had to go ashore while the proper thing
was done, with one of the napkins – clumsy affairs – that
Anna had brought for herself. Roger, who was of course
excluded from this disturbance, fumed and was confirmed in
his opinion, strong already, that women were great nuisances.

Anna and her elder daughter, strongly feminine in the manner of their time, conspired to make Roger feel excluded from something important, and again in the manner of the time, Elizabeth, who was perfectly well, was treated as an invalid for several days, and could not be expected to bail the canoe, which Anna's frequent sloppings made an hourly necessity.

This event caused more trouble than might have been expected, for Anna and her daughter henceforward had to retire twice each month for secret washings of garments Roger was not supposed to know about, and the journey was delayed while the napkins dried, flung over bushes in the sun, when there was sun.

Hannah, sensing that something was going on, from which she was excluded, became even more of a nuisance. She cried a great deal. Cried, not wept, for she was a howler, not a dropper of silent tears. Her teeth hurt, her ears hurt, the motion of the canoe nauseated her and she wanted the others to know that she was in misery, and was in this sense the most important person on the voyage. She possessed in high degree the self-assertiveness of the afflicted.

So she had to be dosed frequently with laudanum, and as the laudanum had to be diluted, water had to be boiled. They drank from the Hudson without scruple, and by ordinary standards it was a clean, fast-flowing river. But the apothecary had decreed boiled water for the cup of laudanum, and thus it had to be; firing must be gathered and coaxed into flame, and a small pot – as small as possible – of water must be boiled to assuage Hannah's pain.

I recall that laudanum was the great specific for pain of all sorts, including heartbreak and desperation, for something like three centuries. It was simply tincture of opium, sometimes mixed with less powerful drugs, and the true laudanum-drinker could get through an astonishing amount of the stuff in a day – quantities that would have killed anyone not habituated to the drug. There was nothing to beat it for toothache, and Hannah was already well on her way to being a drug-taker or, as it was then called, "an opium-eater" for the rest of her life. But what was to be done? It was laudanum or agony, and so laudanum it was.

Coleridge was perhaps the most celebrated of all drinkers of laudanum, and splendid studies have been written of its influence on his Muse. Nobody seems to have paid attention to its influence on his bowels, for laudanum was a rare constipator. How much of *The Ancient Mariner* was the result of intestinal stasis?

Thus, because of landanum, Hannah was pretty seriously plugged up, but as the eighteenth century thought that constipation was a feminine attribute, little notice was taken. Her other function of excretion, however, was in full working order, and imperious in its demands. Far too often for Roger's patience the canoe had to be brought to the shore so that Hannah might be taken into some bushes to pass her water. If he protested, Hannah wept and Elizabeth told her brother that he had made his sister cry.

"The more she cries the less she'll piss," murmured Roger, and Elizabeth was dismayed by his coarseness and cruelty.

This did not add up to adventure in the story-book sense, but *Pilgrim's Progress* did so. Anna had brought three books with her. The Bible, of course, and the Book of Common Prayer; but also Bunyan's great tale of spiritual journeying, and every night, if there was light enough, she read some of it aloud. The young people knew it well already, but they did not tire of it, because Bunyan sweetened instruction with splendid character drawings, and Roger and Elizabeth, and even Hannah when she was not in great pain or asleep, made a game of identifying the people they met on their journey with figures that Christian met on his. Mr. Worldly Wiseman was everywhere, as was Pliable, who always figures heavily in troubled times; Hopeful was certainly Anna herself and Roger, unhampered by modesty, was not sure whether he was Greatheart or Valiant-for-Truth, and decided to be both. He insisted that Elizabeth was Talkative, which grieved her, because she wanted to be Christiana, and thought Bunyan was neglectful of women in his story, as indeed he was. They had had a disagreeable passage with a raucous supporter of the new regime, and decided that he was Giant Despair, as he talked unjustifiably of laying hold of the Gage family and turning them over to people he called The Authorities, but as there were no Authorities within reach who appeared to want them he was foiled. As for the Slough of Despond, it was an almost daily point on their journey, and the Valley of Humiliation came much too often, as they grew dirtier and more disreputable in appearance. But Anna, who had to supply courage to her too easily discouraged children, insisted that they were coming every day nearer to the Celestial City, which was certainly somewhere in British North America, if only they could find Uncle Gus. Their lowest moment was when they made their way inland a few miles to Greenbush, and found that the farms belonging to the Vermuelen estate had indeed been sequestered, and that their former tenants were scornful of them. And so they had to make their way sadly to the point where they turned north-west into the Mohawk River.

(20)

THE FILM-MAKER spared me most of their frequent portages, but I saw something of them. Roger carried the bow end of the canoe on his shoulders, and Anna followed under the stern; Elizabeth remained at wherever they had been forced to leave the water, to attend to Hannah, and guard the bundles, for which Roger and Anna returned as soon as they might. It was weary work, and far from anything Roger was prepared to accept as adventure. The portages on the Mohawk were more frequent, and by far the most taxing was that which led from the Mohawk to Wood Creek. But this was a recognized portage, and not the simple stretches of a mile or so of white water or other obstructions that they could not manage in their canoe, and so there were men to be found who would carry the canoe and the baggage to the Crick, as they called it. To the astonishment of the Gages, they ran, or loped rapidly, over the ground and for a time the travellers wondered if these helpers had made off with their belongings. Carrying Hannah over the long portage was heavy work. Not that the child was much heavier than a bundle from the canoe, but it was exhausting to listen to her cries and complaints, and Anna had begun to fear that too much laudanum was worse than toothache, earache and general debility. But in the end Oneida Lake was reached, and thence the Oswego River and, at last, Lake Ontario, a great inland sea such as they had never seen before.

To my eye, although I suffered with them, after they left the Hudson they were travelling through country of extraordinary beauty. The Mohawk, lying to the south of the mountains, was transportingly lovely in the autumn weather – for it was now autumn and the leaves were turning – but they saw nothing of this, and indeed were fearful of the solemnity and grandeur of the scene. I had to remind myself that these people had an eighteenth-century idea of landscape, and it was not rugged grandeur that moved them. They were creatures of a time before the Romantic Era, during which, and ever since, rough country, mountains topped with cloud, untouched forests, crags and river ravines have been promoted in human estimation into the most splendid sights that Nature can offer. Nature, in its untouched state, was hateful and fearful to these creatures of eighteenth-century classicism. It did not occur to them that these might be the Delectable Mountains of which Bunyan had spoken.

Their greatest dread was of bears, as they slept at night on the leaves or boughs which made their uncomfortable beds. They arranged a rota of watches, when Anna or Roger stayed awake, to give warning if the bears came snuffling out of the undergrowth. What could they have done? What is a pistol to a bear?

Although she had little time to be aware of it, or explore it, this was for Anna a time of incalculable spiritual growth. I would call it psychological growth, but the word would have been unknown to her. God, whom she had worshipped when she was a woman of fortune, though not of the highest station, in New York, had ceased to be a benevolent abstraction, demanding and deserving of reverence, rather like King George III on a larger scale. God had become terrible, but not malignant or unapproachable. The vastness and incalculability of God were apparent to her as she had never dreamed He might be in Trinity Church, or at prayer-time in her New York parlour. And yet, somehow, though she knew herself to be very small in the eye of God, she felt that the eye rested on her, and that it was not an angry eye. It was in the vastness of Oneida Lake that it came to her with a wonderful certainty that God meant her to win this exhausting battle, and that He would bring her at last to – . To Lake Ontario, it seemed, and a long, long journey round its southern shore.

Nor was it Anna alone who grew on the journey. Roger became a man, which is to say that he accepted without demur his place and his duty in the world. Perhaps he was not the best sort of man, but who is to judge? When sieges must be lifted, or maidens rescued, or hardship endured, it is to the Rogers we look, and we trust in their firmness of purpose. The lawgivers, the poets, and scientists are of other breeds, but without the Rogers we should perish.

As for Elizabeth, the tedious care of Hannah made her into a woman. Not a woman of affairs and plans, like her mother, but a woman in another sense, a gentle, nourishing, tender woman, ready to sacrifice herself, not quite entirely, but to the last instant before she was consumed, to duty and charity. She alone felt truly for Hannah. To Anna her ailing daughter was a charge, a duty, someone who must be succoured so far as succour went, but who was not, in the last instance, loved. It was Elizabeth who found love for Hannah, and if it found its expression in childish terms, was not Hannah, in her misery, a child who needed to be cherished like a child? Laudanum could only be used so far, and when it began to fail Elizabeth held Hannah very close and sang a nursery song:

> *Hey, dance a jig*
>   *For the Granny's pig*
> *With a rowdy-dowdy-dowdy;*
> *Hey, dance a jig*
>   *For the Granny's pig*
> *While pussycat plays the crowdy.*

"What's a crowdy?" asked Hannah, many times after she knew the answer.

"It's a little fiddle, darling, such as a pussycat might play."

"Pusscat plays the crowdy," says drugged Hannah. "Sing it again."

How many times did Elizabeth sing the nursery song? There must be somewhere, in our computerized Universe, a record of the number, and all very much to the credit of the gentle-hearted Elizabeth, who never failed her unhappy sister.

(21)

AUGUST VERMUELEN is sitting on the *stoep* of his very decent house at a small settlement called Stoney Creek. He is smoking a long pipe, and resting from a long day at his profession, which is that of a land surveyor. He is very busy, for new lands are being apportioned to new settlers, refugees from the American States. He is a contented, prosperous man.

Who are these tatterdemalions who have opened his gate

and are coming toward him? A woman, brown as an Indian and in rags, with a dirty boy who holds his head very high, and a girl carrying what might be a monkey, but which from its wails he judges to be a child.

The woman is weeping. "Gus," she calls; "Gus, it's Anna."

I too am weeping, in so far as I can as a – shall I say a ghost? A disembodied but not unfeeling spirit, at any rate. God be praised, Anna has made it! This is the end, and I can stop agonizing. For, since the film began, I have felt heartbeat for heartbeat with the actors. Are they actors?

As the scene on the film fades, it is replaced by a notice, a warning, in print:

NO . . . NOT THE END.

For me, the onlooker, how could it be The End? Quite a long time earlier in the film I had recognized that Anna was my great-great-great-great-grandmother. Here she was, risen from the waters into the land which was to be mine.

Not the end. A beginning.

III

Of Water and the Holy Spirit

I HAVE NEVER visited Wild Wales, that northern part of the Principality which I had heard of, vaguely, as the land of my Gilmartin forebears. Only the Welsh Border is known to me, and that from a weekend visit in childhood. How, then, do I recognize the mountain country at once, and with the familiarity I might feel if the screen showed some part of France or Italy, countries I know well? But as the third film in Going's Festival, and the second in what now seems to be a Festival meant for me alone, appears on the screen, I know at once that I am looking at Wild Wales. I am next to Going, impalpable and invisible, eager for more about Anna Gage and her children. This must be a fairly modern film, for scenes of action are to be seen behind the title and the necessary preliminaries. But, as with *The Spirit of '76*, this is beyond question a film peculiar to me, for the Sniffer is watching something different; his film is a prodigious affair called *Shadows of Our Forgotten Ancestors*, the work of the great Soviet film director (and dissident) Sergei Paradzhanov. But there is nothing Russian about what I see. Wales, beyond a doubt. Is there some hidden connection? Am

I really the witness to films addressed to my posthumous needs? It must be so. Is there any other explanation?

(2)

THE ACTION appears at first to be concerned with some horribly bad weather. Here is a mountain pass, through cliffs of the blackest slate, lashed by fierce rain driven hither and thither by capricious gusts of riotous wind. It is dusk above the mountains but in the pass it is already night. There is music; the composer has been given his head, but his orchestral fury is merely an accompaniment to the meteorological tumult. Thunder crashes and echoes from the slate sides of the declivity through which there appears to be a track better accommodated to mountain sheep than to travellers. But – yes – I can just make out the figure of one traveller, a man on foot, stumbling through the darkness, searching for a foothold where the water has washed away the scant soil and the sharp stones that once marked the road. From time to time he loses the path, but he cannot stray far because the way is too narrow and its sides are so steep that only a goat could climb them.

The traveller is drenched. His frieze cloak is sodden and his broad hat, which he has fastened to his head with a long scarf, pours water from all three of its cocks. He wears leather gaiters and strong boots, but they are as heavy with water as the cloak. Is he a brave man, or merely a desperate one? If he does not find shelter soon he will certainly die in this storm.

Has he found shelter? This must be a village, or a hamlet, a single street of perhaps nine houses, the most miserable this widely experienced traveller has ever seen in all his tramping through Wales. In hovel after hovel the windows are broken, where windows have ever pierced those stone walls, and not a sign of life is to be seen.

Not a sign, but does he hear a sound? From one miserable pile of tumbledown masonry there is a sound, and as he draws near, he knows what it is. It is the sound of a harp.

I sigh. Is this to be yet another film in which the Welsh people are shown as unremittingly musical and poetic, assuaging the harshness of their destiny with songs of love and valour and dreams? No, God be praised, it is not. The harp thrums and tinkles, and to its accompaniment somebody is singing a bawdy song, a song of shameful lust and filthy desire, and there is laughter at every evil hint and dirty word. I am astonished that I understand the ancient tongue, even in this disgraceful dunghill stretch of its vocabulary, but I reflect that death is full of surprises. The traveller pauses, to my astonishment, for he seems to be wondering if he can endure such company as this song could please. But a sharp gust almost throws him on his face, and he knows that he has no choice. He finds the leather string that lifts the wooden latch of the door, and as the wind drives it open with a crash he steps inside.

(3)

IT IS, apparently, an inn and the rudest inn that man has known since the inn that, so long ago, refused shelter to Mary and Joseph. The room is not a large one, and the only light is from a poor fire, but the place is full, and warm as much from the heat of the bodies of the guests as from the hearth.

The harper, who is also the singer, stops his ribald tale in mid-verse; he is old, filthy and apparently blind, for a leather shade hangs over his eyes like a penthouse. The other guests, who may number ten or a dozen, are big men who look at the traveller with sour mistrust. They are Welsh mountain men; nothing about them is remarkable except that they all have

red hair. Not ginger hair, which is common enough in all
Celtic countries, but a darker red which, if it were washed,
might be called auburn.

"May I take shelter here?" asks the traveller in courteous
Welsh. "The night is very bad."

"You may, or you may not," says one man, after a long
and inhospitable pause. "Who may you be?"

"I am a traveller, bound on my Master's work. My name
is Thomas Gilmartin."

"And who is your master, that he sends you to such a
place as this, on such a night as this?" says the biggest man, a
giant even among these mountain men.

"My Master is Our Lord Jesus Christ, and I am here and
everywhere on His work, which never ends," says the traveller. He shows no fear.

"Never heard of him," says the big man. "He has no
land here." The other red-haired men guffaw, and repeat the
joke among themselves – *Never heard of him.*

"Then I must tell you of Him. But first may I dry myself a
little? I am wet through. Can I buy anything to eat here? I have
had no food since morning, and I have been walking all day."

"Oh, you can pay, is it? Too proud to ask for a bite, is it?
Where do you think you are, little man?"

"I hoped to reach Mallwyd tonight, but I do not know
where I am. Am I near there?"

"You are two miles or so from Mallwyd, and you will
never get there tonight, or perhaps ever. You are at Dinas
Mawddwy. Does the name of Dinas Mawddwy mean anything to you?"

"The blessing of God be on Dinas Mawddwy, then.
May I stop here till morning?"

"The blessing of God has no meaning in Dinas
Mawddwy. You must be a fool not to know that."

"I only know that I have come from Dolgellau and I am
making my way to Llanfair Caereinion – Shining Llanfair, as
it is called – to carry on my work. Have I taken a wrong road?

And I must tell you that the blessing of God is as powerful here as it is everywhere, say what you will."

It is the blind harper who speaks now. Scarecrow though he is in outward appearance, his voice is finely deep and melodious. "Dinas Mawddwy is not a place of blessings, but of curses, master," says he. "You do not know who is talking to you. That is Cursing Jemmy, the blackest curser and swearer even in this cursing place. So you may stick your blessing up your arse so far that when you want it next it will pop into your mouth all brown and stinking."

The red-headed men are much pleased with this witticism, and the harper bobs his head in acknowledgement of their laughter. The harper goes on; plainly he is Cursing Jemmy's toady.

"Jemmy can curse for five minutes without a pause or taking fresh breath. Jemmy can curse the black out of a parson's coat. The last parson came here ran off with his fingers in his ears."

"That is formidable cursing indeed," says the traveller. "I don't suppose you would oblige me with a sample of it? I have heard some very fine cursing in my time, and though I now preach against it as the Devil's work, I have a right to consider myself a judge."

"You, a judge?" says the harper. "A Methodist preacher? What way would you be a judge, if I may be so bold as to ask?"

"You clearly know nothing of Methodist preachers," says the traveller. "We are not your Church parsons, who have been to college and live snug in grand houses from birth to death. Most of us are saved men – brands snatched from the burning – and before we took up Our Lord's work some of us were very great sinners, I may tell you. Now – you men of Dinas Mawddwy have not travelled far. I can tell, because you say you have never heard of Our Lord Jesus Christ, whose name resounds throughout the whole world. Your ears are stopped against Him. I know. My ears were stopped against Him, too, but He can shout louder than you can stop your ears, and He will. He shouted till I had to hear him. Now, am I to hear your fine curser?"

Cursing Jemmy leaned forward, with his hands on his knees and his elbows spread. He took a great breath, and launched into his aria of finely burnished abuse and blasphemy.

Welsh, like Irish and Scottish Gaelic, is an apt language for scurrilous abuse and bitter condemnation, as it is for poetry and prayer. It is in its heart a language of the Middle Ages, when speech was well-salted and frank, but the Celts brought poetry and rhetorical splendour to it, and an ear for rhyme and assonance that makes Welsh poetry an untranslatable marvel of ingenuity and subtle music. So much I had known, but at a distance, because I know no Welsh and had to take on credit what I heard about it in books. Notice that I *heard* books, I did not scan them with the eye alone, and I think this is what made me a good, and often idiosyncratic, critic. But now, as I watch this film, I understand; the Welsh tongue, after – I don't know how many generations – is mine again. I feel, and I marvel not merely at the sense but at the overtone, the suggestion, of Cursing Jemmy's diatribe. With brutal force he suggests what the traveller might do with his Lord, and he develops fanciful details that could only have been carefully arranged beforehand in his mind. This is no extemporaneous blasphemy. It is the creation of a powerful imagination. Jemmy is long-winded, too. He delivers his blast in a single breath, and he has the lungs and control of a great singer.

(4)

THE TRAVELLER, leaning back in his chair, listens with appreciation, and when Jemmy closes with a fine coda he taps on the floor appreciatively with his staff.

"Well done, Jemmy," he says, in a gentle voice. "Well

done for a mountain man and an unimproved intellect. If you can find an eisteddfod that offers a crown for cursing, you might well chance your luck. I could not have done much better than that in my own best days, and I was a notable curser, let me tell you, before I found my salvation."

"Let us hear you, then," says the harper. "You cannot speak to Jemmy in that voice without proving yourself. Curse, preacher! Curse, you braggart! You shall not eat or rest here till you have made good your boast."

"Nay," says the traveller. "I have forsworn cursing, for it is the Devil's work. Though, I tell you, cursing is also the Devil's poetry, as Jemmy has shown us. I will gladly go without food, and I will go out again into the storm, before I will swear and blaspheme as Jemmy has done. But perhaps I may offer you a real eisteddfod judge's opinion on Jemmy's style. Would you like to hear it?"

"You would not dare," says the harper. A stir and a murmur among the men told of their agreement.

"Indeed, I will dare anything in my pursuit of Our Lord's work," says the traveller.

"Let him speak," says Jemmy. "To find fault with my cursing – it is very great impudence, and impudence too may be a form of poetry if it is bold. Speak, damn you, you black-coated turd from Jesus' arse. Say your say, and then I shall kill you. At a blow! I shall kill you!"

"So I shall, for it is always a pleasure to bring light into darkness and improvement into ignorance. Now, listen to me, all of you. What Jemmy has spoken – with eloquence, I grant you – is not true cursing at all. It is naught but blasphemy and filthy abuse. Jemmy is a mere mountain-cacafuego and no more, good as he is. Do you not know what a curse is? Abuse is trivial sport, for women and children – unless the woman be a witch, in which case her abuse may well be feared, for she has given her soul to Satan and rails in his name – which is no foolish or feeble name, let me tell you. But I wander from my point. A curse is an imprecation, in which the curser outlines and details the future of the accursed, under which he must suffer forever, in this life and perhaps in the next until the curse be lifted. Who taught us to curse, think you? It was God himself who laid the first curse on Cain, the evil-doer and murderer. What did Great Jehovah say to Cain? 'Now art thou cursed from the earth – a fugitive and vagabond shalt thou be in the earth.' And is it not so? Does not Cain walk abroad still, bringing war and rape and villainy and every cruelty to unredeemed mankind? You tell me that you know not Christ, but I am sure upon my soul that you know Cain, for he speaks loud and clear in your filthy songs and your un-Welsh want of hospitality to the stranger among you. Cain is raised here in Dinas Mawddwy, but you are so sunk in your evil that you know it not. God's curse upon Cain was the primal curse, and every curse since then has been in its pattern. Truly to curse is to call down the Divine vengeance, and those who have no light of the Divine, or the blackness of Satan, in their natures cannot curse. They can only spew filth, which Jemmy does very well indeed. Seek the Divine, men of Dinas Mawddwy, if you would learn to curse, but be assured that the better you know the Divine, the less you will be inclined to curse."

There is silence. Neither the harper nor Cursing Jemmy has a word to say. They want time to think about what the traveller has said. But after a few minutes a voice is raised, and it is that of a lad of about fourteen or fifteen who has sat on the floor in a corner. He is the pot-boy of this miserable inn and he has the dark red head of Dinas Mawddwy; he does not look as though his life has been a happy one.

"Tell us more about cursing, master," he says. "Your Bible curse is well enough, but we are Welsh. Do you know of a Welsh curse?"

Some of the men murmur. Yes, tell us of a Welsh curse. They know of the Bible. They have heard of Bishop Morgan's Welsh Bible, though it is doubtful if any one of them has seen it, or could read it if he had done so. These men are as Welsh as Welsh mountaineers could be. For them it is as though the Romans had never brought four hundred years of

European culture to their remote land. Their Wales is an area of perhaps two miles in all directions from the hovel in which they sit. A Welsh curse! Now that would be a fine thing, a comprehensible thing.

The traveller is caught in his own net. He has talked too much, his old fault, against which John Wesley himself has warned him. He will have to pray hard for correction of that flaw in his nature. Meanwhile he must keep his hold over these troglodytes, if he hopes to preach God's Word to them before the night is over. He temporizes.

"For a truly Welsh curse, a curse uttered before there was any knowledge of the Curse of Cain in this land, I should have to go back very far into history," he says.

"Go back as far as you please and we shall be at ease wherever you lead us. We are Welsh history, preacher."

"You are? What do you mean?"

"You have not recognized us?" says the harper. "You have not seen that we are the living Gwylltiaid Cochion Mawddwy? You must have heard of us. We are very famous. Even in England we are known."

"The Red Banditti?" says the traveller. "I did not know that I had fallen into such distinguished company. But surely that was in olden times."

"It was in the days of King Henry the Eighth – and that was a very, very long time ago – that we were heard of in England. The King sent his black devil Lewis Owen to hunt us down and it was on a very famous Christmas Eve he seized eighty of us, and hanged us from trees like the carcasses of sheep. It was then that we forswore Christmas and all it means, because it is the worst day in the year for us. But it was many months after that those who had escaped met with him on the road to Mallwyd – the road you are taking, preacher – and they dragged him from his horse and put more than thirty stabs into him. They still call that place The Baron's Gate, and indeed it was his gate to hell. We are the blood of those men, and we are as good as those men."

"And as red–headed as those men," says the traveller,

and wished he had not, because the silent red-haired men give him a look of unpleasant consideration.

"Yes, as red-headed as those men," says the harper. "And as apt for history as those men. So tell us of this Welsh curse, traveller, and be warned that we expect a good story."

(5)

"YOU SHALL HAVE one," says the traveller, "and from much further back into th. antiquity of this land than Henry the Eighth, who was a Welshman too, and a scourge to us, God forgive him! What I tell you goes far, far back to the time of the great princes, and the old gods. And one of these princes was a mighty magician, and his name was Math fab Mathonwy, and he was a strange one indeed. Only when he was at war would he stand upright, and then he was invincible. But when he was not at war he lay at his ease, and for his greater ease he decreed that his feet must always nestle in the lap of a virgin. There were many of these royal virgins, and when the time came for them to marry, Royal Math would give them fine dowries.

"Now it came to pass that the loveliest of these footholders was a maiden called Goewin, and she was of royal blood, the daughter of Pebin, who was a king."

"By God, if I had my feet in a virgin's lap they would not linger there long," says Cursing Jemmy. "I have a better thing for a virgin's lap than my feet, boys, isn't it?"

"Silence!" says the harper, who seems to have more authority than could be justified by his miserable body. "Let us hear this story. It has weight."

"But Jemmy has spoken well," says the traveller, "for there were men like him at Math's court, and they lusted as Jemmy lusts. Like Jemmy they were great cursers and fighters but there was no light in their souls, not so much as a candle.

It is about them you shall hear, and what their fighting and lusting brought to them. Do you want to hear, or will you listen to what Jemmy thinks he would do with the lovely Goewin?"

These men are true Welshmen. They want the story. Lust can always wait and be enjoyed for itself, but stories like this come rarely.

"At Math's court were two trusted warriors of the King; their names were Gwydion and Gilfaethwy, and they had their magic, too. Now Gilfaethwy was a loving man, and he yearned for the beautiful Goewin, as she lay at the foot of the King's bed, doing her duty by his royal feet. 'How may I win this lovely maid?' he cries, and his brother Gwydion hears his moan and he vows to help him. So – to rouse the King from his bed he contrives a war between Math's kingdom and that of his neighbour, and the King rouses himself and puts on his armour and takes his sword and goes off to fight. So – what follows?"

Without anyone having said a word the pot-boy has put a big jug of ale at the traveller's side; he pauses to take a long, refreshing pull at it. The red-haired men are leaning forward now, for they can guess what is coming, but they want to hear it from the lips of the story-teller.

"Very good drinking, that is," says the traveller. "And more than welcome to a wet and weary man. So – as soon as the King has gone to war Gilfaethwy goes to the royal bed, where Goewin still lies, and in his terrible lust he takes her. She shrieks, but there is no one to hear. Gilfaethwy is very rough, for his lust is his master. He forgets his love, and a very bloody deflowering it is, and when that is done his love-talk is of no help at all, for the girl weeps and will not be consoled. Gwydion, dirty dog that he is, stands by the bed and feasts his eyes on the terrible scene. Ah, a painful tale, my red-haired friends, and it is no pleasure to me to tell it."

The traveller pauses again, for the pot-boy has brought him a big hunk of bread and some cold mutton, and he sinks his teeth into the rude sandwich with the pleasure of a starving man. His hearers must wait until he has satisfied his hunger.

"King Math is victorious, and he returns triumphant, and he sees what has happened. Indeed, he sees it as clearly as I see the bottom of this empty tankard," says the traveller. Jemmy gives a jerk to his great red head, and the pot-boy hastens to refill it.

"That is more like it," says the traveller, and takes a long swig. "Now, I suppose you want to know what the great King does."

The outcry from the men, so silent until now, is loud and eager.

"Well – here comes the great curse. As I told you, King Math is a mighty sorcerer, and when he sees the wretched maid and the bloody sheets, he is cold with rage. Does he rave and scream and strike at Gwydion and Gilfaethwy with his sword? He does not. Unbridled rage is for fools. He lifts his staff, and holds it over the two evil brothers, who are valiant no longer, for what is valour against magic? – I could eat more of this meat, and not so much of the fat this time, if you please."

The excitement of the red banditti is intense, but they must wait until more bread and meat is brought, and the traveller has munched a large chaw.

"Very good meat, this is. Stolen, I suppose? Such sweet flesh is not from any creature on this slatey mountain. – Now, let me think. Where was I? Ah, yes, King Math lifted his wand. 'Now,' says he, 'I do not mean to kill you, traitors and ravishers that you are, so you need not cringe at my feet. I have other plans for you. Let me arrange my thoughts. First, I shall take this poor girl into my bed, not as my foot-warmer, but as my wife, and as my Queen her honour is restored and the evil seed of Gilfaethwy dies in her, and her maidenhead is as it was before.'"

Ah, that was noble. That was indeed royal, murmur the red-headed men, and the harper cries that it was great magic as well, for who can mend a torn virginity but a great sorcerer?

"'My judgement on you, evil brothers, is this. And hear me well, for nothing can recall my curse, once spoken. Behold, I turn you into deer. You Gilfaethwy a hind, and you, Gwydion, a stag, and you shall flee to the forest and there you shall mate all day and all night until Gilfaethwy is big with young. Red deer you are from this time forward. Return to me in a year and a day.'

"And so the evil brothers did, and their mating was very rough and noisy, every thrust a pang, so as to teach them a lesson. It was a year and a day later that King Math's seneschal came to him and said: 'Lord, there is a stag and a hind outside, and with them a sturdy fawn.' The King said, 'Come, my Queen, we have business with these beasts,' and they went into the courtyard where the creatures were.

"King Math was ready to forgive them, but he saw the dark look on his Queen's face, and he knew that it was because after the rape she had been unable to bring a child to full term. So he composed his countenance into a frown of disdain, and said: 'Gilfaethwy, you that have been a hind this year past shall now be a wild boar, and you, Gwydion, shall be a sow. The fawn I shall keep, and he shall be baptized and fostered.' And at once the fawn became a fine boy. 'This boy I name Hyddwn, the deer. Now back to the forest with you, and mate as wild swine for a year, and when the year has passed come to me again and bring the finest of your nine farrow.'

"It was so. Gwydion and Gilfaethwy lived as swine for a year, and Gwydion littered nine piglets. They came again to the King, but his Queen's face was still stern, and the King said: 'The piglet is well enough,' and he struck it with his staff and it became a fine boy with red hair, who was christened Hychdwn – which means pig, as well you know. 'The Queen is not appeased,' said King Math, 'so back you go to the forest, but now Gilfaethwy shall be a she-wolf, and you,

Gwydion, shall be a wolf. You know what you have to do. Be outside my walls a year from today.'

"The year passed and the wolves came to the gate of Math's castle, and it was all as it had been before. The King said: 'Have you had your fill of rapine, you false men? I shall take the wolf-cub and he shall be named Bleiddwn, the Wolf. Is it enough, my Queen?' Goewin nodded, and the King spoke again: 'Go then, my dishonoured kin, and be men again, and marry what dishonoured women will take you. But these three fine boys shall be three true champions – Bleiddwn the Wolf, Hychdwn the Boar, and Hyddwn, the tallest, the Stag, and my Queen and I shall raise them as our own.' And that was the great Curse of King Math."

"But was their mating terrible?" says Cursing Jemmy, with hope in his voice.

"Pain at every push," says the traveller.

"I swear I have sometimes wondered what it is like to be the woman, when I am merry," says Jemmy.

There was a long silence, and then the harper said: "By God, that was a mighty curse. Was ever such a curse heard before or since?"

"Never," said the traveller. "And now I have done my part of the bargain and now you shall do yours. I am about to preach, so settle yourselves to hear God's Holy Word."

Preach he did, so long and so powerfully that when he was finished the light of dawn was beginning to reach even into that desolate valley. Many of the men had fallen asleep, some from drink, and some from weariness, and a few in what was perhaps a holy stupor of astonishment. Never have they been so bamboozled and buffeted with edification.

"That was very refreshing," says the traveller, and he must be speaking to himself. "I am well rested, and I must be on my way." And, damp as he is, but with the heart of a lion, he leaves the awful inn, and sets forth on his path, which is not much easier, but is at least seen by daylight.

(6)

HE HAS COVERED about a mile in his journey toward Mallwyd when he hears a sound at his back, and when he turns it is the pot-boy – a poor shrivelled scrap of a lad – who has followed him.

"What do you want, my boy?" he says, kindly.

"I want to go with you, master," says the boy.

"For why?"

"Because I have never heard such talk in the whole of my life," says the boy. "You have won my heart for Christ, master, and I cannot leave you. Drive me away if you will, but I shall follow you until your heart opens to me. You have made me your servant forever."

"I am no tyrant, boy," says the traveller. "I cannot drive you away. But what am I to do with you?"

"Perhaps God will tell you, if you ask Him," says the boy.

"That was well spoken, and I accept the rebuke," says the traveller. "But I really do not know what I can do with such a boy as you. Have you a name?"

"Indeed I have, master," says the boy. "Poor as I am I am not so poor that I have no name. I am Gwylim ap Sion ap Emrys ap Dafydd ap Owain ap Hywel ap Rhodri ap Rhydderch ap Gryffyd."

"Good lad," says the traveller. "You know your pedigree even to the ninth degree. And do you know your cousinship, as well?"

"To the ninth degree also," says the boy, and I, from the end of the twentieth century, see pride in this sorry creature.

"You are a herald, as the Welsh have always been. But I must tell you, lad, that things have changed in Wales, and in the town the English no longer tolerate our long names and long pedigrees. If you come with me to Llanfair you will have to be Gwylim Griffiths, I suppose. But wait a bit – have you been baptized, my boy?"

"I do not know what is baptized," says the lad.

"The great John Wesley is right when he says that we Welsh are as pagan as Red Indians," says the traveller. "To be baptized, my child, is to be taken into Christ's great family by prayer and sprinkling with water. Now, you bade me ask God what I should do with you, and God has put it into my mind that the first job is to baptize you. So come here by this stream and get into it as deep as you can."

"I can go no deeper unless I lie down," says the boy. "It is just up to my knees."

"Then that will have to do. God gives us what he means us to use, and it seems that he does not want you to be wet all over. So close your eyes, and fold your hands, and listen reverently to me."

What a scene this is! The Sniffer is looking at something else, which is so complex that it must be meant for symbolism, of which he is very fond. The Sniffer would not think highly of the biblical simplicity of what I see, as the rising sun strikes up the cruel valley from which the traveller and his follower have just emerged; they stand by the stream where the slate cliffs give way to green herbage, and there are sheep on the other side of the stream, cropping and uttering their perpetual gentle lament – Baa, baa, baa. I know for the first time how intimately the words of the Bible entered the hearts of the people of Wales, for the Scripture's perpetual symbolism of the hills, the pastures, the flocks and the Good Shepherd were fresh to them as they can never be to dwellers in cities, or in lands that know nothing of sheep. I am in the embarrassing predicament of a man who has all his adult life cherished a gentle, smiling (sometimes foolishly giggling) cynicism about anything that hints of pastoral simplicity, or any simplicity, yet here I am, weeping – in so far as a man with no face and no tears can weep – weeping in the spirit as I see the boy standing with bowed head in the stream, and the traveller scooping up the clear water in his hands, and pouring it over his head as he prays.

No, no; this is not a scene for the Sniffer, but it is truly a scene for me. I feel the icy water pouring over my own head and down my face, to wash away my tears.

The traveller speaks again. "I have baptized you as a child of Christ, by water and the Holy Spirit, and it now comes to me very strongly that I should christen you, as well. Christen you into your new family. Have you a fancy for any particular name?"

"I am well pleased with the name I have," says the boy, stoutly.

"But I have already explained to you that time and history have taken away the name you have. Can you write?"

"No, I cannot write, nor read, though I am anxious to do both," says the boy.

"Then listen to me, my boy, for God is prompting me strongly. You are now in Christ's family, well and truly, but I think you had better come into my family, as well. I have no child, I am sad to have to say, and that has always been a gentle but a real grief to me and my wife. Would you like to be my son?"

The boy's face is all the answer he needs.

"Then bend your head to the water again, and in God's name I christen you Wesley Gwylim Gilmartin. So be Wesley Gilmartin from this day forward."

As they step out boldly toward Mallwyd, where the church tower is now in sight, the boy speaks, and perhaps he is not wholly content.

"I am grateful to you, father. But what kind of name is Gilmartin? I have never heard any such name."

"Well, my son, it is not really a Welsh name, though I count myself a Welshman. It is a Scots name, from the far north, where my people lived a couple of generations ago. But you shall learn English, and keep your Welsh, and you shall be my apprentice."

"A trade? Oh, I dearly want a trade! Which trade?"

"When I am not travelling to do God's work and John Wesley's work, I am a cloth merchant. I buy the good Welsh flannel and I send it to Scotland, where it is needed. It is called the Scotch Trade, and you shall learn it. You shall learn to be a weaver."

So the weaver-preacher and his apprentice enter Mallwyd, and, having had some bread and ale for breakfast, they step out on the twenty miles to Llanfair yn Nghaer Einion, which today is called Llanfair Caereinion.

(7)

Until now the film has progressed as straight narrative, but here it breaks up into the technique that I believe is called Concurrent Action, by knowing ones like Allard Going. Up on the left of the wide screen I see young Wesley Gilmartin hard at the work of the loom; it is a huge affair, and on the beam which is perpetually before his eyes is written, in Welsh, "My days are swifter than a weaver's shuttle, and are spent without hope." But this is not young Wesley's case, for I see that under the care of the preacher's wife he is growing big and strong.

In the lower right-hand segment of the screen he is bent over his book, by the fireside; he is learning English, and writing, though he never becomes a great hand at either.

What is this, at lower left? These must be fair days, when Thomas Gilmartin visits the local towns – Trallwm, Newtown, and sometimes Berriew – to buy the red flannel that is the staple of his trade. It is of the reddest possible red, for that is the colour ordained for petticoats and the Welshwomen's heavy cloaks, and is thought to be sovran against rheumatism and the woollen string disease, as consumption is called. Thomas can command the best because he is a fair dealer, and pays a fair price. Young Wesley accompanies him, to load the pack-horse with the purchased goods for the seven-mile track over the hills.

Here (upper right) I see Thomas preaching in the open

air, as John Wesley did and counselled his preachers to do as well. His hearers wear the heavy clothes and gaiters of the farm; some are in smocks, exquisitely worked at the yoke; many of the women wear the heavy steeple-crown hats, so long the distinguishing mark of Welsh costume. These indestructible hats are heirlooms, passed from mother to daughter. Wet or fair Thomas stands in the streets, and he and the boy sing a hymn, as loud as they can in one language or the other, until they have drawn a big enough crowd to hear the Word.

Now another film technique is used: the screen is black, save for a single face, as some sinner is moved to tears of repentance. These people take their religion passionately, and their protests and confessions are loud and often eloquent.

(8)

WHAT NOW? More of this skilful montage, as I see Thomas Gilmartin grown old, and dying an exemplary death. Young Wesley, always so called though he is young no longer, gives a deathbed promise that he will continue the evangelical work, though he declares himself unworthy, for he has not the preaching gift as Thomas had it. But he kneels for blessing, and henceforth he travels through the towns, to buy the flannel, and to preach as best he can. He is earnest; he never seeks to be eloquent, but sometimes he achieves the eloquence of simplicity.

As I watch this sad scene – though Thomas assures all those who crowd around his deathbed that to die in the assurance of a blessed hereafter is not sad – I see in the other quarters of the screen Young Wesley's concern for his children, his eldest son, Samuel, and a younger brother, another Thomas. Young Wesley has married twice, and the child of his first wife appears to be an exemplary youth, happy to

continue in the Scotch Trade. But the son of his second
marriage is rebellious, and wants something better. He wants
to put his foot on the ladder toward a fortune, and he knows
how to do it. He wants to be a servant.

"Why?" asks Samuel, as the boys lie in bed together.

"Because I have a taste for something better than this,"
says Thomas. "Do you think I want to bend at the loom until
I am bunchbacked like our Dad? A weaver! Do you want to
be a weaver, Sam?"

"Our Dad is not a weaver now. He has weavers to work
for him. He doesn't have to touch his cap to any man. Do you
want to be a cap-toucher, and a toady? Where's your manhood?"

"I'm ready to touch my cap if it brings me to the notice
of people who can lift me in the world. I've a taste for a bit of
life, Sam. Not this endless spinning and weaving and packing
the horses and trudging to Scotland and haggling and being
called a Greedy Taffy by a lot of greedy Scotchmen. Red
flannel's going out, Sam. You mark my words."

"There'll be money in red flannel for a while yet. And
don't sneer at our Dad. He's done very well, look you.
When he goes – as we all must, and God spare him – there'll
be a very pretty little bundle, and some if it will be for you.
How can you be a servant if you have money of your
own?"

"Being a servant is a very good trade. Look at Jesse
Fewtrell. Do you suppose he has no money of his own?"

"Oh, very well, if you want to be a Jesse Fewtrell and
scrape shillings by cheating your master, go ahead, and be
damned to you!"

"Sam – I never thought to hear you curse me. I'll tell our
Dad."

"I didn't curse you, you morlock. I spoke theologically,
which is probably above your head. I said – and I meant – that
if you persist in this headstrong path, your damnation will be
certain."

"Oh? So it's theological, is it? Well, I can be theological

too. I would rather be a doorkeeper in the house of a lord than dwell in the tents of the Wesleyans.''

"Tommo, that's twisting Scripture! I won't share a bed with anyone who twists Scripture. I don't know what might happen in the night!''

"Then get you out of bed.''

"Oh no, my fine lackey-lad. You get out of bed!''

And Samuel gives Thomas a mighty kick that lands him on the floor, where he spends the night.

Why? Because he has a hankering for high life and the only entrance to it, for Thomas, is the servants' entrance. When he is in Trallwm with his father he sees the fine carriages of the county gentry with their splendid horses and coachmen and footmen in fine liveries. He knows them all and identifies the liveries as boys now identify makes of automobiles. Best of all, he sometimes sees a carriage from the Castle, and then there are two men on the box, and two footmen in their places behind, and in the carriage itself the Countess, and now and then the Earl, who seems to see no one, but from time to time lifts a weary finger to the brim of his wonderful hat, as he acknowledges a curtsy from some woman on the street. Virtually the whole town belongs to him, and these people are his tenants; he is upon the whole a popular and good landlord. As Thomas Gilmartin had said of his father, this boy has something of the nature of a herald, and the pomp and splendour of county gentility feeds his imagination and rouses his ambition. He horrifies his father by repeating his perversion of Scripture; he says that he would rather be a doorkeeper in the house of a lord than dwell in the tents of the Wesleyans!

This is abomination! Surely this is Cain raised!

Young Wesley does what he can. He beats Young Thomas soundly, for he that spares the rod hateth his son; but beating is of no avail. He exhorts him, but Young Thomas has a scoffer's way with the Bible, and can quote more Scripture on behalf of the good and faithful servant's life than his father can quote against it. His mother weeps, his brother storms, but Young Thomas cares nothing for words or tears. He cares for nothing but a fine coat, and buttons with a gentleman's crest embossed on them, a hat with a smart cockade, and a face that is shaved every day.

So at last the black day comes when Young Wesley, who is now becoming Grey Wesley, accosts a stout, self-important man in the Trallwm street, and says, "Mr. Fewtrell, sir, may I beg a word with you?"

"Well, what is it, Gilmartin? I'm busy."

Mr. Jesse Fewtrell is a very important man, for he is the Groom of the Chambers at the Castle, and he has favours to give. Favours, but only for the Earl's tenants, and Young Wesley is not one of those. Favours for good Church people, and Young Wesley is a field preacher of that nasty group of craw-thumpers who are beginning to call themselves Methodists, as if John Wesley had not been a good C of E man all his life. Mr. Fewtrell's fat face is sour as he looks at Young Wesley.

"It is my son Thomas, Mr. Fewtrell. He has a great desire to enter service, and I dared to hope that if you had a place you might give him his start, is it?"

Mr. Fewtrell is repelled by such a notion. The idea is preposterous. He has known of Methodists entering service, but only in Methodist households, which were not those of county gentry, to say nothing of the nobility. He wants no praying and psalm-singing among his staff. But when he looks at Young Thomas, who is a well-set-up lad, and whose breeches and stockings show that he has the good calves which are absolutely obligatory in a liveried servant, and a round red face, that looks so respectfully into his, and a great head of deep red hair, that glows like copper, Mr. Fewtrell has an idea. A disagreeable idea, of course, or Mr. Fewtrell would not have it, but an idea, all the same.

"The boy speaks English, I suppose?" he says.

"Oh yes indeed, sir. Very correct English," says Young Thomas. But his tongue is that of someone who thinks in another language.

"I'll take him on liking. I need a lad, but I won't have any nonsense, you hear? Send him to the Castle on Monday next – that's Lady Day; if he lasts for a quarter I'll see what I can do. No pay for the first quarter, mind."

"Oh thank you sir. Certainly not for the first quarter. Thank you, Mr. Fewtrell. You are very kind. And the lad will do everything to please you, I'll go bail."

Mr. Fewtrell nods curtly, and gives another hard look at Young Thomas, and goes about his business. Which is to take his morning glass of dark sherry at the Green Man; he will cut a figure in the bar where the superior tradesmen, as opposed to the farmers, are to be found. They are all tenants of the Earl, and Mr. Fewtrell is a great man to them.

I see, with sadness, that Grey Wesley, who speaks so confidently to God, is made humble by an upper servant at the Castle. But that is the way of the world, and when I was alive I saw much deferential smiling and heard much fawning speech in the New World, where such things are imagined by idealists to have no place.

Thus, on Lady Day, March 25, 1838, Thomas Gilmartin becomes a Castle servant. He receives no pay, but canny Mr. Fewtrell puts an item for his service under the record of Sundries he presents every month at the Estate Office, and pockets it himself. Once again the screen splits into four and I know rapidly what service means, for at the beginning there is no livery, and Thomas is what is called below-stairs "the gong boy." Twice a day he empties the hundred and forty chamber-pots in the Castle, beginning with the elegant porcelain *pots de chambre* in the boudoirs of the Countess and her lady guests, then moving to the heavier jordans in the gentlemen's rooms (some of which, unaccountably, and with no intention of disloyalty, have pictures of Royal Palaces printed inside them), and, last of all, the plain pots that are used by the servants. There are two hundred and eighty pots in all, for every day the pots of the day before must be taken down to a yard in the back premises, and there scalded and set out to air. As well as the pots there are commodes, concealed in fine sets of steps, or chairs of innocent appearance; but in each one there is a removable pewter container – called a Welsh Hat, because of its shape, and perhaps as a jeer at the peasantry – in which the dung of the gentry and their servants lurks, to be coaxed forth with a spatula, and put down an outdoor drain.

"The pots and the hats are your perks," says the head footman, a great joker; "anything you find in them you can keep or sell, as you please."

The system of "perks" runs through the whole domestic staff of the Castle. Mr. Fewtrell's perks are very great, for they are gifts of wine and spirits from the merchants that supply the great household, and he does a lively business in these among the tenant farmers who have money to spare, and like to say to their cronies, "This is a pure drop; comes from the Castle." The chief footman's perks are the candle-ends from the whole great household, for sometimes fourteen hundred candles are lighted in a single night, and the custom is that no candle is ever lit twice. And so his disposal of "long ends" in the town is very remunerative. Just as remunerative is the trade of the cook – for My Lord is old-fashioned enough to employ a woman to do his cooking, and will hear nothing of a French chef – because she sells dripping to those who bring their bowls to the little green door adjacent to the kitchen; where there are so many to feed and so many roasts on the spit every day, there is much dripping. The ladies' maids and the valets, of course, have cast-off clothes. Everybody has perks except the gong-boy, and even he has his hopes, because there is a very old tale of a silver spoon having once been found in a Welsh Hat.

So Young Thomas would have toiled long as gong-boy if the Countess had not happened upon him one day as he was stealing a peach in the glasshouse. She ignores the peach; Countesses have upper servants to rebuke under servants. But she likes the looks of the handsome lad, and gives orders that he is to drive her pony-trap when she jaunts through the park to take the air. And so, to the annoyance of Mr. Fewtrell,

Young Thomas gets a livery after about six months in Castle service.

Just a single livery, that of a groom. But Young Thomas grows in favour with the Countess, who likes handsome young men, and it is not long before he becomes a footman. Not an important footman, but one of the sixteen lesser footmen who do work about the place that would nowadays be expected of housemaids. And that means an advance to three liveries. One for morning, which is plain and is marked by a sleeve-waistcoat, a coat that has no tails; one for afternoon, which means breeches and stockings, and a coat with tails and pewter buttons; but – this is glorious – a full-dress livery for evening appearances in the corridors and in the dining-room, which means white stockings, plush breeches and a velvet coat with silver buttons, and, most glorious of all, powder for his red hair. It takes a lot of powder and pomatum to make his red hair the required white, and every morning his hair has to be washed before breakfast, for powder is not worn during the day. But Young Thomas revels in powder, and his impassivity of face, and his fine bowing – deferential but never personal – carry him far up the ladder of service, and by the time he is thirty years old he is head footman, and Mr. Fewtrell has had his first stroke of the fatal three, and is retired and can tyrannize no more.

Thus Thomas is lost to his home, though there is no cruel break. On Mothering Sunday, when all servants are given leave to visit their mothers, or any credible equivalent, he rides on a borrowed pony to Llanfair, with a present of a Simnel cake, baked in the Castle kitchen, and a gift from the Countess. He regales his parents and his half-brother Samuel with tales of the high life. His welcome is saddened by the fact that he has now embraced the Church of England, because the Castle servants are expected to attend the Anglican chapel-of-ease in the park every Sunday. This is a necessity of his employment, but Thomas does not conceal the fact that he likes it, likes the gentility of it, and the ceremonial of the service. Likes sitting in the servants' gallery, and sharing a hymnbook with the prettiest housemaid.

Worse, he has become a Tory, for the Castle expects any servant to support the Earl's candidate at an election with his cheers, and sometimes with his fists, and, although Thomas is not yet of the financial rank that would give him a vote, he has listened with reverence over the years as Mr. Fewtrell held forth in the servants' hall against the iniquities of Radicals and Reformers, and levellers of all kinds. Thomas has turned his coat, but he knows, and his family know, that he has turned it for a velvet coat with silver buttons, and it takes a great deal of principle to speak against that. Indeed, principle has begun to run low in the Gilmartin family after the death of Young Wesley, by then Old Wesley, in 1850.

(9)

FINELY EDUCATED as he was, it is unlikely that John Wesley paid any attention to that curmudgeonly Greek sage Heraclitus who was the first, so far as we know, to point out the psychological fact that anything, if pursued beyond a reasonable point, turns into its opposite. But John Wesley saw too much of life to escape the fact, and in a moment of terrible prophetic knowledge said: "Godliness begets Industry; Industry begets Wealth; Wealth begets Ungodliness." And I now see this law at work in the family of Old Wesley Gilmartin, who had been baptized by water and the Spirit and accepted into the Christian family by a direct disciple of Wesley himself, a man who had been confirmed in the ministry by Wesley, and had profited by the good counsel of his great master.

Old Wesley had not been an imaginative man, and was little troubled by discontent. He was industrious, and sure enough Industry – all that buying of red flannel in prodigious lengths of 132 yards, all those trains of pack-horses over the hills to Scotland, all that honest, moderate profit – brought Wealth, or what was Wealth in the circumstances in which he lived. His Godliness was, however, the great concern of his life, and when I watch his death I know him to be a truly good man, firm in his faith, if narrow in his intellect.

What about the Wealth? It was plain that Samuel, as the eldest son and his father's right hand, should carry on the business. But there was money – money in a leather bag under the boards of the parlour floor – and when it was all counted up, and Old Wesley's few debts were paid, there was a little more than seven hundred pounds for each son.

Thomas takes his money, and takes the bag, and hides both in a place where he keeps his own savings, from his wages and the tips, still called "vails," that came his way at the Castle.

(10)

SAMUEL NOW has the business, and employs weavers, because he has grown too great for the drudgery of the loom. He also has his stepmother to keep; being the eldest son is not all gain, for she inherits nothing except her clothes and some pieces of furniture which are, by agreement, her own. He also inherits the economic situation of his time, and it is troublesome.

The Scotch Trade is on the wane, for country women no longer wear so many red petticoats or the red cloaks which defy rain and snow. They are even giving up the steeple-crown hats that were handed down from mother to daughter, sometimes for four generations. Cleanliness and dress are taking on new forms.

Is Samuel reconciled to a loss of income? Not he.

Samuel is godly. He gives a yearly tenth of what he

makes to the chapel, for its maintenance and for the poor. He honours his stepmother and she lives a life of ease and contentment. He prays night and morning, but his prayers are not so feeling, so unctuous, as those of Old Wesley. God has brought him prosperity, and it is not surprising that, to a mind like his, prosperity looks like solid evidence of God's favour. God is, in fact, a business partner. Is it God's will that he should cling to a declining trade? God, like fortune, favours the bold.

Thus it is that Samuel looks about him and sees that the trains of pack-horses are giving way to the steam trains that are being built all over Wales. Samuel is not a big enough man, financially, to buy into the railway companies and he has a peasant mistrust of railway shares, which he could buy if he wanted them. But as he rides here and there on his business he sees that the armies of men who build the railways must have food where they work, and it is not easily found in the mountains. So he buys a couple of carts, and makes an arrangement with the gangers who employ the railway builders that the men shall buy food from his carts, and from his alone. Intruders are warned off. It is not more than a year or so before he has pretty much given up the Scotch Trade to those who are so blind as to continue it, and his weavers are now pushing the carts every day to where the workers are, and bread, and cheese, and bacon and beer are sold to the workers in a lively trade, and Samuel is richer than his father could have believed.

He leaves his stepmother in the old house in Llanfair, and moves to larger and more convenient quarters down the valley, in Trallwm, where provisions are to be bought cheaper, and distributed more widely. He lives over his place of business, but his house is finer than his father's, and in the bigger Trallwm chapel he is known as a substantial man and – John Wesley would have frowned at this – he is admired as a Big Giver.

Could he do all this and still be a godly man, in his father's understanding of the term? Godliness has brought

Wealth, and where there is Wealth, Industry takes on another colour.

The colour, of course, is that of Samuel's own nature, and though I can see that he is not, in a coarse sense, a carnal man, he is undoubtedly a fleshy one. He has grown physically big, for, though he is not tall, and he is too hard of body to be strictly fat, he has become a man whose clothes demand a lot of good cloth. He takes to a tall hat even on weekdays. He has a large and impressive watch-chain, of the sort called an Albert, because the fashion was set by the Prince Consort; his watch is of the largest, loudest-ticking, most infallible sort. He even affects a gold brooch in his satin stock, although his wife has doubts about it and wonders if it is not a vanity. A man needs a watch, of course, but a brooch – ? But Samuel is not ruled by his wife and he likes the brooch. It is the headlight of his engine.

For to my eyes, Samuel looks uncommonly like the engine of one of the new railway trains. His broad short figure, crowned by the very tall black hat of the day, and the short steps of his short legs, make him appear to advance as if on wheels, inexorably. He is on his way and no one shall stop him.

Samuel is what the town calls "long-headed." He is a reflecting man, and he reflects a great deal on what may bring him a profit. His fine clothes, which need so much cloth, give him a new idea. The railways are pretty much all built, but in the new world of the nineteenth century people of any account have ceased to wear old indestructible clothes, patched and mended, as once they did. Only the poor continue to wear the clothes that look almost like the costume of a harlequin, so patched are they with any cloth that came handy. Clothes are the thing, and Samuel decides that he will be a tailor.

He will be, moreover, a smart tailor. Not to say fashionable, because that would alarm the farmers and local tradesmen who will be his customers, but he will offer something better than the garments made by the inept botcher whose failing shop he buys, and whose clothes might almost have been made by Robinson Crusoe. He will offer the new cloths, the tweeds from the north and the good broadcloths from London, the fancy waistcoats to wear to chapel and smartly cut, dropleaf-front breeches of whipcord for farmers who are rising in the world and want the world to take notice. He is not appealing to dandies, for there are none; but he is aiming at solid men, below the gentleman rank but of proven worth, like himself. His fine broadcloth is impeccable, but of a provincial cut, and the full copper beard he wears, with a shaven upper lip, marks him firmly as a Trallwm man.

He hires a good tradesman from Shrewsbury to be his foreman, but he has an eye to the future, and sends his younger son David to London to learn the art of cutting. To some extent cutting is a gift, but much may be learned, and Samuel has hopes that the gift may assert itself in David.

That settles his family, thinks Samuel. Walter doing brilliantly at a good school. David launched in a fine trade. Polly, his only daughter, at Dr. Williams's, the best Methodist school for girls in Wales, and headed, assuredly, for a good, prosperous marriage.

David is a mercurial youth, a great jester, so perhaps there may be some hint of the artist in him. At seventeen he is already a pocket version of his father, a stocky, short, copper-bearded fellow who looks almost as thick as he is tall, though this is not really so; it is an impression given by a giant's torso on short legs. He has a moist eye, and is a favourite with the girls, though not the most modest girls. His father does not yet know it, but David drinks, and not beer, but spirits. Mary Evans, the barmaid at the Angel Inn, knows David better than his father does.

Samuel is fond of his dram, too, but he is discreet, as a chapel deacon ought to be. He is a member of a small club, made up of perhaps twenty prosperous tradesmen like himself, who do not care to be seen in the saloon bar at the Green Man, but who own a handsome old place called – nobody knows why – the Mansion House, and there they meet, ostensibly to discuss the politics of the day, but also to wet their whistles with brandy and seltzer. Industry and Wealth are truly lurching toward Ungodliness and Samuel knows it, but he can argue it away when the knowledge becomes too insistent.

His wife rebukes him no longer, for she has died. A good, pious, charitable and loving woman, but Samuel's prosperity was too rapid for her. Moreover she was imprisoned in the Welsh language which, fine as it is, does not agree with Samuel's bustling life. He is trapped in his modernity; she in a feudal world. She strove to speak English, but it was not the comfortable clothing of her mind, or her link with her God. So he rushed into the future and she remained in the past.

(11)

SAMUEL IS a rising man. He is prominent in the Radical interest in the town, and it is growing, for there are more and more tradesmen who are no longer tenants of the Earl, or who have their premises on such long leases that they have nothing to fear from the Castle, so long as their rents are paid. Reform and Dissent are powers to be reckoned with in Trallwm. People of historical bent recall that in 1745 not a man would rally to the banner of Prince Charles Edward in the town, to the indignation of the Castle. Samuel becomes an alderman, and his business sense and long-headedness make him such a good one that, in an overturn that greatly annoys the Castle, he is elected Mayor of the Borough. The first Nonconformist ever to be Mayor of a Welsh borough! Think of that! The scarlet gown and the mayoral chain become his stately, short figure better than the succession of Castle supporters who have gone before him, for as long as the Borough has existed. On great occasions his short legs, beneath the scarlet gown and the fur-trimmed tricorn hat, move so deliberately that he seems to travel on castors.

When Samuel is at his pinnacle, Fate strikes him down. I knew Fate would do it, because when I was alive I was a drama critic, and I had inherited a good sense of melodrama from my father. But Samuel did not know it, because men never do foresee such blows, and are always astonished when their destiny follows some old familiar path. Fate is even so devoted to cliché as to strike Samuel in the three most predictable places: in his family, in his pride, and in his rectitude.

Family first. It is Thomas who makes the name of Gilmartin odious to the godly. He is by now the head foot-man at the Castle, and carries on the trade in "long ends" that goes with the job. It is not to Samuel's liking that his half-brother is a professional bower and scraper, but he can do nothing about it, and he will not turn his back on his brother. But Thomas has for many years enjoyed to the full a foot-man's perk of seducing the prettier maids in the Castle serv-ice, and everybody knows it in the town, but nobody speaks of it except late at night, in the saloon bar of the Green Man, or in hints at Chapel tea-meetings. In those privileged places it is spoken of often.

It is not the local fashion to speak too loudly about such things, as nobody speaks about the disgraceful entries, locally called "shuts," down which a dozen huddled dwell-ings, and perhaps three brick privies, house the hard core of Trallwm poverty. Chapel people of the more practical sort venture down the shuts with baskets of necessities for the wretched women and hungry children, but it needs more than that to make the shuts superfluous. It needs some cure that probably does not exist in a world so economically lunatic as this. It needs, perhaps, a revolution in the nature of man, which will make everybody industrious, prudent, decent and loving. And how Old Heraclitus would laugh at that notion! Prosperity must have its coeval and its opposite, and that is what the shuts are in Trallwm, and in every place bigger than a hamlet.

Everybody speaks of Thomas's hobby, and with indignation, when one of the girls dies. It had always been his custom, if one of his pretty subordinates whispered to him tearfully that she feared she was pregnant, to arrange for her to visit a local Wise Woman, Old Nan, who lived at a nearby crossway called the Brandy Shop. Old Nan has a proven remedy for pregnancy, which she makes from herbs and sells to trusted customers at a guinea a bottle. But the most recent favourite disobligingly developed blood poisoning after a miscarriage brought about too late, and died distressingly in the maids' dormitory at the Castle, and it cannot be kept from the Countess. She is furious, and insists that the Earl's agent, Mr. Forrester Addy, get to the root of the matter, and Thomas is in disgrace. Mr. Addy thinks that legal proceedings would be a mistake, because the culprit is the brother of the Mayor, and the Mayor, as a Justice of the Peace, would either have to sit in judgement – which would be dreadful – or refuse to do so – which would be equally dreadful in another way. But Thomas is cast out, and the scandal is on every tongue.

When Samuel meets Thomas, it is Samuel who feels the disgrace. Thomas appears buoyant. Samuel cannot, of course, ask this seducer to his house; not a seducer, and perhaps not a Castle servant, brother though he may be. Nor can he ask his brother to the Mansion House, for he is a servant, however much money he may have tucked away. So Samuel has to let Thomas into the Town Hall at night, by a side door, and talk with him in the Mayor's Parlour, which is not the luxurious apartment the name suggests. He gestures Thomas to a chair, then walks to and fro until his anger is hot enough for him to begin the interview.

"Fornicator!" he says, rounding on Thomas and glaring at him.

"You have always used hard words to me, Sam," says Thomas, and he appears to consider himself the injured brother. "Years ago you damned me, and I've never forgotten that. I've forgiven you, of course. Oh indeed, yes. But you know what the Bible has to say about a man that damns his brother. You've always been a hard man, Sam."

"I told you you'd be damned yourself, Tommo, and I was right! Here's a pretty kettle of fish! I've managed to keep this from our Mam, but everybody else in the county knows of it, and knows what to think of you."

"Oh, not everybody, Sam. A few gossips, perhaps."

"Yes, everybody. Last Sunday, in Chapel, I had to hear the minister pray for 'one of our brothers who had sustained a heavy blow.' And me sitting right below him, in the deacons' pew, with all the other Big Heads of the Chapel! How do you suppose I liked that? Me, the Mayor, and the first Nonconformist Mayor, look you! And what do I hear but that up at St. Mary's the Vicar spoke from the pulpit of the sorrow of the Countess, who was known for her kindness to her girls, and had lost one of them under circumstances that he could not mention in a sacred place. Oh, you've disgraced us finely, Tommo."

"I don't really see what it has to do with you."

"Do you not? I suppose this is something you've picked up from the English up at the Castle. They don't know what family is. My own brother!"

"Half-brother."

"Who do you suppose thinks of that? You, whose father was baptized through water and the Holy Spirit by a man who had served John Wesley himself."

"There's a bastard in the Wesley family now, did you know? Was that the Holy Spirit, do you suppose? I've no bastards, that I know of."

"That will do! You've a girl's death on your conscience."

"A misfortune, certainly. She brought it on herself, Sam. I couldn't get rid of her. Couldn't get enough, she couldn't. I never forced her. A nice enough girl, but a bit of a fool."

"God forgive you, you heartless villain! But that's enough of that. What are you going to do?"

"Well, I must say Mr. Addy hasn't been as understanding as I would have expected a gentleman to be, and so I've been turned off. I suppose I'll find something hereabouts."

"You will not! You'll get out of this town and out of this borough."

"If that's the way you see it. I suppose with some help I could go elsewhere. I thought that's what you wanted to see me about."

"Oh, so you've come for money? What's become of the money our Dad left you?"

"You'd never understand, Sam. Sometimes we play for pretty high stakes in the company I've been keeping."

"Gambling?"

"Sam, if there's gambling among the guests, there'll be gambling among the servants. A matter of pride, almost, to keep up the tone of society. I've never been lucky with the cards or the dice."

"And you expect me to bail you out, is it?"

"Now look, Sam; let's drop all this Chapel talk and come to the horses. When our Dad died, you got the business, as well as half the money, isn't it?"

"And I got the care, and I got our Mam – your Mam more than mine, look you – and I've had to graft hard to make what I have grow with the times."

"Oh, we all know about that. Do you know, Sam, that they talk about you at the Castle? Listen – I've even heard his lordship himself say to an unlucky player, 'Perhaps you could arrange a loan with our Mayor; he's a very warm man.' A joke, of course, but a joke with truth behind it. Everybody knows about you, and the railways, and the shops. You could buy and sell one or more of our county gentry, I dare say. So don't come it over me about money. I'm prepared to listen to reason."

"And what's reason today, boyo? You've a plan, I can tell. Let's stop all this foolery. What will you take to get out and never be seen here again?"

"Of course, I've been thinking of my future. Now, Sam,

it would suit me very well to have a little public house. Lots of us, when we leave service, go into the public line."

"A pub, is it? What pub? I can see in your eye that you have a pub in mind."

"As luck has it, there's a very nice pub down the road a few miles. Enough miles to suit you, I think. You've heard of The Aleppo Merchant, at Carno? It can be had."

"The Aleppo Merchant? That's no pub! That's a country hotel, and quite a fancy one. And a fancy price, I'll be bound."

"It takes a few guests. For the fishing, you know. A very decent little place."

"How much?"

"Ah, now we're talking. The Aleppo Merchant, and a little over to settle some of my debts, and a trifle to see me set up there would run you – Oh, call it twenty-five hundred."

"Twenty – five – hundred – pounds!"

"Better make it guineas, while you're at it. When we play at the Castle, we always make it guineas."

"That's more than three times what you had from our Dad!"

"Money has lost value, as I'm sure you know. I'm being as conservative as I can."

"Yes – Conservative – you rotten, evil Tory turncoat! Conservative is what you are – a Tory. Oh, if our Mam knew of this!"

"Don't tell her, Sam. You've always taken very good care of our Mam, bless her old heart. I give you that."

Samuel has turned grey in the face, for reasons he knows, but which are happily unknown to Thomas. Wearily – he puts it on a little, for he is a Welshman, and such domestic histrionics come readily to him – Samuel sits at the Mayor's desk, and takes a cheque-book from a locked drawer, and in his careful, round, tradesman's hand he draws a cheque, and tosses it across to his brother.

"Thanks, Sam. Good of you, I'm sure. I'll draw this in the morning, if that's convenient."

It is convenient. Indeed, it is desirable. If the Mayor has to buy off his profligate brother, he has no insuperable objection to Trallwm knowing about it, and banks are leaky, however much they pretend otherwise. Trallwm will know that he has done the painful, but handsome, thing. It will do no harm whatever to his reputation. The story will have a slightly different colour than Samuel puts on it, for the bankers know - as Samuel does not - that Thomas has a very nice little nest-egg; his inheritance intact, and the avails of twenty years of bowing and keeping his mouth shut. These are cynical considerations, but very human, and I, the looker-on, understand them perfectly.

"Thanks, Sam. Done like a brother. And now - good friends, is it?"

Thomas has risen, and holds out his hand to the Mayor. The Mayor is reluctant to take it.

"You won't let me go without a handshake, Sam. Blood's thicker than water."

Among the Welsh it certainly is. Thick as tar. Samuel grasps his brother's hand, and it is from his eyes that the tears begin to flow.

Thomas carefully folds the cheque into his pocket-book and goes, with the soft tread of a footman.

(12)

THE MAYOR sits long at his table. He needs no Bible to fuel his reflections, for Holy Writ is deep in his flesh and bone. "The wicked are like the troubled sea, when it cannot rest, whose waters cast up mire and dirt." Isaiah said it all. But did not John say: "He that loveth not his brother whom he hath seen, how can he love God whom he hath not seen?"

A clincher, that one. Oh, hard - hard to be a Christian in

such a puzzling world. For God, who made the world, and his Son, seem to have been at odds on many important points.

Samuel's pride is that of a successful Radical politician, and a man of growing substance. He owns not only his profitable tailor's shop, but a fine farm, called Gungrog Hall. It is not a "hall" in the sense that the homes of the county gentry are "halls," but it is much above a tradesman's residence, and he owns it outright; he is no man's tenant. It is here that he indulges a lifelong interest in fine horses, which may also be fast horses, and a man who owns fast horses likes to see them win races.

Horse-racing, however, is for men whose knowledge and subtlety is of a different order from that of a successful tradesman, and Samuel has the tendency of wealthy men to think that he knows other men's trades as well as he knows his own. Is a man who enters a fine horse in local races – sometimes as far distant as Shrewsbury – to refuse to back his own horse, and back it substantially? Betting is, of course, dead against Wesleyan principle, and Samuel is discreet in his betting, but bet he does, because he convinces himself that it is not gambling, but a particular sort of investment. And who is a better judge of a horse's ability than the man who has bred it from excellent stock, and seen it trained by Jockey Jones, who is now in his employ?

Jockey Jones is not a Wesleyan. He is not anything of that sort. He was bred and his character was formed up a Trallwm shut, and his favourite place of resort is a local slum called, appropriately, Puzzle Square. Jockey Jones does very well out of the races by taking care that Samuel's horses do not win, or win only enough to divert suspicion. So Samuel loses and loses, and in time Gungrog Hall is heavily and secretly mortgaged to discreet men in Shrewsbury, and Samuel turns too often to the Mansion House and to brandy and seltzer. His friends there know well enough that Jockey Jones is a scoundrel, but they have all the discretion – if that is what you like to call it – of the Welsh, and they say nothing to Samuel.

Nor would he thank them if they did. So they whisper that the Mayor is getting into deep water.

Samuel is still a man of rectitude, and it is this which at last brings him down, and brings Gungrog Hall under the auctioneer's hammer, along with the horses. It even endangers the tailor's shop, but does not quite destroy it, because Samuel has been so long-headed as to make his older son, Walter, a partner with a half-share. But half a share in the tailor's shop cannot save Samuel. The shadow darkens toward night when Samuel backs a note for a fellow deacon at the Chapel, one Llewellyn Thomas, a grocer and provisioner in a very large way. Much too large a way, it proves, for the note is a big one, and Llewellyn Thomas is saved from bankruptcy only by this act of trust and Samuel's lifelong principle that a man must never turn his back on a friend. So the bankruptcy falls on Samuel, who meets the note without a whimper, and is ruined. Oh, Heraclitus; and Oh, John Wesley!

(*13*)

Bankruptcy! The hobgoblin, the obliterating shadow of the commercial world of Samuel's day! For in those days a man could be bankrupt but once; there were no second chances, no histories of repeated bankruptcies. It all happens within a few months. Samuel retires to a cramped life in the premises over the tailor's shop, and the black day approaches when he must, in the local phrase, "go up the Town Hall steps" and be formally declared a bankrupt.

Of course desolation and want do not face him, for Walter would do whatever lay in his limited power to make his father's final years as comfortable as possible. Samuel does not face life in the Forden Union Workhouse, the dreaded "workus" with which children and all improvident persons are threatened. But he has been a great man in his world, and now he faces disgrace deeper even than that brought on by Thomas.

Thus it is that he takes to his bed, and two days before he is to mount those dreadful steps to face his fellow magistrates, Samuel has a very quiet heart attack, and is found dead by his son. Dead of disgrace, which was, and still is, often a fatal misfortune. Fate has once again worked out her old, old plot, which is fresh and desolating to every new victim.

Fresh and desolating to me, too. Me, the patient looker-on. I weep, in my ghostly way, for Samuel, because he is my great-great-grandfather, of whom I knew nothing but his name, but whose dark red hair is mine also. It does not matter that he was really nobody very much – just a man who did well in a small, distant town that I have never seen, and met ruin because he was puffed up, and stupid, and loyal, and good, according to his lights; like me, I now understand. There is no such thing as a person who is "nobody very much." Everybody is an agonist in one of Fate's time-worn games on the earth, and winning or losing is not what it seems to be in the judgement of others, but as judged by the player himself.

So Samuel passes, leaving a mess behind him, and nobody to clear up the mess but his elder son Walter, who is not the man to do it.

I know something of Walter, for a passage of that Concurrent Action, of which this director seems fond, and which crowds so much I need to know into the screen in an astonishingly economical manner, has shown me his boyhood and young manhood, his downfall and his marriage.

(14)

WALTER WAS the clever boy, and David was the popular, merry boy. Walter was devout and studious and went away to a good boarding-school – not one of England's great public schools, but a place devoted to the Welsh Wesleyan interest – where he won prize after prize, and showed uncommon promise in mathematics. He organized prayer meetings among the more devout boys, and was exemplary in his religious observance and his truly Wesleyan examination of his conscience. He was a stoutly built boy, whose uncommonly thick legs won him the nickname of Gate Posts. It was clear enough where Walter was going. Like all devout boys he had a spell of wanting to be a preacher, but he quickly put that aside and set his sights on the Civil Service. There is always a place in the Civil Service for a good mathematician, and Walter was also something of a linguist; he spoke Welsh and English from infancy, and to be born bilingual is a great start on Latin and Greek, which he absorbed almost without thinking. The Treasury, the Foreign Office, the Home Office, all seemed within his grasp, and when at last he won a scholarship to Oxford, the thing was virtually assured.

Fate sees it otherwise. Walter is just eighteen when his mother falls ill, and is about to die. She summons him to her bedside.

"Walter, dearest boy," she says; "I want you to promise me never to leave your father. He needs you. He is not as strong a man as everybody thinks. And you know that David is a great disappointment. Your father needs a stout staff to lean on. Give me your promise, my dear."

Walter kneels by the bed and gives his promise, for who can hesitate when a mother lies so near to death? And that, in a great many important ways, is the finish of Walter. He prays to be given the strength to do what he has promised, to be a staff and a strength, and within a fortnight his mother is dead.

Truly, David is a great disappointment. He has learned the fine points of the tailoring in London, and he is a good cutter, but he spoils a lot of fine cloth because he is never entirely sober. Samuel is sure that responsibility will quiet him, and he sets David up in his own tailoring shop in Machynlleth, where David becomes a great support to the local pubs. Yes, and even to the refreshment room at the local railway station, for in Wales there were no pubs open on Sunday, but a *bona fide* traveller could have a drink at the station. So I see David, a roly-poly red-headed rascal, lurking beside the railway track, an empty portmanteau in his hand, whenever the two Sunday trains are due at Machynlleth; as the train arrives, he runs down the track, climbs the barrier to the station area, and dashes into the refreshment room, as *bona fide* a traveller as ever was seen. Of course the girl at the counter knows him and knows what he is up to, but she is a large-hearted, understanding sort of girl, as barmaids often are. It is not long before the tailor's shop closes its doors, and David returns to his father, a prodigal son, for whom Samuel prepares the thinnest and poorest of calves. More like a black sheep, say the Trallwm wags.

Of course that just man Samuel cannot give David his own shop and ignore the dutiful Walter, so he makes over a half-share in his Trallwm shop, which is henceforth Gilmartin and Son. But Walter is no tailor. He is dutiful, but his heart yearns toward the Treasury in London. When Samuel dies, a broken-hearted man, Walter has that part of the shop that the creditors do not devour, and the humiliation that comes with David.

David is shameless, as career-drunks often are, and on market days he is often to be seen in the street outside Gilmartin and Son, staggering among the horses and carriages as he shouts – "Look at him! Look at my brother Walter, who won't give his only brother the price of a pint o' beer! There's a Christian for you!" The townsfolk turn away their eyes, and the gentry, in their carriages, are disgusted. Walter hides in the shop, in the workroom at the back, among the tailors who sit cross-legged on the "board" – the low platform on which they stitch, and iron garments on boards stretched across their knees. They do not look at Walter, but they hear David and, though they pity Walter, some mud sticks to him, as well.

(15)

W ALTER'S LIFE is not all darkness. He is respected in the Chapel, and his marriage is his great strength.

He has married Janet Jenkins, a schoolmistress and the sister of John Jethro Jenkins, who is thereby Walter's brother-in-law in double strength. Polly, Walter's sister, has been finished, in so far as a girl of her station may be finished, at Dr. Williams's school in Aberystwyth, and it is in that prosperous seaside town that she meets John Jethro, who is in a vague world called Import and Export, and marries him. He is sure to be a great man, for he is a scholar and a thinker, and an eloquent speaker in matters of Reform politics. John Jethro is not, however, a markedly practical man, or he would never have married Polly Gilmartin, whose sole recommendation as a wife is that she admires John Jethro extravagantly.

Janet is a bird of a wholly different feather. Not a richly coloured feather, but a glowing russet feather. She is a sufficiently good teacher, so far as she has anything to teach – reading, writing and some pretty music – but she is devout, cheerful, industrious, and she loves Walter with her whole excellent heart. Walter reciprocates, and it is their domesticity that makes it possible for him to endure the burdens of his life.

He is humble, but he cannot cringe. He is polite but he is not deferential. He hates what he has to do, because now the trade of Gilmartin and Son has shrunk until the greatest part of it is the making of liveries. As a livery-maker he has to visit the great country houses which are owned by members of the Reform Party, and measure the servants for the suits of clothes that are part of the emolument of their service.

These are not Castle liveries. No velvet coats for footmen with powdered hair, but smart outfits for men who wait at table, answer the door, and, most particularly, look after the fine horses. The crested buttons, which are moulded in Shrewsbury, have to be ordered exactly to the last sleeve-button, because they are expensive, and a tailor must have a stock of them on hand at all times, but not too many. The butler's striped silk waistcoat must not be striped in colours seen at any neighbouring hall. The liveries must fit, and the figures of fat coachmen, and grooms with bandy legs – for grooms are as bandy as the tailors who sit cross-legged all day on the board – and footmen who are of all shapes, but must be made to look as much alike as possible, call for the most careful measurement, and the servants can be sharp with the tailor who does not work this near miracle. So Walter must drive out to the great halls in his hired gig, and take what food is offered him in the servants' hall, and kneel in the house-keeper's room, measuring the arms and the inside legs, and the backs of servants who are often not very civil in the way they speak to him.

Walter regrets Oxford, regrets mathematical reckoning beyond the measuring of a footman's leg from knee to crotch, regrets the Latin and Greek which have brought him, so it seems, to this. He never regrets the deathbed promise. Honour thy father and thy mother. Most particularly thy mother. And thy grandmother, for the old woman in Llanfair Caereinion must still be provided for, step-grandmother though she is.

Is Walter therefore a fool, I wonder? Has he not the spirit to throw up this whole miserable life and chance his luck elsewhere? But I know it is stupid to ask, for this is what has been and cannot be changed. Walter is a man of his time and a man of principle even when principle is odious. After a day among the footmen and grooms, who have a servant's scorn for someone who serves them, there is always Janet, when he can turn the horse's head toward home.

Of course they have children, four of them. The boys are Lancelot and Rhodri, the girls Elaine and Maude, and from these names I discern that Janet is of a romantic turn, and reads Ossian, and a modernized Malory, and especially Sir Walter

Scott. She reads aloud to her children, even on Sundays, when Walter is engaged with that improving Methodist publication, *The Leisure Hour*. Without being aware of it, Janet gives her children's minds a colour that persists even down to myself. Romantics all, without being fully aware of it.

Of course Janet never thinks of herself as a romantic. It is doubtful if the word would mean anything to her. She is a committed Wesleyan, and it is not in her welkin to see that Wesleyanism is the Romantic Movement as it manifested itself in religion. I know about the Romantic Movement. Is not my father a professor of English Literature in a fine Canadian university where, the syllabus decrees, the Romantic Movement is a successor to the Augustan Age, and a precursor of Modern Lit.? Romanticism: the subordination of logic and strict reason to feeling, and the elevation of emotion to a dominant place in forming judgements and dictating action, and the source of so much of our finest poetry.

Was not Wesleyanism romantic in its bias? Not, certainly, for that fine classicist John Wesley, but he spoke to people who had no classic restraint on their thinking, and who delighted in the exuberance and refreshment of their unleashed feeling. Theirs was not the coolly reverential tone of Addison, who could write, and mean, of the heavenly bodies –

> *In reason's ear they all rejoice*
> *And utter forth a glorious voice,*
> *Forever singing as they shine,*
> *"The Hand that made us is Divine."*

Wesleyans wanted, and found, a deeply personal faith that the Established Church of England no longer gave. The tone of their worship was –

> *He left His Father's throne above –*
> *So free, so infinite His grace –*

Emptied Himself of all but love,
    And bled for Adam's helpless race:
'Tis mercy, all, immense and free;
For, O my God, it found out me!

It found out *me*, it placed *me* in direct touch with God, it made *me* and my salvation the driving force in life.

How wonderful, how infinitely fulfilling, to know that in God's hand the Earl and the Vicar are no more than I! Erring children, all of us. Here is democracy in religion, and democracy, once the philosophers slacken their hold on it, is a recklessly Romantic idea. The Classic notion of society pre-supposes a hierarchy, and hierarchy cannot be wholly rooted out of a world where some men are, indisputably, superior to others. Had not Samuel Gilmartin become the first Noncon-formist Mayor of a Welsh Borough? That was, when all the heavy broadcloth and meals of boiled mutton are forgotten, a Romantic achievement. Religion and Romance combined – there was an explosive mixture!

(16)

AH, BUT hierarchy cannot be rooted out. Drive it forth in the Chapel and it will rise again in the shop, and the family dwelling over the shop. Elaine and Maude know it, and feel it when, during the shooting season, the Earl's brake drives through the streets leaving a brace of pheasants at the home of every faithful Tory tradesman and tenant, but passing by the door of the Gilmartins. Elaine and Maude are never asked to the summer lawn-party, or the winter Christmas party, at the Vicarage, where Tory girls rejoice sedately and respectfully in their excellent, but not fashionable, party frocks. It is not easy at eleven and thirteen to take solace in the certainty that Jesus loves them just as he presumably loves the Tories and the Castle hangers-on. It takes some gritting of teeth, and gritted teeth sometimes give rise to a spiritual pride.

For the boys, things are a little easier. They attend Mr. Timothy Hiles's school in the Oldford Road, and have occasional fights with the lesser boys of the National School where the teachers do not teach in cap and gown, as Mr. Hiles does, as he lathers a little Latin into them. Enough Latin, anyhow, to enable them to call their parents "the Pater" and "the Mater," which is swanky and a cut above the National School. To wear the cap of Oldford School, and to know the scant French that poor Monsieur Boué attempts to teach, amid the clamour of boys who think Frenchmen and their language just silly, is to be educationally a Cut Above. But Lancelot and Rhodri never fail to lift their caps when the Castle landau passes, because the beautiful Countess is Romance personified. She is the even younger wife of the Young Earl, who has succeeded his childless uncle; the Countess is a great London beauty, the loveliest of her "Season." It is rumoured that she is a mighty gambler, and that a lot of the Earl's huge rent-roll goes to pay her debts. That is certainly Romance, as the Chapel never provides Romance. Boys are never very good at resisting either Romance or spiritual pride.

As I look on I wonder how so many people can be accommodated in that little shop and the rooms above it. From the street one enters the front shop; it is not a large room and it is dominated by a round mahogany table on which the bolts of cloth from the shelves may be unrolled, displayed and consideringly thumbed. Behind it is the larger workroom, where the five tailors sit on the board, smoking their stinking pipes and amusing themselves with indecent stories when Walter is not there to check them; a little charcoal stove keeps hot the goose-necked tailor's pressing-irons; the apprentice rushes a goose as soon as anyone calls for one, because every seam is pressed as soon as it is sewn, on the ironing-board the tailor keeps across his folded legs. These, and the big table for the cutter, crowd the room to its uttermost.

The dwelling over the shop is reached by a discreet private door, into a tiny hallway, with a twisting stair. Above the shop a living-room occupies the whole of the front, overlooking the street; behind it are bedrooms, one for parents, one for girls; above is a room with a low ceiling, little more than a loft, where the boys sleep, and family luggage and unused furniture are stored.

The kitchen, of course, is in the basement, a damp, flagged hole where Liz Duckett, the slavey, prepares all the meals, serves breakfast and luncheon to the children, and from which she scrambles up two flights of stairs to the living-room, with food for the parents. She also carries water to the bedrooms, and brings the slops downstairs, to empty them in the brick privy in the yard behind the workroom. Great ingenuity is demanded of Janet and her daughters when they wish to visit this retreat, lest the evil-minded tailors should suspect them of unmentionable physical functions. Their usual device is to bring in something from the line that stretches from house to back wall, and on which clothes are always hanging out to dry, without ever quite doing so. Liz makes no such pretence; she is too humble to afford shame. She usually has a black eye, the consequence of her Saturday night rejoicing in Puzzle Square, or up the shut where she lives in the few hours that are her own. But I see that one must not pity Liz; she is a working woman, and has her own pride.

I innocently imagine that the house is full, but visitors are frequent. Charity – Wesleyan charity – cannot turn anyone who needs food or drink from the door – within reason, that is to say, and reason is extensile, like a concertina. An evangelist, visiting the chapel on one of his tours of preaching, may pass a night or two. He usually sleeps on a shakedown in the living-room, and is glad to get it. From time to time, when he is in a sober – or soberish – period, Uncle David stays for a month or two, until he falls again from grace, and sleeps God knows where and with God knows whom. He shares the bed of the two boys, or with Rhodri when Lancelot has gone to boarding-school in Llanfyllin.

Uncle David is not an easy bedfellow, because he insists on the middle of the bed, where he lies reading the *County Times*, with an oil lamp balanced on his broad chest. There is constant danger that he will fall asleep and overturn the lamp, but somehow he never does so. He regales the sleepy boys with bits of news, upon which he offers comment greatly at variance with what the paper says, for he is privy to all the underworld gossip of Trallwm, and is ribald. He is also a dreamer, and shouts in his sleep.

(17)

ALL OF THIS can be borne, until Auntie Polly arrives from Llanrwst for a long stay, because she is "lying up," which is the local term for pregnancy. She brings little Olwen with her, because the child is not yet two, and needs her mother. Her other four children have remained in Llanrwst, presumably under the cloud that now hangs over the fate of John Jethro Jenkins. He has retired to that modest village until certain disagreeable affairs are put right in Aberystwyth, where the Import and Export languishes in the current depressed state of trade. Nothing positively dishonest is imputed to him, but a certain fine carelessness has brought about embarrassment and hard words from coarse-minded men who do not understand shades of guilt, and see everything in black and white, and pounds and pence.

A woman who is lying up has to be protected from such slights. "Oh, Janno, you'll never know what I've been through in Llanrwst!" Polly says, rather oftener than is needful. Janno's tender heart responds eagerly, and the patient

Walter is resigned to moving himself and his wife into the girls' room, because a woman who is lying up clearly needs the best bed.

Elaine and Maude are somewhat restless under the necessity to sleep on a shakedown, hidden away every day, in the living-room, but Janet explains to them about Christian obligation. However, they find it necessary to intrude frequently into their parents' room, once their own, to fetch clothes from the press. This can be inconvenient for Walter and Janet, but the girls feel that Christian obligation requires that inconvenience should be shared. They have the inconvenience of having to take little Olwen for walks in her baby-carriage. Little Olwen is not an appealing child; she whinges a great deal and obtrudes herself amazingly for one so young.

Worse is to come. A general depression has seriously slowed all business activity in the British Isles; there are great numbers of people who have no money, and those who have money are determined to keep it. Walter feels the pinch. The pinch grows more painful when John Jethro Jenkins and his four sons arrive from Llanrwst, which he has decided to leave to its mean-spirited inhabitants, and to "bivouac" as he expresses it, with his brother-in-law and sister for a time, until his new venture is transformed from a dream into a reality.

"It is an extraordinary thing, Walter, how blind people can be to opportunity, when it is staring them in the face. Now, you know me. You know my views. Utilitarian – that sums it up. Whatever provides the greatest advantage for the greatest number. But somebody has to take the bull by the horns, and bring the advantage into focus, and that demands two things – Vision and Capital. The one without the other is unavailing. Utterly unavailing. I have Vision, and I am confronted by Opportunity – such Opportunity as comes rarely even into the life of an exceptionally fortunate person, like myself. Capital's the problem. Now, I don't know how you are fixed personally, but I should imagine you were pretty snug. Fine situation, fine shop, a large surrounding district to draw from – if you're not doing very well, something must be radically wrong. How *do* you stand, if I may ask?"

"John, you'll have heard that there is a depression across the whole country. Times are difficult. And clearing up after the Pater's trouble has consumed a lot of money. In dibs and dabs, but it all adds up to a surprising sum."

"Ah, but don't you see, Walter – no, of course you don't see, because you have let little Trallwm blind you – these so-called depressions are passing things. But to the man with Vision, they spell opportunity. Anybody can strike while the iron is hot. It's the man of Vision who strikes just before it cools, and astounds all those who have been alarmed by a fleeting recession. You say you can't raise any capital?"

"Not a sixpence."

"That's what you think. But you're wrong, Walter, you're wrong. You have immense capital. You have your good name, your credit, your reputation as a man of exceptional probity. You can borrow. When you tell your banker what I'm going to tell you now, he'll overwhelm you with offers. Bankers aren't stupid, you know."

"Not more than most people, certainly."

"Now listen. And please, I beg you, regard this for the present as *sub rosa*. On the q.t., you know."

"I have a little Latin, John."

"Of course you have. It's another aspect of your Capital that you don't put to use. Now pay close attention to what I am about to say: I have a business associate – I haven't known him long but he is one of the most impressive, far-seeing men I have ever encountered – and he has just come back from Canada. A golden land. The opportunities there are staggering, and men of all kinds are rushing to seize them. The big chances are going fast, but there is still time to do very great things. Now, Walter, think carefully: what is it that the world needs most at the present moment?"

"I wish I knew."

"You do know. Think. Coal! That's what's wanted! Coal! The black diamond! Industry is grinding to a standstill for want of coal. Canada is absolutely chock-a-block with coal, and very little has so far been done about it. Now this man – can't tell you his name, because he insists on the strictest confidentiality – is acting as agent for a very big interest, situated in Liverpool, and he is offering large tracts of coalfields in northern Manitoba at a laughable price per acre. He can let me have five hundred acres of an immensely rich coalfield in a northern area which is remarkable because the coal lies so near the surface. You can almost pick it up. Mining ceases to be a costly job of excavation. And the coal, when it has been assembled – assembled, look you, not laboriously mined – can be shipped south down the Nelson River to the thriving settlement of Winnipeg, whence it can be easily dispersed all over the world. Not just Great Britain, you see, but to the whole world which is craving for coal. This is one of those astounding circumstances where Opportunity and Vision await only the quickening touch of Capital to create vast fortunes. It's stupendous! Now, what do you say?"

"I have learned that I am not a capitalist, John."

"But you will be! You'll come round. You're prudent, but you're no fool. Meanwhile, I'm going to see who can be got to come in with me around the county. I think of trying some of the big Liberal county families, as a starter. Men of vision. I assume I may mention your name?"

"I'd rather you didn't, John. For your own sake. Since the Pater's trouble the Gilmartin name doesn't ring quite as clear as it did. But I wish you well. You know that."

"It's very big, Walter. Huge. I'll go farther – it's overwhelming. I stand in awe of what Canada will mean to us."

Meanwhile, John will "bivouac" until the time comes for him to take Polly and the children to Canada – to the New World, where he will be forever quit of the pettymindedness and social restrictions of Great Britain. John Jethro is, all the family agree, a man of remarkable, dauntless spirit. This is all the more praiseworthy as he is known to be somewhat "touched" in his lungs. Just a hint of tuberculosis, the scourge of Wales, and in the nineteenth century a scourge every bit as alarming as is AIDS in my time. One of its characteristics is the ebullience it often brings with it – a quickening of the mental faculties. I see John Jethro in the little sitting-room, carolling with true Welsh rhetoric about the fortunes that await them all. Walter listens with the sad reserve of a man who does not know how to meet his bills, and whose debtors are slow to pay what they owe him. Maude and Elaine yawn behind their hands, wondering when they can put up their shakedown and go to bed. Only Polly and Janet listen enraptured, with the confidence that girls of the nineteenth century grew up to repose in their wonderful brothers and husbands.

Even I, with my poor command of geography, know that if the coal were any good – which it is not – the Nelson River, so turbulent and fraught with rapids, is quite impossible as a route for heavy barges. Anyhow, it flows the wrong way, and how do you portage a coal barge up rapids on a river that has no locks? I am watching one of those scenes, so common in the history of Canada, where high hopes soar on the wings of ignorance, and high adventure leads to disaster.

John Jethro naturally shares the bed of Polly, who grows huge much sooner than most women who are pregnant. The softness and generosity of her nature find a physical counterpart in this swelling. Little Olwen sleeps in a basket on the floor. Sleeps, that is to say, when she is not howling, as she cuts her teeth. But in the best bedroom John Jethro and Polly sleep the sound sleep of the confident and the trusting.

The boys – Albert, Thomas, Harry, and Lloydie – cannot be accommodated in the premises above the tailor shop. They have to be boarded down the street with Mrs. Joe Davies, a cousin in the fourth degree; Walter pays the few shillings that keep them in Mrs. Joe's garret, for John Jethro, the entrepreneur, is temporarily embarrassed, and cannot quite run to such expense. But of course all seven Jenkinses eat at the Gilmartin table, three times a day, and growing boys are prodigious eaters. Janet laughs at their monstrous appetites, even as she stretches the shillings to find food to put on the crowded table.

(18)

Dear Janet! I find myself falling in love with her – yes, with my own great-grandmother – as I watch these scenes, where her bravery and sweet temper keep afloat this household of raving optimist brother, dispirited mathematician-turned-tailor husband, her sister-in-law Polly – a soft machine for replenishing the earth and not much else – and nine children, clamorous and egotistical as children are and must be if they are to save their souls in an adult world. Janet is not especially intelligent, not physically strong, not of the Joan of Arc mould, but through her faith and her simple goodness – a quality not much in evidence in the world as it was when I so hastily quitted it a few days before seeing this film – she somehow keeps them all afloat, and frequently laughing.

She can be a strict teacher, look you – there I am, falling into the cajoling Welsh trope – but she is a loving teacher, and her children heed her. She teaches faith and goodness, in so far as she comprehends them. She has a store of lessons, and some of them are songs. One favourite, from a Christmas Supplement of *The Leisure Hour*, runs thus:

> *There's an excellent rule*
> *I have learned in life's school,*
> *And I'm ready to set it before you.*
> *When you're heavy at heart*
> *And your world falls apart,*
> *Do not pity yourself, I implore you.*
> *No, up with your chin,*
> *Meet bad luck with a grin,*

And try this infallible trick:
 It never will fail you,
 Whatever may ail you –
DO SOMETHING FOR SOMEBODY QUICK!

OH –
Do something for somebody quick,
It will banish your cares in a tick
 Don't fret about you
 There's a Good Deed to do –
DO SOMETHING FOR SOMEBODY QUICK!

Janet pounds the galumphing, two-four tune out of the senile Broadwood, bobbing her head and smiling as she sings, a pattern of Methodist goodness. And she practises the lesson she teaches. She thinks as little of self as a human creature can do – which, as everything has to be seen from the watch-tower of self, and as every action is a demonstration of self, is not as great a victory as the dear soul hopes it is.

Oh, if only John Jethro were not a man of such determined spirit and firm opinions! He attends the Wesleyan Chapel, of course, for everyone must go somewhere on a Sunday, but he goes in a contumacious spirit. He sits in the Gilmartin pew with folded arms and a look of bottled-up contradiction on his face. It is clear that he disagrees with everything the minister is saying, and can face him down with information out of the advanced books he reads. The story of the Creation is all nonsense; Darwin has put paid to that. When Moses saw the Burning Bush any jackass knows that what Moses saw was an oil-gusher on fire, and what he heard came straight out of Moses' Tory head. How can sensible people in the last decade of the nineteenth century believe such stuff?

When a powerful evangelist – none other than the redoubtable Gipsy Smith – comes to the Chapel to preach a series of week-night sermons to strengthen the faith of the already faithful, John Jethro causes a scandal. On the last night of his mission the evangelist urges all those who feel themselves to be Saved to stand, and there is a rush and a rustle as everybody stands, and many sob in the joy of their zeal. But John Jethro remains seated as if he were a figure moulded in lead. His sister and his wife tremble for him. Polly, unwieldy as she now is, is nevertheless on her feet, weeping for her uncontrite husband. Afterward, at a light supper above the tailor's shop, he explains his position. How can a man be saved who has no intimation that he has ever been lost? Is he not a portion of the grand process of Evolution, which wastes nothing? If there is a God, Darwin has given Him a new meaning. He refuses to run with the crowd, has no wish to give offence, but cannot submit to manifest nonsense. God does not wish John Jethro Jenkins to be saved, but to be expended to the uttermost of his possibilities.

Walter secretly half agrees with him, but he has stood up among the saved because he is a man of peace, and hates rows. Walter's God is still the merciful God of John Wesley, about whom wrangles like this are needless and unseemly. Walter's God is the God of a man who, without knowing it, is a Romantic.

(19)

WALTER'S ROMANTICISM expresses itself in politics. He is a determined, but not an obstreperous or contentious, Liberal and his god on this earth is Mr. Gladstone. A portrait of Gladstone hangs in the little sitting-room on the wall beside the engraving of John Wesley that has come down in the family from Wesley Gilmartin, once the pot-boy of the inn at Dinas Mawddwy. An election is near, and Walter longs with his whole soul to see the return of Stuart Rendel, the Liberal candidate who contests the seat against the candidate of the powerful, ancient and formidable

Williams-Wynn family. John Jethro, of course, is on every platform that will accept him, to speak in the Liberal cause. But he is too vehement, too rancorous, and is almost a liability to his party. It is Walter who takes determined action.

He has a cousin – in what degree it is difficult to say, but within the nine degrees – who is what is called at the time a colourman. That is to say, he deals in paints, which he mixes himself and applies wherever they are wanted with assurances that they will last a lifetime. To this cousin, Ned Thomas, Walter confides his great scheme, and Ned is delighted to assist, for it is directly in his line of work. Thus, after they have all seen their families to bed and said evening prayers in the manner of the time, with Tom Evans, another cousin, Walter and his cronies creep out into the darkness of a Sunday night, and work a transformation in Trallwm. They wear old clothes, and have blackened their faces with soot. With the hardest-drying red paint that Ned Thomas can mix, they paint "Vote for Rendel" on every pavement in the town in gigantic letters.

On Monday morning – a fair-day when the town will be full – there is outrage in every Tory heart. Nothing has been painted on any private wall or building, so nobody has a clear cause for action, but the principal Justice of the Peace hastily assembles four trustworthy citizens to decide what must be done. One of these pillars of society is Walter Gilmartin, and he agrees with the magistrate and the others that this is a very serious matter indeed. An outrage, in fact. His indignation, as might be expected from Walter, is tempered with practicality, and it is his suggestion that a group of out-of-work men be assembled and outfitted with brushes and solvent (vinegar is the best they can think of) to cleanse the streets. And so it is. But Ned Thomas's paint is not to be scrubbed away, and all that market-day the sweating scrubbers scrub, and Tory partisans urge them to scrub harder, until the whole town reeks of vinegar, and by afternoon the whole town is dissolved in laughter. A novelty has crept into the solemn business of politics and it finds a welcome. Some-

one has shown ingenuity and spirit. The impertinent message will not yield, and when voting-day comes Stuart
Rendel is elected by a margin which is rather less than 250
votes, but a margin nevertheless, and Castle influence, and
Williams-Wynn influence, has been shaken once again.

Nobody ever discovers who the culprits were, and it is
not until long after the Gilmartin family has removed to
Canada that Walter ever confesses to his sons that he was at
the root of the great scandal. Even Janet does not know, for it
is not the sort of thing one tells a woman. Twenty years later,
when Trallwm has long been a Liberal borough, traces of red
paint may still be seen on some of the quieter streets.

(20)

WHY DID THE Gilmartins
emigrate to Canada? It is John Jethro Jenkins who goes first.
He needs to go to those coalfields in which he has sunk quite
a lot of other people's money, to find out why nothing is
happening there. He never reaches them, but go to Canada he
does, and discovers a new land in which his rhetorical powers
and his unquenchable optimism are badly needed. For a
time – it is merely to fill in while he looks about him – he
accepts (as he puts it) a minor post in a lawyer's office, and is
so delighted by all the prospects that lie before him that at last
he sends for Polly and the six children and somehow Walter
finds the money for their passage, in the humblest accommo-
dation any ship affords. It is not a lot of money, for the
children travel at a very low price and the littlest ones travel
free, but it is not easily found among the profits of the failing
tailor's shop.

Failing it is, and Walter knows it, but what is he to do? It
is not that business is bad; it is much as it has long been. It is
payment that is bad, for the depression does not lift, and

money is very slow. Even the county families, which have always paid up about once a year, are now forgetful, and Walter hates to dun them. It seems such an ugly thing to do. That he, a stalwart of the Liberal cause, should send dunning letters to highly respected landowners of the Liberal persuasion is something that goes painfully against the grain with him. That he, who knows Latin and Greek and does mathematical puzzles as a recreation, should come down to such a pass is more than he can stomach.

Meanwhile until the blessed day when John Jethro sends for them, there are the Jenkinses. "The Jenkins tribe," as Rhodri calls them, and is rebuked by Lance. While John Jethro is looking about him in the new land the Jenkinses are still in Walter's house, where Polly regards herself as a guest; she suckles little Eden, the baby, and, as she says, it takes a lot out of her. She reads novels of an improving sort and *The Leisure Hour*, while Janet and Liz Duckett do all that is necessary for thirteen people. Of course the Gilmartin girls help as much as they can, but they are schoolgirls, and have work of their own.

As for Rhodri, he enjoys all the delights of boyhood. Mr. Timothy Hiles has now sold his school to Mr. Anthony Jones, M.A., and Tony Jones is chiefly interested in playing the flute and dreaming of Miss Guenevere Gwilt, a local beauty who will have a very respectable inheritance when she marries. To delight Miss Gwilt – and other guests, of course – Tony gets up tableaux at Christmas, in which Rhodri figures as Queen Elizabeth the First and, with his red hair, augmented by a few "switches" and "fronts," is thought to be an amazing reincarnation of the great queen. Education is gnawed by the death-watch beetle of aestheticism under the rule of Tony Jones.

Walter does not complain. His hopes are set on his older son, Lancelot, who is doing great things at Walter's old school and, though it costs him more than he can afford, Walter is determined that Lancelot shall not miss his chance in life, as he did. Lancelot shall figure brilliantly in the examination results and shall go to a university. No deathbed promise shall ruin him, as it has ruined Walter. Already, as a schoolboy, Lance is developing the remote politeness, the immovability, and the gooseberry eye of the Civil Servant.

Can it be managed? Walter's situation is becoming desperate. The domestic hullabaloo attendant on the birth of little Eden has told heavily upon him. Polly, a natural mother, is certainly not a compliant one, and her labour is long and clamorous, and is followed by a number of disobliging circumstances; teetotal as she is, she must have porter – the best – to get her milk going, taking it strictly as medicine, with much protestation; she must have quiet in the house, and Elaine and Maude and Rhodri must be sent to Cousin Gringley's for a fortnight, where they speculate ignorantly about what awful goings-on are attendant on the birth of a child; Polly's appetite, always hearty, must nevertheless be "tempted" with dainties from the butcher and the pastry-cook. Polly is what anthropologists might call an earth-mother, and so far as she can manage it, the whole earth comes under her domination when she adds to its population. And somehow it all costs more money than anyone might suppose.

Janet knows that things are bad, but not how very bad, and she prays that Walter may yet get his head above water. Polly reads aloud the exuberant letters that John Jethro sends every week from Canada. Letters written small, and then "crossed" in the economical style of the day, so that they are to be read only with difficulty. In every one of them John Jethro urges Walter to bring his family to Canada. There is a temporary lull, it seems, in the need for coal, but time will take care of that; other opportunities abound and a man of Walter's abilities will find his feet in a fortnight, and prosper greatly.

Is the fine, winey air of Canada working with deceptive charm on John Jethro's affected lungs? He grows lyrical as he writes of the new land.

(21)

Not without effect. Walter sees, as he puts it to himself, the handwriting on the wall. The biblical phrase is not comforting. MENE, MENE, TEKEL, UPHARSIN: *Thou art weighed in the balance and art found wanting.* Yes, indeed: wanting several hundred utterly unobtainable pounds. *God hath numbered thy kingdom, and finished it.* This, it appears, is God's reward for a man who has been faithful to a promise given to his dying mother. We must not dispute His will. *Thy kingdom is divided and given to the Medes and the Persians.* Certainly this will be so very soon, for the Medes and the Persians of Trallwm, themselves hard-pressed for money, will force the action that will get them at least some of what is owing to them. In short, bankruptcy impends. After that disgrace, repeating and compounding the disgrace of Samuel, might the new land offer something of balm for a hurt man?

Walter confides in Janet, and as always she is hopeful.

"Oh, my dear, if Canada does little for us, it might be a wonderful place of opportunity for the boys," she says, as they lie in their cramped bed above the shop.

For the boys, of course. I know that it is not the fashion of these Victorians to trouble too much about the fate of the girls. Elaine and Maude will do what all good girls do; they will marry good men, like Walter, and live happily, even if in pinched circumstances, forever after.

The parents suppose that their secret is inviolable, but they have reckoned without Rhodri, who is already, at the age of fourteen, long-headed as his father has never been. Rhodri knows that his father has already made the first moves toward that awful journey up the Town Hall steps, and has declared whatever he has that may go to his creditors. Innocent Walter, honest Walter, thinks it must be every penny, the uttermost farthing. But not Rhodri, and he goes to work as soon as the declaration has been made. He knows it has been done, for the boys who go to school with him have heard it spoken of by their parents. The bankruptcy will not come like a bolt of lightning. Walter is too well respected, and his fellow-townsmen are too compassionate, to move rapidly.

That is why Rhodri absents himself from Tony Jones's slack-twisted school on market-days, and darts to and fro among the crowds, confronting farmers who owe for two, four, and even six suits of clothes, saying, "Excuse me Mr. Thomas (Mr. Jones, Mr. Williams, Mr. Griffiths, or whoever it may be), Mr. Walter Gilmartin would like a word with you, sir, before evening, if it's convenient." And the debtors, knowing very well what is in the wind, quite often do have that word with Mr. Walter Gilmartin, and pay something, though never all, of what they owe. They are not treacherous or defaulting men, though they are close with money, when they have it.

"Rhodri, I will not have this. It's not honest and you know it's not honest. I can't explain why – not just at present – but in time you will learn that all my money, wher-ever it comes from, must be put into a certain fund. I am not in a position to collect debts at present. You disgrace me by what you are doing."

"Pater, it's the law, and if the law thinks it's honest, why invent scruples? Anything you can get now doesn't have to go into that fund you speak of. It's yours fair and square. Do be prudent, Pater, and don't think you have to go farther than the law insists."

The truth of the matter is never admitted between them, and Walter reluctantly acts on the advice of his long-headed son, though nothing in the world would make him say so. Advice goes down the generations, not backward from son to father.

So, at last, there is a little money, and places for Lance and Rhodri are taken in the steerage of a ship bound from Liver-pool to Montreal. Walter, and Janet, and the girls, will follow later, when they can. The money, when it is all in, will just get the Gilmartin family to Canada after the hateful disgrace that follows mounting the Town Hall steps. That day has been set, and nothing can change it.

Godliness begets Industry: Industry begets Wealth. But how – by Who's doing – does bankruptcy come into the story? Perhaps Heraclitus might have had something to say about that.

(22)

I LAST SEE the boys on the deck of the S.S. *Vancouver*. It is the least amount of deck made available to any passengers aboard ship, because it is for steerage passengers. Lance is looking pale and the cold eyes of the embryo Civil Servant are moist.

"I say, Lance, have you got yours safe?"

"Have I got my what, safe?"

"Your fiver. You know, the money. The Mater sewed it into your coat, didn't she?"

"I'm going to have to use some of it. Sixpence, I expect. Everything on these boats is expensive. But I've got to have some ginger ale. I don't feel at all well."

"Oh, buck up. Think about Canada."

"What can I think? I don't know anything about Canada."

"Well think of that poster at the station. You know, the one with the huge man in smart breeches looking out over a field of wheat."

"I don't remember it."

"You must. You couldn't forget it. Huge field. Bigger than the whole of the Home Farm at the Castle. Just one field. That's Canada. It'll be ripping, you'll see."

IV

VI

The Master Builder

AM I AT LAST catching the
drift of this film festival which seems to be devised entirely
for me? Am I stupid not to have understood that, whatever
Allard Going may see and write about for *The Colonial Advocate*, I am seeing something wholly personal? Unless I am
entirely out of my mind, this is something which sets before
me the core of my ancestral experience, captured, as a film
captures experience, in a narrative that is coherent as what we
call real life can never be. But why? Is this what happens to
people when they are dead? I cannot tell. I only know that it is
happening to me, and the Gages and the red–haired Gilmartins, whom I had known only as names and whom I had
dismissed as long dead, seem to have life; and indeed seem to
have done much that I may be proud of – I, who had never
thought about ancestors, or expected to be proud of ancestors, while I was living.

This morning, therefore, on the third day of the Festival,
I am a lively spirit as I find my way to the cinema that has
been reserved for these old films, these jewels from the history of that art which is so much of our time and so generally

taken for granted, and so roundly trounced by intellectuals like Going because it does not adopt the wholly serious line he would decree for it if it lay in his power. Going is deeply suspicious of popular entertainment. He wants it to be – no, not educational, and certainly not uplifting, but what he calls "significant," by which he means full of dainties for such rare souls as himself. What is Going to see this morning?

Apparently it is a real gem, rescued from oblivion by some Norwegian archivist. It is to be a film version of Ibsen's *The Master Builder*, made in 1939 by the playwright's grandson Tancred, and thought to have been lost in the Hitler War and at last seeing the light. I look forward to it, for the play was a favourite of mine when I was able to have favourite plays, and I am thrilled when the first moments of *Bygmester Solness* flash on the screen, and translations in messy white type appear at the bottom of the pictures. But of course I am not to see it, except in occasional stolen glances, and these become less frequent as I am caught up in the film which is only for me, which is also called *The Master Builder*, in which the actors – if they are actors – speak in English.

As the film which Going sees is busy with a townscape in which appear buildings, presumably designed and built by Halvard Solness, I am watching another townscape, not at all Norwegian in character. Indeed, I know it to be Canada, and Canada in winter, which is just as bleak as Norway can ever be. My town has the real Canadian look, for there is not a building to be seen that is earlier than 1860 and few so old; it lacks the dignity, the coherence, the sense of importance that even modest European towns manage to convey. Yet it is not without its pretensions, straggling and spotty as it is. There are substantial houses, built as if to endure forever, houses for bankers and well-to-do merchants, and several of these houses are marked by a strong but aesthetically deplorable signature; it is a front window – obviously a parlour window – shaped like a horseshoe. As the camera moves about this Canadian town, which I judge to have about twenty thousand inhabitants, it pauses for a more than passing look at a large and I must say hideous church, built to the greater glory of a grouchy Victorian God. This church is the background to the opening titles. There is no music but the howling of a January wind, which is music of a melancholy kind.

At once we cut – how I am catching the film vocabulary as I watch these things – to a young man who is walking with some difficulty through the night and into the face of the wind, along one of the streets in which large and substantial houses stand side by side with one-storey dwellings, humble and chilly to the eye, that are clad in lumpy whitish stucco, like the droppings of large birds. This is apparently what would have been called a "good district," though not as good as the district further up the river which borders and defines the town. At the end of the nineteenth century this town has pretensions, but has not fully attained them. The wind is not so fierce that the young man needs to struggle so. I know that it is reluctance to do what lies before him that makes him walk with such uncertainty. But he must achieve his purpose, or he will not be able to face those who have sent him here.

He stops in front of one of the houses with a horseshoe front window. This is the one. He goes to the front door, which is at the side, up a few steps, and twists the handle of the bell. He can hear its iron clatter echoing in what sounds like an empty house. He rings until he knows that ringing is useless, then he knocks, and knocks again, and is at last hammering on the dark door. But no one answers.

(2)

RESOLUTE, EVEN if un-happy in his resolve, he trudges through the deep snow to the horseshoe window. He shades his eyes and peers inside.

Nothing but blackness. And then –

I jump, and I know that the film-maker, whoever he is, has meant me to jump. The young man's face is almost against the glass, and suddenly there is another face on the other side, nose to nose with his own. A frightening face, for it is framed in lank dark hair; its haggard, wild eyes and hook nose rise above a straggling beard. I know a little about classic films, and it is so like the face of the Russian actor Nikolai Cherkasov, in *Ivan the Terrible*, that I wonder if there has been some muddle, some mixing of films. Does the face mean to be frightening? A hand is just visible in which a large carving-knife gleams. The young man is frightened out of his wits, but he stands fast, and for the first time since the film began a voice is heard, and it is his.

"Mr. McOmish! Mr. McOmish, it's Gil! Your son-in-law. Will you let me in? I must talk with you."

The face continues to stare, but slowly another hand comes into sight, and it beckons; the hand that holds the knife gestures toward the front door. The young man, shaken but determined, trudges back through the snow, and after a pause the door is opened, and the owner of the face, and the knife, may be seen at full length. He wears a nightshirt and a long, shabby brown dressing-gown. His large, scrawny feet are bare.

"You come from the women, I suppose," says Mr. McOmish and allows Gil to follow him into the dark house, and into the fitfully moonlit front parlour. The cold there is not the blustery cold of outdoors, but a stuffy, still cold that smells of mice. There is not a stick of furniture, but Mr. McOmish disappears into a back room and after a time returns with two kitchen chairs. Then another journey into the darkness and he brings back a coal-oil lamp, and places it on the floor. He gestures to the young man to sit down.

"Well?" he says.

"I hope you understand that I come as a neutral person, and not as somebody who wants to take sides," says the young man. "But there is some business to be done, and Mrs. McOmish and the girls have asked me to talk with you, and get you to sign a few papers, so that everything can be put in legal form. As I am the only other man in the family," he adds.

"Is that a fact?" says Mr. McOmish. "What about that tribe of Dutch uncles and Dutch brothers? Are they dead, all of a sudden? You, a mere son-in-law, the only man in the family?"

"I suppose they mean in the direct family. Your family." And then he stops in confusion, knowing how tactlessly he has spoken.

"Man in my family," says Mr. McOmish with a disagreeable smile. "The only man left in the family; is that what they say?"

"Well, something like that," says the young man.

"You know I never thought of you as belonging to the family," says Mr. McOmish. "I never completely recognized you as part of my family."

"But I did marry Malvina," says the young man. "I would have thought – "

"Yes, I suppose you would," says Mr. McOmish. "But it isn't as easy as that. I never thought you were fit for one of my daughters. It was a sneaking kind of marriage. Wasn't it?"

"Mr. McOmish, I wish you would put that knife down."

"Do you wish that? Well, my wee man, I'll put it down. What did you think I meant to do with it? I was just cutting some kindling for the fire when I heard you creeping around outside. I can do wonders with a knife, you know. Or don't you know? I cut kindling by shaving a stick of cedar till it's like a feather – all beautiful curls, and all precisely the same width and length. Precisely. But if my knife makes you uneasy I'll put it right here on the floor, you see. Handy in case I want it for anything."

"Thank you."

"No thanks needed. None whatever. No need to be grateful. Not a particle. But I can see you have ideas about my knife. Haven't you?"

"Oh no. None at all."

"Don't lie to me, Gil. She told you I took after her with this knife, didn't she? Did she tell you how she squawked and shrieked for her old sister, and pleaded with me not to slit her yellow neck? I guess she left that out, when she told you the story."

"I'd rather not go into that, Mr. McOmish. I want to be as neutral as possible. I'm just here to ask you to sign some papers. That's all I'm after."

"And you thought it would be easy, did you? Just catch the old man when he's in one of his quiet moods and get his name on a few papers. Gil, you know, you're a simpleton. All you Old Country fellers are simpletons. That's why I didn't want you to marry Vina. Only man in the family! Fiddle-sticks! Virgie has an army of Dutch brothers, why didn't one of them come? Eh? Because they've ratted on her, that's why. So it has to be you. I've always despised you Old Country fellers. Stuck-up, know-it-all fellers, every one of you. You know what we say here? 'You can always tell an Englishman, but you can't tell him much.' Doesn't apply to the Scotch, of course. An entirely different breed of dog, the Scotch."

"I've told you often, Mr. McOmish, I'm not really Eng-lish. I'm Welsh."

"A poor excuse. What are these papers? I'm a bankrupt, I know it. Been through all that, pestered and questioned by fellers I wouldn't say How-d'ye-do to in the ordinary way. What papers have you got?"

"Well, if you'll let me explain – Mrs. McOmish and the girls – "

"And old Cynthia Boutell, I'll bet."

"Mrs. Boutell has been with Mrs. McOmish for a few days, certainly."

"Do you want me to tell you something, Gil? Some-thing you're too simple to have found out for yourself, I'll bet. Cynthia Boutell is an interfering, nose-poking, mischief-making old Bee Eye Tee See Aitch. That's a word I'd never use against a woman except under great provocation. But I use it of Cynthia Boutell. All my life I've been against swearing and foul language. But there it is. No other word for her. And you won't hear me use it again."

"That's very delicate of you, Mr. McOmish. But of course these papers have nothing to do with Mrs. Boutell – "

"Gil, anything that's within twenty-five miles of Cynthia Boutell has something to do with her, because that's how she is. I suppose these papers make over the house to Virgie?"

"The house she and the girls are in at present. It's all that's left, I'm afraid."

"Are you afraid, Gil? I'd be afraid if I was in your shoes. Afraid they'd let me in for supporting the whole boiling of 'em."

"No, no, Mr. McOmish. The girls have their jobs, you know. They'll take care of their mother. But the house – I'm sure you see that she has a claim on the house."

"Is that what the lawyers say?"

"Yes. Everything's gone, you know. Even this house – "

"Oh, I know that. When they come to get me in the morning it'll be the last I'll see of this house. Or any of the fine houses I've built in this town. Except I suppose I'll see 'em from the outside. So Virgie wants that rotten little bungalow made over to her, does she?"

"She must have somewhere to live, Mr. McOmish, and it seems to be all that's left. You know what the lawyers said: you are separated but not divorced."

"No, Gil, nothing of the kind. A marriage is a solemn oath, boy. Nothing can dissolve it. Virgie and I have our differences, but, mutual hatred apart, she's my wife just as sure as she was the day we were wedded. Even at the worst – and this isn't the worst, not by a long chalk – she's my wife. Tell her that. Remind her of that. If she thinks any of this money stuff, or that pow-wow in court has dissolved our marriage, she doesn't know law. And I do."

"Then you'll sign, Mr. McOmish?"

"Boy, you don't know what you ask. It isn't the house, the dear Lord knows. I wouldn't claim such a jerry-built old razee as that for my own. I've built better hen-houses than that, in my young days. But signing isn't the house. It's my life, Gil. My life."

"Mr. McOmish, can I get you anything? You look poorly. Is there any water back there?"

Mr. McOmish is gasping.

"I am poorly, Gil. But I don't want water. I must have some of my medicine."

"No, please, Mr. McOmish!"

But Mr. McOmish has risen to his feet and now he is gasping loudly, like a horse with the heaves. The young man is terrified of what he sees, as the older one grows ashy-white. He struggles toward the kitchen, and Gil follows him with the lamp, desperate but quite unable to think of anything he can do to meet this crisis. In the kitchen, on a table, lies a neat package, and Mr. McOmish makes for it with a certainty of purpose that shows he is not so near collapse as he appears.

In the package is a phial and a hypodermic syringe; with the skill of long practice Mr. McOmish fills it full. He drops his miserable brown bathrobe to the ground and lifts his nightshirt up to his neck; but as it bunches up so that he cannot properly see what he is doing, he pulls it over his head and stands in the kitchen, in the half-light, stark naked.

Stark indeed, for he is so thin that his ribs show and his hip-bones protrude. He looks like one of Grünewald's horrifying Christs; that is something I know, and that the film-maker certainly knew, but which Mr. McOmish and Gil do not know. His diaphragm is covered with tiny spots of dried blood, and looks like nothing so much as a pincushion. He stabs the needle into his flesh with a little whimper, and pushes the plunger home slowly. He withdraws the needle, and wipes it carefully on the fallen nightshirt.

"These needles getting dull. Have to rasp them up," he says, in a far-away voice, as if to himself. "Help me dress, Gil; can't stand here bare-naked. Glory, it's cold."

Indeed it is cold. Gil helps Mr. McOmish to put his gown and his robe back on, and assists him into the parlour, to one of the kitchen chairs. Gil sets the lamp on the floor, and takes the opportunity to put his overcoat back on.

"Do you feel well enough to sign now?" he says.

"Give me a few minutes, so the medicine can work. No hurry. Not a particle. I want to talk. There aren't many I can talk to, but I'm going to talk to you, boy. You've got to know what's what. You think I'm an old devil, don't you? That's what my daughters call me. The Old Devil. Don't dispute it. Isn't that what Vina calls me? Eh?"

Gil does not reply.

"See? You daren't deny it. In a court of law, you couldn't deny it. Their mother taught them that. Virgie has turned my own flesh and blood against me, to call me an Old Devil. Do you know how I got to be an Old Devil?"

Gil shakes his head.

"Well, you'd better know that they're right. I am an Old Devil, now, and when I was young I was a Young Devil, which is a totally different thing. I wouldn't give a York shilling for any feller that hadn't some devil in him. I've always had plenty of devil, and I came by it honestly. Do you know how I come to be here? Here with you? Sitting on this poorly made chair?"

Gil shakes his head again. Mr. McOmish is amazingly recovered, and is sitting up quite straight on the wretched chair. His eyes glow and his voice is resonant in its nineteenth-century Ontario speech – sharp, clear, Scottish with a Yankee twang and now and then a whisper of Irish. He gestures, jabbing a forefinger at Gil, extended from a hand that is plainly that of a superior craftsman, a strong, skilful, big hand with knotty knuckles and strong black hair on the phalanges. On this skeletonic wreck of a man the hands, like the head, are still impressive.

As Mr. McOmish speaks the pictures leave the parlour and show me what he is talking about. But his voice explains them. I believe movie people call this Voice Over. It is illustrated narrative, and Mr. McOmish's tale is gripping.

As for poor Gil, he is slumped, in so far as a strong

young man can slump, on his comfortless wooden chair. He cannot escape the narrative of Mr. McOmish, his father-in-law and a self-confessed Old Devil.

(3)

"Long ago and far away," says Mr. McOmish, and Gil can hardly believe this bardic introduction to what surely cannot be a heroic tale, "my people, my ancestors – yes, I'll call them ancestors because there's no reason in the world why only big people should have ancestors and people like me have none and be robbed of our past – lived in Scotland, right up in the north-ernmost part of the West. They were farmers. Crofters, they called them, and a lot of them were shepherds, as well. Had been since Noah saw the waters subside, I'd reckon. But for some consarned legal reason, that nobody ever wholly understood, the local big man took the land and what do you suppose he did that for? To turn it into moors where he could pasture his sheep, that's why. And that was when this country needed settlers. It was a hundred and fifty years ago, or more. Probably more because I don't know exactly. So the local big man heeded the call given to him by an even bigger man – Lord Selkirk, he was, and very kindly assisted the people off the farms to go to the New World, as they called it then, to make their fortunes. There were fortunes everywhere in the New World, for the taking. And off they went, crowded into a sailing-ship."

I see the crofters and shepherds, with their bundles, being rowed out to the ship, which is certainly small enough. They are clothed in homespun, and are the colour of the earth. The very earth of Scotland is being moved to the New World. The children are rosy, but the faces of their fathers and mothers are already brown and marked with hard work. The clothes they wear are not picturesque Highland dress. Not a kilt is to be seen. But they wear the blue bonnet, and their cloaks are plaids, sure enough, not in the tartans of a later date, but in dark browns and black-and-grey checks. A sober people, dark and thrawn as their own soil.

I see something else. This is an indoor scene, in what is doubtless the Big House of the district, though it looks meagre enough, and there sits the laird on one side of a table and on the other is a man who looks like a lawyer, and whose speech shows him to be an Englishman. The laird signs a paper – he is not a ready hand with the pen – and the lawyer pushes over to him a bag which chinks as it moves on the table. I know that in the bag there is a guinea for every crofter the laird has cajoled or bullied into the ship; a guinea for every woman. Nothing at all for the children, who do not count. There are far more than thirty pieces of silver in that bag, but the laird, though he is a truly religious man, never thinks it is the price of betrayal. These are pieces of gold, and his reward for assisting his country to people the new lands to the West.

"Do you have any idea where those poor wretches were headed for, Gil? It was a terrible place, in swamp land north of Lake St. Clair, called Baldoon, after Selkirk's place in Scotland, and they were invited, oh so genteelly, to take up farms. What could they have farmed? Not sheep, unless the sheep grew webbed feet and turned to a diet of reeds and grass that was as sharp as knives. And cold! Scotch cold is like a cold linseed poultice all over you from head to foot; but this cold was like being slashed every quarter of an inch of your body with sharp razors."

And indeed the screen shows me something of that cold place and I can sense the raw chill, spirit as I am.

"But there were some of those Scotchmen who had the devil in them, and they saw half the shipload die in the first winter of cold and starvation and even phthisis, but mostly of misery and exile, and they made up their minds to get out. There must be something better than Baldoon, even in this

God-forsaken country, they thought. So when spring came, they set out to walk – to walk, mind you – south-east. Not knowing south as anything but a portion of the compass. Not knowing what there was in the south, except that it had to be a better land for sheep than Baldoon. So they walked, and they walked, and men carried bundles of a hundred and fifty pounds weight, and women carried children who were too little to walk, and they lived on God knows what – oatmeal, I suppose, and what roots they could find that weren't evil to the taste – and those that didn't die on the way made it. And my great-grandfather made it, and I had the tale from him. Often and often.

"Any idea how far that was, Gil? No, and I haven't either, but it was five hundred miles if it was an ell, as the crow flies, and they weren't crows. Do you suppose they made twenty-five miles a day, through the wilderness, and getting over rivers somehow, and creatures they'd never seen busting through the undergrowth and staring at them? Indians, too, I reckon, and they'd have taken the Indians for enemies, though I don't suppose they were. Indians are mischievious, and I've no doubt at all they played them some tricks. But the ones with the Devil in them made it, and my Devils made it to not far from here. And they worked! How they worked! But it was Heaven for them, because every family had its Location, as it was called, free and clear. No laird to turn them off it at his pleasure. So after some farming my grandparents set up a tavern, and the woman kept the tavern while the man worked the farm. Hard, hard work, but to them it was thriving, after the awfulness of Baldoon.

"It was in that tavern, Gil, that I played when I was a little shaver, and it was from my grandmother's tavern slate, where they kept score, that I learned to reckon, and reckoning come so easy to me that I've lived by reckoning pretty much ever since. I got to be a Devil at reckoning. A lot of the scores were paid off in barter, so you had to have a good notion of values."

I see the tavern, and the plain dull room that is the bar.

Every wall is lined with cupboards, and little William – as he then was – plays at crawling among the cupboards, to see how far he can go from one side of the room to the other, without being baulked by the cases of liquor. There are not many of these, for the whisky and the rum stand in barrels behind the bar, and it is from them that the grandmother – who keeps a very strict barroom and permits no smutty stories or swearing – serves generous measures at a penny a glass. As the whisky is purchased at twenty-five cents a gallon, such a price for a dram yields a good profit. There are jugs of spring water on the tables, but few men want water. The liquor is good, of its kind, but its kind is not the modern kind, for the whisky is given colour and savour by generous additions of tobacco leaf and salt. There are low taverns where whisky contains a little opium, as well, but Mrs. McOmish will have none of that, and "McOmishes" is known to be a decent place. Decent or not, a great deal of whisky is consumed, for the men who come here are farmers who could drink lye without taking much harm, and the travellers in the uncomfortable, bone-racking stagecoaches, who want a potent drink to warm them. But drunkards are warned off, and Mrs. McOmish sears them with biblical admonitions that *wine is a mocker, and strong drink is raging*. Not whisky, of course. A few drams after a day's work is no more than a man needs, for his comfort, but orray-eyed drunkards are not tolerated.

(4)

THUS MR. McOMISH continues, delighting in detail and scraps of minute information that would have been golden to the young listener if he had been an historian, but he is impatient and his attention wanders. What was this long, rambling chronicle like in his expe-

rience? In substance, if not in high-flown language, it was like
the poems of Ossian, which his dear mother used to read to
her children at bedtime. Yes; Ossian, whose tales of long ago
and far away had held him spellbound as a child. Ossian,
probably a fake, though his mother knew nothing of that,
and she loved those fine tales as the great Emperor Napoleon
had loved them; the poems of Ossian were what he took with
him on his campaigns, and Ossian inspired him to splendid
enterprise. But Gil, who has had a difficult day with Mrs.
McOmish and the girls, falls asleep, until he almost falls off
his hard chair, and starts into wakefulness, to hear what, in
Ossian's bardic vein, would have been a tale of love.

"You'd never believe it, Gil, to look at her now, but
when first I set eyes on Virgie she was the loveliest little thing
you ever saw. Slim and supple as a willow, and the lightest
step – ! Saw her in church, of course. Where else would I meet
anybody of her stamp? Old Loyalist family and such? But I'd
seen her before church, when she didn't know it, and I saw
her bare foot and it nearly finished me, it was so slim and
white.

"You see, we all walked to church – never travel on Sunday except on foot and to worship – and I was making my
way along Fairchild's Creek, because that was the shortest
from the farmhouse where I boarded, and I came on a bunch
of five or six girls sitting on the bank of the creek, pulling on
their stockings. They walked barefoot until they were almost
at the church, y'see, then they washed their feet in the stream
and pulled on their shoes and stockings, so they'd not be
dusty when they met the congregation. Oh, there was vanity,
even among Wesleyan Methodists, let me tell you! You can't
quell vanity, because the Devil won't have it, that's why. I
heard them laughing, and I didn't show myself among the
bushes, and I peeked. The Devil, you see. I didn't know what
they might be up to, but I wanted to see it. And Virgie was in
the midst of the group, waving her bare feet to dry 'em, and
chewing something. And do you know what it was? A ribbon. A pink ribbon and she was chewing it to make it wet and

then she was dabbing her mouth with it, to make her lips a pretty pink! The Devil! And I thought that's the one for me, the girl with the Devil in her! She was sixteen, but she was developed. You know what I mean? Developed, but not over-developed like some of those girls that had breasts like four-quart pails. And that was it. I was a goner.

"But how would a young sprig like me, just out of apprenticeship to a carpenter, get to know a girl like that? She was a Vanderlip, and that meant a lot in those days and in that place.

"Oh, I found out about her, you can bet. Asked everybody, and I thought I was cute and nobody'd guess, but I suppose they did. Love and a cough can't be hid, as they say. The Vanderlips were part of the Vermuelen and Gage tribe, and they were the biggest people in the district. Old Gus Vermuelen was dead, but he'd made a pile, let me tell you, as a land agent. His sister Anna had died not too long ago, a very old woman, and by Gum she was a tough old party! By the Eternal, she was! Escaped from the Yankees after the Revolution in the States, and licked it up here with her children in a canoe – think of it, in a canoe – and got her Loyalist's rights in money, and cracked it all into a general store. And she throve, boy, she throve! Richer than Gus, even. Her daughter Elizabeth was Virgie's grandmother and Elizabeth married Justus Vanderlip – the Dutch stick to their own, you bet – and Elizabeth had eleven children: seven boys and four girls, and every one of the boys got to be a rich farmer, or a lawyer, or a doctor, and all with solid money. Even the girls had money promised, when they married. One of the farmer sons, Nelson it was, was my Virgie's father, and had his own money as well as whatever old Justus might leave him. So who was I to dangle after an heiress? Eh? A young carpenter, just out of apprenticeship? Eh? What was I?

"I'll tell you what I was, Gil. I had the Devil in me as big as theirs. I could reckon. Not much education, but I made the most of what I had, and I was lucky to have one good schoolteacher, a young feller named Douglas; he was teaching for a year or two to get some money to go to college, as they all did then, and he was a bear for reckoning, and he saw the promise in me and he taught me all he knew. Ordinary reckoning, of course – storekeeper's stuff – but beyond that he taught me algebra and Euclid. That name mean anything to you?"

Oh yes indeed. Gil had heard of Euclid, the father of geometry. It was at that moment I was certain that Gil was my grandfather. So Mr. McOmish must be my great-grandfather, the family scandal.

"Yes, I had Euclid behind me, and I was all set to be a builder. Not just one of your hammer-and-saw carpenters, framing barns and hen-houses and putting up little square hutches for humble people. I burned with ambition, boy, and I wanted that girl, Vanderlip though she might be. But how?

"Get her attention, that's how. So I joined the church choir. Not much of a voice, but loud and shrewd. After I got to know her she told me I could be heard way above the rest. She said that when it was that old Methodist favourite

> Oh for a thousand tongues to sing
> My dear Redeemer's praise,

everybody gave thanks that Will McOmish had just the one tongue. She was a wit, that girl. We didn't sing difficult music, like the Anglicans; they sang in parts; Tonic Sol-Fa they called it, or some such nonsense. We just sang the tunes, as loud as we could, to pull the others after us. I could see her, down in the church, laughing at me while I strained and hollered. But I got to be a figure in the Wesleyan Methodist Church. Loudest voice and pious. I didn't think much of Reverend Cattermole, the preacher, but I put on a serious face and never missed a word he said, and that counted with her parents. So one day after church Mrs. Alma, Nelson's wife – very fine woman, always had a fine silk dress – asked me home to Sunday dinner, at the family place, old Justus's house, the palace of the dynasty.

"I went, and I minded my manners. Didn't eat like a wolf, though the food was way above the level of my boarding-house. Always said 'Please' and 'Thank you kindly ma'am' and 'Splendid victuals these are' and 'No more thanks, I couldn't eat another bite,' and listened respectfully to the old folks. Old Elizabeth sat at one end of the table and Old Justus sat at the other and all the kin and in-laws on each side. I was the only stranger and I declare I felt I'd been singled out. These were silver-fork people and I minded my p's and q's. Never cast a glance at Virginia, down the long table. But before I went home, as soon as I'd et, I shook hands all round, and when I took her hand it was like the handle of one of those electric batteries. So I was emboldened to ask Mrs. Alma if I might call again, and she said of course.

"That was how it began. Before autumn I was walking out with Virginia . Telling her about my ambition, and boasting, I guess, as young fellers do with a girl. Those were glory-days, Gil. I don't imagine you ever felt anything like that. It was unique, as we say of a particular architectural problem."

Mr. McOmish, in his arrogance and egotism, underestimated Gil. Underestimated every young man who has ever been in love. Gil could hear his mother's voice, raised in the words of Ossian:

> *Fair rose the breasts of the maid, white as the bosom of a swan, rising graceful on swift-rolling waves. It was Colna-dona of harps, the daughter of the king! Her blue eyes had rolled on Toscar, and her love arose!*

"So at last it come to the point where I had to speak to Nelson Vanderlip and ask for Virginia. By the Eternal, Gil, but I was scared! I don't suppose anybody in all history has been so scared. He had a black silk waistcoat, and a watch with a fob with a good many seals on it, and old-fashioned whiskers; not a beard but big fuzzy things growing out of the side of his face. What sailors call bugger-grips, whatever that means. And he sat there after a Sunday dinner, in the parlour, just looking at me with his eyes half-shut."

Yes, thinks Gil, just the way you looked at me when I asked for Malvina. And you told me not to think above my station, you – you *failure*!

"It worked out, though. He said I'd have to wait. Prove myself. Serve seven years for Rachel, he said; he was full of Bible sayings. But that was all I needed. He hadn't said No. I suppose he saw the good stuff in me. Knew I was a sure thing.

"Soon it was all round the family, and they were nice about it, except for Cynthia, who was the only girl still not married, and with a game leg, and a disposition like a box of broken bottles. And I set out to prove myself. And by the Eternal, I did!

"Had to get away, of course. I'd learned everything that could be learned there. Went to Hamilton, and got myself taken on by a really big builder, one of the Depews. And there I learned not only joinery but a lot of the cabinet-work and the real heart of building. And everything I did profited by the reckoning I could do, because many a good workman can't reckon for sour apples. Haven't got the head for it. Because it's a gift, you see. Any fool can learn the basics, but they can't apply them. Can't see where they fit into a piece of work. And I did some very sweet work for the Depews, till I knew the time had come to go and claim my bride from Nelson Vanderlip. I'd saved. Scrimped and denied myself, and in that whole five years I only got to see Virginia five times, but she was true to me. Pretty true, I suppose I should say.

"Not that she strayed. Not a particle. But she was young and lovely and young fellows hung around, and there was one schoolteacher wrote her some poetry, and she showed it to me and we laughed over it. I should have heeded that, Gil. What kind of woman laughs at a man's heart, however rotten his poetry is? I found out, later on, when it was too late. But I laughed with her. 'He may be a half-cut schoolteacher, but he's a flat-cut poet,' I said, and I thought I was pretty smart.

Lucky devil, he was, though he moped a good deal when she gave him the gate.

"Not that he ever got near her. It wasn't the fashion of the day. I was her accepted sweetheart, but I hardly dared put my arm around her, and as for the kissing – I tried that once but she jumped away mad, and said, 'You mustn't kiss me without you ask me first, because I mightn't want it.' Jackass that I was, it never occurred to me that if she loved me the way I loved her, she darned well ought to want it. We had great ideas about the purity of girls in those days. They didn't want it and they didn't want it after marriage, a lot of them, and how they ever had babies I couldn't figure, but I found out later.

"So at last I had a few hundred dollars, and Virgie and I were married in the Wesleyan Methodist Church, and there was a big supper at the Vanderlips', and I was astonished to find how many relatives I had all of a sudden, and how kind of few-in-the-pod my parents looked as they sat at that table, which had been moved out into the yard for the occasion. I made a speech that I'd sweated over, about how good it was of the Vanderlips to let their last daughter go to a poor feller like me, but how I'd try to be worthy of her. For our honeymoon we went to Buffalo on the old stern-wheeler *Red Jacket*. I don't recommend a stern-wheeler or Buffalo for a honeymoon."

(5)

ALL OF WHICH, as Mr. McOmish talked, was unfolded before me on the screen, so much more revealing than anything he said. Because he was the narrator, of course, I saw that the Vanderlips were glad enough to be quit of their sharp-tongued daughter, and now that Cynthia – not the most desirable of brides, because of that short leg she got when it was caught in the wheel of a hay-wagon – was married to Daniel Boutell, who was a showy fellow with a big moustache, who travelled in dry-goods – they had at last discharged their nineteenth-century parental duty to their children.

Before the buggy with the ribbons tied around the whip took off for the steamboat wharf, Nelson Vanderlip handed William an envelope, with a richly paternal smile, for it contained Virginia's marriage portion, a cheque for twenty-five hundred dollars, and not a trivial fortune in terms of the times and the bridegroom's deserts.

(6)

Some grey warrior, half blind with age, sitting by night tells now his deeds to his son, and the fall of the dark Dunthalmo. The face of the youth bends sidelong toward his voice. Surprise and joy burns in his eyes! . . . I gave him the white-bosomed Colmal. They dwell in the halls of Teutha.

Thus the words of Ossian rose, half-understood, into the memory of Gil. Were they apt to this wretched tale of a carpenter and a rich farmer's girl? To his own situation, listening to Mr. McOmish? It depends, surely, on how you choose to see it.

"Let's forget the honeymoon and what came of it for a while." Mr. McOmish is almost genial; the drug is making him expansive. But, oh! how cold the unfurnished room is, and how eerie the light from the lamp. Am I to be here all night, thinks the red-haired young man. He fears Mr. McOmish, and with reason, for his father-in-law has a reputation for violence that has ruined his marriage and terrorized his daughters. His servitude to morphia has devoured his substance. His family wish only to be quit of him, and Gil has been sent to get a legal assurance of that. It is plain that nothing will be signed until the tale has been told, and how long will that be? From time to time Gil nods off, to awake with a start to find himself once again facing the terrible old man – old? he is not so old; he is fifty-six or -seven – who has hitched his chair so near to Gil that now they are sitting almost young knee to bony knee.

"I was crowned with success, Gil. Success, that's to say, in so far as it was open to a man of my talents, a builder who knew his work thoroughly, as few builders do, let me tell you. With Virginia's marriage portion I was able to set up in business in a solid way. I could command the best workmen and the best materials, and I could get the best out of both. Whatever I built then is standing today, and will stand until some fool pulls it down. Do you know what they say, Gil? They say that a builder who builds houses to last is a traitor to his trade, but that's scoundrel's talk. Is there anybody who is anybody who does what he does less than the best he can? Where's the morality in jerry-building? I was a moral builder, Gil. Always have been a moral man, whatever Virgie may say of me. Virgie was poisoned by old Cynthia Boutell. Virgie isn't a bad woman, but she's a sour one. Old Cynthy's the bad one.

"Right from the start, I was a success, and everybody who wanted good work wanted me. But my great send-off came about eighteen months after I started in business, and that was when I was given the job of building a mansion for Mrs. Julius Long-Pott-Ott.

"That name makes your eyes bug, don't it? But she was the great social leader of this place, and rich as they come. She'd been Louida Beemer, but she married Mr. Long, who was an old storekeeper with a pile of money, and he choked on a fishbone within a year of the marriage, and not long after she married Mr. Pott, who owned the big China Hall on Colborne Street. Louida was a pretty girl, and a nice girl, too, which doesn't always follow, but she was either lucky or unlucky in her husbands whichever way you want to look at it. It wasn't two years before Mr. Pott fell downstairs – he was a secret drinker – and broke his neck. So Louida didn't even have to buy new weeds, because she could have her mourning for Mr. Long made over. And she looked so fetching in her weeds that the obligatory year was only just up when she married old Ott, who was a German with more money than you could shake a stick at, which he made out of hogs. And there was Louida, three times a widow, with three big fortunes, and not yet thirty when Ott died – died of too handsome a wife, people said, but that's what they always say in such cases – she was such a nice woman that she didn't drop a single one of her husbands' names, and Mrs. Julius Long-Pott-Ott she was and still remains, and a real high-flyer with her own saloon.

"The high mucky-mucks insist that it should be called a 'salon,' with the weight on the first syllable, but that's just French for saloon. I always said saloon, and after a while she gave up correcting me. They get together there every Friday at four and they drink tea and talk politics or the theayter till half past five. Very select. Frank Schalopki's string orchestra plays in the background, and now and again Ida Van Cortland, the actress, puts in an appearance when she's in town. They accept actresses – married ones. Very open-minded.

"I built the house where all that goes on. There was an architect, a Toronto man, who drew the plans, but I was able to correct a lot of his mistakes. You know – doors that opened into one another, and parts of it that you couldn't heat, do what you might. He wasn't pleased to be shown up, but I argued him down, and Mrs. Long-Pott-Ott was on my side. She had a very practical streak, even if she didn't recognize that her maid, Ola Millard, had been at school with her. Ola used to laugh sometimes, because Louida Beemer had flown so high that she ate what she called her dinner at half-past six at night, when everybody else had et theirs at noon, and had a hot supper at half past five, and she never sat down to it without first making a toilet, which was what she called changing her duds. But for all of that, she was a sensible woman and knew value and good work, and I did my best for her.

"You wouldn't believe what the ordinary sort of builder would get up to, in those days. One of the great tricks was to finish the doors and joiner's work in some trash-pine or fir and often not half-seasoned – and then the painter would do it up with a special paint of lead and oil and cinnabar, and it was supposed to look like mahogany, till the heat came on in winter and the balsam began to leak out of it. Dragon's-blood finish, they called it. Trumpery!

"That was not for William McOmish. Best wood, best workmanship clear through. Didn't come cheap, of course. The Long–Pott–Ott house came out way over estimate. But what could you expect? The architect found out about my skill with stairs, so he put in a real beauty, standing free of the wall and curved, and when he showed me the drawing I knew he expected me to be flummoxed. 'Oh yes,' I said, cool as a cucumber, 'but this isn't just your $T = \frac{R}{\tan (R\text{-}3)}$ 8 deg. job, is it? I'll look at my table of tangents and have it worked out for you in the morning. All those kite-winders call for some careful calculation. And the rail? Secret dovetailing will do it, I reckon. I'll attend to that myself, to be sure it's right.' By golly, you could have knocked him down with a feather. He'd never met a craftsman like me. Consequence of that, I got my way about the horseshoe window in the front parlour. He didn't want it. Said it was vulgar, but that was jealousy. Mrs. Long-Pott-Ott wanted it, because nobody else she'd ever heard of had one and she said it was a Moorish touch. So in it went, and it became my trademark in every house I built after. You see the one here, in my house, till they come for me.

"After that house there was no holding me. Everybody wanted me. But I didn't want everybody. I'd only build for people I respected and who respected me. They didn't need an architect. I could do better than any architect they were likely to find. I did some lovely work. Made wood and brick do things nobody'd ever imagined they could do. There were some in that saloon who said my work was over-

ornamented, but what did I care for them? They weren't the
kind of people who build houses. They were the kind of
people who infest other people's houses when they're built.

(7)

"I CAN LOOK back over a
remarkable career. Not only did I build – I advised other
builders. Would you believe it, Gil, I was the only man
around who knew how to cast a stair? Even a miserable
stair*case* – you know, one of those things that goes up with
walls on both sides. They'd struggle and mess around, and in
the end they had one riser too high at the top, or the pitch was
so steep it was like a ladder, or the treads were too narrow –
that's fatal to old folks, you know – you'd never believe the
trouble they could get into with that simple calculation.
Because they were just carpenters, you see. It would be crazy
to call them *builders*, let alone master builders, like me. And I
put it to 'em, you bet. 'If you want me to plan your stairs, it'll
cost you twenty-five dollars," I'd say, and they'd shrink back
as if I'd stabbed 'em. But if they didn't want a stair that was a
disgrace, they had to pay up. I've made a hundred dollars in a
month, just that way, in my time.

"But every career has to have a pinnacle, and mine came
when the Wesleyan Methodists decided they had to step out
in front of the Anglicans and the R.C.s and have the finest
church in town. The Wesleyans had always been looked
down on as poor folks, but times had changed, and they had
some of the solidest people in town in their congregation and
they wanted a big, fine church. So of course they got an
architect.

"I must say he did a pretty good job. The design was in a
style he called Mauro-Gothic. The Gothic part meant that he
put in arches and pillars everywhere, though the pillars didn't

hold anything up, and the arches were just for show. And he had an atrium, and he had a belfry, and he had an apse, and a jagged thing up one side of the belfry that he said was Saracenic."

As Mr. McOmish speaks I see the church. Time has given it a charm of its own, though it is a nightmare of needless ornament. All the styles the architect had mixed up in this Mulligan Stew of a building have blended at last; it is a Victorian Methodist Church, and could not be anything else. It looks as if it would defy an atom bomb, and it would cost a fortune to dismantle it. As it appears before me, I see that the Heritage Foundation has put a plaque on it, declaring it to be an architectural treasure. From purse-proud temple to architectural horror to national treasure in a little over a century; a truly Canadian story.

"That architect was a learned man, as architects go, but he was not dealing with learned people but powerful people. So he came to grief. They let him have his way with the outside, but the inside was another matter. They wanted it with a raked floor, for one thing, and he said that was wrong in a church. He wanted a central aisle, and they said, What for? Do you think we are going to have any processions? None of that Romish stuff here. He wanted the Communion Table right in the middle of the apse, and that was intolerable; the pulpit had to be the focus of the church and no nonsense about it. The pulpit, from which God's Holy Word is expounded to His people. What about tradition, he said, and they said, What tradition? This is our tradition coming right from John Wesley, and we know what we want. He had put the choir at the back of the church in a gallery – in a gallery, can you believe it – with the organ up there too, and the elders of the church just laughed. Listen, they said; our daughters sing in that choir and we want to see 'em doing it. And we're not paying through the nose for a big Casavant organ with a harp stop and a euphonium stop and even a contraption that makes a noise like a drum and the dear knows what else, to have it hidden in a gallery.

"He sulked, of course, and kind of hinted that they were ignorant. You can guess how that went down with the elders, any one of whom could have bought him up and never noticed the cost. And in the end it was a proper Protestant church, with the pulpit in the middle of the business end, backed by a beautiful set of organ pipes – decorative, of course, because all the real whistles were behind it, made of metal and wood – and the choir in front of it in curved pews, so the congregation could get a good look at 'em and price their hats, and the organ sunk in front of 'em, so that you caught sight of the organist's head over a red curtain. And then came the real Donnybrook.

"It was just about a piece of carving, that ran over the top of the organ pipes, and made a kind of canopy over the pulpit, to conceal the lights that shone down on the preacher. The architect had designed it to be of carved oak – I was to carve it – and he wanted *Ad Majoram Dei Gloriam* on it on a background of carved leafage.

"Latin! You could have heard the screams and shrieks clear to Hamilton! Latin! In a Wesleyan Methodist Church! You'd have thought the Pope was going to move in the very first Sunday. It only meant *To The Greater Glory of God*, of course, but it said it the wrong way. There was a terrible rumpus, and the architect quit.

"Good riddance to bad rubbish," they said, but when they had cooled down in the same skins they got hot in they realized that the interior of the church wasn't finished and they had no architect! Of course the level heads knew what had to be done. They had to call on me to finish the job, and do it properly.

"He'd grabbed up all his plans, and skedaddled, but that didn't bother me. Not a particle. I could make plans just as well as he could, and in two weeks I had an interior that was just what they wanted. Just what I wanted, too.

"You see, I was the great stair man, and I'd always wanted to build one of those pulpits with a curved stair on either side, so the preacher could have a choice. Go up one and come down the other when he'd finished his sermon. Real style and not a Papist hint about it. They bit. They didn't know how expensive those free-standing curved staircases could be. But I had 'em where I wanted 'em, because I'd changed the wording on that piece of carving over the pulpit so it read: *The Lord Is In His Holy Temple: Let All The Earth Keep Silence Before Him.* Very choice and doctrinally correct.

"That's what I built. The finest mahogany, the real thing – no pine daubed with cinnabar – and the rails of those curved stairs were secret dovetailing such as you've never seen – because you weren't meant to see it. And that piece of carving! I declare it took me a month, because it all had to be in the most almighty-twisted Gothic lettering you ever saw, and so overhung with leafage you couldn't hardly read it. I even put a wooden dove, right over the preacher's head, among the leaves. There were mockers who said it looked as if the dove might drop a mess right down on his pate, but they were properly scorned as what they were – mockers. It was a marvel.

"And the first service in the new church was the highest point in my career. I was there, in a frock coat, and at the proper time I offered the plans – not really the plans, which weighed about a hundredweight all told, but a few plans bound in morocco leather – to the preacher, and he blessed them, and made a very handsome tribute to me, as a great Christian builder. I had to have a powerful injection of my medicine that day, I can tell you, or I might have dropped down in a swoon from the sheer glory of it."

Yes, the scene appears before me even as he speaks, and I can see that William McOmish's eyes are wild, the pupils so small that they seem like black pinpoints, and he sways a little. He feels the glory of the moment, the people in the packed church think, but Virginia McOmish, and the Misses Malvina, Caroline and Minerva McOmish, who are sitting near, know better and one might almost say that their eyes express fear, as the Old Devil yields up the plans, and returns to the pew, unsteady and breathing thickly.

I have not seen Virginia McOmish since the courtship scenes and as I look at her now I wonder how anyone can ever have thought her pretty. But I look again and see that her features are good, even delicate; it is her expression that chills, so cold, so minatory has it become. In the pew behind her sits her lame sister, Cynthia Boutell; same features and the same expression exaggerated. She looks, as her brother-in-law often says, as if she could chew nails. Beside her sits her husband, the unsatisfactory Dan; he looks a jolly man, who has spent a good deal of time on his moustache. He wears a large Masonic ring and is running to fat. Of the three McOmish girls Malvina is handsome, for she has her mother's fine features; Caroline is not at all handsome, for she has carroty hair and a pudding face, but her expression is sweet and diffident; Minerva, the youngest, is plump and pretty but must not be exposed to excitement as she suffers from *petit mal*, and might do something embarrassing.

Sunday dinner after the great service of inauguration shows me in brief what is wrong with the McOmish family. They walk home, William in glory, for he has been congratulated again and again on the steps of the church – his church! As soon as they reach their home, which is the spacious, hideous house that I have already seen, stripped of its furnishings and without fire, as Gil and Mr. McOmish talk their way through a long winter's night, Virginia goes to her bedroom, to take off her hat, an uncompromising black straw. William follows her, steps behind her as she looks in the mirror, and attempts to kiss her.

"Oh, don't maul me," she says, and twitches away from him. I see jealousy in her face. His face shows humiliation and anger, as he walks away, and down the stairs, where not one of his daughters has a word to say to him. Caroline feels that she should say something, some word of praise for the great church, but the three girls have been so rigorously indoctrinated by their mother and Aunt Boutell, that she cannot do so. When you think what Ma has to go through, day after day, it would be disloyal to show any warmth toward Pa. Nor does Pa invite warmth, however much he may desire it.

Rhodri Gilmartin is joining the McOmish family for Sunday dinner. He is the unwillingly accepted suitor of Malvina. Neither of the other girls has a beau, so they unite to make great sport of Rhodri, and I see that it is not pretty sport. Jealousy, and a hinting, sniffing, smirking suggestion that there is something not quite nice about the whole business of being engaged, lie behind the sport. When dinner is over – roast pork, boiled potatoes, applesauce with the pork, squash pie, and what would now be called doughnuts (but which the McOmishes call fried cakes) consumed in silence and washed down with strong tea – Malvina and Rhodri are permitted to retire to the parlour. They sit on the sofa together and converse discreetly, because they are aware from various scrapings and sniggerings that Caroline and Minerva have pulled a chair up outside the door of the parlour, and are peeking at them through the transom. To see – what? Nobody would ever say what it was, but it might be something that God has somehow made necessary, but of which God certainly has no reason to be proud.

(8)

T HE GREAT CHURCH having been built, the great church must now be paid for. *Of course* several rich men of the congregation had pledged money before the first sod was turned, but the pledges would not cover a third of what the great church had cost. That gave no concern to anyone. *Of course* the church must have a mortgage for, as the Reverend Wilbur Woolarton Woodside very wisely said, a church without a mortgage is a church without a soul. Without a mortgage to be paid off, how could the congregation be spurred to organize all the bazaars, fowl suppers, home-talent concerts, and other affairs that would raise money, and also generate Christian enthusiasm? If people cannot be goaded into doing something for the church, they may quite probably lose their zeal for the church. As the pastor put it, they might be at ease in Zion, and nineteenth-century Protestantism had no use for ease. Not a particle. Stress and struggle was what was needed to keep people alive in their faith. A mortgage; pointed toward that great day in the distant future when the mortgage would be paid off, and a great service organized so that the congregation might see the mortgage burned, by the minister and his elders. They would, in a few months, inaugurate a new fund to build a Church House, for young people's meetings, Sabbath Day school, and a round of bazaars, fowl suppers, and home-talent concerts which had formerly taken place in the church basement. People must be kept at the job of raising money, or they may forget Christ.

Just at the moment, however, a lot of bills have to be paid and *of course* those bills must be shaved as close as can be contrived. William McOmish, that great man, has built a splendid edifice, but as the elders and the minister remind him, it has run way over the estimate. But there never was an estimate, says William. He didn't take any stock in estimates, which were always wrong. He simply did the best work possible, cost what it might. Was anything else fit for God's service? Certainly not, reply the elders, some of whom are bankers, but we have to keep our feet on the ground. So how about reducing some of these bills for timber, and decoration, and lighting, and a furnace, and that huge bell – first-class bell, *of course*, but who would have thought a bell could come to so much – and *of course* the vengeful bill the offended architect has rendered for his part of the planning? How about it? Surely Mr. McOmish, a bred-in-the-bone Wesleyan, can do something?

What William can do is sharply limited by what his suppliers will do, and several of those suppliers are not Wesleyans, and want all their money. It comes out that he has even bought some fine mahogany from a Catholic firm, and what could you expect from such want of prudence as that?

Pride is a costly possession. That is doubtless why the Bible is so rough on pride, and why it is first among the Deadly Sins. William is too proud to stick out for full payment. He won't give it to the elders to say that he has to have money to keep his business going. That sort of close reckoning is mean, and nobody has ever said, or ever will say, that William McOmish is mean.

So he cuts what he can, and that means, in the end, that he cuts his profit to next to nothing at all, and all his fine carving, and concealed dovetailing, and superfine finishing are for the greater glory of God and, as a minor matter, for the ruin of William McOmish. The nights pass when he figures and figures – and he is too gifted a figurer not to know what lies ahead. Ruin. Lesser men, who cannot figure so brilliantly as he, but who will not reduce their bills, will not suffer, or not suffer extremely, but he knows he is finished. No; never finished. He can build again, and perhaps build better. But he will have to have credit at banks, and he detests credit, which puts him in the power of little men whom he despises.

Needs must when the Devil drives. And this is not his personal devil, that makes him a remarkable man, but the Great Devil, Old Horny himself, who is the Contrary Destiny of so many proud folk.

William, not looking at all like a petitioner, confronts Mr. Bond, a powerful banker and a hard-praying Wesleyan, one of the real old school who may be heard to murmur *Amen* and *Praise the Lord*, during an especially powerful sermon.

"Oh, Mr. McOmish, times are not as prosperous as they may appear, and we have to be particularly careful at present about loans. And you are asking for a long loan, of course. Speaking simply for myself, there is nothing I should like more than to oblige you, but as a banker – no – I fear I could never justify it to my Board. It's not a personal matter; it's *policy*, you see."

Thus it is also with Mr. Murdoch and Mr. Nickel, Wesleyans and bankers both, and elders of the church William had built. It isn't personal, it is *policy*, that holy word.

(9)

Ī̲T IS AT THIS time that William meets with Mrs. Julius Long-Pott-Ott on Colborne Street, as she is stepping into her fine barouche; Sam Clough, her coachman, is holding open the door for her, and her foot is on the step. But she turns toward William, who has raised his hat.

"Oh, Mr. McOmish, I hoped to meet you! I have so much wanted to congratulate you on the new Grace Church. A truly fine building! Gives our little city a whole new appearance. And it makes me prouder than ever that it was you who built my house."

"Very good of you to say so," says William. But he does not smile. Is anybody watching him talking to this fine lady, whose scent of violets he detects? Will there be any talk if he is seen with her, lallygagging right in the street?

"I've thought –" says Mrs. Long-Pott-Ott, "I've thought now and then, that I'd like a new interest. If you ever considered becoming a limited company – everything in your control, of course, but with a source of capital – I'd be glad to talk about it."

"Never thought of any such fool thing," says William brusquely.

Mrs. Long-Pott-Ott has been snubbed and she knows it. But she is too clever and too rich to show resentment. Furthermore, she knows a thing or two, and is what the town calls "long-headed." She smiles, and she has nice teeth, as well as hair that receives more than local attention.

"Well, think about it now," says she. And steps lightly into the barouche.

The hussy, thinks William. To propose such a thing in the street! A sleeping partner – because that's what everybody would call it. William McOmish has taken Louida You-Know-Who as a sleeping partner! The filth! No use even thinking what Virginia would say if she heard about it, even as a suggestion. A man as a sleeping partner, that's business. But a woman! The business term takes on quite another significance, breeds filthy talk.

Meanwhile Ruin. What else was there?

(10)

L IKE SO MANY people who are obsessed by their personal problems, it never occurs to William that anyone else may be aware of them. But when William is known in every drugstore in town, and visits some of them as often as twice a week, with his somewhat dog-eared prescription signed by Dr. George Harmon Vanderlip, his brother-in-law, he cannot expect it to be a secret. Drugstore clerks will talk; they know who puts faith in a special liver-pad, who drinks Peruna Tonic for Female Complaints (presumably unaware that it is simply sherry with a few herbs to make it bitter), who favours which of the sixty or more cathartics that they have on their shelves; much of their social success depends on their seemingly unwilling revelations of these interesting facts. And they know who asks for morphia. Asks for it repeatedly. Morphia is not a restricted medicine, although some caution is advised in supplying it. But when a man has an open prescription from a well-known physician, is a drugstore clerk to raise a question?

Thus everybody knows that William McOmish is an opium-eater. The expression has a horrendous, darkling sound, greatly appreciated by the gossips. Of course William does not eat it, nor does he smoke it, or drink it as do the users of laudanum. He injects it, for a reason that seems to him, and to Dr. George Harmon Vanderlip, his wife's own brother and surely a man to be trusted, to be entirely sufficient. William is an asthmatic, and has been one since childhood, the illness increasing until it becomes intolerable.

So it was that the evil day came, several years ago, when Dr. Vanderlip, having given William a relieving jab in the solar plexus, said: "It's absurd, Will, for me to have to come here to inject you every time you have one of these spells. I'll give you an open prescription and a syringe, and you know by now what has to be done. The dose should be kept as low as possible; never more than seven grains a day, at most. And only when you need it, of course. You're a man of good sense. You'll be all right."

William was not all right. The pressure of business, the excitement of doing his finest work, and the misery of his domestic life make his "spells" more frequent, and long before he has finished the great church he is taking thirty grains a day and often more. He needs it in order to keep himself up to the mark, because under the pressure of work he finds himself becoming dull when he needs to be sharp for his calculations. Sometimes his hands tremble, and a man with trembling hands is not in any state to do hidden dove-tailing. Also his digestion is in bad order; he has a sour stomach, and he belches when he has eaten nothing and therefore has nothing to belch about. His natural irritability is becoming uncontrollable and he snarls when he does not mean to snarl. Almost the worst thing is his constipation; he takes a highly regarded aperient, a real blaster, but it is power-less, and his straining in what is delicately called "the little house" seems sometimes as if it would rupture him, and his heart protests.

All of these things are plainly the result of demanding work, and his only recourse is to the syringe and larger doses of his one friend, who brings calm, freedom from worry, freedom from pain, freedom from the terrible gasping when his lungs are filled to bursting with air which he cannot force out, when his head seems about to burst, and when he is afraid of death. Yes, afraid of death; he, a strong, highly intelligent, resourceful and skilful man.

It is astonishing that he thinks nobody notices. But as he laboured at the great church the Reverend Wilbur Woolarton Woodside and the banker-elders saw his inexplicable excitement, and his strange eyes, and because the word had seeped up through the social structure from the drugstore clerks, they know what is wrong. Mrs. Julius Long-Pott-Ott, who has broad experience of husbands and knows a man with a secret when she sees one, guesses what is wrong. But nobody likes to speak to Mr. McOmish about it, because he is forbidding and has a sharp tongue. And nobody speaks ill of Dr. George Harmon Vanderlip, because nobody who is not at least equally loaded with science and arcane knowledge likes to criticize a doctor. Doctors rank just below parsons in their special sanctity.

Bankers, too, are priestly men; priests of Mammon, that popular deity. Bankers never talk. Of course, being human, they may murmur something to their wives, who may say something under the seal of strict confidence to a friend. How then does the news spread so quickly that William McOmish, long known to be an opium-eater – that poor woman, those sad girls – is on the brink of ruin? Even more astonishing, that Louida Long-Pott-Ott has offered to bail him out, and he bit her nose off, right on Colborne Street. So Sam Clough says, to a few confidential friends, strictly under the rose, of course.

(11)

LIKE GIL, I am growing restless under the unrelenting, self-justifying narrative of Mr. McOmish. Like Gil I sense that there must be other ways of looking at this story. Now, suddenly there flashes on the screen what is plainly a group photograph of a family reunion; out-of-doors on a farm lawn, about forty or more men and women are standing in front of a house, from the upper windows of which hangs a banner which says, "Welcome Vanderlip-Vermuelen-Gage Family." The colour is sepia – a light gingerbread brown. In the back row stand the men, most of them with their arms folded; the only fat one is obviously the detrimental Dan Boutell, and he is also the best-dressed. In front of them are the women, in chairs, dressed in everything from what was fashionable at the time and the place back to garments well-preserved for fifty years and perhaps longer. Among them I recognize my grandmother as a young woman, her gaze concentrated by a pince-nez; she is the only one of the group who wears spectacles. In age they range from youth to two old women, at the extreme ends of the row, who wear the frilled white caps, the shawls and the ample black skirts of a much earlier day. Sitting at their feet are children, the little girls dressed heavily and wearing button boots; the boys wear roundabouts, breeches, Windsor bows, black stockings and button boots as well. They all stare fixedly at the camera, except for one blurred child who has moved during the "time exposure," of at least twenty seconds, demanded by the photographer.

I know them instantly, and with a certain shock. These are my forebears, on my father's side, at least, and a severe group they seem to be. Is the severity the result of the "time exposure"? Is it merely the fashion of the day? Or have these people no wish to seem happy and approachable? It is easy to identify William McOmish, whose scowl marks him as a man to be reckoned with, a man of intellect, a man who can cast stairs that would defeat a lesser builder. But there are others whom I recognize, from half-remembered family tradition. There is Great-great-grandfather Nelson (born Trafalgar year), a beard well down on his chest, standing behind his wife, Alma Devereux; at the far left of the women's row, that she-ancient must be Granny Sands, his great-aunt, whom he likes, purely in jest, to threaten with his buggy-whip. ("I'm going to touch you up, Granny; here I come; step lively, Granny. Dance, Granny!" "Oh, git along with you Nelson. He-he-he, my dancing days are over Nelson, and you know it!" "Come on, Granny, give us a little jig!") Nelson was the joker of the party. The man with the long scar on his face must be Bug Devereux. So called because, when he was seventeen, his face swelled hugely and at last burst, and a great black bug crawled out of it, spread its wings, and flew away. It is received belief that at some time an insect must have laid eggs in a small cut on his face, and hatched there, and the bug is his sole claim to distinction. But there is a man widely known as Forty-Pie Doane, because he once devoured forty pies in a church pie-eating contest, and survived, as undefeated champion. He is as thin as a rail, and looks hungry. Only related by marriage but a man of grotesque distinction. There is Cousin Flint, short, small-headed, scowling; not a man I should like to meet in a dark wood. There is Ella Vanderlip, celebrated for her goitre, which is indeed prodigious. There is Cynthia Boutell, the sister-in-law whom William McOmish detests with his whole soul. And this old woman at the far right – it cannot be, but it is – Hannah Gage, last of the tribe to remember that long journey from New York to Canada; Aunt Hannah, now well over one hundred if she is a day, and famous for her determination to undertake any disagreeable task – "If anybody has to suffer, let it be me; I'm broken to it" – but who is never allowed to suffer because everybody knows that Aunt Hannah's life has been a martyrdom to rheumatism, asthma, bad stomach, and immovable bowels. She is the improbable survivor of Anna Gage's adventurous brood.

Some in the picture have dim remembrance, through family legend, of Hannah's brother Roger, who had died at the Battle of Queenston Heights, in 1812, repelling the Yankee invaders who had come to liberate Canada from the British yoke and got a surprise. Roger's name is on the monument on that victorious field. But virtually everyone in the picture remembers Grandmother Elizabeth herself, who, with her husband Justus Vanderlip, grew richer even than old Anna, from clever shopkeeping and land deals, and never allowed the memory of her brave brother Roger to grow dim. Elizabeth, in the memory of all in this picture, finished her life as a smiling matriarch, sitting in her parlour, passing the time agreeably with pinches of snuff from her tortoise-shell box, interspersed with peppermints from her other box, which was of real old American silver, brought from New York and one of the two treasures to make that far-off voyage. Elizabeth left the management of her household to her four daughters, while she gloried in the achievements of her seven sons – farmer, lawyer, doctor, two parsons, and two members of the newfangled Legislature (with their hands, said the envious William McOmish, deep in the pork-barrel). Is it by chance alone that none of these are present at this family affair? Busy men, of course, but surely they could have put in an appearance.

My forebears. I know that I am blood of their blood and bone of their bone, but they seem as far off and strange as so many Trobriand Islanders. Their clothes are good. That is to say, they are of hard-wearing, sturdy materials. But who can have made them? They do not seem to fit anywhere, and they have never known the touch of the presser's goose. The men wear vast cravats, and some of the older ones wear black satin stocks, in which there are horseshoe pins, presumably of gold. Do they brush their hair, or claw it into a rough semblance of order? They have glaring-clean linen, though they are bathers-once-a-week – if so much; the Dutch concept of cleanliness. And the women! They seem not to have prided themselves on their appearance, though many of them wear heavy jewellery of jet and gold, assurances of substantial means. Only my grandmother and her sisters seem to have given any thought whatever to their appearance. Everybody over forty in the picture has a ravaged mouth, suggesting that few teeth have survived so long. Did these people know love, or laughter? Have – or had – these people wombs, testicles: it must have been so, but who would guess it from their outward being?

Then the rigid picture breaks up. The figures move, and I see them differently, though they are still strange.

Strange because they are chronologically absurd. There are people in this assemblage who have no right to be here, or certainly no right to appear at the ages they seem to have reached. I must remind myself: am I watching a movie, a work of art or at least of artifice, and has not the Director a right to do what he pleases with Time? Is not the cinema the place of dreams, the place of once-upon-a time? What I am seeing is not Ibsen's *Master Builder*, which is apparent to the Sniffer, beside whom I am seated, or perched, or however my condition must be described. Nor is my time the chronological time he sees on his screen. Is this what McWearie, in his attempts to explain Tibetan belief to me, called the Bardo state? Am I not in pleromatic time, that embracing element which has nothing to do with the processional tick-tock, tick-tock of our time when we are – as we vaingloriously describe it – alive?

I cannot protest or question the truth of what I see. Whatever truth it possesses is certainly not the historical truth I have been educated to think of as alone worthy of trust. In what I am watching, Time is conflated, as indeed it must be in any work of art. It is merciful of Whatever or Whoever is directing my existence at this moment to show the past as a work of art, for it was as a work of art that I tried to understand life, while I had life, and much of my indignation at the manner of my death is its want of artistic form, dimension, emotional weight, dignity.

(12)

I FOLLOW THE figure of my grandmother. She moves with a self-conscious dignity that goes with the pince-nez. She is "a working girl" and proud of it, for that was not the condition of most women of the time. She is a secretary, invaluable to her boss, Mr. Yeigh, who is, like herself, of Dutch descent and often says to her, "We Dutch must stick together, Miss Malvina." She knows not only the inner working of the large carriage and bicycle works of which Mr. Yeigh is the manager, but also the details of Mr. Yeigh's hobby, which is bee-keeping. "Order me six five-banded Italian queens to be delivered as soon as possible, Miss Malvina," says he, and she knows precisely what he means.

Why is she a working girl? Why is her sister Caroline also a secretary, working in the insurance company that is dominated by the energetic Dr. Oronhyateka, notable as one of the Mohawk aboriginals who has "made good" in the white man's world? Why is their young sister, although only sixteen, already apprenticed to the millinery trade – for the poor child has *petit mal* which unfits her for secretarial work? I know, of course, for have I not seen Mr. McOmish, a wrecked and ruined man, haranguing his son-in-law in the depths of the winter night? But how did it come about, what went before, what explains Malvina's exaggerated self-confidence and propriety? What explains the look of fixed outrage, of monstrous affront, that I see on the face of Virginia McOmish, my great-grandmother?

(13)

Now APPEARS a series of brief scenes from Malvina's childhood and girlhood.

Here is a fine house in the clapboard mansion style of the early nineteenth century; it would have charm and an air of welcome if the blinds were not drawn to the sills, and the knocker on the front door muffled in crêpe. Inside, members of old Elizabeth's family are gathered for the funeral of the matriarch, one of the survivors of the great flight from New York. In the parlour the men of the family are gathered, talking in hushed but not reverential tones, as the undertaker's milliner takes their hats, one by one, and wraps them in the obligatory long crêpe "weepers" for the approaching funeral. Another milliner takes the sizes of their hands, and outfits them with new black gloves – for this is a first-class funeral and no expense is spared. Old Elizabeth's two black servants, Angeline and Naomi (themselves fugitives long ago from the Slave States), pass trays on which are small glasses of Elizabeth's personal cordial, cherry whisky, made by steeping black cherries in the whisky-jug for six contemplative months. Sparingly taken it has prolonged Elizabeth's life, and it now comforts the bereaved, some of whom require three glasses to steady their nerves.

"Now Mother's gone, I reckon you to be the oldest stock, Nels," says a younger brother, oddly named Squire Vanderlip. (He is not a squire but a lawyer.) Nelson nods, assuming the role of seniority with becoming gravity.

Upstairs the women are gathered in what had been Elizabeth's personal parlour. On the wall hangs the other treasure that had come from New York, so long ago. It is the portrait of George III, so dear to Major Gage, and now framed in Victorian style, heavy with ebony and gilt. The women are chatting, sipping the cherry whisky, and now and then wiping their eyes with handkerchiefs broadly edged in black.

Confusion! Old Hannah is bursting in with fearful news. (She is not the "oldest stock" despite her great age, for she is a woman and, at least in theory, could change family alliance.) She whispers to Nelson, the oldest male stock.

"Nelson, what do you suppose those young 'uns are at?" She hisses the news in his ear, in a gust of evil breath.

"What in Tophet!" cries the oldest stock, forgetting the solemnity of the moment. He hurries out on the *stoep*, which is what these people, true to their Dutch ancestry, call the broad verandah or gallery that runs around three sides of the house.

What indeed? The children are following a wheelbarrow in which Flint pushes a large doll. They are weeping loudly and brandishing the black-bordered handkerchiefs with which they have all been supplied. They are playing funeral!

Uncle Nelson descends upon them, roaring, followed by a dozen outraged fathers. The children are seized and roundly tuned. Their weeping is passionate, for they do not fully understand how they have sinned, but they know that it must be sin that brings this sudden and painful public correction.

Only one of William McOmish's girls is in this horrid mockery of a great occasion, and like a good father he seizes Malvina, turns up her skirts, and beats her soundly. She is profoundly humiliated, not only by the beating but by the horrendous fact that her drawers are thus exposed before the boys, although they themselves are being beaten and have no time to jeer at her.

The mothers, and aunts, and the minister, watching this massacre of the innocents from the *stoep*, agree that right, and justice, and morality have been vindicated, for the only way to bring up children is to beat the Old Ned out of them whenever He asserts himself.

"He that spareth the rod hateth his son," says the minister, to general approbation, and, lest a few children dare to look resentful, he adds, "Honour thy father and thy mother, that thy days may be long upon the land that the LORD thy God giveth thee."

This assertion of proper feeling gives added solemnity to the subsequent funeral, as the plume-decked hearse, with its four plumed black horses, precedes the black carriages to the church and the churchyard where the matriarch is to lie.

(14)

NOT ALL OF Malvina's childhood is bitterness. I see her now, not much older, holding her father's hand as they make their way to the principal hotel of the little city, where there is a wonder, very suitable for children, to be seen. William is pleasantly aware that he is providing his child with a great educational opportunity.

For who is holding a public levee, to which all comers, upon payment of a modest fee, are welcome? None other than General Tom Thumb, the famous dwarf. He is declared by his escort, the great P.T. Barnum, to be only twenty-five inches tall, though in fact he is thirty-one. But there he is, before Malvina's wondering eyes, standing on a red-carpeted dais, with his tiny wife, Lavinia Warren, and his dwarf aide, Commodore Nutt (who is somewhat taller than Tom, but obligingly stands on a lower level). Even as the newspapers have reported, "his clothes are the production of the most distinguished tailors, and his gloves are of necessity furnished to order, for nothing so small and fairy-like were ever manufactured." As for Lavinia, she is splendid in her wedding dress, a miracle of tiny ruffles.

William and Malvina join the queue who move slowly forward to shake hands with the living marvel. Or rather, to be touched lightly with his extended forefinger, because a rough handshake could hurt him.

Neither William nor Malvina see the look of fixed sadness in the eyes of the General and his lady who, like many artists, get their living by exploiting their wretchedness.

There is an occasional flash of romance in Malvina's life when, in the streets of the town, she sees the four daughters of the Chief of the Six Nations Indians. These handsome girls wear splendid riding-habits – green velvet turned up with red – and have fine horses. The Johnson girls are certainly not squaws. They are princesses.

Was it the visit to Tom Thumb and the dashing Johnson girls that awakened Malvina's appetite for marvels, for strange epiphanies and, as she grew older, the theatre? She yearned toward the theatre, without ever daring to imagine that she might herself be a part of it. Methodism had no place for any make-believe but its own, though from time to time entertainments took place in the basement of William's great church that were theatrical in a gelded, sanctified way. Such a performance was an operetta for children called *The Land of Nod*, and Malvina, who could strum a little, coached Georgie Cooper, a limp boy with a poor ear, in his principal song:

> *I'm the jolly old King*
> > *Of the realm of dreams,*
> *The dear little Land of Nod;*
> > *And whatever I say,*
> > *Or whatever I do,*
> > *My royal old head*
> > *Is depending on you;*
> *Now isn't that awfully odd?*
> *Amusing, yes funny, and odd?*
> > *Whatever I do,*
> > *I depend upon YOU –*
> *For – I'm King of the land of Nod!*

Georgie's voice was very near the adolescent break, and on the high note of "YOU" he was apt to be flat, or crack, but Malvina worked over him as if he had been a star of opera. After Georgie's solo twelve little girls in cheesecloth executed the Dance of the Dreams, to a slow waltz. Malvina had trained them, and it was agreed that in this task she "showed talent." Among the Methodists talent might show itself, but ought not to be dangerously encouraged.

When she began her working life even the McOmishes had to admit that some portion of her wages (she got four dollars a week) should be kept by herself, and out of this weekly dollar she spent twenty-five cents whenever it was possible on a ticket to the theatre. Her parents disapproved, but at seventeen she was hardened to disapproval and at the theatre she could ease her spirit, for two hours at least, in the presence of her idol, none other than Ida Van Cortland, leading lady of the visiting Tavernier Company. Oh, Ida Van Cortland, exemplar of womanly dignity and allurement to a hundred thousand spiritually starved girls as she bodied forth the miseries of *Camille*, that noblest of fallen – but spiritually exalted – women! When Camille expired in the arms of her Armand, Malvina experienced that sweet deliquescence of the loins which the truly sensitive feel when something profoundly affecting is made palpable on the stage.

Malvina cherished in a secret pocket of her purse the lines that had appeared in the local paper, the work of a poet who wished to remain nameless, but was easily recognizable:

> *TO MISS I ✶✶ V ✶✶ C ✶✶✶✶✶✶✶*
> *(after witnessing her mighty performance in "Forget-Me-Not")*
> *Touched by the fervour of her art,*
> *No flaws tonight discover!*
> *Her judge shall be the people's heart,*
> *The Western World her lover!*
> *The secret given to her alone*
> *No frigid schoolman taught her: –*
> *Once more returning, dearer grown,*
> *We greet thee, passion's daughter!*

The poet, as everybody knew, was none other than the man who had, so many years before, wooed Virginia Vanderlip, suffered her scorn, and lost her to William McOmish.

Fallen women exalted on the stage! Malvina had cause to know how ill that sat with the McOmishes. At seventeen she had suffered one winter from "a gathered throat" which the doctor (not Uncle Vanderlip) diagnosed as tonsils, and said that they must come out. So one Saturday afternoon, when she was free of the bicycle-and-carriage works, she made her way to the doctor's office, and he removed her tonsils, without anaesthetic, for, as he explained, it was a quick operation and the discomfort trivial.

Walking home afterward, spitting blood into her handkerchief, she was overcome with pain and weakness and collapsed against a green picket fence, vomiting blood and losing consciousness. The woman who was sitting on the *stoep* behind the fence hastened to her assistance, took her into the house, and sent a messenger to William McOmish. In due course he arrived with the family horse-and-buggy, and took his daughter home, refusing to speak to the kindly woman. And when he reached home his wrath, and his wife's, was terrible.

If Malvina had to faint, did she have to do it outside Kate Lake's? A known house of ill-fame, where Kate Lake kept shameless girls who did unspeakable things for men of low character – the Mayor and two aldermen, among others – and was known to be a common recreation for the roisterers of the town? She had allowed herself to be taken up onto the *stoep* of that house where the Lord knows who might see her. Moral indignation clouded the McOmish home for days to follow.

Poor Malvina! My own grandmother, whom of course I had never known in this younger and tenderer aspect but whom, as I watched this film, in its dismal sepia shades, I suddenly knew as I had never known her in life. Knew that she had lived in the fear and bitterness of that loveless household and – it seemed to me now – had felt that fear and lovelessness even before she made her sad entrance into this world. Had known it perhaps in the womb.

(15)

IT WAS McWEARIE, that avid collector of scraps of information which, when gathered together, made up his outlook on life, who had told me that it was now believed by some medical scientists, and the psychologists who were unknown in the nineteenth-century world of Malvina's girlhood, that children in the womb are, in their enclosed world, nevertheless conscious of the atmosphere of the greater world that they would join after the months of gestation; join with deeply implanted feelings that they would never be able to shake off in the seventy or more years that lay before them. Children in the womb know no language but they hear sounds, tones of voice, sense calm and also turmoil and rancour. Malvina had been begotten in a world without love and, whatever her aspirations nurtured in the theatre and in happier circumstances, would never truly be at ease in a world where love in its manifold forms is the begetter of all that makes life sweet. Malvina might yearn for love, might try her best to engender love and stimulate it in her own life, but would never be free to trust love or give herself to love without fear.

How many children are doomed before they make their entrance into this world to live with fear that lies so deep that they do not recognize it for what it is, having never known anything else? Ghosts cannot weep, or I would weep at what I know now when knowledge comes too late.

Knowledge that comes to me in scenes interspersed with scenes from Malvina's youth, for as she makes her way toward whatever of love life has in store for her, there are scenes from the life of her parents, loveless and embittered. But, nevertheless, loyal. William and Virginia "stand by" one another, as they say, and call their quarrels "differences of opinion" and will not put a name to the hatred that possesses them. Marriage may not appear sacred, but it is certainly inviolable. William will not hear a word against Virginia, for that would reflect badly on his choice, his home, his way of life. The master builder, who is so deft with wood and brick and stone, so apt in the mathematics of stress and strain, of angles and oppositions, has no skill in matters of flesh and blood. It must be said that it would take a mighty man to soften Virginia, who is too witty and sardonic to yield readily to any kind of softness, and from the outset of the marriage she takes pleasure in planting barbs in her humourless, vulnerable husband.

(16)

Not surprisingly they find a figure who can take on all of William's anger and frustration, and all of Virginia's self-righteousness, and exemplify both to the satisfaction of the warring parties. This is Virginia's limping sister, Cynthia Boutell, known to the whole family as Aunt. For Virginia anything from the choice of a green kerseymere for a gown, to the daily iniquities, unreasonable demands, and shortcomings of William, and of course the bringing-up of her daughters, must be submitted to this oracle of an older sister, and what she calls Aunt's Judgement is solicited every day of her life, for they are near neighbours. To William, Aunt is the mischievious old bitch of whom he spoke to Gil, during their midnight colloquy. In the fashion of the day he must submit to Aunt's presence at his own table every other Sunday; on the alternate Sundays he and Virginia must have midday dinner with the Boutells and he must endure not only the acerbities of Aunt, but the unceasing good-nature and jocosity of her husband, Dan Boutell.

When dinner is over Virginia and Aunt settle to a satisfactory canvass of the week's gossip, all of which passes under their unforgiving eyes in a passion of disapproval. Nor is current gossip alone the subject of their talk. They go back for years and even for generations, reconsidering and re-judging the faults and mishaps of others, the failures and miscalculations and, of course, the follies of people now middle-aged, who once were young. This is called by William "threshing old straw" but to Virginia and Aunt it is the cud of life, which they chew and re-chew with unfailing relish. The girls, Malvina and her sisters, "do the dishes" as girls should, for neither of the Vanderlip sisters can tolerate the slopdolly ways of a "hired girl," and William in his decline could not afford one. The men, William and Dan, go for their inevitable Sunday walk, and Dan smokes one of his expensive cigars, which are not permitted in either house, and which William will not touch. Opium-eater as he is, he despises Dan's slavery to the weed. Their dull walk circles a vacant lot that Negro children use as a playground; it is known as The Devil's Half-Acre. What do they talk about?

"Ever think of joining the Oddfellows, Will?"

"Why would I want to get mixed up with that Tribe of Manasseh?"

"Well, the Masons, then? I could put you up, you know, whenever you say the word."

"You know I don't hold with secret societies. Nothing about me has to be kept secret."

"Aw, come on! It's just a way of getting together without the womenfolks. After Lodge the boys have a high old time. Keep it up till the last dog is hung, some nights."

This expression refers to the Feast of the White Dog, an occasional ceremony of the local Mohawks; no non-Mohawks are admitted, but rumours – inevitably scandalous and derogatory – are current, including tales of the sacrifice of a white dog, but how or for what reason nobody knows, but everybody suspects.

"Why would I want to keep it up with Jem Hardy and Bob Holterman and that tribe? Let 'em wear their little white aprons and play the fool by themselves."

"It's more fun than a barrel of monkeys, sometimes. I've known the meetings to adjourn to Kate Lake's. Ever been to Kate Lake's, Will?"

"I should say not. What makes you think such a thing?"

"Oh, a lot of it is quite innocent. Kate sings a good song."

"I can imagine what kind."

"You're too strait-laced, Will. Never let yourself off the chain. Say, last week I had to get down to Detroit on business, and overnight I seen this show, *The Mulligan Guards at Atlantic City*. Those girls! Lot of 'em and not a plain one in the lot. I bought a few postcards. Here, take a look."

"You know I don't hold with the theayter."

"Well, then, here's a few that ain't from the theayter. I picked these up from the candy-butcher on the train, a couple o' weeks ago. Ever see anything like that?"

These are cards of plump girls, wearing a look of simple innocence combined with allurement, and they are naked, though some of them wear black stockings.

"Put those things away, Dan. I don't want to see 'em."

"Come on, Will; you'll want to see these. This set cost me five dollars," Dan whispers. "Six ways o' doin' the Dirty Job. Did you know you could do it like that?"

"Dan Boutell, you ought to be ashamed! A married man!"

"Not all that married, Will. I don't get much o' that. Cynthy says it's disgusting, even among marrieds. These cards sort o' help out, when a fellow's lonely. You get much o' that, Will? – Aw come on now, don't walk away mad! Wait for me, Will!"

(17)

Dan has grazed Will on a very sore place, because Will doesn't get much of that. Virginia's ideas about the intimacies of marriage come directly from Aunt: even among marrieds, it's disgusting, and the fact that it leads to children – and a man has a right to expect children, however shameless their begetting – is just one of God's mysteries, and makes a decent woman wonder sometimes what God can have been thinking about when he set it up that way. As a temptation to men, Aunt says. Aunt has no children, for the best of reasons.

A man has "marital rights," and William often reminds Virginia that it is so. Their bodily unions are infrequent, and since the birth of Minnie have been wholly discontinued. But in William, that gaunt, strong Highlander, desire has not died, and there are frequent scenes of proposal – never pleading, for why should a man plead for his rights? – and contemptuous rejection. William will not force her, though there are times when he wonders if he might not kill her.

His desire is a torment, and the last such scene, two years after the birth of Minnie, is brief and bitter.

I see it in full, for I cannot turn my gaze from the cinema screen, much as I wish to do so. I am condemned to see. The unhappy couple are preparing for bed. Both are in their nightgowns, and before she retires Virginia squats over the chamber-pot, for there is no modesty between them about this necessity. The sight strikes up the flame in Will, for it is one of his oddities that his wife in this position appears deeply erotic to him. As she is giving her hair a final brush – a hundred strokes each night, to brush in the bay rum she uses as hair-dressing – he approaches her, his arms reaching out to enfold her. She can see him in the mirror, and sees that the front of his nightgown pokes out comically over his erection. With a scowl she turns and strikes him on his penis with the ebony back of her hair-brush, with more force perhaps than she intends. He makes no sound, but retreats, nursing his hurt, doubled over in pain. That is the last instance of sexual activity in the McOmish household.

> *Heav'n has no rage, like love to hatred turn'd*
> *Nor Hell a fury, like a woman scorn'd.*

So wrote an English poet who would perhaps not have thought that people like the McOmishes had any right to noble passions. But if he had known more about people – and he knew much – he would have known that a man scorned is also a prey to fury.

From that moment, William was a man melting in fury. It was at best a silent, unsleeping fury, but it disposed him more and more toward asthma, his ancient enemy, and asthma turned him to the needle, and after the needle his fury spoke loud and long. Scenes of the bitterest abuse were frequent, and as he stormed Virginia sat silent, a figure of mute martyrdom and hatred for her tormentor.

William did not rant about sex – certainly not – but he abused his cold, unloving wife and what he could not bring himself to say about her he said about Aunt.

Poor Mrs. McOmish! Who could believe what she went through? To come to such a pass – she, a woman of good family, a Vanderlip – and to put up with it without a word! *Of course* she spoke to her minister, the Reverend Wilbur Woolarton Woodside, and he gave the best advice he could, which was shallow and inept. *Of course* she had to speak to her brother, the Doctor, who shook his head and said that Will had let his medicine become his habit, and he had known dreadful cases of that. He gave his sister a silver teapot and sugar bowl, which did not have much effect on the problem. *Of course* she spoke to Aunt, who declared that she had always thought there was bad blood in William McOmish, and she wished she had spoken more firmly before Virgie had married him. But the very best of us can't always know what's best for others, and Virgie had refused to listen to hints. She had made her bed and now, Aunt supposed, she must lie in it.

Nobody but these intimates were supposed to know what was going on, but of course everybody knew it, for the clerks in the drugstores to which William went for his supplies told this one and that one, always in strict confidence. On the q.t. Part of the bitterness of bourgeois life is that there are really no secrets.

(18)

THUS MALVINA grew to be twenty-eight, the calm, dignified Miss McOmish, so active and popular in church work, especially in getting up entertainments. Malvina also sang. She was a contralto, and it was through her singing that she had met Rhodri Gilmartin. It was some time before their friendship reached the point where she dared, greatly fearing, to ask him to her home.

Rhodri was very popular in singing circles, for he possessed a fine, natural tenor voice. Of course he had his limitations, for he was just a journeyman printer, and his family had come within living memory – which was to be a raw newcomer in those old Ontario towns – from what a lot of people still called the Old Country. The Dutch backbone of the town, and all the country round, knew that it was not *their* Old Country, which they had not forgotten in the almost two hundred years since they had set out from Amsterdam, and Rotterdam, and The Hague. Perhaps they had sided with the British during the regrettable revolution, and had had to make a run for it to Canada, but to them Englishmen were still suspect: foreigners with peculiar ways. So a growing sympathy between a good Dutch girl (a little flawed by a Highland father but still so Dutch that the Scots blood hardly counted) and a johnny-come-lately was not regarded with favour.

Malvina, in the manner of the day, was becoming rather desperate; she was just over thirty, after which anniversary a woman became a certified Old Maid. In her mind, also, there was a war of fidelities: she must certainly honour her father and her mother, but they gave her no honour in return, and she faced a life of office work on their behalf; she did not strongly want a husband and children, but she very strongly wanted not to be an Old Maid; she had some romantic ideas about love, picked up from novels and the plays in which her

ideal, Miss Van Cortland, figured but she had never experienced love in her own life, or seen it evinced in the lives of
others in any way that made it look attractive. Under such
pressure of conflicting ideas, she fell in love with Rhodri
Gilmartin.

He was good-looking, he dressed well, and in the fashion of the time and the place he had an elegantly waxed
moustache, not tortured into ridiculous bodkins of hair, but
discreetly pointed at the ends. He sang, movingly, the ballads
of the time by Fred E. Weatherley and Guy d'Hardelot; and
there was one of a somewhat earlier time –

> *I fear no foe in shining armour,*
> > *Though his lance be swift and keen;*
> *But I fear and love the glamour*
> > *Through thy drooping lashes seen.*

– that Malvina found irresistible.

He talked. He did not talk tediously about the Japanese
War, like William McOmish. He did not thresh old straw like
Mother and Aunt. He talked about really interesting things –
books and music and church picnics, and bicycle races and of
course the theatre (he had seen Henry Irving and been profoundly influenced by that charismatic actor), and, best of all,
he made jokes. He also made grave social errors.

"Have you thought of trying your hand at making ladders, Mr. McOmish?" he asked one Sunday at midday dinner. "Ed Holterman has done very well with ladders and
nothing else, I understand."

Matters were very much on the downhill grade for the
McOmish family; indeed, it was the combined earnings of
the three girls that was keeping it afloat, for William had had
nothing to do for months, and had been incapable of doing
anything well for at least two years. He gasped continually
with asthma, and sought the relief of the needle several times
a day. Most of the time he sat at the table glassy-eyed, and
pushed his food into heaps with his fork. But this well-meant

suggestion from the Englishman (the McOmishes had no truck with Welsh pretension) in reply to some comment about the scarcity of building contracts roused him to a Highland blaze.

"Are you suggesting that I'd lower myself to the level of a common carpenter like Ed Holterman? Make ladders? Me, that built Grace Church, and finished it when the architect threw in the sponge? Me that's built half the finest residences in this city? You don't know who you're talking to, young feller. It looks as if you don't know who I am."

Then gasping, and the awful pallor of the face, and the retreat to the bedroom, for what everybody at the table knew about, and what nobody at the table wanted to give a name.

Gilmartin's apologies were unheard by Mr. McOmish, and received with grim silence by Mrs. McOmish. Nobody, of course, might leave the table until Mrs. McOmish had drunk the last of her unnumbered cups of strong tea. When, at last, it was possible to leave the table, it was understood that the girls should wash the dishes. Virginia and the silent figure at the table, who was Aunt, went to the back-parlour for the threshing of some agreeably new straw, for of course Aunt's judgement on the unhappy remark of Rhodri Gilmartin must be heard and chewed over. Had his eye on Malvina, had he? Had too much to say, if you wanted Aunt's opinion. Been hovering around for at least two years. When was he going to pop – if he meant to?

Aunt was now alone. It was five years ago that Daniel Boutell had left the house one day with a carpet-bag, since when neither hide nor hair of him had been seen, nor so much as a postcard received. But Aunt had her dowry money still, and on that she "managed," making a great deal of self-honouring fuss about it. After all, as Virginia often said in these sessions, had anybody expected anything better of Dan? He had married Cynthia for her dowry, but she was one too many for him, thank the Lord. What had she ever seen in him?

Malvina and Gilmartin as usual retire to the front-parlour, well in view of Mrs. McOmish and Aunt, and after some quiet talk they go for a walk, and it is on that walk that Rhodri proposes and is accepted. He has, in the cant of the day, popped.

What then? Marry? Malvina *marry*? The thing is too big for comprehension. Marry, when the family fortunes are so low, and her salary needed? Marry, when Pa is so ill and needs so much money for his medicine? Marry, and leave Mother, who has to put up with the Lord knows what, when Pa is not himself? How sharper than a serpent's tooth, says Mrs. McOmish, thinking she is quoting the Bible. Hadn't Malvina seen enough of marriage, asks Aunt, who has now set up as a great expert on the married state. As for the sisters, Caroline and Minnie, they are stricken, for if Malvina leaves the household, however will they manage Ma and Pa alone? Not to speak of the money. Marry the Englishman? It is out of the question.

(19)

M ALVINA IS DRIVEN to devise a stratagem. She has a talk with her mother and, in language that is the more horrible for being veiled, suggests, without really saying, that she *has* to be married, or disgrace will overtake them all. It is not really a lie, because it is not precisely framed; it is a tissue of hints. She has said nothing of this to Rhodri, who would despise it as a lie, deeply discreditable to Janet's son. As for Virginia, she will say nothing to William. This is women's business. Thus it is that in the McOmish front-parlour shortly afterward, the Reverend Wilbur Woolarton Woodside unites Malvina in holy matrimony to her hoodwinked bridegroom, and the register is signed by the bride's hoodwinked parents and by Aunt. No relatives of the bridegroom are present, nor have they been

asked. The evening ends in profound gloom for the
McOmishes. The bride and groom have taken the night train
to Niagara Falls.

All of this I see, filmed in sepia, a colour which seems to
put the action at a distance, and lessen its emotional impact.
But not for me. These people are my people and I suffer with
them, and I do not take sides. I feel the ruin that faces William
and Virginia as poignantly as I understand the predicament of
Malvina and Rhodri. This is no tragedy of star-crossed lovers, nor are the elders of a stature to achieve tragic proportion.
Theorists of the drama may deal in tragedy and comedy, but
the realities of life are played more often in the mode of
melodrama, farce and grotesquerie.

Grotesquerie – and now, briefly, terror. One night Virginia turns on her husband and, as she tells Aunt, later, lets
him have the rough side of her tongue. Sick, is he? Maybe he
is sick, but it isn't the asthma that ails him. It's *that stuff*, which
has made a slave and an orray-eyed tyrant and monster of
him.

Wasn't it her own brother who introduced him to it, he
counters. Yes, and didn't her brother think he was man
enough to use it prudently? And what has he done? He's
become a – she can't bring herself to say it, but he knows well
enough what she means. That's what he is now, and well he
knows it. And hasn't her brother washed his hands of the
case, says William, because he's too God-Almighty righteous
to come and look at what he's done? Oh, for the Lord's sake,
be a man, she cries. Be a man? Is that it? How often has she
given him a chance to be a man? Because he's too good a
Christian to gad up to Kate Lake's with her rowdy old goat of
a brother-in-law, he's lived in a hell that only a man knows. A
hell of her making. Her, and that Lapland witch of a sister of
hers. Don't talk to him about being a man! What about being
a woman? Has she been a woman? Eh? Has she? Seven times
in thirty years of marriage. She can count as well as he can.
Seven times, and three children! And every time with tears
and reproaches, as if he was some kind of a dirty beast.

Doesn't she read her Bible? Isn't the woman the servant of the man? Isn't he the head of the household? Hasn't he loaded her with every luxury a decent woman can want? Hasn't she one of the finest houses in town, built with all the skill Almighty God blessed him with? He's a man in the street, but in his own home he's a dog, because he's a Christian man, and won't force a woman.

Street saint and home devil! That's what he adds up to! Street saint and home devil!

Virginia screams it. She is dressed from head to foot in mourning for one of the Vanderlip brothers who has been gored by a bull, but William is in his nightshirt, barefooted, and at the disadvantage of the naked when faced with the clothed. In his rage he seizes a carving-knife and pursues her around the dining-table, not rapidly, but slowly and with menace.

"Devil, am I?" he says, in a low voice. "Well then, a Devil I'll be."

She retreats in horror. For several seconds she cannot scream, but when her voice returns to her she screams loud and long, and screams again and again, until Caroline and Minnie, white with terror, rush into the room and join her in screaming. They dare not seize Pa, or protect Ma, but they can scream, and they do.

William is not Devil enough to hold out against such screaming. Like many another man, he is terrified of the maenad shrieking of women. He drops the knife and rushes from the room to the chest of drawers where he keeps his only remaining treasure.

(20)

THE CULMINATION of this is that next day Edmund and Dr. George Harmon Vanderlip come to their sister's aid at a family conference, and read the

Riot Act to William, who is hardly in a condition to understand it. The upshot is that Virginia and the girls are moved into a humble house that was William's when first he married – an old razeee, William calls it, and from his master builder's point of view that is what it is – and Dr. George Harmon Vanderlip handsomely agrees with Brother Edmund to pay what it costs in taxes. The house, by law, may be rescued from the ruin of William's fortunes. Of course furniture for this dwelling must come from the big house with the horseshoe front window, and Virginia and the girls contrive, somehow, to take most of what there is, leaving William alone in a house that is empty of all but a bed and a few chairs and some pots and pans.

It is there that William is bivouacked on the night when Gil visits him, and I first see them at their midnight conference.

Final ruin impends. Every penny that William had is gone, and of course all Virginia's dowry money has gone with it. Bankruptcy is to be completed in a few days, and everybody, greatly assisted by Aunt's judgement, has agreed that Virginia must be legally separated from a bankrupt, for bankruptcy in that society is one of the darkest sins, and almost the ultimate disgrace.

(21)

As DAWN SHOWS its first grey light through the horseshoe window, Gil at last has his way. William signs the papers. The indivisible marriage is no more.

The day following William is to be seen, dressed in his best black, riding in a carry-all driven by an aged pauper, accompanied only by the sheriff of the county. He is being taken to the county home for paupers and the mentally unstable. Everybody knows where that carry-all hails from.

Is he sunk in shame? No, as the old Devil makes this decisive journey he smiles sardonically to right and left, and raises his battered top hat to anybody he recognizes. Lifts it with a special sweep to Mrs. Long-Pott-Ott who passes in her barouche. She smiles and nods, good woman that she is.

Lifts it to whatever power it is that has used him so capriciously. William has faced ruin in several different guises, and the old Devil is showing the world precisely what he thinks of it.

Happy are they who die in youth
when their renown is around them!

Is it so, Ossian? Always?

V

Scenes from a Marriage

WHEN I WAS ALIVE I sometimes tried to read those books that sought to explain what Time is, but I could never make head nor tail of them. They asked for a mathematical ability that was beyond me, or for some philosophical flight which I could not accept. But now that I am dead, what is this element in which I live if it is not Time? For a while after my death things were easier, and what I apprehended was attached to the ordinary Time I had known while I lived; that Time is no longer mine, for now I recognize neither night nor day, minute nor hour. All measure of Time is slipping away and my glassy essence, as Shakespeare calls it (and I can do no better), knows no measures, no boundaries. Surely what knows no bounds must be Eternity.

Not Eternity yet. Not quite. I know these films, that I watch in the company of the Sniffer. He sees another film, somewhat kindred to my own, and it has a beginning and an end; as I take my place when he takes his, and leave it when he goes back to the *Advocate* offices to write his review, there is at least that much measure of time.

What is the film today? He is to see something more recent than the films heretofore; it is Ingmar Bergman's *Scenes from a Marriage*, which dates from – when was it? – 1972. I saw it before I was married. Before I met Esme, indeed. What I saw was the trimmed version that was shown commercially; this is to be the full work as Bergman conceived it. Something recovered from a film archive.

I know that I shall not see that film. And yet, as the cinema darkens and the screen comes to life, I see, on my own personal screen, the same title: *Scenes from a Marriage*. Something from my personal archive.

What marriage? My own? Not in the scene that appears. That is certainly the library at St. Helen's, my grandparents' house in Salterton, which I remember from boyhood visits. It was on the lakeshore, and the sound of the waters of Lake Ontario is part of my memory of it, and part of what I see and hear now. Who are these people, sitting by the fire? Grandfather, Rhodri Gilmartin, now in his early sixties, a rich man, a powerful man, an owner of newspapers, a man with political influence and, as the world measures success, a success. One would hardly recognize this sturdy man as the slight youth who passed a miserable night with his father-in-law, William McOmish, it must be – what? – more than thirty-five years ago.

Who is that old woman – older, probably, than her years – in the rocking-chair on the other side of the fire? Malvina McOmish she once was, and I sense that she is so still, in the depths of her being, as Rhodri is still the long-headed Welsh lad who gathered some alms from the wreckage of that failed tailor-shop. Malvina is plainly an invalid, but what is her illness?

She has an attendant, the fat woman who sits in front of the fire at work on a jigsaw puzzle representing, when completed, The Entry of King Charles II into London after His Restoration. Do I know her? Yes, she is what has become of Minerva McOmish, now a dependant and companion to her invalid sister. In her lap nestles a fat little dog, one of the terrier breed called Black-and-Tan. The infamous Janie, with whom I was not allowed to play when I was a boy, because Janie had delicate nerves, as overfed pets so often do.

"Brocky, Janie wants out," says Auntie Min. A young man, who sits further from the fire, rises and shepherds Janie to the front door, where she ventures into the cold night, urinates weakly by the front steps and waddles back to the warmth, and the lap, and the frowst to which she makes her doggy, gaseous contribution.

I know the young man. My father, as a youth. Brochwel Gilmartin, whom I knew only as a moderately successful university professor, who wrote a psychological analysis of *The Ring and the Book* that sustained him in a profession where some such publication was obligatory.

He hates being called Brocky. He hates Aunt Min and he hates Janie. He hates the illiteracy of "wants out." He does not hate his parents, because that would be wicked and, although he fancies himself to be an atheist, he cannot escape from the indoctrination that bids him honour his father and his mother. Honour them he does, as dutifully as he can manage, conscious that such honouring has a whiff of superstition about it. He hates a great many people, tolerates many people, but he loves only Julia, and his passion for her is a torment.

How do I know what he hates? How is that knowledge communicated to me? I understand with a sinking heart that in this film I am to know whatever I am to know not by the actions and the words alone of the players, if I can call these forebears of mine players, but by sharing their thoughts and their feelings.

How in the world am I to know those things from a film? Films are not adept at conveying thought and feeling without words or actions. How does one become privy to the thoughts of those who do not speak or move?

Writers have tried to convey such knowledge by what they call Inner Monologue. Joyce wrestled with the problem in two great, long, dense books. He was not the first, and his followers have been many. But words cannot give the fullness of feeling; they can only struggle to arouse some echo-feeling in a reader, and of course every reader must comprehend in terms of what he has himself felt and known, so that every reader feels the essence of Joyce and his imitators in a different way. An echo is a diminished voice.

Musicians have done better. With voices and huge orchestras – or possibly with a string quartet – they have aroused greater depths of feeling than most writers can hope to do. Wagner, to name but one, has done it with shattering impact. But even Wagner, with his magnificent music and his rather less worthy pseudo-medieval words, is never wholly successful. Why? Because a work of art must be, in some measure, coherent; but thought and feeling mingled, as all of us experience them, are surging and incoherent. Thought and feeling trimmed into coherence in a work of art are still far from the reality, still far from the agonizing confusion that rises like a miasma in what a great poet has called the foul rag-and-bone shop of the heart.

And not just the heart. The guts, the bones, the physical being of the human creature, which, alone of all creation, is given the sense of a past and a present, and the apprehension of a future – gifts that agree so oddly with the mind, the heart, the soul and the body, all combined. Oh, what a god we have made of the mind, the understanding, which is so necessary to life, but which hangs like a cloud in the sky above the physical world which is the totality of every human creature! The mind: a trifler! Feeling is more than what happens in the mind; feeling possesses the whole living being.

Can this film succeed where other arts have failed? Never. Not a hope. But this one will try, and I must watch and feel so far as I can, for in my disembodied state feeling is still my last hold on life as once I possessed it. Feeling, as though I still had a body, a mind, and all that makes a living creature thrill with joy or writhe in pain.

Nobody in the room I am watching thrills or writhes. They might perhaps be said to stew, to bubble deeply and

with terrible purpose in the gumbo of their emotions. Three
of them appear to be reading, and so they are, but the reading
is no more than the uppermost layer of their reflections and
emotions. Rhodri seems to be busy with his favourite author,
P. G. Wodehouse. Malvina is reading *St. Elmo*, an almost
forgotten novel of her youth. Brochwel is chewing doggedly
away at *The Faerie Queen*, of which a portion is required
reading for his literature studies at Waverley University, but
which he is determined to read in its entirety, for already he
detests half-heartedness and superficiality. Auntie Min is trying to find the moustache of King Charles the Second for her
puzzle; five hundred pieces in all, and a terror, as she frequently tells anybody who will hear.

The books and the puzzle occupy the upper layer of their
minds, various as these are. Each of the four is conscious of a
musical accompaniment to reading, and reflection. With
them I – the patient looker-on – read, and listen and experience their deeper monologue.

(2)

AUNTIE MIN: *(Music: "The Honeysuckle and the Bee," played
on a banjo, minstrel-show style.)*

This it? No; won't fit. Must be hair off one of the girls. He
had plenty of girls, they say. Can't really see. Of course
they've all got lamps, but nobody imagines I'd like a lamp.
Where did this fellow come? Brocky would know, but I
daren't ask him. He'd jump down my throat, or else heave a
sigh and tell me in that "Poor old dumb Minnie" voice he
puts on. Lordy, Lordy, the young! When they're babies they
love you and you can't do enough for 'em, but wait till they're
grown up, and then they seem like they can't stand you. Even
if they're your own. Brocky is like that to Viney. Coldly civil.

No more. What went wrong there? Why doesn't he love his
Ma like a real son? Viney and I loved our Ma. Couldn't have
loved her more. Poor Ma. What she went through with that
Old Devil. He died in the Poor Farm. Long after Ma, too.
The Devil looks after his own. Of course all Brocky can think
of is that Julia. Well, that's how it goes. That was the way it
was with me and Homer. . . . *You be my honeysuckle, honey, I'll
be your bee.*

Homer was undoubtedly the neatest man I ever saw.
Shoes always shined like glass. Always a clean white handkerchief in his breast pocket, too. And one in his hip pocket.
"One for show and one for blow," he used to say. He had
more jokes. . . . ! Called his hip pocket his pistol-pocket, as if
he was a bandit! I loved just walking down Colborne Street
with him, he was so classy. And believe me I dressed up to his
style, you bet. Great big hats. He used to call them my
Gainsborough hats. A painter. Must have liked big hats. A
big hat, and a dress made up in a good Dotted Swiss, silk
stockings and patent leather pumps so tight they nearly had
me crippled. Lots of beads. Always *have* loved beads, and that
was the time of the really Big Bead. Those red ones! I have
them still. Some place. Yes, the Big Bead was The Bead of
Choice, as Miss McGovern at Ogilvie's used to say. And
scent! He used to give me scent after we were engaged, when
it was all right. *Djer Kiss* – that was the name of it. Spicy.
Black box with a parrot on it. A small man. Good gifts come
in small packages, he used to say when he gave me a quarter-
ounce of *Djer Kiss*. Small, and bald in front. A distinguished
baldness, not that scabby baldness. And pince-nez. French
for pinch nose. Of course he was an optometrist and always
in the height of the fashion in eye-wear. Pince-nez, and the
lenses tinted just a hint of violet. It rested the eyes, he said. He
pioneered tinted lenses in our city. Sometimes I asked him if
he wasn't afraid the violet tint would look like an unhealthy
shadow under his eyes, but he would chuck me under the
chin (if we weren't in the street) and say they made him look
passionate. Pretty strong talk, but after all, we were engaged,

and when he kissed me . . .! Brocky was playing that song last week on the Orthophonic as they call it now. Taken over from what we called the phonograph. That song when the girl sings about her lover and bursts out, "And Ah – his kiss!" It brought it all back, and I had to pretend I'd got something in my eye. That phonograph Homer gave me the Christmas after we got engaged. An Edison. Thick, heavy records. Like stove-lids, Ma said. Some records came with it. "Gems from The Yokohama Girl." . . .

> *In your silk pyjama*
> > *Go and tell Mama*
> *You will be happy with me –*
> > *My little Japanee!*

And "Cohen On The Telephone" – we *laughed*. . . . "I vant a carpINter to mend de *shutter* that hangs on the side of mine house, because de vind come, and de shutter *clutter*." Clever, real clever, taking off the Jew. Homer was clever, too. He included a record of hymns for Ma, and that sort of made her hesitate to condemn the phonograph, because it sang "The Old Rugged Cross" and "Life's Railway to Heaven." . . .

> *Keep your hand upon the throttle,*
> *And your eye upon the rail.*

Ma liked anything that was religious. We used to joke about it. She'd sit in the parlour window, all Sunday afternoon, so's people could see her, with her specs on and her Bible in her hand, and then she'd doze off. But of course she was really religious. I guess. . . . She said I oughtn't to take such an expensive gift as the phonograph. Said I was making myself cheap. Keep your hand upon the throttle. But Homer got round her. Said as we were engaged it was really for our future home. Not that it ever got there. We couldn't marry until his mother went. It would have killed her. Or so she gave out. I don't think so. She was as tough as old boots. But anyhow, Homer had to believe

her. She was his mother. And of course at last she did die, and
we were ready to get married till Ma said – with tears in her
eyes, and it was the only time I ever saw Ma cry – "I'd hoped
you would have waited till I was gone." That clinched it, of
course. We couldn't wait for old Mrs. Hall to die and then marry
right in Ma's face, the way Viney did. So we waited and Ma
certainly took her time. But she went at last – not that I ever
wished for it, nobody could say I did – and then Homer got
pneumonia before the year of mourning for Ma was out, and he
died, and that was that. He left me everything, but not the
business, of course. His cousins saw to that. I've got his cuff-
links and watch-chain still, and I guess they'd better go to
Brocky when I'm gone. Never mind; Homer's few hundred set
me up in business for myself. The Home of The Hat Beautiful.
Everybody said it was a wonderful name. And I knew the
business. Hadn't I been buyer for Ogilvie's for years and for
your straws and your felts and your feathers and your Bohe-
mian ornaments – cherries, little apples, flowers of all kinds –
there weren't many who could beat me. Creative, they call it
now. That was what I was; creative. An artiste of the hat. . . .
Damn cars! As soon as they got popular, and everybody had to
have one, and women started to drive, and girls wanted to drive
with the top down and the wind blowing, that was Good-bye,
Hat! Of course the older women went on wearing hats, but
time took care of that. I'd put a hat in the window that anybody
would be proud to wear, but unless somebody wanted to wear
it to a wedding, or maybe a funeral if it was a crushed velvet,
let's say, there my hat would stay for weeks. Got under my skin,
and my trouble got worse. I had to turn to Rhodri for extra
capital, and why not? Wasn't he my brother-in-law? He came
through, in the end, but not warmly, it must be said. I suppose
Viney made him. She knows how to get what she wants and
Rhodri's weak, under all that bluster. Weak, and I'm not afraid
of him. Not a particle. He's done well. I grant you that. But he's
had the luck, and not everybody does. How did Viney get him?
That was a mystery, but some of the girls said she caught him on
the bounce, from that Elsie Hare. He was too proud to be jilted.

Always thought of himself as a great one with the girls. He had
a kind of a come-hither combined with a touch-me-not look
about him that was like catnip to some of 'em. Still is. And
Viney's jealous, don't try to tell me any different. She's still
jealous and there's women around this city who would grab at
him. And maybe they do. Some of those women in that Drama
Group, as they call it, always wanting him to be in plays. Luckily
he's too busy for much of that. And what parts could he take,
anyway? Old men. He'd not thank you to be asked to play an
old man. But wouldn't surprise me if . . . Dresses younger than
his age. And what he spends on clothes the Lord only knows.
I've always been poor, and when you're poor you see life from
underneath and you notice things other people miss. I've tried.
I've certainly tried. But nothing seemed to work, and I lost
heart and more money from Rhodri couldn't do anything
against cars and flappers who didn't know what a hat was.
Young de'il-and-go-flickets! What would people have said in
my day if we'd carried on like that? Rolled stockings! And the
War hardly over! Like this Julia. Oh, Brocky doesn't kid me.
Not on your life! I see that look in his eyes when I'm not
supposed to see anything. . . . Viney's beginning to nod. She'll
want to go upstairs soon. Maybe I'd better go and heat the milk.
Hope those ugly foreigners are out of the kitchen. They look at
me as if they'd like to kill me. . . . But I'd like to find the King's
moustache first. What was it we used to say? A kiss without a
moustache is like an egg without salt.

(3)

MALVINA: (*She is reading* St. Elmo *by Augusta Jane Evans;
             below her reading is music; a song, "Could I," as sung
             by Emilio de Gogorza on a Victor Red Seal Record;
             further below, her brooding.*)

Glad to see *St. Elmo* again. Down under all that trash of

Rhodri's out in the end room. Min found it. What was she doing rummaging around out there? Snooping. A snooper even when she was a young one. Must be fifty years. Bought it after I saw the play. Ida Van Cortland. Most elegant woman I ever saw. That last scene, where St. Elmo says: "Is Edna Earl more righteous than the Lord she worships?" – then that pause, and she looks him in the face and says – "Never was more implicit faith, more devoted affection, given any human being than I now give you, Mr. Murray; you are my first and my last and my only love." People don't talk like that any more. But you see the reality. Yes sirree! Brocky laughed when he saw me reading *St. Elmo*. But I've read more books in my life than he has, though he's going through them fast enough. I know that the heart of a book isn't just what you get from the language. Not that I suppose they care a particle for the heart of anything at the university. All head; no heart. They sneer at *Les Misérables* now. Well, let them better it, I say. Music, too. That stuff he buys and plays. Not a tune anywhere. Some of the songs are good. That one he played that made Min cry. She thought I didn't see, but I did. Thinking of Homer, I suppose. Min's had hard luck. Her trouble, to begin with. I saw her yesterday when she had one of those spells at the table. She thought nobody saw, but I saw. *Petit mal* the doctor calls it now. Used to say epilepsy, but that's *grand mal* now. I wish she wouldn't lock the bathroom door when she goes in. Might have a seizure right there on the seat, and how would we get at her? But you can't break an old maid of that habit. Old maid. I was the only one of us three to get married. Consumption was the great fear. We've all got poor lungs. Min didn't have the gimp to outface old Mrs. Hall, and poor Carry was the real breadwinner after Pa went smash and I married. Ma never really forgave me, even when I sent her money on the q.t. Poor Carry. She could play the piano like a professional. Might have been a professional, with better luck. She'd rip through that "Grande Paraphrase de Concert sur le Faust de Gounod" so your eyes would blink. Wonderful waltz tune in that. Ed Gould used to sing words to it –

> *"I can sing like a nightingale,*
> > *My notes are clear and bright."*
> *"You don't mean like a nightingale,*
> > *You mean like a gale in the night."*

He thought that was great till one day Mr. Yeigh turned on him and said, "Jeering at High Art leaves High Art untouched, Mr. Gould, but it shows up the quality of the mocker," and Gould just shrivelled up like a leaf. Everybody respected Mr. Yeigh. That Christmas he gave me *Les Misérables* with a nice inscription. He knew I had a leaning toward a really good book. I've read it, oh I guess five times. Beats *St. Elmo* into a cocked hat. Reality! That's what Victor Hugo had. Reality. He knew the human heart. Gould! Oh he thought he was a card! That day he brought the chocolates to the office and treated all the girls. They were cubes of soap he'd had coated at Alf Tremayne's Candy Kitchen. But girls were a curiosity in an office in those days, and we had to put up with a lot. I wanted to get out of it. To get married. Not just to get out of it. I wanted some romance in my life. Carry wasn't the only one who had art in her. I could sing. Haven't sung for years. Asthma. From Pa, I suppose. Worse now than when I was young. We all have poor lungs. But I love a good song. De Gogorza –

> *Could I but come to thee once,*
> > *But once only,*
> *As you sit, so sad and lonely*
> > *With your head on your arm*
> *So weary-hearted –*

What a voice! Rich baritone. Heard him sing that in recital. But every time he left the stage he strutted out ahead of his accompanist, and she was a woman! A gentleman would have let her go first. But he was an artist, of course, a Great I Am, and I suppose you have to make allowances for that.

Could I but come to thee
When night is falling
In the old sweet way
Just coming at your calling
And like an angel bending down above you
To breathe into your ear
"I love you –
I loooove you."

I suppose the man had died before they were married. De Gogorza sang it almost like a ghost, soft and mysterious and very tender. Before they were married. Like poor Min. Not that Homer Hall could sing a note. Tin ear. Does Min ever hear a ghost like that? Don't suppose so for a minute. No imagination. I was always the one with the imagination. But what could I do with it? Three girls, left with Ma, after they dragged Pa away to the Poor Farm. Making a show of himself in the street, right up to the end. You don't keep your Ma as she's been used to on imagination. I wrote some poetry. No good, I suppose. After I married Rhodri I even wrote stuff for his first paper. For the Christmas Issue. How we worked over that! I don't suppose the subscribers gave a continental whether they had a Christmas Issue or not but Rhodri was determined they should have one. He was proud, and wanted to show 'em. And he did. He's done well. Rich, now. I wish Ma could have seen. She never had any time for him, and I know he didn't like her, though he never said so to me. I give him that. Proud! And how he could sing!

I fear no foe except the glamour
Of the eyes I long to see;
I am here, love, without armour –
Strike, and captive make of me!

Used to sing that at concerts, looking straight at me. All I could do not to blush. He used to talk stuff like that to me even after we were married. Welsh blarney, of course. I never let myself set too much store by it. But it brought warmth into a cold life. My life. Why cold? If I knew. Ma and Pa, I suppose, but it's disloyal to think so. Talked that way right up to that awful row we had. Was I to blame? He never understood. There has to be some reality, say what you like. Not all romance. That old music-hall song he used to sing –

> It ain't all lavender
>> Don't you think it is
> There's fish and there's corduroy trousis!

Well, it's all done now, but things have never been the same since that awful row. A marriage is for keeps, and I was always loyal. Never mind about the other. Is he loyal? Sometimes I wonder. That woman who comes to him at the office, and whines about the hard luck she's had in her marriage. Well, if she married a jackass, whose fault is that? She picked him. Complaining to another man isn't loyal. She got a bad house over her head. Let her live in it, *I* say. Of course he makes fun of her when he tells me about it, but that could be to cover up something. I know he lends her money. And those others. Think they're high-flyers because their husbands are professors or in the Army or some such nonsense. Haven't enough to do to keep them warm. I've heard them boast about their "affairs" as they call them, though I wonder just how far the affair went. All that hugging and kissing at Christmas parties. Enough to make you throw up. "How we apples swim, quoth the . . ." That's an old one. Ma beat me when I was four because I used language I heard around the blacksmith shop. . . . Does he get up to any of that when I don't see? He's always had a way with women, though underneath I know how shy he is. A lot of women don't think a man can be shy unless he's a fool, but I know better. Sometimes the shy ones get into the biggest messes. . . . . God, sometimes I burn with hate, and the worst of it is I don't know who I'm hating. But I hate till it gives me a headache, and now I can't even get out into the garden and take it out on the weeds. Is it imagination? That's been my curse – imagination. Sometimes it nearly kills me. I sit here and I imagine things that disgust me, sometimes. Where does all that awful stuff come from? Is it being a woman? A woman with imagination and nothing to use it on but hate and suspicion? Hate is a poison, and once it gets thoroughly into your system there's nothing to be done but to hate till you're sick and exhausted. Hate is an addiction. Brocky's doing a course in psychology. Do you suppose they ever tell them that? Brocky gets his imagination from me, though he thinks he gets it from his dad. As a girl, I tried to write. Poetry, but it was never the real thing. Forced. But I felt something real. His dad was never a writer – except for news-papers, and he was good at that. Political. Editorials that he used to say were dripping with blood. Did he get that from his uncle? Old John Jethro Jenkins? He could write and he wrote letters to the papers that blistered the government, for what-ever good it did. Which was nix. An old blowhard. How Auntie Polly respected that man! "Malvina you mustn't con-tradict the Master," she'd say, whenever I couldn't put up with his rubbish. The Master! Master of that house, which was mortgaged to the hilt, and falling to pieces from neglect! The fire black out and there he'd sit in bed with his overcoat and hat on reading the encyclopaedia! I know Rhodri helped him, on the q.t. Thought I didn't know. Well, blood's thicker than water. With the Welsh it's thicker than tar. I wish it was thicker between me and Brocky. My son! Gets his imagination from me, I know. Could I have been a writer? A woman Victor Hugo? What went wrong? What's gone wrong, all down the line? I liked being a working-girl. My own money. Not to do what I pleased with, of course. Had to go to Pa and Ma as long as Pa was around, after he went smash. Ma needed it even more when he was out of the way. Never mind. It was my money, and I made it myself. What money have I got now? Stacks of it, but it's really Rhodri's. I have nothing to do with it. Of course I'm a director of a couple of his companies, but what's that? Sometimes he puts a paper in front of me and says,

"Sign there –. . . You don't know it but you were at a directors' meeting this morning." He means it kindly. Doesn't
want to give me trouble. But that's the kind of trouble I'd really
like. Always hated keeping house, and when we were poor
sometimes I'd find I was crying while I swept the floor. Not
now. Haven't swept anything in years. Have to make those
foreigners do it. They're all right, I suppose. You can trust
them, and they keep a pretty good house. Not the old style, of
course. Not the Dutch style. Not Ma's style. Clean out the
keyholes once a week with an oiled feather. That was Ma's
style, and she saw we did it. Of course she couldn't do much,
except make the odd pot of tea. After Pa went to the Poor Farm
she lost all heart for any kind of household work. Said her
powers had completely gone. . . . Who looks after that house
in Wales, I wonder, now that I can't get over and see to it?
Never could get any decent help there. Not just for the summer months. Farm girls and old cooks like gypsies. And dirty!
They hated it when I used to go into the kitchen when they
didn't expect me, and caught them all sitting around drinking
strong tea and stuffing themselves with bread and jam and
gossiping. But it was my house, wasn't it?. . . No, it never was.
It was Rhodri's house. It was Wales to him. Cold, wet country
even in June. Never took to the people. Gasbags. And insin-
cere. You never knew what they were saying about you behind
your back. County gentry! Down on their luck, most of 'em.
And the people in the town were worse. He'd sit in some dirty
tinsmith's shop, because he'd known the tinsmith when they
were boys, and chew the rag and thresh old straw, while I sat
outside in the car, getting one of my headaches. And then next
minute it'd be the county. La-di-da till you couldn't bear it!
How we apples swim! A headache, then my asthma. Might as
well admit it, I hate Wales and the hold it has on him. Those
women he meets. Gigglers. And he likes to giggle with them.
Like that Julia. A giggler. I'd like to get her by that long hair of
hers and give it a good yank! I've got to stop this, and go to
bed, or I'll make myself sick. Oh hate – hate! The poison of my
life, and the worst is that I'm not stupid enough not to recog-

'nize it! There's no medicine for hate, and that's what my imagination has turned to. . . . I've read six pages of *St. Elmo* and haven't taken in a word. Am I getting simple? No, by gum, I'm not, though sometimes Rhodri treats me as if I were. I can see what's in front of me. I can see Brocky looking at me, when I try to talk some reality to him. I suppose I'm an ignorant old woman, in his eyes. But I still know more Latin than he does, even if I never finished High School and had to do that secretarial course. Pitman's Shorthand. I can write it still, and sometimes I leave little notes to myself around the place, to show Brocky I can write something he can't read. Mr. Yeigh said I was the best shorthand writer he'd ever employed. And that was where my imagination went, I guess. Reality took over. Now it's all gone to seed and dreams. I think things happened that I've read in books. Like this book. *St. Elmo.*

> *And like an angel bending down above you*
> *To breathe into your ear*
> *"I love you.*
> *I love you."*

I'm getting silly. More of this and I'll be crying and nobody would ever understand why. Bed, now.

"Min, bring my hot milk upstairs in about five minutes, will you? No thanks, I can manage the stairs alone."

(4)

I SHRINK FROM watching this film; it is deeply embarrassing. Getting painfully near the knuckle. The Loyalists fleeing to Canada and the gradual rot after that great expenditure of spirit. Yes. The hegira from Dinas Mawddwy to Trallwm and the rise and fall of a Methodist family. Yes. But this – that young man who seems to be reading *The Faerie Queen* but is really stewing in his own juice, like the other three, is my father and I don't want to know about his involvement with anyone called Julia. My mother's name was Nuala – Nuala Connor from Dublin, a female academic and a cool but kindly and sufficient mother. There was no extreme heat between my parents. Sixty-eight degrees Fahrenheit, I would reckon it. The heat in the library at St. Helen's – the palpable, real heat – must be well over eighty F. and the psychological heat is just below boiling – a slow simmer. But I cannot escape the film.

Can it be called a film, this extraordinary evocation of things that go far beyond the photographable, physical presence of these people? This film that gives the truth of temperature, of smell, of the sense of physical sickness that hangs about my grandmother and spreads through the room, of the subhuman life of the dog Janie who can know nothing of the complexities around her but, as dogs do, absorbs them all and makes them manifest in her somnolence, feebleness and gluttony; Janie is sick with the life of that house.

The technique of the film is advanced beyond anything I ever saw in my days of life as a film critic. The screen divides and shows many images, or a number of contrasted images that comment upon one another, or swells to one monstrous and frightening close-up; the colour ranges from the dim sepia in which the sad life of Min is seen to the rich Caravaggio palette of my frustrated, imaginative grandmother. This is a film that reaches all the senses including smell. Smell – which our age has made the least acceptable of the five, but which rouses emotion with a painful immediacy. We are not supposed to smell people, and millions of dollars are spent on various devices to kill human smell, either at its source, or in the nose of the proximate companion. But to the aroused, the truly curious, the enchanted or the enchained, is there any better revealer of truth than a smell? As now, when a smell of health, soap, bay rum, and expensive clothes assails me, and I know it is my grandfather.

(5)

RHODRI: *(The music which supports his thoughts is from a musical comedy of the twenties, called* Lady Mary; *the voice of Herbert Mundin, a comedian of the day, is heard:*

> *What do the Yanks know of England*
> *Who know not Austin Reed?*
>   *They may have the dollars*
>   *But they buy their shirts and collars*
> *From the Boys of the Bulldog Breed.*

He is rereading, for the sixth time, a story by Wodehouse in which Bertie Wooster reflects on his one-time love for Cynthia, "a dashed pretty and attractive girl, mind you, but full of ideals and all that. I may be wronging her, but I have an idea that she's the sort of girl who would want a fellow to carve out a career and what not. ")

Carving out a career. That's what I've done, I suppose. But what a release to read about somebody who had no need to do it, and not the slightest intention of trying. What a holiday to read about people who have no real problems, who are not chained to day-to-day, year-to-year obligations. What a satisfaction to read about aristocrats whose chief concerns are growing flowers, or prize pigs, or simply having a good time. What do the Yanks know of England? What do the Canadians know of England? Come to that, what does P.G. Wodehouse know of England? Because this isn't England, it is a fairy-tale land, an England that never was. Brocky tells me that somebody has said that Wodehouse's stories are musical comedies without music. That's their charm for me. That, and the magic of the language. Escape from reality. And what's wrong with that? Haven't I had plenty of reality? Or what people call reality, which always seems to mean something nasty? I took on reality when the Pater announced that we were emigrating to Canada. *(Music changes to "Yn iach i ti,*

Cymru," a *farewell to Wales.*) Lance and me first, to spy out the land, he said, but in reality I suppose to be spared the final misery of selling up the shop, and the furniture, paying debts – he paid every penny, good man – putting up the shutters and leaving the place he loved. But I seized on one reality, and that was that twelve pence made a shilling and twenty shillings made a pound, and an extra shilling made a guinea. Where did I learn that? Is a sense of money inborn? The Pater had none. Uncle David certainly had none, though he had the craftiness to marry Mary Evans the Angel, who had money. Grandfather had a sense of money, but not enough sense of how to hang on to it. Backing that debt for Thomas! Couldn't he sniff that Llewellyn Thomas was unsound, if not actually a crook? Sanctimonious old twister! Religion was like a drug to those people. It could blind them to anything. A great day for me when I put it aside. Yes, put it aside without giving up the outward forms, because it would have grieved the Mater if she thought I wasn't a Methodist from my crown to my soles. Was it hypocrisy? Hypocrisy is a necessity if life is to be endured. All hypocrites: some hypocrites for God's sake. The Mater. The finest woman I've ever known. The last time I met Lance, when I went to his sixty-fifth birthday party, he said, "Rhod, our Mater was the dearest and best" – then he wept. So did I. Her prayers were what saved our skins in this awful country. (*The music changes to "Do Something for Somebody Quick."*) That was a silly song, but she wasn't a silly woman. Every night in that awful first year, before a poor supper she made us all kneel, and she would pray – the Pater couldn't pray, he was too low in his mind to pray aloud – that God would bless us in the new land. Which He did. No getting away from it. That night in December, when Lance was late for supper and for prayers, and he suddenly burst in and interrupted the prayer – which showed how overwhelmingly important it was – saying, "Pater, there's a sign on the door at the Plough and Harvester saying they want an accountant," and the Pater jumped up in mid-prayer and ran out, and came back later to say that he'd just caught Mr.

Knowles as he was locking the door, and landed the job. Knowles told him to take down the sign and be there at eight in the morning. I suppose he was impressed by the Pater's good speech and honest look. A great night for us, that was. The Mater didn't actually say that God had answered our prayers, but we didn't need to be told. Even I believed it. And from that day we never wanted. The Pater was accountant in that factory till the day he died. It was below his abilities, but it was a job, and he never knew how to capitalize on his abilities. That deathbed promise to his mother. His ruin, in a way. I'll never forget the moment Lance broke into the Mater's prayers with that promising news. Has my career been evidence of God's goodness? Or luck? Or my way of capitalizing on my abilities? Nobody can say, but I know what the Mater would have said. . . . A little intelligent hypocrisy might have saved the Pater. Too good. Excess in virtue can be ruinous. . . . Those awful first days on the job. The men at *The Courier* used to tease the life out of me. "Rhod, is that woman that wears the dog-muzzle really your mother? What's wrong with her? Does she bite? Is that why you left the Old Country? She bit somebody?" I couldn't mention it at home. I couldn't ask her not to wear that damned wire cage over her mouth and nose when she went out-of-doors. Packed with some sort of mentholated wool that she was sure was a protection against the Canadian cold, and a certain remedy against her asthma. She never thought it made her look strange. To make fun of a boy's mother! They were a rough lot. It hurt me in a special way. An intrusion into my deepest feelings. My home. . . . The Pater, too. That ad he made me put in the *Courier*:

> *Bespoke tailor desires employment. Eighteen years experience as cutter and fitter. London (Eng.) training. Letters to Box 7, this journal.*

"What's a bespoke tailor, Rhod? Are those pants you're wearing real London bespoke pants? Do they wear patches on the

knees in London now, Rhod?" What I went through with the
Courier gang! Not bad men – though Beak Browder and
Charlie Delaney were not much above the criminal class –
but men from another world. Not the world I grew up in. So
far as I'd grown up. Fifteen, and raw off the boat. . . . That ad
was the nearest thing to a lie I suppose the Pater ever allowed
himself. He was never a real tailor, and his London training
didn't go beyond a few wrinkles Uncle David showed him,
from time to time. But he had to have a job, and as a failed
man I suppose he thought he had to go right back to the
beginning, and that was the tailor's bench. Pitiful. But could I
say so? To my own father? Unthinkable. . . . I've helped quite
a few immigrants in my time. I know what they feel. The
desolation of leaving home and facing the worst – the
bottom – of a new country. . . . Can I ever forget the first day
at the *Courier*? Lance and I arrived on a Saturday, late in the
afternoon, and Uncle John said he had jobs for us and we
started Monday morning. I was scared out of my life. There I
was, a printer's devil, and I'd never seen the inside of a print-
ing office in my life. Delaney was first: "Get the lye bucket
and scrub out the urinals." That was the way with a new
apprentice. Give him the rottenest job first, to humble him.
As if I needed humbling! The lye skinned my hands, and the
stink made me vomit. Printers. Great beer-drinkers. Stinking
piss. Then it was, "Get over to the market and get us some
fruit for dinner." "What fruit, sir?" "Any fruit, you stupid
little bugger." "May I have some money, sir? For the fruit,
sir?" "Do you think we pay for fruit? Grab what you can, and
run. And if you're caught, don't say you're from here, or I'll
beat your brains out." So I stole, and it nearly killed me. A
thief! Had I come to this? If Hell is any worse than that first
week at the *Courier* I'll be surprised. Not just the cursing and
filthy language and the perpetual dirty jokes about women,
and the tobacco-chewing and the reek of men who never
seemed to wash, but what they used to call in the Chapel the
Abjection of Soul, the fear that God had deserted me. That's
when I learned that God has two faces. I'd exchanged the

Wesleyan chapel for a chapel of the Typographical Union.
. . . That was my Canada. That was the vast wheatfield and
the sturdy farmer in elegant breeches. Lance and I lived with
Uncle John and Auntie Polly. And every week we gave them
most of our wages to put aside to buy furniture for the house
when the Mater and the Pater and the two girls followed us
out to the new land more than a year later. And when the day
was near and we asked Uncle John for the money, what did he
say? "Don't trouble about it, boys, I'll make it right with your
father." And that was all we ever heard about it. He'd used
our money, the damned old scoundrel. – Ah, well; not a bad
old stick. Just untrustworthy about money. When we told the
Pater, he looked pretty sad, but he never said a word of blame
to John Jethro. Uncle John was the Mater's brother and he
couldn't bear to grieve her. I've never mentioned that to a
soul. Not even to Vina. To cheat a couple of boys – how could
he? And in other ways he was so much above the rest of us.
Educated beyond us. But education never seems to have
much to do with money matters. Nor with common sense
. . . Look at Brocky. A really intelligent fellow, you would
imagine. Certainly Jimmy King says so. But he seems ready
to sacrifice it all for that damned Julia. What does he see in
her? Stupid question. What does anybody ever see in someone else's love affairs? But is it love? Looks like rank infatua-
tion. He's a slave. Thinks I don't know it, but I do. Perhaps
because I've been a slave a couple of times myself. Perhaps
that kind of slavery runs in the family. Do we overvalue
women? Perhaps it would be different if there weren't madness in Julia's family, but there is. The mother. The old grandfather. They're not locked up, but above a certain level of
income we don't lock such people up. They're not crazy,
they're neurotics. Until they burn the house down, or
threaten somebody with a knife, that's to say. Like William
McOmish. There was a nice neurotic for you! And I suppose
I have to understand that Brocky is his grandson, as well as
the Pater's. There's a strain – Do I see it in Vina? No, no; that's
ridiculous. There never was a more level-headed woman

when we were young. Now, of course, things have changed. She has so much illness to bear, poor woman, and illness eats into the mind as well as into the body. Not neurotic, but has too much to bear. . . . Is Brocky leading an immoral life? Has he gone the limit with that girl? That can be a frightful trap, and the man isn't always to blame. It's horribly coarsening. Does he take any precautions? Ought I to speak to him? He'd probably laugh at me. If the woman drinks a glass of really cold water right after – that does the trick. That's what Vina and I have always done. Birth control. . . . If only she didn't hate the Old Country so. Every year I want her to come with me to Belem. But after the first few years she has always said it's too much for her. And I know she doesn't want me to go. But I do go, and I live there by myself – unless I take Brocky with me – and I swear it saves my life. It's peace and happiness and a blessed rest from perpetual illness and from old Min. . . . Min. There's that in the family, too. Min lacks a round of being square, and that's all there is to it. She thinks I didn't see her at dinner last night, in one of her fits, one hand scrabbling in the mustard pickles. Oh, what a heritage Brocky has – asthma, on both sides. *Petit mal* likely to be *grand mal* at any time. Failure. Bankruptcy. Disappointment and bitterness of heart. That terrible thing about Vina. – That won't do! Back to Wodehouse.

What do the Yanks know of England?

No, not England. Not even the Never-Never Land of Wodehouse. The Old Country. The Country That Never Was. What does that poem call it? The Land of Lost Content. . . . What was it, come to that? Not all lavender. Don't you think it was. *The fish and the corduroy trousis.* The dirty stories of the tailors, which I wasn't supposed to hear. Nasty Bowen, who hung around the Lion Yard and would drink a cup of his piss for a penny. And many a penny he had, from boys like me who wanted to see if it would kill him, as it was supposed to do. Fred ffrench and I clubbed together a ha'penny each, for a try. And we made sure it was the right thing, and not some beer he'd substituted on the sly. Did Nasty drop dead? Not he. Lived to drink again. Liz Duckett and Jack the Jockey – I knew something about them, sure enough. Sin, but they seemed to thrive on it. Poor old Liz. The Pater used to send her money he could ill afford, every month, because she'd been faithful when we were down on our luck. I took that over, as soon as I could afford it. Till she died. Lance would never send her a penny. Lance became hard. Or maybe just sensible. I never help the weak, he said, when I put it up to him. Hard. But there's good sense in it, too. No amount of help can make the weak strong. A good heart, old Liz. Died of syphilis, I suppose, as anybody might have foreseen. But even syphilitics know what it is to be hungry. . . . Struggle, struggle, struggle. That's what it's been. Brocky laughs when I say so. You must have had some fun somewhere along the way, he says. But I emphasize the struggle with him. He's had an easy passage, so far. Education. Mind you, he seems to take to it. I can't say I ever did, though I've picked up a few things here and there on my way. I'm surprised sometimes how much I know that people with far better chances than I ever had don't know. Poetry. Always liked it, though Brocky says I have a sweet tooth. *A Shropshire Lad*. Yes, I find myself in a lot of that, though I was a next-door Montgomeryshire lad. The other side of the Wrekin. Yes and the Breidden, too.

> *What are those blue remembered hills,*
> *What spires, what farms are those?*

But that came later. When I tackled education, I was sure education had to hurt. . . . The books I bought! Ten-cent classics. *The Meditations of Marcus Aurelius*, the very first, and I have it still. Somewhere. I couldn't get beyond page three. Jimmy King tells me Marcus Aurelius was a Stoic, and a tough old bird. Preached detachment from the outer world, and the brotherhood of man. Fat chance I had of detaching myself from the outer world! I had to struggle not to be eaten alive by it. But the brotherhood of man – yes. I liked that better than the Methodist doctrine of Christian love, which always seemed a bit sticky to me. You can love a brother, but you don't have to crawl all over him and lick his sores, like that Francis of Assisi. I had a shot at him. A nut. I even bought Kant's *Critique of Pure Reason*. Second-hand, but still a full seventy-five cents. Couldn't understand a word. That convinced me that I was really stupid. But somehow I managed to get along. I wish I had been able to get a real education. But look at Jimmy King. A professor, but what has his knowledge made of him? Tries to borrow money from me. Has never put by a penny in his life. Work! . . . Night school. Hard sledding after a full day at the *Courier*. But it was there I discovered the reading I really liked. Poetry. Not many people in the class cared about it because most of them wanted accounting and shorthand. I did those, but I squeezed in Literature. Tennyson, Swinburne. The poetry that was nearest to music. I suppose music and poetry took the place of religion, for me. Do so still, I think, though Brocky says it's cheap music and cheap poetry. How easily the educated young dismiss your props and stays! Religion had withered for me. As if a bunch of flowers had turned into those rustling, dry corpses of flowers that Vina keeps all winter and calls "everlastings." Dust-catchers. Poetry and music . . . Of course music was what we had at home. My sister Maude, a fine musician. Church organist at seventeen. Could play anything at sight. What evenings we had, every Sunday! We all sang. Lance and I were best in "Watchman, What of the Night?" There was a duet! A real bowel-shaker, as Hardy makes somebody say. I was the fearful, despairing Soul, in the tenor, and Lance was a terrific bass as the Reassuring Spirit.

Tenor: *Say, watchman, what of the night?*
   Do the dews of the morning fall?
Have the orient skies a border of light
   Like the fringe of a funeral pall? –

Bass: *The night is fast waning on high*
          And soon shall the darkness flee
      And the morn shall spread o'er the blushing sky
          And bright shall its glories be.

Me, pathetic and in dread of death, and Lance like great, powerful Hope, and Maude thundering away in that rich accompaniment when we joined voices and I plucked up spirit and we really brought the roof down on

That night is near, and the cheerless tomb
      Shall keep thy body in store
Till the morn of eternity rise on the gloom
      And the night shall be no more!

That always made the Mater weep. But happy tears, because it was the Christian promise made into music. Poor Mater; the first to go. And Elaine would sing Tosti's "Good-Bye," and we all had wet eyes. Happy misery, Brocky calls it. Happy Welsh misery. But it fed us as his taste in music certainly doesn't. Nobody sings that stuff any more. Indeed, I never hear anybody sing now, who isn't paid to do it. We sang because we couldn't help it. . . . Vina sang at some of those evenings, after we were married. A really good contralto. Her star piece was something German by somebody called Böhm. "Still Wie die Nacht." But of course she sang it in English:

Still as the night,
      Deep as the sea –
Should love, thy love e'er be!

That's asking for a good deal, certainly, from a talkative Welsh husband. But when she sang

Glowing as steel
      As rock firm and free
Shall love, my love e'er be!

I had a sense that she was singing from the heart. As rock firm and free. That's her loyalty, and mine as well. Because through all the ups and downs we've been loyal. Except for that one thing. But there's no point in worrying about that now. . . . Poor Maude. Died young. Consumption, of course. Runs in the family. Jimmy King calls it the disease of romance, but it doesn't look very romantic when you see somebody near the end. Horror and pain. Could hardly bear to be touched. But poor Maude had a terrible blow. Cruelly jilted, not a month before the wedding. Now, it seems, consumption is pretty much a thing of the past. Brocky is sometimes near it. I know the look. Julia. Why are so many in our family fools about women? . . . I was certainly a fool about Elsie Hare. But when she dropped me and married Elmer Vansickle I got over it. Wouldn't be beaten by a girl. That marriage never prospered. Vansickle couldn't hold a job. A boozer. Met Elsie a few years ago at the Toronto Exhibition. Wouldn't have known her if she hadn't told me who she was. Had run to fat and she'd lost a front tooth, and stuck a piece of adhesive tape over the hole. Pathetic! She had a kind of soothering way of talking. Not humble, but respectful. Respectful to me! When I'd been a slave to her, and she certainly must have remembered that. A lucky escape. Her grammar was terrible. She'd have disgraced me, which Vina has never done. Vina was on the upward path, like me, and for a while we climbed together. Twin Battleships, as Bernard Shaw says in that play. What happened? That awful row, I suppose. Nothing could have been quite the same after that. But she's been loyal. We've both been loyal. I know she frets about the women I meet, and certainly some of them are charming, but they haven't got what she's got. Inherited from Loyalist forebears? Possibly. I believe heredity is discredited now by the people who think they know. But I have a tailoring background, and I know that the best broadcloth isn't made of second-grade wool. . . . What will become of Brocky? He's got good stuff in him, on both sides, though he makes fun of his mother's ideas, and mine. But he's not really

close-woven. A bit slack to the hand, as Uncle David used to
say when he fingered a piece of stuff. He knew, even if he did
finish up married to the Angel. Mary Evans the Angel. Not
that she was an angel, but she owned the Angel Inn. A good
pub. Right by St. Mary's Church, where the Angel Inn has to
be. The Angel of the Angelus, named in the days when
churches and pubs weren't as far apart as the Methodists
thought they should be. The Angel was a happy pub. I hope
old David lived happily, rotten though he was to the Pater.
Old David liked freedom and a merry life better than respect-
ability. . . . I've read this story to the end, and I don't think
I've taken in a word. But of course I've read it many times.
Wodehouse never fails. Like music, almost. Meaning, but
never an exact meaning that you can seize. Just feeling. That's
what I read him for, I suppose. He makes a reality of the Land
of Lost Content, or a part of it. . . . Vina's gone to bed, but I
know she's not asleep. She's waiting for me to come up and
say good-night. Min's taken up that bloody hot milk. I tell
Vina it's constipating, and constipation breeds God knows
what illnesses, but nothing will break her of the habit. Auto-
intoxication.

"Well, I don't know what you're going to do, Brocky,
but I'm going to bed."

And I know what you'll do, my son. You'll play music –
Tchaikovsky – very quietly, and feed your misery about Julia.
Happy misery, and don't think you've escaped it, because I
know better. It's just that you feed it with different music.

(6)

BROCHWEL: *(When his father has left the library, and has had*
time to mount the stairs and reach Malvina's bed-
room, where he will chat for a few minutes before he
puts out her light, Brochwel does indeed put a record
on the Orthophonic, turning the volume down low.
It is not Tchaikovsky; it is a record he takes from his

university briefcase; its title is "June in January" and
it is played and sung in the weakly plaintive, almost
whimpering style of the time.

> *It's June in January*
> *Because I'm in love –)*

"Extraordinary how potent cheap music is." Noel Coward. Place the quotation, Mr. Gilmartin. *Private Lives.* And how right he is. This gets to me as better stuff doesn't. Because my feelings are cheap? No; because this is the voice of my generation and all popular romanticism inclines toward cheapness, and I can't expect to escape it. Not completely, or I'd be a prig. I know better, or think I do. When I want the music of romanticism I turn on the Big Boys and my elders think

> *If that's not good enough for him*
> *Which is good enough for me,*
> *Why, what a very cultivated kind of youth*
> *This kind of youth must be.*

G & S. And very good stuff, too. A lot more wisdom in it than most people think. What's that –

> *The pain that is all but a pleasure will change*
> *For the pleasure that's all but pain –*

Nobody includes *that* in his *Oxford Book of Victorian Verse,* Sir Arthur Quiller-Couch, editor. But old "Q" has room for some stuff that isn't nearly as close to the mark. I wish Frosty wouldn't always call him "Q" as if he was an intimate friend. Doctor James Pliny Whitney Frost, the eminent poet and lecturer, Professor of Eng-Lang-and-Lit at Waverley University. The personification of poetry and good taste, as presented to the young. Never try a quote from Noel Coward on Frosty. Not a bad guy, if only he wasn't so bloody impeccable. Give me old Jimmy King who will always be Number

Two to Frosty because he Drinks. I've seen him Drinking right in this room. Dad keeps very good Scotch. . . . "I'm a teetotaller, but not a bigoted one," Jimmy says, when his eyes are swimming, as if we'd never heard it before. I'm the pride and joy of both Frosty and Jimmy because I know how to write the kind of essays they like; impeccable for Frosty, and rather more peccable, but funnier, for Jimmy. I understand very well how to be a Pride and Joy to my teachers, and I play it to the hilt. But not a pride and joy to Dad and Mother. I'd have to be something other than a Grade A student of Eng-Lang-and-Lit to make the Grade A with them. I'd have to give up Julia. . . . Why does Mother hate her so? Because she does, though she's all good manners and "graciousness" when I have the nerve to ask Julia here. That's when Mother speaks with all her nineteenth-century clarity and correctness. It's that ass Bidwell who keeps telling me that Mother is "gracious," which he thinks is a very fine thing to say about an older woman. Bidwell: my rival in Eng-Lang-and-Lit, but he never quite tops me. Can't, because, although he knows everything and has read everything, and reads Virginia Woolf and gives papers about her to the English Club, he's never had a real feeling in his life. Or if he has, he takes good care to keep it out of his essays. That time he made Frosty furious by hinting that there was something dicey about Tennyson's friendship with Hallam – that was when the shit hit the fan! . . . "I'm not sure I fully understand what you are suggesting, Mr. Bidwell, but if what I dimly apprehend is correct I must ask you never to make such a suggestion in this class again." I knew better than anybody in the class what Bidwell was suggesting because he suggested it to me one warm spring night and I hope I was tactful in my refusal. Don't want to hurt his feelings but No Thanks! . . . Bidwell knows all about Oscar Wilde, who must be handled with kid gloves, at Waverley in this year of grace. Bidwell has read about Wilde's trial in the Notable British Trials series, which he wormed out of the Reserved Shelves in the library. But he didn't know that the person who lured Wilde into those treacherous bypaths was a Canadian. Yes, Robert Ross, a member of one of our First Families. An odd footnote to Canada's meagre association with Eng-Lang-and-Lit, but this is an odd country. Wilde, betrayed by those errand boys and out-of-work valets. Why didn't he see through them?

> *An habitation giddy and unsure*
> *Hath he that buildeth on the vulgar heart.*

Place the quotation, Mr. Gilmartin. Yes sir. *Henry IV, Part 2.* Do you think it means that Shakespeare was a snob, Mr. G? Not necessarily, Professor JPWF. Maybe it just means that Shakespeare knew his onions, and how many beans made five and a few things like that. Anyway, snobs aren't always wrong. Q: Are you a snob, Mr. G? *A:* From time to time, sir, as occasion serves and the situation demands, like yourself and the rest of us. . . . There's nobody who doesn't hold himself superior to somebody is there, sir? We academic snobs, now. Not that I class myself with you, sir, but I am beginning to see people in terms of what they know about Eng-Lang-and-Lit. That isn't easy. . . . My mother, now, thinks Thomas Hardy is the bee's knees and the feline's slumberwear, but I notice that she turns to *Les Misérables* and tonight she was reading *St. Elmo* which must surely hold some sort of award for the Most Awful Novel. What am I to make of that? There is no accounting for tastes, to which Aunt Min invariably adds, "as the old woman said when she kissed the cow." And my father, who reads P. G. Wodehouse over and over again, and then stuns me by coming out with a scrap of Ossian that he learned at his mother's knee. I've never read Ossian, though I suppose I ought to take a peep, some time. . . . What did I learn at my mother's knee? *Swiss Family Robinson,* which isn't too bad, and *The Water Babies,* which bears the Prof JPWF Stamp of Approval as genuine Eng-Lang-and-Lit and which must also be one of the beastliest, most finger-wagging books ever written for children even by a Low Church parson, but also *Sammy and Susie Littletail*

and *Bunny Fluffkins' Birthday Party*, which aren't any kind of
Lit. . . . Q: Has anybody, possibly excepting you, sir, Prof
JPWF, ever been brought up on a strict diet of the Best That
Has Been Thought and Said? We all need to take aboard a
certain amount of rubbish to keep us human (again excepting you, Prof). Like "It's June in January," so let's have it
again, shall we? Would it surprise you to learn, Prof, that I
grew up on a heavy diet of the comic strips – yes, the despised Funny Papers – and that I still gobble quite a few of
them every day? *Mutt and Jeff* has provided me with many a
treasured phrase. "Such ignorance is indeed refreshing,"
says Mutt, when Jeff has insisted on spelling Eugene with a
U. And Jeff says, "Mutt will throw a jealous fit," when he
has himself engaged the affections of that fair enslaver, Miss
Klutz. And "Insect!" and "Lowbrow!" as Maggie says
when she beans Jiggs with the rolling-pin. I have to have this
stuff as the drug addict has to have his snort. It keeps me
from sinking under the sheer weight of excellence, of aspiration, of insight, of transcendent beauty, which is Eng-Lang-
and-Lit. The mind can only endure so much grandeur. Or
my mind, anyhow. Obviously not yours, Prof. . . . Q: Tell
me Prof, how in God's name did you come to be saddled
with the name of James Pliny Whitney? . . . Not that JPW
was inconsiderable. By no means. He was no slouch, and his
finest achievement was to bring Niagara Falls right into
everybody's room, like Love in Bloom, twinkling and
shuddering into a glass bulb with a tiny prickle on the end.
Yes, our never-sufficiently-to-be-praised Hydro Electric
Power System sprang from the loins – pardon the seeming
indelicacy, Prof – of James Pliny Whitney. . . . Q: Was that
it? Did your parents foresee in a vision, when you were still
snoozing in the womb, that you would bring another kind
of light into the lives of Young Canada? The Light of Eng-
Lang-and-Lit? The light that never was on sea or land until
chaps like you channelled it down into a thousand shimmer-
ing, shuddering light-bulbs like me, to say nothing of an
infinitely greater number of dim bulbs, fit only for the

clothes closets and the boarding-house-back-halls of academia? And all with our little prickle at the bottom, for piercing and deflating people who question our authority, as you yourself so efficiently do, Prof? Ah yes, I see it now. Your name, James Pliny Whitney Frost, is one of those splendid puns that life delights in and that only a few people see. People like me. . . . "June in January" has ceased to feed my melancholy. So what now? "Love in Bloom"?

> *Can it be the Spring*
> *That seems to bring –*

No, not since Bidwell parodied it the other day in the Union dining-room:

> *Can it be the breeze*
> *That seems to sneeze*
> *Its germs right into my room?*
> *Oh no, it isn't the breeze –*
> *It's Love in Bloom!*

A parody can shake a trifle like that, but it has no strength against anything of real worth. . . . Do I want a drink? Daren't. Old Min measures the decanters, I swear she does. Old snooper. If I want a drink I have to get some rye from the government store and drink it with Bidwell in his boarding-house room. Half a bottle. A Baby Bear. Drunk out of tooth glasses with water from the tap. Not for the refined palate, but what the hell. How awful those student boarding-houses are! And what sharks the landladies are. They shouldn't be called boarding-houses. They are rooming-houses. They provide no food. Students who aren't able to live at home, like me, room in a rooming-house and eat at the Union. Donkey's liver fricassee, and orange Jell-O to top off. When Dad was a young printer he lived in boarding-houses, in Toronto and for a while in New York. Three-fifty a week for a room and three meals a day. Laundry extra. Sheets changed fortnightly. He says the food wasn't too bad but apt to be monotonous.

> *There is a boarding-house*
> > *Far, far away,*
> *Where they have ham and eggs*
> > *Three times a day.*
> *Oh, how the boarders yell*
> > *When the ham and eggs they smell*
> *Oh, how the boarders yell*
> > *Three times a day.*

Another parody. Of a hymn. How those sanctimonious Victorians loved parodies of what they were supposed to hold in respect. Boarding-house songs. There was –

> *If you don't make love*
> > *To the landlady's daughter*
> *You will never get a second piece of pie.*

Dad says he never saw a landlady's daughter in all his experience that offered a pennyworth of temptation. Characteristic that after all these years in Canada he still says "penny-worth." . . . Of course he's never really lived here. Not in his heart, he hasn't. It's always Wales. The Land of Lost Content. Does everybody have one? With Professor JPWF it's Harvard, where he did his doctoral work. With Professor Jimmy King it's Edinburgh, where he seems to have lived contemporaneously with Burns and Sir Walter Scott, and Byron dropping in now and then on his way to Newstead. And Mother – I know where her Land of Lost Content is. Her days as a "business girl" and the first years of her marriage, before everything seemed to go amiss, and Dad somehow got away from her. He has the adventurous mind, you would think, but sometimes I wonder about her. Something got lost, or destroyed, by the way. . . . If not a drink it must be more music. Tchaikovsky. The received wisdom of the moment is that he's second-rate. Ah, critics! How unforgiving they are toward anything that isn't, in some special way, known only to them, absolutely first-rate. Do they ever guess, I wonder, how much energy and guts and sheer talent it takes to be second-rate? Which Tchaikovsky? The Sixth, I suppose. The good old *Adagio lamentoso*. Look at this stuff included in the album! "His music, with its strange combination of the sublime and the platitudinous, will always touch the average hearer to whom music is more a matter of feeling than of thought." Christ have mercy! And this: "As long as the world holds temperaments akin to his own, as long as pessimism and torturing doubt overshadow mortal hearts and find their cry re-echoed in the intensely subjective, the deeply human music of this poet who weeps as he sings and embodies so much of the spirit of his age – its weariness, its disenchantment, its vibrant sympathy and morbid regretfulness – Tchaikovsky's music will survive." What wizen-scrotumed ninnyhammer wrote that, I wonder. He probably thinks that's very classy prose. . . . The Sixth begins with a groan. Very properly. I often groan. Seventeenth-century writers often say they "groan in spirit," and that's what I do when it would just make trouble to groan aloud. I groaned in Introductory Psychology when Martin invited us to bring him our dreams. Oh, not for revelation in class! No, no. Just so that he might, in his office, explain the dream process and the dream work *à la Freud*, and of course in complete confidence. But how can it be confidential when Martin knows it, and has mauled it over, and made God knows what of it? He's no psychoanalyst. Just a junior prof, not yet thirty, and nervous as a cat. Repressed sex, I suppose. Wants to and daren't. Anxious to get on intimate terms with the girls, obviously, and I suppose some of them will fall for it. I expected Intro Psych to be about a few basic things – theory of learning, and whatnot – but he makes it a half-baked exploration of anything and everything. Would I take him a dream? Not for any money. I don't want him sticking his nicotine-stained fingers into my mind. . . . Now we've

stopped groaning and are getting into the *Allegro non troppo*.
My dream. Last week. A gleaming snow scene, and the time
dusk, closing in toward night. I am in a wood, through which
runs a narrow track. I stand beside a bare tree, and hear sleigh-
bells. Up comes the sleigh, and who are in it but Mother and
Julia, together and very affectionate. They are dressed in
magnificent furs. The driver, on the box, is also in heavy furs,
à la russe; he is impassive. The sleigh stops and both women
smile with affectionate warmth at me. I step forward toward
them, and as I do so Julia opens her fine fur cloak and she is
totally naked, and as lovely as I have ever seen her. Mother
smiles approvingly, seems to bless us. Julia draws her wraps
about her, the whip cracks and the sleigh moves on. I am left
with an intense feeling of rapture and fulfilment. . . . Why
has this dream so strong a Russian atmosphere, and why does
it seem to belong in the nineteenth century, although all the
people in it are of today? The intensely northern atmosphere
of Canada, I suppose. We have hot summers and resplendent
autumns, but it is winter that establishes the character of our
country and our psychology. The Canadian mood. Canadian
love, not cold but certainly not Mediterranean, as so many
people expect love to be. Is it because I have been reading so
many Russian novels and found myself in them as I never do
in novels about the south? That's the kind of psychology that
I want to learn about, and I don't suppose Prof Martin would
understand a word I was saying. Who would? Jimmy King, I
think, the old Scots romantic. . . . That day in class, when he
was lecturing on Byron; he paused for a full two minutes. A
long time for a pause, but he stood staring out of the window
into the snowy campus, playing with the plastic acorn on the
end of the blind-cord. Then he turned to us and said, in a
terribly sad voice: "I don't suppose that one of you mutts has
understood a word I've said." Everybody came to with a
start. Now that was real education! He woke us up to a sense
of our insufficiency. But – Byron and probably Pushkin,
strained through the Scots-wool sensibility and life experience of Professor James Alexander King, late of Edinburgh,

were made real to me, and I think I undoubtedly understood
what he was saying, mutt though I freely admit that I am. . . .
Would I tell Prof Jimmy my dream? No need to do so. He has
been there himself, and he would have the sense to leave what
is inexplicable unexplained. Romance can't be laid on the
table and carved up like a cadaver, to see what once made it
live. . . . Here's the second movement. *Allegro con grazia*. One
of Tchaikovsky's amazing waltzes, speaking of elegant melancholy, refined sensibility, love and everything that goes
with it turned into a dance. The sort of thing ballet does,
when it goes past the technicality of hopping about on tippy-
toe. Ballerinas always looks so unapproachable, yet infinitely
desirable. Because they are abstractions, of course. Abstractions of what a beloved woman looks like to her lover. . . .
Says Prof JPWF: "All great art is an abstraction from life, a
purging of superfluities." Yes, a purging from all that can-
you-get-the-car-tonight and let's-make-it-a-date and no-
I've got-to-stay-home-and-study-and-anyhow-I'm-
getting-the-Curse and God-you're-an-awful-dancer-you-
were-born-with-two-left-feet. This waltz is an abstraction
moving into nobility of aspiration and tender feeling. Tender,
not soft. Nobility is not a characteristic of the modern world
or of student life, but how are we to live at our best without
it? Without nobility the love-path is inevitably downward
toward something that can become very mean and
grubby. . . . She is driving me mad with desire. Not just for
the lay – God what a word for it! – That means nothing
unless it is the counterpart of an emotional coming-together.
But if she won't have it, why does she keep teasing with it,
like somebody teasing a dog with a scrap of raw meat? She
allows me every familiarity, every intimate knowledge and
caress except the final one, because that would be conquest
and to her the idea of conquest is unbearable. She plays with
me dangerously. That night when I almost strangled her –
but of course I'm not a strangler and didn't finish the job. The
look in her eyes before I let her go. Fear. I couldn't bear the
thought that she was afraid of me. But it was a near thing.

Should I have raped her? That would have been the end of
everything. I've never been quite so much off my head as
that. But I can endure a surprising amount of midnight torment without being absent from class sharp at nine the next
day. I suppose that marks me as something not quite up to the
Byronic standard. Not enough steam in the boiler?. . . Madness in that family. Everybody hints at it without ever saying
it full out. The old grandfather. Once an admired professor.
Now a prisoner in his own house, and begs that he be not left
alone for fear he might attack the housemaid. At his age! That
night we were having a party in his house, where Julia was
acting as keeper. I suppose we were making so much noise we
penetrated even his extraordinary deafness. Perhaps he
sensed something he didn't really hear. Appeared in the arch
leading into the drawing-room, like mad Lear, white hair and
beard wild and tumbled, and his dressing-gown hanging
open so that we saw his ancient body, yes and even his
withered parts, like the sons of Noah beholding their father's
nakedness. Staring at us with blind eyes, the cataracts seeming to give off a blue light. "Have these young men taken up
their permanent abode here?" he asked, with astonishing
authority in such an apparition. We scampered. Like ghosts
from an enchanter fleeing, as Bidwell said later. Always ready
with the neat quote. And there are others. Grandfather is just
the obvious one. But that hint of madness is the wormwood
in the gin. The subtle, dangerous, irresistible savour. I may
lack the steam but I have the dangerous imagination of the
romantic. And where does it come from? . . . I wish it wasn't
necessary to change these records so often. But it can be done
without breaking the mood. Now for the *Allegro molto vivace*.
Is that madness in the music, that skittering, undignified
disorder, resolving itself now into a determined theme that
suggests doom? A procession? Not an obvious one like the
Symphonie Fantastique, but surely those trumpets are urging
the listener on toward – what? Not a gallows, surely, but a
rejection. A rejection by what is dearest in life. Astonishing.
The drag of the music until now has all been downward.

Themes that seem to pull toward an abyss. But now it is all upward chromaticism, furious and unnerving. But of course. It's the famous manic-depressive temperament, about which Martin chatters and explains so shallowly, as though everybody above the level of a turnip didn't have some experience of it. Down, down, down – then upward suddenly, bringing on mental seasickness. And so to the final movement, the *Adagio lamentoso.* . . . Here it comes. Can I bear it? Of course you can bear it, you jackass. You've invited it. You could smash these records if they were really unbearable, but instead you've suborned the dead composer to ravage your feelings, and you're enjoying every minute of it. The pain that is all but a pleasure is changing to the pleasure that's all but pain, as the cranky old cynic tells you. Was he a cynic? I rather suspect that in him the cynicism was the crutch of the lamed romantic. But this music – Abjection before the Beloved. Does romanticism offer a more wretched, more ignominious state of soul? Manhood in abeyance. Manhood in chains. What is Tchaikovsky talking about? Resignation, and that laudanum of the romantic spirit, Renunciation. But not quite. There is protest against Resignation in what I hear. And then, defeat and the final succumbing to Destiny. *Amor Fati.* The final throwing in of the towel. . . . Then what? For the true romantic it's the dagger or the poison bowl. But sodden and disordered by romance as I am, I'm not quite ready for that. What would it look like? Like the feeblest, wildest folly, and even those who understood some part of it would think I'd crazily overbid my hand. They would say she wasn't worth it. Is she? Is she worth a life? . . . Am I crazy to see the Sphinx in a Canadian university girl? The Sphinx, nobly breasted, with the haunches of a lioness and a smile of maddening tenderness on lips that ask the great question. But what question? That's what I shrink from. There is no question on the lips of the Julia-Sphinx. Whatever question there may be is my own; I ask it myself, and pretend it is hers. And if I killed myself, would it be for her or for the answer to a question I had posed myself? In the end, though I love her as much as I could love anyone, it all comes down to myself. And that's why all this Hamlet-like nonsense about suicide is self-indulgence and I am simply playing dangerously on my own feelings. Like all romantics, I suppose, I stand alone, and see Julia in a light that I give off. Men have died, and worms have eaten them, but not for love. . . . A quotation again. I feed my fires with quotations. Nobody else's life is worth my life, and that's that. I am too anxious to see what happens next to apply an arbitrary closure. Better to suffer and live, and taste the full bitterness of suffering, than to hop the twig – for what? Julia would be wretched for a week, and later in her life I would be a sad incident and perhaps, if she saw it that way, a scalp at her saddle-bow or a notch on her rifle. But Mother and Dad would be desolated. I know that. The bystanders get most of the splashed blood. Deep-deep inside me, there is something that says No to that. I want to see what comes next, whatever the cost.

> My soul, sit thou a patient looker-on;
> Judge not the play before the play is done:
> Her plot hath many changes; every day
> Speaks a new scene: the last act crowns the play.

There's the satisfaction of Eng-Lang-and-Lit; somebody else has said everything for you, and said it better. Is it living at second hand, then? No, you must feel things for yourself or you can't truly understand what the Great Ones have said before you. It's only the easy acceptance of literature that reduces it to a triviality and a self-indulgence. Literature is an essence, not a piquant sauce. . . . One o'clock! My God, and I have an early class! Hungry. It's humbling, and salutary as well, that emotion and reflection beget hunger, and the flesh and bone and lymph and blood that are partners and partakers of emotion must be allowed their say. . . . Plato said the soul sets its seal upon the body; isn't it time we recognized the seal the body sets on the soul? My soul cries, Die for Julia, but my liver and lights say, No, live for me, and I will reveal what

I have for you. The body is no fool. . . . Put the screen in front
of the fire. God, it's close in this room. Then the kitchen. Feed
the animal. My animal. Bed. And after Tchaikovsky and a
snack I shall soon sleep.

(7)

So, FOR THE MOMENT I
have seen the last of my father. My father! I never thought of
him in this way. But then, who really knows his father, or his
mother? In our personal dramas they play older, supporting
roles, and we are always centre stage, in the limelight. And
Professor James Pliny Whitney Frost, who is cast as Polonius
in this provincial, Canadian *Hamlet* – probably a very different creature, if one knew more about him. Polonius must
once have loved, before he became a wise counsellor to King
Claudius and so an old ass to the Prince. After all, he begot
the fair Ophelia.

On this amazing screen I have seen the Sphinx-smile
that torments young Brochwel, and I have seen that identical
smile on the lips of a dozen young women. Saw it, now and
then, when Esme smiled in just that way. What does it mean?
A comprehension beyond the wit of the protesting lover, or
simply nothing at all, or What on earth does he think he is
talking about? There is a gap of understanding that the extre-
mest achievements of Feminism will never bridge. Women
love, too, and love deeply and often bitterly. Women understand the body better than men do. Men bully it or neglect it,
but women take it into full partnership. So, when a woman is
simply the screen on which a man throws some fantastic
image from within himself, what has the woman to do with
it, and what is she to make of it? Julia – a pretty girl, and no
fool – is to be pitied, I think. She has to carry a burden which
she has not asked for, but which she cannot quite bring

herself to thrust aside, because her body, too, makes its demands, and love is very flattering. Not a goddess or a cock-teaser, as Brocky sees her, but another creature, locked in another life.

St. Helen's sleeps by the water. Not so the household in *Scenes from a Marriage* which the Sniffer is watching and which I now glimpse from the corner of my eye. In that film the couple are at it hammer and tongs, rolling on the floor, punching and jabbing like gutter children. Decidedly not my couple. Not Rhodri and Malvina, who have never exchanged blows in all their married days and would be horrified at the thought of descending to such rough-house. Am I mistaken or has physical violence come up the social ladder? Every day one reads in the papers of well-placed people who have fought with fists and flying crockery over some marital point of difference. In St. Helen's Rhodri and Malvina are asleep in their separate rooms, for Auntie Min has a bed with Malvina, who might need her in the night, and Rhodri's habit of waking at three o'clock to read and drink milk and eat arrow-root biscuits would certainly be disturbing.

How unlike themselves people look when they sleep. Or do they look like their real selves, or the selves they do not exhibit when awake? The merry man who sleeps with a fixed scowl, the beauty who pouts discontentedly – surely there is some truth in their sleeping faces? Is it the body's memory, surely as real as the mind's, that reveals itself in sleep? Is it the chaos of the dream world, upon the surface of which some buried recollection rises, then sinks again? Rhodri, as I see him in his big bed, looks not successful, not the lecturer of the improvident Jimmy King, but a wistful man, rather like the boy who passed those wretched days on the *Courier*. Malvina looks noble, which astonishes me; her high arched nose, without its accustomed pince-nez, is almost eagle-like. Auntie Min is, quite simply, a baby; a sad baby, quite unlike the fatly smiling, covertly snooping, jealous, biddable Min of the daylight hours. And Brochwel sleeps like a youth not quite twenty-one, wearing no signs of a breaking heart.

Is his pain, therefore, nothing but romantic affectation? No, but I sense that in Brocky there is much of the survivor, something of the spirit of Anna Vermuelen, who will not be downed by misfortune, however painful.

Is his aching desire for Julia an illusion? Not in the least. It is quite real, but it is not altogether what he thinks it is. It is a rite of passage, an introduction to full manhood, just as surely as if in some primitive society he was obliged to go through a brutal circumcision with a stone knife, or in the classical world to endure an alarming death–and–revival ceremony that would make him a partaker of one of the ancient mystery cults.

Brochwel was my father and, although I never knew him any better than any man knows his father, I see now what it was that made him a successful professor, and a man with a reputation based not on *The Faerie Queen*, with its wondrous assemblage of noble knights, cruel temptresses and impossible loves, but on the works of Robert Browning, the great poet of the ambiguities of human experience. Do the ancestors, fleeting and heavily cloaked, visit us in sleep and speak in voices partly understood?

VI

The Land of Lost Content

T HESE FILMS ARE becoming
uncomfortably personal. I am not unstirred by what has gone
before. I felt anger and danger and anxiety with Anna Gage; I
was saddened by the vicissitudes of the Gilmartins, for every
rags-to-riches tale is a new one, and the later drop from riches
to rags is always deflating; the bitterness of William and Virginia McOmish woke my pity. William – that wretched creature, a soured idealist. Virginia, that hater of Venus, what
would she have been in our more liberal age? But these tales
wore the softening garb of distance, of "period costumes," of
folk unknown, though I understood now how powerfully
they lived – or had lived until the Sniffer pulled his bludgeon
out of its elegant casing – in me. But Malvina was my grandmother, and to think that she had once been thirty, and had felt
the awful approach of Old Maidery so keenly that she had
even been prepared to lie – no, not quite lie – to hint – about the
necessity for getting married, seemed to me to violate everything I had ever felt about her, or about grandmothers in
general. A grandmother ought to be a monument of probity,
and a doubtful grandmother is almost like a counterfeit coin –

certainly was so in the WASP world of my childhood. And Rhodri – how well I remember my eighth birthday, when he gave me a five-dollar bill, and shook me by the hand; until then he had always kissed me when we met, and that handshake marked an important step in my journey toward manhood; I was now too big a boy to be kissed by my grandfather. Could this confident old man, who wore such fine clothes and smelled of French toilet-water, have been the unhappy boy who suffered a descent into Hell when he became an apprentice at the *Courier*? Had that deep, still musical voice in which he spoke once been the silvery tenor that went straight to the heart of Malvina, secretary to Mr. Yeigh, and seemingly so impregnable behind her silver pince-nez?

Quite the most troublesome figure was my father. That the man I knew as wise should once have been so confused, so bamboozled by Cupid, so befooled by a girl, so dominated by his instructors, so wanting in self-determination, was unbearable. What had given him strength? What had hardened this seeming putty into steel? Was I to learn?

How far was this voyeurism to go? I knew now the shame of the sons of Noah when they beheld their father's drunkenness.

Yet – was I really such an unreflecting, uncomprehending jackass when I was alive that I supposed the sufferings and inadequacies of humanity came for the first time in my own experience? No; not wholly. But I had never applied what I knew as general truths to the people without whom I should never have experienced life; I had taken them for granted. As McWearie used to say, one's family is made up of supporting players in one's personal drama. One never supposes that they starred in some possibly gaudy and certainly deeply felt show of their own.

McWearie used to talk a lot about the personal drama. He liked to call it the Hero Struggle, and when I protested that the term was grandiose for what he was describing he rebuked me with the sharpness of a Scots schoolmaster banging his ruler down on the fingers of a stupid boy.

"You're that dangerous class of fool, a trivializer, Gilmartin! To the human creature nothing that gets strongly to him is trivial. It is all on the heroic scale, so far as he can grasp it. What a fuss about the Oedipus Complex – the fella who wants to possess his Mum! What about the Hercules Complex – the fella that must grapple with his Twelve Labours while his wife and kids go by the board? What about the Apollo Complex – the fella that thinks you can have all light and no releasing darkness? And women – our towns and villages are jammed with Medeas and Persephones and Antigones and God knows who not, pushing their wire carts in the supermarkets unrecognized by anyone but themselves, and then probably only in their dreams. All engaged in the Hero Struggle!"

"So far as they can grasp it," said I, to cool him.

"They don't have to grasp it, you gowk, in the sense you mean. They just have to *live* it, and endure it so far as they can bear. You suppose you're a thinker, Gilmartin, and what you are is a trivializer because your thinking isn't fuelled by any strong feeling. Wake up, man! Come alive! Feel before you think!"

That seems to be what I am doing now, as I watch these amazing films, so much better than any I ever saw when I was a critic. I am back in the Fun House, for the last day of the Festival, with Allard Going, that combination of villain and low-comedian in my personal drama, on which, so far as the world is concerned, he dropped the curtain with a rush.

(2)

THE FILM LEAVES ME no time to speculate. What is this? Far from the frowsty library at St. Helen's, and the noise tells me at once that this is war. A bombardment is in progress. What I see is a small cellar under a ruined house; some remaining timbers provide a roof for part of it, and under this are huddled five men. They are Canadian soldiers – gunners from the symbols on their shoulders – and they are trying to snatch some rest after their day's work of manning the guns that attack the German artillery which is now returning the attack with professional accuracy. There is nothing unusual in the situation. A certain amount of night bombardment is to be expected. This night the Germans seem to have a better focus on their work and shells are dropping very near. But what is to be done? Run to some other cover, farther in the rear? The risk is just as great as if they stay where they are. Under regular bombardment, men become fatalists. If it finds you, it finds you, and if it doesn't, you man your own guns for the return match.

One of the five is my father, Brochwel Gilmartin. He is nervous, but not afraid. The prevalent fatalism has claimed him. He wants to sleep, knowing that sleep in such noise is impossible. But he composes himself to rest as well as he can, seated on a heap of debris, wrapped in his overcoat, and with a Balaclava helmet over his head, upon which his tin hat is somewhat absurdly placed. The bombardment will probably last for half an hour, and already twenty minutes have passed.

Suddenly, the unmistakable hissing, whistling sound of an approaching shell. Nearer it comes, and it will explode somewhere very close. With a heavy thump it lands dead in the middle of the cellar, and lies partly buried in the earth, but still visible. A big one.

The five men freeze, their eyes fixed on the monster. They are beyond mere fear, for they know that instant death is at hand, and all their bodies and souls and minds are waiting. How long? Nobody can say. A few seconds, at most. Then it is obvious that owing to some unaccountable chance the shell is not going to explode, and dissolve them in red rain. Or not at once. Without a word they scramble out of the cellar and run.

Each runs in a different direction, and I see only Brochwel, pelting along what had once been the street of an Italian hamlet until, when he has run possibly half a mile, he sights a church that he has observed several times during the last week. It is a ruin, but quite a lot of the walls are still standing. He does not enter the ruin, which could be dangerous, but seeks shelter in the churchyard.

What he finds is the wreckage of a tomb. Not a grand tomb, set up for some nobleman, with his armorial bearings carved on it and perhaps a stone figure or two, but a lesser tomb of the sort that is built above the ground, so that the corpse does not have to be lowered into the dampness and possible flooding from the nearby river. These affairs are sometimes called altar tombs. This might have been the tomb of some minor local grandee, a wealthy notary or a man with a good vineyard. It cannot be less than a hundred years old, and was never built to sustain bombardment; although it has not been struck directly, one side has fallen away, revealing the cavern within. It is into this that Brochwel creeps, and makes himself as comfortable as he can.

Is it the lawyer or the lawyer's wife whose bones and ruined coffin he disturbs? Pardon me, signora, if I creep into your bed. Nothing personal intended, I assure you. Your virtue is perfectly secure with me.

It is not, he reflects, a bad hole. "If yer knows of a better 'ole, go to it." A First World War joke, that has endured. He knows of no better hole. Dampish, but not wet, and out of the wind, and alone, which is a great thing. For him, one of the chief trials of war is that it is never possible to be alone, and his temperament requires a certain amount of solitude. Not that he is morose, or misanthropic. He gets on well with his fellow gunners who are, he finds, recruited chiefly from men who would, in civilian life, be working for the telephone company, or the hydro-electric power company, or in some similar high-grade technical jobs. Men of excellent character; men of superior intelligence; men who are, he soon learns, fully as complicated in their real nature as himself, the young university teacher. But if Brochwel found himself fighting, eating and sleeping with the members of the Royal Society, he would still need to be alone from time to time. *O beata solitudo, O sola beatitudo*! And here, in the tomb, he enjoys this luxury, undisturbed by his quiet companions. If only there is no serpent, no scorpion, sharing these quarters, he is lucky indeed.

(3)

I, THE PATIENT looker-on, know where he is probably better than he does himself. This is the Italian Campaign of March 1944, and the Allied Armies in Italy, under the command of the redoubtable Alex (which was what his troops from Britain, the U.S., India, Canada, New Zealand, South Africa, France, Poland, Italy, Brazil and Greece called their commander-in-chief), are pressing toward Rome. The present obstacle is the Gustav Line, anchored at Monte Cassino, which Field Marshal Albert Kendring is defending with tenacity. The town of Cassino is in ruins, as is the great Monastery that towers above it, but the German line holds. It cannot hold out forever, but it will block the road to Rome as long as it can, and machine-gun pillboxes, mobile steel pillboxes, anti-tank emplacements and now and then some bitter hand-to-hand fighting are giving the Allied Armies a hard time. But the Gustav Line must break, at last. Meanwhile these regular bombardments are routine warfare.

Brochwel can never wholly reconcile himself to the fact that the gunners, of whom he is one, are hurling shells one, two, three and even five miles at troops they cannot see, and whose position they discover by a variety of ingenious devices which he does not pretend to understand. To fight men one will never see – is this modern war? Indeed it is. He has always known it, but now he comprehends it. His job is to do what he is told, which is to stand at a large affair like an architect's desk and calculate how, and where, his particular group of guns must fire. Do they hit anything? He hopes so, and if they do he will know it in time. If they are falling short, and endangering the Allied troops ahead, he will undoubtedly hear it at once. He is a minor figure, doing an important job like many others, but without personal initiative. He does as he is told.

He likes that; likes it very much. To know what is to be done, and to do it with all the efficiency he can muster, as part of a huge organization, is luxury. He understands, without approving, what the German Reich has been doing for so long. Obeying orders, without any necessity to ask questions or have reservations, can be deeply satisfying. Alex is running the show. Our Leader.

Brochwel knows this rather better than the men around him, for he has been, until recently, doing a job at Headquarters, likewise in a minor capacity. Without having seen the great commander more than a few times, and at a distance, he has been on the inside of the great campaign, where many like him also serve in what would, in time of peace, be thought of as lesser office jobs.

Then what is he doing lying in a tomb with a long-dead lawyer and his wife, under bombardment?

(4)

Brochwel is young, though older than when last I saw him, and he is romantic. Intelligently romantic. Nothing of the D'Artagnan about him. But he has decided that he must see service not as a superior clerk, which is the sort of thing his Army betters think befits a man with an excellent education and poor eyesight, but as a man in battle. "Every man thinks meanly of himself for not having been a soldier," said Dr. Johnson, and

Brochwel is very fond of the great Doctor's sturdy wisdom. So, a soldier he will be, in the true sense. He will confront the foe. By some wangling – for he knows a few people in the right places – he has managed to get himself transferred to the gunners, and here he is. Miserable though it may be, and deprived of the regular solitude that is so much a necessity of his nature, he does not regret the change. Does not even regret the danger, for, although he will take every precaution he can against being killed, he will risk even that in order to be part of this experience. So far as he can achieve it, he is in the thick of the great events of his time. He does wish, however, that he could see the men he is trying to kill.

Unlike most of the gunners, he knows what he is firing at. In his student days, seeing as much of Europe as he could manage in two months, travelling by bicycle, now and then by train, with a pack on his back, he had visited the great Benedictine fortress of learning at Monte Cassino. There he had seen what was on display of the 1400 great patristic and historical codices, marvelled at the vast library, the treasures, the evidence of long custodianship of Western culture, gained some understanding of what the Benedictine Rule had meant in bringing discipline to intellectual life, sensed the reluctance of the monks of the Middle Age to destroy Greek manuscripts which they did not comprehend and suspected of intellectual enormity – had learned indeed what could be learned from guidebooks and guides who were talking to tourists who could not be expected to understand or sympathize with much of what Monte Cassino had meant in creating the North American life of which they were proud, but unthinking, partakers. What he had seen had seized his imagination sufficiently to keep him in the town of Cassino for several days, in order to learn more.

What he had learned, and what he now recalls as he lies in the lawyer's tomb, a part of the force that has reduced the great monastery to rubble, gives him hope. What if the monastery has been knocked down, once again? Has it not been knocked down in the past by the Lombards, the Saracens, the Normans, suffered a great earthquake and been knocked down once more not long since – yesterday as history goes – by the French in 1799? The treasures of the monastery have undoubtedly been spirited away as soon as the present invasion of Italy became a certainty, and will return again, and the great walls will be raised as soon as the present war is over. The splendid Doors of Desiderius will once more be put in place. The substance of Monte Cassino may be beaten to rubble by bombs, of which previous despoilers had no understanding, but the spirit of Monte Cassino is unconquerable. And of that spirit he, Brochwel Gilmartin, a humble instructor at Waverley University in far-off Canada, is a partaker, and will be so as long as he lives.

(5)

GOD BE PRAISED for the ingenuities of modern film! As my father reflects on what he knows I, the patient looker-on, see it revived in a score of images on the huge, many-imaged screen. Just as well, for I did not know what Brochwel knew, and his musings would have meant little to me if I had not been able to see Lombards, Saracens, Normans, French and all the other wreckers at their work, and had not had it brought home to me that they were all, surely, the same men, different in dress and weaponry, but as one in their determination to break down civilization wherever they found it. Always in history there are those who are impelled, by reasons they think sufficient, to ruin, in so far as they can, what the patient, indefatigable warriors of civilization and culture have built up, because they value other things and worship other gods.

This is the history of civilization; building, wreckage, and rebuilding, century by century. Not because civilization conquers in a series of jerks, but because it never rests even when it is apparently thrown down.

Nor are all the despoilers men of war. Some are men of meddlesome idealism, like those who sought, in the nineteenth century, to remove all the scholarly treasures of Monte Cassino to an up-to-the-minute National Library in Naples, where they could be cared for by industrious technicians according to the most advanced archival principles of the day. And who was the doughty fighter who put a stop to that nonsense? None other than William Ewart Gladstone, a British Prime Minister and a staunch pillar of the Church of England. An extraordinary champion, surely? But Gladstone was a most uncommon politician because he was a man of imagination. His concern was certainly not inspired by the splendour of the Abbot of Monte Cassino, who had been for centuries one of the great swells of the Church of Rome, answerable only to the Holy See, and privileged to wear seven different precious mitres in succession whenever he celebrated Pontifical High Mass. As the lion-like face of Gladstone flits across the screen before my eyes, I see in him a man possessed by the romantic continuity of history and of intellectual persistence. Seven precious mitres are very fine in their way, but they are best understood as symbols and adjuncts of the continuity of spiritual and intellectual tradition.

Did that tradition really stem from the great St. Benedict of Nursia? Brochwel (I cannot be quite so free with my father as to think of him as Brocky: I leave that name to parents and old aunts) certainly does not think so. When Benedict – not then a saint but an energetic zealot – decided to found his monastery, he chose the place on Monte Cassino because it was the site of a temple of Apollo that had survived into the sixth century of our Christian Era. Benedict's first act was to smash the image of the god and destroy his altar. Benedict was himself one of the smashers.

Did he utterly banish Apollo from Monte Cassino? He thought so, but we may wonder now if the Apollonian spirit did not live on, under the Benedictine robe. Things are never so clear-cut as even a great sage like Benedict believes them to be. Did not his sister, later known to the pious as Saint Scholastica, set up her nunnery five miles away, and meet with her brother once a year to discuss holy matters? Hindered as it was by the difficult five-mile journey, the feminine spirit-still asserted itself at Monte Cassino, and one wonders whether Apollo, wherever he was, did not smile that it was so. Even Benedict could not drive femininity out of the realm of the gods, though he might banish it five miles away from his House of God.

The light of the spirit, as Apollo knew then, and probably still knows, was not the privilege of a single sex, and Benedict and his followers had to pay a heavy price because that idea never occurred to them. Nevertheless they travelled far, walking as they did, on one leg.

(6)

WHAT IS HE, Brochwel Gilmartin, lying awake in somebody else's tomb, unable to sleep after the bombardment, and his astonishing escape from death – what is he? A young Canadian. A tiny cog in a vast machine devoted to the apparent destruction of a great monument of culture, one that has no significance for the warriors but that of an impediment in the Allied march upon Rome. Brochwel is a man fated by his time to be one of the wreckers, though he hopes, if he survives the war, to return to his Canadian university job as one of the builders. As a Canadian, he is inescapably a provincial, like the New Zealanders who were the first to reduce the great monastery to rubble. But we provincials, he reflects, have our place, and an important one, for we are not beguiled by the notion that the fate of mankind and of human culture lies wholly in our hands. These others – the French, the English and even the Poles – probably enjoy some such delusion. The Americans certainly do, for they are natural-born crusaders, forever in the right, even when they are least aware of what they are crusading about. But we provincials, who are compelled by a dozen reasons, some of them not wholly mistaken, to tag along in such crusades as this, are also in our way the patient lookers-on in these political and cultural convulsions, and perhaps we have cooler heads when it comes to weighing the importance of what is being done.

No, I am not Prince Hamlet ... A literary tag, highly appropriate for the young professor.

If I survive this war, thinks Brochwel, I shall still be standing on the doorstep of my life and my career, whatever that may prove to be. What sort of world have these smashers and destroyers made for me?

A world without faith. Or so everybody says. The century past has been a great age of the God-killer. Nietzsche, who was as mad as a hatter, but had some arresting madman's ideas, and without our splendid madmen our culture would be a pretty arid affair. Freud, who asserted with the persuasive cunning of a powerfully gifted literary man that all faith, all belief, is an illusion, bred of childhood fears. Bertrand Russell, who has no time for faith, but all the time in the world for a variety of Noble Causes, and innocently believes that their nobility resides wholly in their usefulness to mankind. They all want to bring everything down to that – to Man.

Can one blame these greatly gifted, persuasive people, if they were sick to death of the faith that has sustained a large and influential portion of the human race for nearly two thousand years? How does it show itself? Is not Christianity edging close to senility? Christianity: an essentially Oriental and Mediterranean structure of belief that begins to spring at the rivets when it is stretched around the globe among people in cold climates. A belief that cannot be reconciled to any workable system of government, or economics, but which others say has none the less revolutionized our notions of a just society, and brought compassion into a world that possessed only the scantiest notion of any such thing. Argument along these lines can go on forever.

One thing, however, is radiantly clear to Brochwel: if he gets out of this mess with a whole skin he cannot embrace the reductive spirit of his age. The reductive spirit that shows itself so trivially in trivial people, and has made some of the most persuasive thinkers of the past century embrace a man-centred world, will not do for him. He does not want a world that prates solemnly about Science, without any understanding of the doubts that haunt great scientists. Science, which seems to offer certainty, is the superstition of ignorant multitudes, who think it means toothpaste and tampons. The hungry sheep look up, and are fed foul air and poisonous garbage. Eng-Lang-and-Lit, the joy of his life, never grew in that soil. What can he believe?

(7)

THE MANICHEES had an idea that was by no means absurd. Theirs was a world that lived under the heaven of the Warring Brothers, Ormuzd and Ahriman, or call it God and Satan, if that pleases you better. The brothers were of wavering but almost equal power, and they slugged it out for the domination of our world. Sometimes Ormuzd the Light One seemed to have the advantage, but never for long, because Ahriman the Dark One would gain a fresh hold, and all the splendours of Light were endangered and some were extinguished.

Of course Christianity wanted nothing to do with such an idea and condemned it as a heresy. Christianity rested firmly on the idea that the Right must always triumph, and Christianity knew beyond any doubt what Right was. But these awful, wrenching wars in which we embroil ourselves are far more easily understood in the Manichean figuration than in the socially concerned sentimentality into which Christianity appears to have fallen. Christianity, now too much a kingdom of this world.

Am I a Manichee, Brochwel asks himself. Thank God I don't have to answer that question. I take refuge in what I believe to be the Shakespearean world-outlook: credulity about everything, tempered by scepticism about everything. Credulity and Scepticism, my Warring Brothers.

I, the patient looker-on, I, Connor Gilmartin, son of this young man whom I now see at a time in his life which far antedates his begetting of myself, find that I am laughing. Yes, laughing for the first time in all this Festival of deeply personal films. Laughing for the first time since my funeral. How can I help it? Brocky – I feel that I may call this young man Brocky, since he is not yet my father – is no philosopher, and certainly no theologian, but is he not the better for that? He is open to contradiction on just about every point in his reflections that I have overheard, and seen projected as images on the screen that is the correlative of his mind. He is really not much more than a boy, and loaded as he is with Eng-Lang-and-Lit he has had small experience of life, although this war is maturing him rapidly and roughly. But I like him – love him, indeed – as I never did when I knew him simply as my father. He is not the slave of his intellect; he has a heart and – what am I saying – a soul.

Has death and my personal Film Festival brought me to a belief in souls? I cannot recall ever having thought much about souls before, for when I lived I was undoubtedly one of the people Brocky has been thinking about – the spiritual illiterates. Though my body is unquestionably gone – cremated – everything that drove the engine and steered the course seems still to be with me, and I can't think of a better word for it than soul. We live and learn, yes. But we die and learn, too, it appears.

For how long? Surely I am not to go on forever, looking

at recreations of my nearer forebears in all their variety and vicissitude? An eternity of movies – I can't face it. Stupid thought: I have no choice in the matter.

There seems to be an interval in the *Maxim Trilogy*, the masterpiece of Leonid Trauberg that the living audience is watching. They have had *Youth of Maxim*, and *Return of Maxim*, and now there is a pause before *The Vyborg Side*. The Sniffer is walking toward the foyer, where he will exchange guarded commonplaces with his fellow critics. They never talk about the film they are watching. Somebody might snatch a precious idea or simply a good phrase. They eat dry sandwiches and drink the thin white wine that seems to be bottled solely for such occasions. They retire to the restrooms and I recall that in Shakespeare's day such an interval was frankly called "a pissing while." Now the critics return morosely to their seats, and the Sniffer sits sighing at my side.

(8)

T HAT IS MY FATHER, certainly. But not the young soldier. No, this is a professor, forty perhaps. And who is that melancholy-looking man with whom he is talking across a table?

Of course, I know that room. It is the library at Belem Manor, my grandfather's Welsh home, where I once spent a weekend as a boy of twelve, on my first trip to the Old Land where my parents were doing some research in the British Museum. How well I recall my astonishment at how big it was! It was on a quite un-Canadian style of amplitude.

What a change this is from the crowded little house in Trallwm, where I saw grandfather as a boy; the stuffy quarters above the tailor's shop, where so many Gilmartins and Jenkinses somehow found places to rest their heads. This room – how shall I describe it – is so handsomely got up with

fine upholstery, linenfold panelling, velvet curtains, antique
furniture and a heavily carved marble fireplace that it pro-
vokes an aesthetic indigestion. Its presentation cannot be
described in terms of interior decoration; it is the spirit of a
very rich fruitcake, made habitable. Or so it was when my
grandfather lived in it. Now, as the two men sit on either side
of the big desk, it seems diminished, and the room is not
bright, although there is full autumn sunshine outside.

"How exactly would you wish us to describe the house,
Mr. Gilmartin?" says the melancholy man.

"Victorian Gothic, I suppose," says Brochwel.

"I should recommend something else," says the man.
"That is not a term we like to use. The associations are, let us
say, unfortunate."

"But that's what it is," says Brocky. "We think the architect was Barry, who designed the Houses of Parliament, you
know."

"Well – that's not the best association, either," says the
man. "Not many people would care to live in the Houses of
Parliament. Except the Speaker, of course. He does so rent-
free."

He smiles a wan smile at his little joke.

"This isn't the original house, of course," says Brocky.
"It's on a very old site. Used to be an old black-and-white
manor, some of it dating from the time of Robert de
Belème."

"Aha. Historical interest. That's a bit better. Roger
de – ?"

"Robert de Belème. He was Master of Horse to Henry
II."

"Do you recall the date?"

"Henry II reigned around – oh, 1160ish – I think."

"Better and better."

"Robert de Bèleme bred fine horses for him. Had a big
farm hereabout; the King was mad about Spanish horses.
This was a stud-farm."

"Very good. And a manor?"

"Yes. That's why the house is called Belem, of course. And the village is Belem-en-le-Dyke. Offa's Dyke, that was."

"Don't recall Offa."

"Well, he was a king of Mercia about – I think – 750. Built the Dyke to keep the Welsh out, or to show them where they were supposed to stop. Not that they did. There's still a few hundred yards of the Dyke on this property."

"I see. Well – we don't have much call for history as early as that. Queen Elizabeth is about as far back as house-purchasers usually like to go."

"Archaeologists are very interested, Mr. Crouter. They come here all the time for a look, and sometimes for a dig."

"Ah, but archaeologists are rarely purchasers, Mr. Gilmartin. Scholars, you see. Not well-off. We're talking pretty big money, here. When it comes to house-property archaeologists rarely rise above what we call an Old World Cottage. Something half-timbered, and easily convertible to modern dwelling. Not destroying the authentic atmosphere, of course, but quaint. Now you couldn't call this place quaint, could you?"

"Not unless you call the Houses of Parliament quaint. But I have always understood that your people sell every-thing and anything."

"Oh, of course we do. Butler and Manciple can, and do, sell residences all over the kingdom. We yield to no one."

"Then what's the objection here?"

"No objection. None whatever. But of course we have a strong sensitivity to the pulse of the market-place, and I won't pretend to you that we could consider this place a property of the very first class – first-class demand, I mean. No suggestion that it isn't a splendid place – in its own way."

"Then what's the trouble?"

"There will be no trouble, Mr. Gilmartin. Butler and Manciple never think in terms of trouble. But a top price might not be practicable. Its location, you see."

"But for something like eight hundred years it has been considered rather a good location."

"No, Mr. Gilmartin. I'd better explain. In the real estate business, you see, we always say that there are three primary concerns in selling a property. Location, location and again, location." Once again Mr. Crouter smiles his ghost of a smile, at this much-admired house agent's joke.

"And you don't like the location?"

"Not me, Mr. Gilmartin. Our buyers. The buying public. Look, I'll tell you how it is. People with substantial money to spend on a property nowadays are predominantly business people – London people – and what they are looking for is some place not more than fifty miles from London. For weekends, and easy holiday-access. For entertaining their business friends. Now I've seen a castle, especially if it has a moat, go for a really big price. A plum, in fact. But only if it's in the Home Counties or close to the London area. An Elizabethan manor – especially if Queen Elizabeth ever slept there, ha, ha, and she was certainly a great lady for sleeping around – in a royal sense, of course – we can place one of those in a jiffy. A nice William-and-Mary, or a Queen Anne, or a Georgian – no problems there. There is a very big movement at present in restored vicarages. You understand; big places with grounds, that vicars can't keep up, now that gentlemen with private money have pretty much ceased to go into the Church. A fine vicarage is catnip to plenty of people slightly below the country-house level of income."

"But Victorian Gothic is coming into great popularity. Have you seen Kenneth Clark's book?"

"That's scholarly, of course, and the scholarly buyer isn't usually well-fixed. Strictly Old World. Cottage and quarter-acre of garden. And there's location, in the present instance."

"What's wrong with the location? Look outside. A superb day. A splendid view, right over toward the Red Castle."

"I'll be frank with you, Mr. Gilmartin. It's Wales. Wales is too far, and too wet, and too unfashionable."

"But you sell places in northern Scotland, for God's sake! What's fashionable about that?"

"That's sporting. Grousing. Deer. Those big creatures – what do they call 'em? Stags. They kill stags. Just between ourselves, there are two people up there breeding stags, to keep the mountains well-stagged, for the sportsmen. A good stag fetches quite a figure."

"I believe there are a lot of otters in the stream here."

"Otters don't pull, Mr. Gilmartin. You have to walk too far to find 'em. And in water. Otters are not a major enthusiasm among the Stock Exchange set."

"This is very discouraging."

"Sorry. But I know you want me to be realistic."

"What does realism suggest, then?"

"We'd have to explore that. Suppose we run a picture in *Country Life*; and that means substantial investment on our part, as I'm sure you'll understand. What does this place look like to the casual eye? What can a photographer get hold of? It's not really a castle, though those towers are castle features, certainly. And it's not ecclesiastical – not an old abbey or anything of that sort – though there's an ecclesiastical air about it, especially the windows. And it's bloody well not domestic, if you'll pardon my French. Doesn't look homey. Not at all. So what can we hope for? Might go for a school, but they never have any real money. Might go for a nunnery, and those R.C.s are sharp dealers, let me tell you. I don't suppose you have any objection to an R.C. sale?"

"I'd sell to Old Nick if he would pay a good price."

"I'm glad to see you're free of religious prejudice. That's always troublesome in a vendor."

"You tell me that location, and location, and location are your standards. A good price is mine. Or rather, I should say it's the standard the Inland Revenue have imposed on me."

"Ah, it's a forced sale, is that it?"

"Indeed it is. And I'll tell you why. My father was born in this county, very near here, and he always wanted a house here. Always wanted this house, in fact. But he was a citizen of Canada. He knew what the situation was: he was liable for estate taxes in both the United Kingdom and Canada, and on his full estate. You can guess what that would mean. Taxes far exceeding even his substantial means. After a lot of haggling and costly legal process he got an agreement from the tax people here that if he lived in this place for seven years after the agreement was signed, his estate here would be taxed only on what he owned in the United Kingdom. But that agreement came too late. He died five years later, and now I have to arrange to pay full estate tax in both countries, even though he never lived here for more than six months in any given year. The Canadians are very decent as tax-gatherers go, which isn't far. So are the people here. But they are not so decent that I don't have to find a hell of a lot of money – so much money that when it's all paid there won't be much left, if anything is left at all. It's *policy*, they tell me. He left some substantial bequests, though not to me. So you see how it is. I've got to squeeze as much money out of this house and its estate and its furnishings as I can possibly get, or I'm ruined. Worse than ruined, because I live on a professor's salary. I belong to the kind of people who buy Old World cottages if they buy anything at all. I may have to sell my modest, modern Canadian house to make up the final sum. The lawyers! They get their big slice, win or lose. So I'm avaricious, Mr. Crouter. Avaricious as only a cornered man can be. And I'm asking you, what can you do for me?"

"My very best, Mr. Gilmartin. Butler and Manciple always do their very best and you can be sure I'll tell my principals everything you've told me. They understand about estate taxes. A lot of our business comes from people who've been taxed out of places they've lived in for – nearly as long as Robert de Belème's time ago. I suppose you hate selling this place?"

"Frankly, Mr. Crouter, I don't. It would never be mine, however long I lived here. This place represents a dream of my father's, and it was a dream that did not make my life easy, I may tell you. This was his Land of Lost Content, which he managed to turn into a sort of Paradise Regained."

"You don't say so! Okay Mr. Gilmartin. I'll do the best I

can, as I've said. And I can tell you – I've a romantic side to my character, my wife keeps telling me – we at the firm know that we do quite an extensive business in dreams. That's what estate-agency is."

(9)

However boldly, and indeed cynically, Brochwel speaks to Mr. Crouter about selling Belem Manor, his thoughts when he sits in the big, now somewhat dismal, library that night, having supped on cold lamb with salad, followed by Old Rose's notion of coffee, are in a very different strain.

Paradise Regained, he had called the Manor, and doubtless for Rhodri it had been so. The powerful Liverpool owners of Belem Manor, the Coopers, had obeyed the ancient law of Heraclitus, that excess in anything eventually runs into its opposite, and their wealth had brought ease, refinement, an illusion that wealth needs no shepherding, and eventual ruin. For him to be able to buy the Manor – that was a stroke of quite unforeseeable good fortune. To have the Canadian dollars to restore the splendour which the Coopers had allowed to run to seed, and to be himself the master of a great house for which his father, the unfortunate Walter, had once supplied the liveries – was that not a Paradise Regained, an adjustment of the balances of Fortune?

To be able to indulge the hobby of his middle age, and fill Belem with handsome antiques had given him unceasing pleasure. His own taste was fair, and he had the guidance of his old school friend Fred ffrench, who had become something of a notability in the world of antique dealers. (Was he not one of the committee who vetted the furniture that was shown at the annual Antique Dealers' Fair in London? Was he not a regular supplier to the great Bond Street dealers of antiques that he bought in Wales when Wales was still unknown territory to the English buyers?) Yes, Fred ffrench, who had gone to school with Rhodri. Fred had come up in the world, and converted his father's undertaking business into one of the finest provincial antique shops in the Kingdom. On the way he had abandoned the English spelling of his name, and Fred French became Fred ffrench, which was authentically Welsh, and looked well on his letterheads. Fred ffrench was happy to put his taste, his knowledge and, of course, his professional scale of fees to work for his old friend.

Old friends; there were plenty of them and Rhodri never turned his back on one of them, however humble. But there were new friends, as well. County people, many of whom had been brought to straitened circumstances by wars which claimed cherished sons; that ill-fortune worked hand in hand with rising taxes, and the temper of a time which was sour about their sort of privilege. They were pleased to welcome the new owner of Belem Manor; his lavish spending looked like an assurance that the old days, when county was county, had not wholly disappeared. There were those, of course, who despised him as an upstart; they were county people who did not like his New World ways, and townspeople whose long Welsh memories went back to the days of drunken Uncle David, and the disgrace of bankruptcy. But on the whole Rhodri had managed very well as a county landowner, and his open-handed support of local causes salved the feelings of the gentry whenever those might be rubbed a little raw.

Oh, he had enjoyed a happy old age, had Rhodri. He had returned to the Land of Lost Content and found it still a land of present content. But now the setting in which he had played out his comedy must be disposed of, the fine antiques must be sold, the rapacity of the tax-gatherers must be appeased.

The auction impended, and Brochwel dreaded it, for he saw it as the piecemeal destruction of his father's dream. The dreamer now slept, never to wake again, but after every life, some wretched dispositions must be made, and somebody must see them through. And so – an auction.

(10)

T HE AUCTION. This film represents an extraordinary variety of techniques; the scene with Mr. Crouter, for instance, was as direct as it could possibly be. The war scenes with Brochwel in the cellar and the altar tomb were wonders of rapid cutting and montage, and now as I first see the great auction at Belem Manor I know that there are to be even more, even dizzier, evocations of fact mingled with feeling, superimpositions, distortions, and all the riot of *épopée cinématographique* as the great Abel Gance and Leonid Trauberg conceived it. If, during my lifetime, I had been confronted with the job of reviewing this film, what could I have made of it in my useful journalist's prose? Its import is amply clear – much clearer than straight narrative could achieve – but its technique is the phantasmagoria of the human mind, of human perception, of human thought as poets of the film understand it.

The auction – what a festival it turns out to be! A big tent, an ornamental tent like a wedding marquee, has been set up on Belem's lawn, and at one end of it two kitchen tables have been put together to form a platform, and covered with a handsome Turkey carpet; the auctioneer now takes his place; he is not that genial figure, a country auctioneer, but Mr. Beddoe, one of the high priests of the great Bond Street auction house of Torringtons, and his mien is serious. He is, in himself, an assurance that fine things are to be sold, and fine prices expected. Before he begins he glances over the assembly who sit in the folding chairs on the grass. Mr. Beddoe is an old hand, and knows precisely who they are.

The local gentry, of course; come to see the fun, to marvel at the prices people will pay for chairs and tables they have known when Rhodri Gilmartin was dispensing his considerable hospitality. Some of them have pencils ready to mark prices in their catalogues. (Catalogue on request, from Torringtons; price one guinea.)

The visitors, some from quite a long way off, in Cheshire or Shropshire; they think they know antiques, and hope to pick up good things at less than shop prices; they study *Connoisseur* and Frank Davis's column in *Country Life* and they have been busy on the view-days, taking note of what they think they will bid for. They have vainglorious hopes of getting the better of Mr. Beddoe, of scoring off Torringtons, and boasting about it forever after.

The Ring. Mr. Beddoe knows the members of the Ring very well, but he does not nod or acknowledge their presence. These are the professionals, the men from the big antique dealers, who attend every significant sale, buy all the best things, and know to a farthing what every object will sell for when they have got their hands on it. They hate and despise the visitors, those simple amateurs, and sometimes when they feel mischievous they trap one of that gullible tribe into a contest of bidding, and then leave him with a piece they have never seriously thought of buying, which has been run up to an absurd price. It is possible – even though it is illegal – that the Ring will let one of their number buy a good piece at a low price, if he can, and then, when they meet at night at the Green Man in Trallwm, they will have another auction, and one of their number will buy it at a greater price, for sale to a customer he knows wants this very thing; the precious object will at least double its money, on Bond Street.

The Ring are the old hands at the antique business. Not well-dressed or remarkable men to look at; they do not seek to call attention to themselves. But they are the nourishing root of a complex trade. They are not in the least like the glossy young men with cut-glass accents who will eventually sell the antiques (polished and repaired where necessary) in Bond Street, in Cheltenham, in Oxford or wherever people seek the very best survivals from the furnishings of an earlier age.

The Ring are not the eager bidders – the catalogue-wavers, the putters up of hands, the head-bobbers. Mr. Beddoe knows them, and a wink or a raised pencil is signal enough for Mr. Beddoe.

Mr. Beddoe, and his colleague Mr. Wherry-Smith, are prepared to steer a careful course over the three days of the Belem Manor Sale. There is a lot of Victorian Gothic and some earlier Gothic Revival stuff in the catalogue; it remained in the house when Rhodri bought it, because it was too big, too grandiose for the dwellings of the remaining Coopers. That style is now well advanced in the antique market as collectable. It will not draw the visitors, but the Ring will pick up the best of it. Mallatt's, on Bond Street, is already doing very well with Gothic Revival, and it will be a rage for a few years.

The hour strikes from the Belem stable clock, and Mr. Beddoe taps on his desk with a ball of ivory which he holds – not for the likes of Mr. Beddoe is the conventional auctioneer's hammer – and silences the crowd, which Brochwel, standing alone at the back of the marquee, judges to be no less than two hundred and fifty.

"This is an important sale, ladies and gentlemen, and Torringtons are very happy to be offering some exceptional pieces, including many in the Gothic Revival area. The terms of sale are printed at the front of your catalogue, and I expect you to have familiarized yourselves with them. So without more ado [Mr. Beddoe relishes 'ado' as a word congruous with the antique trade] let us begin, and I think we may as well start with the famous Belem Clock, which you have undoubtedly examined in the Great Hall."

Indeed the audience has gaped at the astonishing Belem Clock, much too big to be brought into the marquee. Whoever buys it will have to pay a handsome price to take it away.

"Made in 1838 by Hausburg of Munich; strikes the

hours on one bell and the quarters on four others, each quarter differently. An eight-day movement, and the dials on the
façade show seconds, days of the week, the days of the
month, the months, the four seasons, the signs of the zodiac,
the time at Belem Manor – which is, of course, the time at
Greenwich – as well as the phases of the moon. The pendant
escapement is on Graham's principle. The case finished, as
you have seen during the view days, in fine bronze and
ormolu.

"But the special feature of this clock is its assembly of
chimes, thirty-seven in number, operated by sixty-two
exquisitely tuned steel keys. There are seven changeable cylinders, and the chimes will play four English airs, four Irish
airs, four Welsh airs – and I know that many in this audience
have just heard it play 'Of noble race was Shenkin' – and four
patriotic airs. There are two cylinders of Scottish airs – the
Cooper family, who commissioned this remarkable clock,
were proud of their Scottish ancestry – and of course in the
best nineteenth-century tradition there are four Sacred airs.
Cylinders cased in oak boxes lined with velvet. More than a
clock: a musical instrument of unique quality.

"The ornamentation is in the finest early-nineteenth-
century style. Figures representing Day and Night; two
heads of Time in youth and age, and medallions of the Seasons, all rendered in verd-antique. Dial enriched in gold and
fine enamel. An unique piece, ladies and gentlemen; a triumph of horological skill and in itself a splendid evocation of
the mid-nineteenth century. Somewhat large, it must be
admitted, but many of you have very large houses, I know,
and we now ask for your bids on an exceptional timepiece."

Silence.

"Nobody likes to be the first to bid on the first item. I
know that well. So shall I propose a figure? Shall I say five
thousand pounds for a beginning? You would not, as I am
certain you know, reproduce this clock today for five times
that figure. There simply aren't the workmen. Five – do I hear
five? Does anyone say five, to start the bidding?"

Nobody says five. Or anything at all. Mr. Beddoe comes down, and down, and down, until one of the Ring (who knows an American with a place in Scotland, who will pay ten thousand for the clock) gets it for five hundred pounds.

Is Mr. Beddoe dismayed? Not he! He knew that monstrous clock would go very low, but he knew that the buyers would thereby be encouraged to think that everything that came up subsequently would go low. And he is right. The next item, an angle ottoman – "upholstered in China Damask trimmed with silk gimp and cord, finished with silk tufts and rosettes and a shaped valance trimmed with bow gimp and fringe" – goes for exactly twice what he had mentally decided he might get for it. All is going well. The crowd thinks it smells bargains. The ottoman whispers of Victorian flirtations, of crinolines wooed by drooping sidewhiskers.

Mr. Beddoe offers what he calls a Portfolio Stand in oak, with brass ornamentation and crimson tassels. A century ago the pious Coopers used it not for portfolios, but for a gigantic Bible, which was thus displayed, opened each day to some edifying passage, in the Great Hall. Mr. Cooper read from it when the forty indoor servants were assembled for morning prayers. The Coopers had great faith in daily doses of religion for keeping the maidservants sweet and the menservants chaste, and upon the whole it worked – the daily prayers, Sunday processions of the whole household to church, and a decidedly un-Christlike severity toward any backsliders, pregnant housemaids or light-fingered footmen. This object, which Brochwel thinks a monstrosity, fetches a very good price from a visitor who wants it to display his art books, which exemplify the religion of his very cultivated style of life.

Rhodri, assisted by electricity and modern refrigeration, had managed Belem with five indoor servants.

Upon the whole, good objects, conformable to modern life while bringing to it a whiff of Gothic Revival romance, fetch good prices. Two hall seats, upholstered in Utrecht velvet which, though faded, is still sturdy, bring a surprising figure. They look like something on which Sir Walter Scott might have sat – but he hadn't.

A pianoforte by Broadwood, the case of which is gussied up in elaborate marqueterie of an eighteenth-century savour, but standing on Gothic legs, causes a contest of bidding that looks as though it might bring two ladies to blows. It is not offered for view by the porters who move the furniture in and out of the tent with expedition, stage-managed by a senior man who is rather past heavy lifting; the piano may be seen in the drawing-room in the house. The bidders know that the innards of the piano are in ruins, but they want the extraordinary case, for reasons best known to themselves. The members of the Ring are not interested in this one, and watch the bidding with the amused despisal that is the mark of their profession when amateurs are vying for anything they themselves do not want.

Two suits of full armour, which are obviously phonies but would look impressive on a fine staircase, go very well indeed. They seem to speak in steely voices of Romance – Abbotsford style. The atmosphere in the marquee is now at a heat very agreeable to Mr. Beddoe, and to Brochwel. The dismantling of Rhodri's dream is going very well.

Brochwel does not stay for the luncheon which is offered at the back of the marquee by a firm of Shrewsbury caterers at a reasonable price. Some of the visitors have brought their own flasks of sherry and are greedy after the excitement of the morning. He does not want to mingle with them, or answer questions, and so he wanders through the gardens.

(11)

THE GARDENS had been old Rhodri's special enthusiasm, for to him they spelled luxury and superiority of station even more than the Manor, with its mixture of Gothic Revival stuff and the very good antiques he had bought himself, helpfully guided by his old friend Fred ffrench. Rhodri's pieces of old oak and good eighteenth-century chairs and tables were selling briskly under Mr. Beddoe's guidance, and the Ring were picking them up at sums that had to be considered fair, even by London standards. In the gardens Belem Manor still survived as Rhodri had known it, and Brochwel thought he might still encounter a spirit which the confusion wrought by Torringtons' men had banished from the house.

The gardens were extensive and, though the year was now well advanced, were still bright with autumn flowers and shrubs. The Coopers had fitted them out with garden figures of shepherds and shepherdesses carved in stone, not at all bad of their kind, and for their period.

The Coopers – who had they been? A wealthy Liverpool family of ship-owners whose desire it was to lift themselves in the world by the possession of a fine estate. Wales was near, and they lived before the time when all desirable estates had to be near to London, or in the Scottish Highlands. To judge from their taste in furnishing, they must have been devout, but not devout in the Methodist mode. Oh no; they were Church of England, but Low and Evangelical. The source of their money was a great merchant fleet, trading with the West Indies, and there were rumours that they had begun life – two or three generations before the family that destroyed the old, worm-eaten, dry-rotted Manor of an unguessable antiquity – as "blackbirders" who had transported slaves from Africa to the American Colonies, at a high profit, even when the spoilage of slaves who did not survive those terrible voyages was taken into account. There were jealous locals, inspired by the spite which lies at the heart of much Welsh wit, who had spoken of Belem Manor as Blackbird Hall. Probably the tale was untrue: people are apt to think that anyone with a lot of money must come by it in some discreditable way, but they are not always right. The Coopers had lived at Belem Manor in high style through most of the nineteenth century, until only one old Miss Cooper was left, writhen by arthritis in the Welsh damp and cold, and with just enough money to see her into her grave. She died at a great age, and Rhodri bought the Manor from a group of distant cousins, who had no hope of keeping it up.

Here was the bench on which Brochwel had sat five years ago, during his last visit to Belem in Rhodri's lifetime, and it was here that Rhodri had told him the Great Secret. I see them sitting in the sunshine – for in Wales sunshine must be seized on the fly and must never be taken for granted – Rhodri so smartly dressed in white flannels and a blue blazer, my father somewhat rumpled and greyish, as a travelling professor usually is.

"I miss your mother, of course."

"But she never came here."

"No, no; she was here a number of times, when she felt up to the journey."

"But you came, nevertheless, whether she came or not."

"Yes. But you see, I had to look after the place. Couldn't leave it unoccupied for a year at a time."

"There are lots of servants to keep an eye on it. And Norman Lloyd is your agent, isn't he? He wouldn't let it come to harm."

"Not the same thing. No manure like the foot of the master. A place loses heart if it's not occupied."

"Not loved, you mean."

"Yes, that's what I mean."

"Mother never loved it."

"No."

"But she came here, all the same."

"Yes. She wanted to see what I was doing with it. She loved all that sort of thing. Inherited from her father, I sup-pose. He knew what building was."

"But he came to grief?"

"I'm not sure that I'd call it grief."

"The Poor Farm? Wasn't that disgrace?"

"For the old woman and the girls, it was. But I heard

tales about William McOmish having a high old time out there. He was a man of some intelligence, you know. He kept the books for the Poor Farm better than anybody they could hire. And he used to give lectures – yes, lectures – to the paupers on stresses and strains, and geometry as applied to building, and the stupidity of the Russo-Japanese War, and all sorts of things. He was an old gasbag, but not a fool. Loved to talk. So he ended up as a kind of parody of what you are now – a professor, a knowledge-box, a professional Wise Man."

"Thanks, Dad. You certainly give me a build-up."

"Oh, go on with you! You know I'm really very proud of you."

"Nice to hear that. I'll make an exchange: I'm proud of you."

"I've not done too badly, considering what a poor start I had."

"Was it so poor? I've heard you quote Ossian. Not one of my colleagues has ever done that."

"That was the Mater. A dear, good soul. We'd have sunk without her. The Pater lost all heart when we went to Canada."

"It was very bitter for you, those first years?"

"Cruel. We were humble people at home, but I'd never been used to filth and wickedness. Those first months at *The Courier* – ! You spoke of Ossian; a line of his recurred to me every day at that time –

Blind, and tearful, and forlorn, I walk with little men.

Beak Browder and Charlie Delaney were little men, sure enough. Somehow I had to get out of that."

"And you did. You fought the hero-fight."

"Get away with you! There was nothing heroic about it. Just hard, hard work and a lot of personal sacrifice."

"Every man's fight is the hero-fight, wherever and however he meets it. If he has the courage to face the dragon, or destiny, or whatever it may be, and whether he wins or falls

in the battle, it's the hero-fight. Dad – tell me – I've always
wanted to ask – what pushed you on to make a success of
your life? The kind of success that sees you at last here at
Belem Manor?"

"To be wholly frank, Brocky, I think it was laziness, of a
kind. You see, there was one thing I always wanted, and held
ahead of me as a great thing to be achieved. I always wanted
to have a twenty-minute nap after lunch, every day of my life.
Now, it was obvious that a journeyman printer, or a Mono-
type man, couldn't do that. Even the Union hadn't the nerve
to ask for that, if they had the imagination to conceive of such
a thing. It was obvious that I had to be self-employed or – no
nap. Never. So, I saved, and scraped, and your mother went
without things, and at last I was able to buy a half-interest in a
little weekly paper for a few hundred dollars. The nap was
mine at last. And after that it was simply a matter of hard
work, as I said."

"In certain ways that is a shamefully immoral story.
Desire For Nap Leads to Success: how would that look as a
headline?"

"Terrible. Misleading the young. But true, as so many
terrible and misleading things are."

"And Mother supported you and stood by you through
all that?"

"Like a warrior. No man ever had a better wife."

"Then what went wrong?"

"Wrong? I don't understand you."

"You do, you know. Ever since I can remember, you two
were pulling different ways. When did you stop pulling
together?"

"I don't know that I can tell you."

"You don't know?"

"Oh yes, I know. But I've never told anybody. And you
are her son, after all."

"Is it something very shameful? It wasn't another
woman, was it?"

"Brocky, what a common mind you have! If anything

goes wrong between husband and wife, it has to be another woman. You, a professor of literature! Is that the only story you know?"

"Easy with the Welsh rhetoric, Dad, and tell me. Do you think I'm old enough to know?"

"We were very close. Not Hollywood close but really close. Before you there was another child. About fourteen months after we were married. We didn't tell you. A girl. Stillborn. That was a blow, but we survived it. What happens to stillborns, I wonder? The doctor took it away. Probably put it under his roses. He murmured something about the danger of pregnancy after a certain age, but I didn't pay proper attention. I had your mother to comfort. Then John Vermuelen wrote his family history."

"I never knew about that."

"I didn't keep it around the house, and I don't think your mother did either. But I had a little job-plant in the newspaper office I owned then, and John asked me to print the history for him. It wasn't much bigger than a pamphlet. It included a family record up to the time of publication, and that was when I discovered about your mother."

"What about her, for God's sake?"

"When we married, she lied about her age. She was a full ten years older than she had admitted to. I was so furious I cried. Cried right there, standing beside the make-up stone. I remembered the Pater saying to me, 'Rhodri, you must surely know that Malvina is a lot older than you are. People around town know it. Haven't you heard?' But I was headstrong and told him to mind his business and I'd mind mine. We had a terrible row when I confronted your mother with it. Went on for days. She didn't defend herself. Just wept. She'd deceived me, and I thought I could never forgive her. But I did, and you're the evidence of the forgiveness. When you were born your mother was nearly forty-five, and in those days – how old are you now? Forty-five yourself? – that was considered very risky. But you seem to be tidy enough. Long-headed, as the children of old parents are supposed to be."

"But how can you have quarrelled so bitterly about such a trivial thing?"

"Trivial! You can't mean that! Trivial! My God, Brocky, it was a failure in truth, and in loyalty. What do you suppose a marriage is, if it isn't rooted in truth and loyalty?"

"People do speak of love, from time to time."

"Is love anything but truth and loyalty?"

"Nowadays the stress seems to be on the physical thing."

"Exactly! They mean sex. Sex is an instinct, and for some people it seems to be the supreme pleasure, but what can you build on it? Forty or fifty years of marriage? No, that means truth and loyalty, when sex has become an old song."

"That's very Confucian."

"From what I hear, Confucius was no fool."

"Women want love."

"Is that what they want? I've always wondered."

"You and Freud."

"Surely he knew. I thought he knew everything."

"He said he didn't know that."

"He was the great mental-health man, wasn't he?"

"I suppose you could call it that."

"He was rather after my time. Never read him. Read about him, now and then."

"He said the measure of psychological health was the ability to love and the ability to work."

"I certainly have had the ability to work. And I really loved your mother very much, in the beginning. Real love, not just pillow-love."

"And did she love you?"

"As much, I suppose, as that terrible home and those awful parents made possible. I realize I was very green when I married. Things were very different then. We were both virgins. Do you know that in all that long marriage I never saw her naked? Never knew at the end how horribly her left breast had decayed? When the doctor told me, I was as much in the dark as any stranger. Of course that was the way her parents had lived. Her mother – an old tartar. Tongue like a two-edged sword. I hope you had a good look at Nuala's parents before you married her."

"Very nice, jolly people. Father a lawyer in Cork."

"And Catholics?"

"Lapsed."

"Well, there it is. Now you know."

"Really, Dad – about her age – I don't see that it was all that big a thing."

"It was a failure of truth and loyalty."

"Oh, come on!"

"Christ forgave the adulteress, but I don't recall that he ever forgave a liar. And there was the other thing, of course."

"What other thing?"

"This thing. Wales. When it became possible for me to come back here every summer she set her face against it. It was a land where she could not follow. She didn't even try."

"Her family were Loyalists. Canada was their country."

"She wouldn't understand that this is my country. That was a loyalty she wouldn't permit, but she couldn't stop it, so it was the irresistible force and the immovable object. . . . Result, deadlock."

"I didn't see it that way. It seemed to me it was Pull-Devil-Pull-Baker, and you both were fighting for my adherence to your particular loyalty. Have you any idea how difficult that was for a child, and even more difficult when I was growing up?"

"For a while, we thought your only loyalty was to Julia."

"Perhaps it was. But if so it was an escape from the tensions at home."

"Tensions. What tensions?"

"That house was a warring camp. A psychological battlefield where not a shot was fired, but hostile feeling and determined opposition spread like poison gas."

"You're exaggerating! Who's the rhetorician now?"

"I am. And for good reasons. Only exaggeration can

give any idea of the day-to-day, year-in year-out quality of the feeling in that house. Mother was determined to win me for Canada. You were always dangling the romance and beauty of Wales before my eyes. When you offered to send me to Oxford, Mother knew exactly what you were at. And she played the invalid, and insisted that I go to Harvard, so that I could dash home if she thought she was dying. You know what I mean – she had more near-deaths and recoveries than Harry Lauder had farewell tours. Harvard wasn't Canada, but at least it was New World, and she was New World to the soles of her feet."

"All right. As we seem to be getting down to cases, tell me, and tell me true. Which side have you come down on? Are you New World or Old?"

"Sounds like a novel by Henry James."

"Never read him."

"Don't. But that was his question and he plumped for the Old."

"And you've plumped for – ?"

"Both. Or neither. I suppose my real world is the scholar's world. What we used to call in my Waverley days Eng-Lang-and-Lit. Not a bad world. That's my homeland."

"A bit dry-as-dust, isn't it? All in books, I mean."

"A little dryness doesn't hurt. Mother used to talk to me, when I was a child, on Dominion Day as a usual thing, about loving Canada. But I couldn't love Canada, though I did my dutiful best until I was about fourteen. You don't love Canada; you are part of Canada, and that's that. Mother talked about loving Canada as if it were a woman. A mother, I suppose. She wasn't strong for my loving a woman as a mate. Never. Other countries may be like women. France makes a great thing of Marianne, or whatever she's called, and the English still sing sometimes about that big helmeted bruiser Britannia. But Canada isn't like a woman; it's like a family – various, often unsympathetic, sometimes detestable, frequently dumb as hell – but inescapable because you are part of it and can't ever, really, get

away. You know the saying: My country, right or wrong –
my mother, drunk or sober.''

"I see. Well, you'll never be able to live here, that's one
certain thing.''

"No.''

"When I'm gone, you'll sell it up, I suppose. If your
mother sees, down through the Gates of Pearl, she'll dance a
jig for the granny's pig, as she used to say.''

"That was one of her Old Ontario expressions.''

"Well, to use another of hers, I'm hungry enough to eat a
horse and chase the rider. What about getting in for lunch?''

"Yes, if we're late the kitchen staff will be annoyed, and
there'll be wigs on the green. That's another of mother's.''

"Oh, not while Rose is there. She'd cut a dead dog in two
for me.''

"With a dull knife, I have no doubt.''

"Extraordinary how your mother's Old Loyalist turns
of phrase keep cropping up, even here in the Old Country.''

"She was a very powerful character, whatever you may
have against her.''

"Don't say that! I have nothing against her. That's all
done with. Never harbour grudges; they sour your stomach
and do no harm to anyone else.''

"Lunch?''

"Lunch.''

(12)

THERE HAD BEEN many
conversations during the last visit, for Rhodri seemed to be in
the confessional mood that comes with age, when a life's
accounts are being made up. Recollections and scraps of family lore kept asserting themselves in Brochwel's mind as he
followed the fortunes of the sale.

Rhodri's old Welsh chests, of sturdiest oak and carved with symbols recording their first owners' loyalty to the Stuarts, fetched very good prices, though it was a period when oak was not "in" and the big money was in mahogany and walnut pieces. And how they gleamed, not as shiny objects, but as rich things that spoke from the heart of the wood and the craftsmanship that had determined its present shape. Old Rose, the housekeeper, and the last of the servants to be "kept on" as a caretaker, was in ecstasy as each treasured piece went, usually to a member of the Ring, under Mr. Beddoe's skilled direction.

"That's my polishin' brought that £800!" she hissed to Brochwel. "That's my Lavendo and elbow-grease that fetched that £800; and for that little side table! Who'd ever have thought that!" And she was probably right. Auctioneers know that a piece that has been in loving and careful hands for years brings far more than the supposed "treasure" that has been hoiked up from storage in the back of a stable, unloved and forlorn.

Unlikely objects fetched unexpected prices. There was keen competition for a "prie-dieu chair," upon which a petitioner could undoubtedly have knelt, but it is far more likely that one of the Cooper daughters had sat on the cushioned kneeler to put on her pretty stockings. The Victorians and the designers of Gothic Revival furniture had a curious trick of adapting a medieval object to a domestic modern need. There were "aumbries" for instance, made in imitation of the cupboards in which the chalices and patens of the Communion service were kept, but which the Victorians used for their teacups and milk jugs. Silver especially came in for this sort of transformation and many a jam-spoon took the form of a spoon for the holy oil at a coronation. Commodes, chastely concealing a chamber-pot for use in a lady's bedroom, might have quite a Gothic air about them, so that the infrequent pleasure of defecation – the displacement of the Victorian female tappen – was enhanced by a sense of historical continuity. These po-boxes – as the Ring called them – went very well in the antique shops of the kingdom. They made pleasing occasional rests for lamps. Belem offered several examples of all these things, remaining from the high and palmy days of the Coopers.

The prie-dieu chair; as the bidding became quicker and keener Brochwel thought about the religious associations of his family. Janet – the Mater – whom he had never seen, had apparently been deeply devout in the Evangelical, Wesleyan manner, as had Walter, who also had died before Brochwel was born. Great people to pray, both of them. Great people to set aside a tenth – the biblical "tithe" – of their little income to be given to church and charity. Rhodri had been only an occasional church-goer, but he was a generous church-giver. A salve to conscience? Malvina had long ceased to go to church, even infrequently, before her death. An invalid. Sometimes the minister came to call, and drank tea, and laughed more often than the conversation seemed to make necessary. But in one of these Belem Manor conversations, during that last visit, Rhodri had said something significant.

"In all our life together, I never saw her pray," he said, with a wonder that made it plain that he himself did pray, perhaps furtively but none the less with true intent. If they had shared a religious life, would the need for insistence on truth and loyalty have been less avid? If they had had a belief in which they could, so to speak, turn easily and draw full breaths, would they have needed so strict a world of duty?

I, the patient looker-on, think I know the answer to that. Rhodri and Malvina had come at the end of the great evangelical movement in Christianity, when the immense impulse given to it by John Wesley and his disciples was running down and no longer infused those who believed they believed. Could Malvina, whose family had been ruined by church ambition and church hypocrisy, have been a strong believer? She was not a saint and it would have taken the zeal and fortitude of a saint to believe devoutly and humbly in a faith that had brought ruin and humiliation and a sense of treachery.

As for Rhodri, his relinquishing of the church – though not wholly of belief – had a different, a comical, an entirely understandable and forgivable origin. He simply outgrew Methodism. He possessed a strong, though not a cultivated or refined, aesthetic sense, and the hideous temples of evangelicism, like William McOmish's Grace Church, made him laugh. If that was God's house, God must have appalling taste. If the people God assembled there were His chosen, God was welcome to them. Rhodri the journalist knew too much about many of them to accept them as intellectual or ethical equals. There was no spite in this, just a little snobbery of a not wholly discreditable kind.

Snobbery, like every other social attitude, takes its character from those who practise it. The snob is supposedly a mean creature, delighting in slight and trivial distinctions. But is the man who bathes every day a snob because he does not seek the company of the one-bath-a-week, one-shirt-a-week, one-pair-of-clean-drawers-a-week, one-pair-of-socks-a-week man? Must the gourmet embrace the barbarian whose idea of a fine repast is a hamburger made from the flesh of fallen animals, and a tub of fries soaked in vinegar? Is the woman who wears a first-rate intaglio to be faulted because she thinks little of the woman whose fingers are loaded with fake diamonds? Rhodri had outgrown the kind of people who exemplified – no, not the faith of his fathers, but what remained of that faith in the modern world.

Doubtless it is the Devil's work to nibble away at a man's belief in such a fashion, but it must be admitted that the Devil is a fine craftsman, and so many of his arguments are unanswerable. Probably Heraclitus would have had something to say about that. Everything, in time, begets its opposite.

(13)

I F IT IS TRUE, as the song says, that "Love and marriage, love and marriage, go together like a horse and carriage," it is equally true that art and snobbery, art and snobbery, go together like a highway and robbery. On the second day of the sale Mr. Wherry-Smith, one of Tor-ringtons' best men when it came to pictures, takes the auctioneer's elevated desk, and sets to work with professional geniality.

As a joke, he opens with two pottery caricature figures of Gladstone and Disraeli. A member of the Ring is annoyed when an eager outsider pushes the price up to twenty-five guineas (for Mr. Wherry-Smith does not admit the existence of any lesser unit of currency), but the Ring man knows where he can get rid of those things for sixty, without a murmur.

Then come the pictures, some of which are better than Rhodri ever knew, or the Coopers ever foresaw. A Gainsborough called *The Beggar Boys*, with an indisputable pedigree, went for thirteen thousand guineas. The county spectators gasp, for they had always liked that picture, as they sat under it in the dining-hall at the Manor, but they had never *respected* it, and were humbled by their own lack of prescience. A portrait by Millais of his wife – the former Mrs. Ruskin, and a stunning Scots beauty – brought five thousand, and another Millais, of pretty children, brought two. Noblemen fetched less. A reputed Kneller of the Marquess of Blandford (John Churchill, but not *the* John Churchill) fetched a mere seven hundred and fifty guineas and an Earl of Rochester (which one? the one who wore a white periwig) went for a miserable hundred. A Poynter of squeezable but obviously virginal girls in a classic setting, with plenty of sun shining through their flimsy garments, brought twelve hundred guineas from a wistful local bachelor who had always fancied it, but a gloomy Watts called *Love and Death* went for a risible sixty. The very next picture, a rousingly romantic portrait by John Singleton Copley of the twelfth Earl of Eglinton, glorious in Highland chieftain's dress, created a furore, and the Ring quickly ran it up beyond the reach of any but very serious buyers; it went at last to one of themselves for thirty-five thousand guineas. There was a round of applause in the marquee, and Mr. Wherry-Smith, smiling as though to say, "Nothing to do with me; I am but the humble broker of the Muses," bobbed his head in acknowledgement.

Some of these pictures came with the Manor and represented the taste of the Coopers, who had bought fashionably in their time; their Victorian pictures have come into favour again. Some of the pictures had been bought by Rhodri, whose simple principle it was to buy what he liked, and that meant pictures of men who looked as if they held their heads high in the world, and ladies who had beauty in the style of one age or another. He liked to surround himself with pictures of people who might have been his ancestors, if he had belonged to the class that has ancestors, and not just forebears. He never pretended that these odds and ends from sales were connected with himself by anything other than right of purchase. But in a way he was right. These were pictures of people successful and important in their own time, and as a successful and important person he might be considered their descendant and modern exemplar. Some of the pictures were good – in the world of Mr. Wherry-Smith and the Ring – and some were scorned in that same world. Some fetched substantial prices. Some went for under £100, which in modern terms is ignominious. To Brochwel everything in the sale was part of the milieu Rhodri had created for himself, the stage-setting against which he had played the final scenes of his hero-struggle, and it was painful to see prices put on the fabric of a dream.

Mr. Wherry-Smith bent his neck to the rougher yoke of two depictions of Napoleon, copied from French originals by one of the Miss Coopers who had a talent – though not a large one – in that direction. Napoleon apparently thinking; Miss Cooper has left the nobility of the Emperor in abeyance and has emphasized the simple Corsican; his eyes are dimmed and he seems not to have shaved lately. There is about him the air of a bandmaster ruined by drink. *Napoleon Crossing the Alps*; after Delacroix – a very long way after. Can the Emperor not ride? Why is his horse being led by a picturesque guide? Of course this permits the Emperor to look out of the picture, straight at the audience, so to speak. One hand is thrust into his bosom. Neither of these pictures reaches twenty guineas. They will end up in third-rate schools, to impress third-rate parents, who know Napoleon by sight.

Worse is to come. *The Temptation of Christ* which had hung in a place of honour in the Great Hall is a very flat picture, and in many respects inexplicable, for Christ seems to have spent his forty days in the wilderness in a pink tea-gown. His face is that of the usual nineteenth-century Bearded Lady, and the hand with which he gestures toward the heavens is apparently without bones. The Fiend is the colour of dirty bronze. Naked, but decently vague about the crotch, he points below, to the Kingdom of this World. The Fiend, undoubtedly by accident, is handsomer than Christ. No bids, and the picture is withdrawn.

Nor has Mr. Wherry-Smith any better luck with the statuary with which the Coopers had ornamented their house, and which Rhodri had found too heavy to remove. Mrs. Cooper, in Roman dress, teaching two small sons in Roman tunics from a marble Bible; classically, but without obvious erotic effect, her nipples are discreetly hinted at under her drapery. Nipples are of course very maternal, but they have other significances, and perhaps Mr. Cooper had not been indifferent to these. Clever, is it not, to suggest the human form below the garments, and in *stone*? But not clever enough for anybody in the marquee. Mrs. Cooper is too big, too marmoreal, too holy, even for a garden ornament. Besides, how would you ever get the thing home? Mr. Wherry-Smith, in answer to a question, denies any knowledge of B. E. Spence, the sculptor, who has signed the piece and added "Fecit Roma" to show that it is right from the nineteenth-century fount of all great art.

Showing no emotion, Mr. Wherry-Smith passes on to Eve, a bluey-white marble effigy of our First Mother. She is reaching upward, presumably for the apple, but the whole tendency of her body is downward; her mouth droops and her flesh seems heavy as if more than ordinary gravity were dragging it to earth. She is fattish, but her breasts are globular; her hips are broad and suggest squelchiness; her mount of Venus is chastely imperforate and has the bald impersonality of a blancmange. She has long, ladylike fingers and prehensile toes.

"You have seen it in the Library Garden, ladies and gentlemen. What am I bid? Shall I say a hundred guineas, for a start?"

He is permitted to say it, but nobody seconds his optimism. Eve will remain where she is.

Rhodri had rather liked Eve. A nude, but biblical and thus permissible.

(14)

THE THIRD DAY of the sale is reserved for what the auctioneers call "domestic" objects, and it is not the distinguished Beddoe or the aesthetic Wherry-Smith who preside, but a Mr. Boggis, whose realm this is, and who brings Torringtons a considerable sum each year by selling what would never appear in a Bond Street shop. The contents of servants' rooms, piles of excellent bed-linen, Turkey carpet – worn but with many a year left in it – stair carpets and gleaming brass stair-rods for those who can still persuade maidservants to polish them, sixty-eight yards of Brussels carpet from an upstairs corridor, long runs of magazines for decades out of publication, lowly po-boxes from the domestic quarters, a cheval-glass at which the servants have smartened themselves before going through the baize door which divided their world from that of the gentry, towel-horses, sets of jugs and basins and chamber-pots (florists sought chamber-pots because, when discreetly used, they are excellent for middle-sized "arrangements"), sets and sets of chairs in dozens and half-dozens from all parts of the house and especially from the back quarters where forty domestic bottoms had to be accommodated for meals and for rest, the Aga cooker, the sale of which makes Rose weep, for it has been her domestic altar and she knows its every whim. Mountains of things, and money in every one of them, which Mr. Boggis can charm out of them as deftly as anybody in the auctioneering world.

Surprises, of course. An oak bidet is put up, and to many of those in the marquee its purpose is unknown. They do not associate the Victorians with those objects that appear so mysteriously in the bathrooms of hotels when they venture "abroad." But some female Cooper must have been so Parisian in spirit as to desire such a thing, and here it was, from Gillows of London. It brings an astonishing sum from an antique dealer from London, who sees a future for it. Who collects period bidets?

Equally astonishing prices are paid for the piles of velvet curtains, supplied long ago by John G. Grace of 14 Wigmore Street. When the Coopers built their new Gothic Belem, Mr. Grace's men spent fifty-six days hanging curtains and laying the carpets. Mr. Boggis has unearthed much information from some records still in the house, which lends an inexplicable authenticity and antique charm to what might otherwise appear to be second-hand domestic furnishings. Oh, he is a shrewd man, is Mr. Boggis! Splendid stuff here, even after more than a century; some amber China damask brings ahs and oohs from those who know fabrics. Much of Mr. Grace's work goes to a London costumier, who will reshape it as costumes for plays and films.

The greatest surprise of all, perhaps, is the Orthophonic; such a novelty when it first appeared at St. Helen's,
so full in tone, so deft at allowing the "inner voices" of
complex music to "come through," as earlier machines had
not been able to do. Rhodri never noticed that it was growing old, as he was increasingly deaf, and that other record-
players had succeeded it and improved on it; he had brought
it from Canada because he was not quite sure where he
would buy such a thing in the United Kingdom. Now, it
appears, it has risen again from its lowly estate as an outworn instrument, and become valuable as an antique, capable of being put in first-rate condition, and of course the
very thing for playing your seventy-eight revolution
recordings, ladies and gentlemen, which will not function
on your new high-fidelity machines.

Not just the old Orthophonic leaps into life, but also the
scores of records that go with it. Many of these are now
collector's pieces. Georges Barrère playing "The Swan"
exquisitely on his gold flute, Melba singing Tosti's "Good-
Bye," Evan Williams singing a Welsh song of parting, "Yn
iach y ti, Cymru," Gogorza singing "Could I," singers forgotten, like Cecil Fanning and David Bispham, and "Hearts
and Flowers" played by the Victor Salon Orchestra. There are
five enthusiasts in the marquee, and the Ring is not
interested – indeed has come today only for a bedstead in the
Gothic taste, with hangings reputedly designed by Morris –
and the bidding is keen and rapid. The watchers are excited.
Old gramophone records! Who would have suspected! Have
we anything at home like this? Brochwel is pleased that the
record of "Gems from Lady Mary" brings £8. "What do the
Yanks know of England?/That know not Austin Reed?" A
man who is an enthusiast for forgotten musicals bids it up
and is pleased to get it. Mr. Boggis, crafty man, puts up the
best of the records one by one, and not in batches. Mr. Boggis
is just as highly esteemed, at Torringtons, as either Mr. Beddoe or Mr. Wherry-Smith, because Mr. Boggis believes that
at an auction sale there is no such thing as something nobody

wants. He might even have sold Eve if she had not been Fine Art, and thus Mr. Wherry-Smith's.

He proves it in the last lot of all that comes under his hammer. A quantity of garden equipment has gone, at reasonable prices, and assemblies of odds and ends – "job lots" is the term – for reasons that can only be known to the buyers. This final lot is made up of a hand lawnmower in poor order, a trousers press, a quantity of burlap wrapping, and a zebra-skin rug. It goes to a farmer for eighteen shillings and, as Mr. Boggis will tell you, every eighteen shillings is eighteen shillings you didn't have before.

By five o'clock the sale is over. Brochwel cannot bear to walk again through the empty rooms; the house has the ravaged, unswept air of a place that has been looted by an army; nothing remains but odds and ends of rubbish in corners. He finds Old Rose in what used to be the Servants' Hall, empty now except for the old woman who is weeping into her apron. She is to be the caretaker until a new owner is found, and she will live at her cottage down near the gate with her nephew, who is not a good fellow, and exploits her. Brochwel cannot think of anything to say, but he takes Rose in his arms and kisses her wildly rouged cheeks, and walks the two miles back to Trallwm.

(15)

Brochwel is staying at the Green Man. He drinks a couple of whiskies and then resigns himself to the dinner; some sort of unidentifiable warm flesh, vegetables cooked to mush, and stewed prunes with chemical custard to conclude the feast. The vile coffee – gravy colouring and hot stale beer, it might be – is an extra, but he has it because it is expected of him. He is, after all, the gentleman who has come all the way from America to close up Belem

Manor. The Manor has figured in the history of Trallwm in the past, and the inn has no doubt that it will rise again after some temporary lull in its fortunes. Though who will keep it up in the real old style, as the late Rhodri Gilmartin has done, is certainly a problem. Rhodri Gilmartin had a very long purse, no doubt of it. Gave to everything, and his annual lawn-party – plum cake and strawberries unlimited for the old men and women from the Union (no longer called "the workus") was famous. Had a real feeling for the workus, had Mr. Gilmartin. This gentleman, his son, will certainly be very rich.

Brochwel knows for a certainty that he will be nothing of the kind. Two governments will contend and at length make some sort of agreement about how much "the grim wolf with privy paw" – the unappeasably covetous tax-gatherers – will demand, and how much will be left over for Rhodri Gilmartin's heir. They will probably not despoil him utterly. They will leave him a few thousands, but not many. If only Rhodri could have contrived to die in Canada, some sort of case against the highest British taxes might have been made. But he did not. He died at Belem, and Trallwm gave him a splendid funeral, at which the Mayor spoke eloquently of this native son who had after so many years come back to the place of his birth. Rhodri, if he were aware of that (and I, the looker-on, think it very likely that he *was* aware of it), would have liked his funeral very much. Everybody who was anybody in the county was present, and the Earl, though too old and unable now to venture out on a wet day, had sent a handsome tribute of flowers; had he not, during the past few years, been on excellent terms with the dead man? The boy who had run to open the gate for the Earl's Countess had quite disappeared in the prosperous man who restored Belem Manor to something very like its Victorian splendour.

Brochwel was not greedy for money, but how many people are utterly indifferent to it? He needed nothing, and if he had inherited all his father's wealth he would undoubtedly have continued to be a professor of Eng-Lang-and-Lit because that was what he knew, what he liked best, and what afforded him refuge from aspects of life he did not want to face. That was indeed the land of which he was a country-man. Not for him the struggle, the hero-journey of old Rho-dri's life, in which so many external enemies had been met and defeated. His struggles were within, and it was Rhodri and Malvina who had chosen the battleground. The Old World, or the New? Was it utterly imperative that there should be a final decision? Was Eng-Lang-and-Lit really a solution?

Brochwel leaves the inn, and in the dusk he rambles through the Trallwm streets, and although he does not know it, they are not greatly changed from the days when Rhodri ran, and revelled and rollicked in them as a boy. The dreadful "shuts" have been somewhat improved, though they are still not desirable residences. Automobiles now spread their per-vasive stench through the streets where, in Rhodri's time, the stench of horse dung was just as pervasive. At the Town Cross the old, battered stone pillar, part monument and part pump, still marks the heart, though not the centre, of the town. The Mansion House, where Samuel Gilmartin had lorded it among his prosperous companions, is now the premises of a county office, but its pillared entrance has not changed. Brochwel walks down the Salop Road – so called because it comes from Shropshire and is thus Salopian – and looks at the humble shop where, a lifetime ago, Walter Gilmartin and Janet and their children, and as many Jenkinses and other Gilmartins as could thrust themselves through the easy door, had played out their domestic tragedy, or melo-drama, or farce, or whatever you choose to call it.

Nobody appears to live "over the shop," for the win-dows are lightless and uncurtained. Probably the stationer who now rents the premises keeps extra stock up there. It was behind those windows that Janet Gilmartin – she who had been Janet Jenkins – read Ossian to her scarcely comprehend-ing children. And yet, when Rhodri was a crusading political writer, had not some tropes and rhythms of Ossian given substance to his prose? Who ever knows what children hear and make their own forever? Did not Brochwel himself sometimes hear his voice urging his students not to leave completion of their work "till the last dog is hung"? A phrase of Malvina's, that was, coming from who knows what Vermuelen past, when it referred to the Mohawk Feast of the White Dog, about which the white man knew nothing, but where they suspected that dogs met a harsh, ritual quietus. Well, well; he must not walk the streets of Trallwm till the last dog was hung; he must get back to the Green Man, and try to rest before setting out tomorrow on his return journey to Canada.

To Canada. To familiarity and his own sort of ease in life. To Nuala whom he loved with all his heart, and now and then told her so. To Nuala who had healed the wound left by Julia, though nobody could erase the scar. How painful it had been! During one of their many wretched scenes of parting (for he never had the resolution or the good sense to break the thing off abruptly) he had so far sunk as to complain of the way she had used him. "Surely in things of this sort it's the man's job to look out for himself?" she had said. It was only one of many observations of hers that made it plain how impossible it would be for him to confide the best of his life to such a person. But he must not begin that old story now, or he would get no sleep. And if he was to sleep, he must first read. Must. It was a lifelong habit, not to be broken now.

The Green Man, like virtually all inns, hotels, motels, lodging-houses and places of their kind, has no idea that anybody reads in bed. Bed, to the innkeeping trade, is a place for fornication or for sleep. This is why people like Brochwel develop a contortionist's talent that enables them to read in extraordinary positions, in light which, by the time it reaches the page, is not more than twenty-five watts in strength. With his head where his feet should be, with his book held high and askew, Brochwel settles himself to read Browning, his professional companion, his enthusiasm, his philosophy and, in the lingo of professors of Eng-Lang-and-Lit, his "field." He reads *Shop*.

> *Because a man has shop to mind*
> *In time and place, since flesh must live,*
> *Needs spirit lack all life behind,*
> *All stray thoughts, fancies fugitive,*
> *All loves except what trade can give?*

Browning was right, as he usually was. A life spent in "trade" like that of Walter, or a life spent in journalism, which was half-trade half-profession, like Rhodri, need not be mired in trade alone. Brave thoughts and high aspirations can rise above almost anything. Had not the wretches in the Nazi prison camps kept hearts and souls above their torment by clinging to their philosophy or their religion?

He had taken leave of Rose, good old soul, in the empty Servants' Hall at Belem. It was a room he never entered if he could help it, because of a story old Rhodri had told him on one of his visits to the Manor.

"I was a boy of twelve, I suppose, and I was here in the Servants' Hall with my father, who had come to measure the menservants for their annual livery outfit. I remember I was eating a big slice of bread and jam the cook had given me, and my father was kneeling on the floor, measuring the inside leg of a groom, a miserable bandy-legged fellow with a boozer's nose. He pushed the Pater with his foot – not hard, not a kick, but a nasty nudge – and said, 'Make haste, tailor, I haven't got all day.' And the Pater looked abashed, but said nothing. I put down my bread and jam and swore in my heart that some day I would be somebody important, and never – *never* – would I speak like that to anybody. Never be insolent to a man who had to serve me. And I never have."

No indeed. Stray thoughts, fancies fugitive, had illuminated his life. As indeed stray thoughts, fancies fugitive, had illuminated the life of his wife, though he had never understood her any better than she had understood him.

They were held together by a loyalty which was more than love – which may, in fact, be the distillation of love. He had taken the light way because, as a man of his time and place, it lay within his grasp. She had taken the dark way because, as a woman of her time and place, there was no other way for a woman of her imagination, her intuition, her witch-like sensibility and vision of life. Between them they had made Brochwel the queasy but resolute creature that he was.

He thought he was reading, but he was musing – not thinking, not deciding anything, not seeing anything afresh but just bobbing up and down in the dark tarn of his feelings. Of course he fell asleep and Browning fell forward on his face and woke him up sufficiently for him to extinguish the feeble interference with darkness that the inn called electric light, and sleep again.

The last thing I see in the film is Belem Manor, its Victorian Gothic turrets and vaulted windows picked out in dim moonlight. It sleeps, too, and when it wakes again it will not be a Gilmartin who kisses it back into life.

(16)

ON THE SCREEN in the usual white print, appears the formal closure

THE END?

And then, suddenly a message –

NOTHING IS FINISHED TILL ALL IS FINISHED

VII

...To the Wind's Twelve Quarters
I Take My Endless Way

THE FESTIVAL IS OVER. Not just the wondrous festival of rediscovered films that Allard Going has been gloating over in the pages of *The Colonial Advocate*, but my personal festival that ran beside it, visible to me alone, and significant to me alone. But is my festival over? What of that gnomic conclusion – "Nothing is finished till all is finished"? What am I to make of that?

More film? I dread it. My festival has taken me into the past, though not really very far into the past, of my own forebears. Taken me into the eighteenth century, which is no distance in the procession of human history, but far enough to tell me more about the American strand and the Old Country strand which, in me, were woven into what is now indisputably a Canadian weftage. Given substance to people, many of whom were strangers to me, or at best names to which no special character attached, but whose courage and resource, loyalty even to the point of self-destruction, crankiness and meanness, despair and endurance are now known to me, and arouse my admiration, my pity and – I must say it, strange as it seems to me – my love. Yes, love, for I know more

about them than I suppose they had ever known about themselves, just as I now see I have known so little about myself,
have so scantly loved myself.

Love myself? I have never thought of such a thing. It
seems indecent. My parents, kind and indulgent as they were
to me, would never have proposed love of self as a possible or
desirable state of mind. They were both – are both, I should
say, for they live and I am dead as the world thinks of death –
of Puritan strain. My father, a highly educated man and, like
so many highly educated men of our time, still an undevel-
oped child in matters of the spirit, is nevertheless unswer-
vingly honourable and the Methodist strain in him persists as
a strong, if desiccated and almost wizened, morality; he is a
man with a powerful sense of what he calls "the decent
thing," and he can always be depended on to do it, even
when it costs him dear. My mother, brought up a Catholic in
the harsh Irish tradition, is at root much the same sort of
creature. They abandoned religion, the comfort and joys of
religion as well as its night-terrors and absurdities, but its
morality lives on without any emollient faith. It is a morality
into which no thought of self-love ever intrudes, and even
self-approval is looked upon with humorous suspicion. Self-
respect – ah yes, that is another thing, a cooler thing.

From them, from the atmosphere of my home, I took on
this condition of mind without ever giving it much serious
thought. Not love, but a sort of amused tolerance, has been
my conscious attitude toward myself. By love, of course, I
mean charity and forgiveness, not a foolish egotism. In my
life I suppose I was not a bad fellow. Of course I had my
lapses, rooted in stupidity rather than evil, but on the whole I
tried to do the decent thing. But now it is as if my heart has
been painfully enlarged, and in this swollen heart I must find
a place for all that I have seen of my forebears, their vanities,
their cruelties, their follies, which were, at least in part,
explained and made to seem inevitable because of their circumstances. And, in addition to these, something splendid –

the stuff of life, indeed. Will the world that I no longer share think of me with love?

Is it all gone, this love and understanding of those who are no more? I don't hope for primitive or bygone things. I don't want anybody to light candles on my grave on All Souls' Day, or sob for me on a midnight pillow. But will they include me in their charity? In the light of what I now see, the chances are slim.

(2)

WHAT DO I now see? My wife, sitting opposite her agent in his office. The room is meant to look like business premises, but there are too many piles of dusty typescripts on a side table, too many unsightly photographs of authors (men scruffy and dishevelled, in turtle-necks and jeans, women, many of decidedly unattractive mien, wearing huge spectacles, some holding cats), too much literary mess and too powerful a stench of good, but pungent, cigars.

"I have to be careful, Rache. If we rush this book onto the stands, isn't it going to look too calculating, as if I hadn't really undergone a terrible experience, and was just out for money?"

"Esme, you've got to understand, this is why an agent is your best friend. An agent can see things you can't. An agent can see ahead to the paperback, the lecture tour, maybe – if things are handled right – a really big TV series, enlarging the book, making it even more personal, grabbing an audience of millions. It's a very fluid picture."

"Well – do you think I could handle that?"

"Esme, you don't need me to tell you that you can, and you will. Look at yourself objectively. I know it's hard, but you're an intelligent woman and you can hack it. What are you? First of all, I don't need to tell you, you're a looker – "

"Oh Rache, that's nonsense – "

"Baby, listen to Old Rache. He knows what a looker is in modern-day terms, and you're it. Those pictures in the fashion magazines, those models – grouchy-looking girls, some with crazy squints, some that look as if they'd poison you if they bit you – but hair! Jesus, the hair! And the bones! This is the day of the Anorexic Look, but with a big bazoom. A really great pair of maracas – and you've got 'em – "

"Oh, Rache, business is business – "

"You don't have to tell me! I'm being completely objective. You've got everything it takes, and if you'll just let me handle it, Christ knows where it will end."

"Well – if you say so."

"I do say so. I can see the thing in a way you can't. Don't imagine I've forgotten your bereavement, under those terrible circumstances. Jesus – Gil lying there, covered with blood, and you shrinking back against your pillow as the murderer makes good his escape! Do you think I've forgotten that? Maybe in the TV series they might even have a re-enacted scene of the murder – not you acting, of course, because that would be in the worst possible taste and would alienate the over-thirties – but enough actualization to hammer home the immensity of your tragedy."

"It would be powerful, as you say. But of course I'd just do the talking. Right? Wearing a dark ensemble. Not black. That would be coming on too strong as a widow for modern viewers."

"And your hair down. You'd better start growing it right now. The longer the better."

"It's fairly long now."

"Get it longer. There's time, if you're a quick grower. But the first thing is to get the book out. I've put out feelers – "

"So soon?"

"Not a bit too soon. You forget how long it takes to get a book out nowadays. Even on a rush job, it'll be months. So get busy on the script and don't waste a minute. The thing could go cold on the plate if we don't move fast. This outline you've given me – it's okay but it lacks something. I want another two or three days to decide what, but I'll find out, and I'll be in touch with you at once. It doesn't have to be a long book, you know. You're not writing *War and Peace*. A hundred and twenty-five pages, well spaced out, with a socko cover, and a really great picture of you on the back. So go home now, Esme. Take a deep breath, and then get going on the word-processor. We have no time to lose."

"Well Rache, if you say so – "

"I do say so. And don't think I'm rough. I bleed for you, baby. But getting down to the writing will comfort you like nothing else could. Writing is the best therapy when your heart's broken."

"My heart's all right. It's my digestion, really."

"Of course. Shock. Bereavement goes right to the gut. So write! That's the therapy for you."

"I suppose really – maybe it's presumptuous to say it – I suppose really I'm doing it for others."

"For other broken hearts. For other bereaved people. Exactly. That's the way you've got to look at it. I'll get through to you early next week."

(3)

"CALL IT A WHIM, if you wish. But I'm sure you understand how imperious a whim can be. I don't know that I could face it, otherwise." The Sniffer has assumed an air of gravity.

"You mean that if you have to move into Gil's office you refuse to take over Gil's job?"

"Not *refuse*. No, no Chief – I didn't mean *refuse*. It's a

remarkable opportunity to shape the Entertainment Department into a coherent whole. Poor Gil hadn't much idea of
coherence."

"I wouldn't go too far with that, if I were you. The
Department is pretty well received just as it stands."

"Oh, quite. Quite. Gil had a touch; I don't deny it. But
there are things that could be done. So you see – "

"What I see, Al, is that you want Gil's job, but you make
it a condition that you won't occupy his office – "

"It's full of his stuff. He was a terrible magpie, you
know."

"Maintenance can clear it out in half a day."

"Yes, certainly. But his ambience will remain."

"I don't understand. What ambience?"

"You know – his feeling, the essence of him that has
been caught up in the walls, the drapes–"

"Maintenance can give it a coat of paint. Dry–clean the
drapes."

"I'm not getting through to you, Chief, I'm afraid."

"No, frankly Al, you're not. Tell me – what in hell do
you really want?"

"I really want an office that isn't full of the spirit of a
dead man."

"It's news to me that our offices have that kind of spirit.
You talk as if this place was Dracula's Castle. My God, Al, it's
hardly been built seven years. The editorial private offices are
all the same. But I can see that something is troubling you,
and I'll go a reasonable distance to help you. If you don't want
Gil's office, what office do you want?"

"I'd rather thought of McWearie's."

"If you're worrying about atmosphere, McWearie's
room practically *is* Dracula's Castle. I never saw so much
peculiar junk in my life. That skull on his bookcase! But he
does a first-class job. His series on the ordination of women –
got a Newspaper Award. Why disturb him?"

"As a matter of fact, if I were to take over Entertainment,
I'd like to talk to you about McWearie. He doesn't really

belong in Entertainment. I'd be glad to see him moved to another department."

"And you'd start by hoofing him out of his office. Isn't that a bit rough?"

"His office is at the end of the corridor. Quiet. Just the place for thoughtful work. That's what I'd like."

"Well – I'm damned if I'm going to tell McWearie that you have a whim for his office, and he has to get out. I can't treat staff that way. The Guild could kill me. He'd have a very legitimate grievance, and we don't need grievances in senior writers. But I'll tell you what I'll do. *You* go to McWearie and tell him very nicely – pretty please – that you're going to succeed Gil as head of Entertainment, and you'd be grateful if he could see his way to let you have his office, for which you have a special soft spot. If he agrees – all right. If not – nothing doing. But no iron hand, Al. If Hugh says No, it's No. And don't use my name, because I want no part of it."

So this was how it was! I didn't in the least mind that the Editor-in-Chief was appointing my successor so soon after my death. A daily paper is exactly that – daily – and there is no time for sentiment in such matters. That he was appointing Randal Allard Going did not greatly surprise me, because he is the most likely candidate on the staff as it stands. Going's inherent odiousness did not stop him from being a pretty good journalist. I suppose I have a right to dislike him personally, considering that he has seduced my wife and murdered me in consequence. These are not winning traits in a man. Now he wants to get rid of McWearie and grab his office.

The meeting between them soon lost any pretence of amiability.

"So what it comes down to, Mr. Going, is that you want my office, because you have a fancy for it, and for no better reason."

"I've explained the reason. If I am to do the work of Entertainment Editor, I can't do it from my present office which I share with four other critics."

"But you can do it from Gil's old office,"

"I've told you, I don't like Gil's old office."

"It's a senior man's office. It has a place for a secretary. Where's she to go if you come way down here?"

"She isn't – wasn't Gil's secretary only; she's secretary to the department. She can stay where she is."

"I see. Well, the long and short of it is that I don't choose to move, Mr. Going."

"Hugh, we are going to have to work together. Inevitably I must be in the driver's seat, and I think I'd like the driver's seat to be right here, in this office. Can't we settle this thing amicably?"

"Meaning settle it your way? What's the alternative? Would you like my resignation, perhaps?"

"Now Hugh – remember the old saying: 'Never threaten resignation unless you are prepared to carry it through.'"

"What makes you think I wouldn't carry it through?"

"I don't want you to do anything rash."

"I won't, never fear. Have you talked to the Chief about this?"

"That's beside the point – "

"No it isn't. I'll bet anything you did and he's said he'll have nothing to do with it, and you must get it if you can. Well, I've answered that, Mr. Going."

"Hugh – can't we be friends?"

"What for? I'm paid to be a colleague, not a friend. I was a friend of Gil's, but that was another thing. Because you're standing in a dead man's shoes, don't expect to take on his friends, as well."

Oh Hugh – you shouldn't have said that! But when your Highland blood is up you say cruel things, and you don't understand how dangerous "dead man's shoes" is, in these circumstances. You've made an enemy of the Sniffer, and I can understand why, but it is a mistake, all the same.

(4)

THE SNIFFER IS in no condi-
tion for a professional row. He seeks Esme, as he has done
rather too often since the funeral. She has not been coming
into the *Advocate* offices. Although she is entitled to whatever
Bereavement Leave she wants, she has missed only one week
with her column – a week during which the news pages have
kept her name well in the public eye. She has let the Chief
know that she will have a column ready for the week to come.
This is gallant. It is also assurance that her readers will have
no time to forget her. The Sniffer has called her every day, and
every day she has refused to dine with him, and has told him
that he is not to come to her apartment. Surely it would
appear simply as the condolence of a family friend, he pleads.
She thinks otherwise.

This time his pleadings are so pitiful that she consents,
and when they meet at a quiet table in Le Rendezvous I am the
invisible third party, and I find it a delightful evening.

"You can't imagine what I've been going through,
Esme."

"Can't I? Do you suppose I've been having a high old
time?"

"No, no; but you know what I mean."

"I can guess. But I don't think you know what *I* mean."

"Dearest one – "

"Al! Cool it, will you. Just keep it on a friendly footing.
Don't you know that waiters have big ears?"

"Esme – dear friend – our positions are rather different – "

"Perhaps not as different as you imagine."

"Meaning? – Oh, no. You have no guilt in this affair."

"There are other things than guilt."

"You're being mysterious."

"And you're being self-centred."

"*I* am! Listen – it's all over the office that you are going to write a series of articles on bereavement. Fine! You're in a great position to do just that. But I'm a writer, don't forget, and I know how much objectivity and calculation it will take to do a series and do it right. You aren't just going to spill your guts. You're going to do it with very tidy journalistic calculation."

"Therapy for a broken heart."

"What! That doesn't sound like you."

"It isn't me. But that's beside the point. There are considerations you don't know about."

"Such as?"

"I haven't been quite myself lately."

"Not surprising."

"That's what my doctor said. He was all sympathy. But he said he'd like to run two or three routine tests, and he phoned me yesterday."

"Oh, darling! I've been unforgivably inconsiderate! You're ill."

"Not ill, exactly. I'm pregnant."

The scene gives way to an interval of low comedy here, because the Sniffer does a very complete job of what was called, in my boyhood, the Nose Trick. He whoofed upward through a mouthful of the Cabernet Sauvignon, sprayed a good deal of it over the table, but shot quite enough through his nostrils to make him howl with pain. Two waiters rush to his aid. As Esme mops her frock with dignified restraint, they beat the Sniffer on the back and offer him a glass of water, but without much effect. He continues to cough and blow his nose, which hurts him abominably. The Sniffer is one of those men who always blows his nose one nostril at a time – poof-poofty-poof – and he does so now, and mops his streaming eyes, and tries to apologize through involuntary little yelps of pain. It takes some time to calm him. The *maître d'hôtel* hastens to the table with a measure of cognac, and urges the Sniffer to sip it with the uttermost caution. Another tablecloth is brought, and deftly laid. At last the helpers and servers go away, the other diners stop staring, and the couple regain their privacy.

"You said – ?"

"I said I was pregnant."

"But – but – "

"Yes, I know. I suppose I'd been a little bit forgetful about The Pill. One gets tired of that nagging obligation, you know. So there it is."

"And there we are."

"And there I am."

"Oh, me too. *Mea culpa, mea culpa, mea maxima culpa!*" The Sniffer beats his breast, ritually, like a priest at the altar.

"For God's sake shut up! Let's not have another scene."

"But I'm in this, too."

"No, Al. Not you."

"Esme – what are you saying? Who else could it be?"

"My husband, you fool!"

"You don't mean to sit there and tell me that while we – you and I – were lovers, you were allowing Gil to – "

"Of course I was! Do you suppose that because of you I would put Gil on the Indian List? I was very fond of Gil."

Oh, Esme, you can't believe how overjoyed I am to hear you say that! My dear, dear wife, how I love you at this moment! And – and Anna, and Elizabeth and Janet and Malvina and Rhodri – yes, and I suppose the McOmishes, will all, in some measure, live on. I see the continuance of life as I never did while I was a part of it.

The Sniffer is utterly unmanned. He is eating nothing, though Esme is getting through a very respectable meal.

After a pause he says, in a low voice, "You'll be attending to that, of course?"

"Attending to what?"

"Your condition. It's not a problem nowadays."

"I don't follow you."

"Esme – this pregnancy. The sooner you have it terminated, the better."

"Better for who?"

"For us. Then later, when and if we marry, we can start with a clean slate. Presuming we want children, of course."

"When and if! Al, we might as well get this straight right now; I'm not going to marry you. That's the craziest thing I've ever heard. Do you want to marry me?"

"I have an overwhelming obligation to you. And I'm certainly not going to back off from it. I must take care of you, but I don't want to take care of a child that might just possibly be Gil's."

"It is Gil's. Do you think I can't count? The doctor says he thinks it's about ten weeks. Well – ten weeks ago you were in Europe for a month, casing the world theatre and telling the *Advocate* readers how lousy it was. Now look; we had better get this straight. I'm going to have this child. It's a perfectly okay child, lawfully begotten by my now dead husband. What used to be called a posthumous child. Is that clear?"

"Esme, do you really want a child?"

"I don't know, but I'll find out. And this child makes all the difference to the articles I'm going to write. Rache Hornel says it's the cherry on the cake. And you don't come into it, except perhaps as jolly old Uncle Al, who turns up with a teddy-bear once in a while."

"Esme, you're being very unkind. Because of this mess we're in – "

"You're in. I'm fine."

"Have it your own way. But there was something else, you know. Something you seem to have forgotten. I was going to try to interest some television people in you."

"I think you have, Al. By conking poor Gil. Now – if you can catch the waiter's eye – "

(5)

RACHE HORNEL IS NOT one of your simple, businesslike literary agents who gives advice only when asked for it. Writers are creative, he says, but they need the creativity of the business man, the man of long vision and wide knowledge of the world, if they are to achieve what he calls their full potential. Rache learned his craft as an agent in the place he always calls L.A. and he has brought the spirit of L.A. to Toronto, where it does not quite fit. If Rache could have been at the side of Virginia Woolf she would never have confided to her diary that she thought a sale of five thousand copies very flattering; Rache would have developed her until she was writing for the movies, with a weekly salary in five figures, ten per cent of it for him, the creative entrepreneur. I am aware that he is shining the full glare of his creativity on Esme, and I am present at the luncheon – Rache liked to do big things over food – where he bursts his inspiration full on her.

"But Rache, I don't see this as me at all."

"It's the new you, Esme. The Esme you've never explored."

"But it's the occult. Not a bit my thing. I've always been very feet-on-the-ground."

"This is feet on another kind of ground. I'm not proposing some teacup reader or back-street medium. Mrs. Salenius is the best there is. State-of-the-art, I swear it."

"You've talked with her?"

"I've visited her. Put our case. No names mentioned, naturally. She'll see what she can do. She makes no promises."

"What is she going to attempt?"

"Communication with Gil. A message from the Beyond."

"She isn't going to try to find out who killed him, is she?"

"Not unless you want it. A message is what she thinks of."

"I don't want to talk about the murder."

"Of course not, baby. Too painful."

"What'll it cost?"

"Nothing. She doesn't take fees. You can make a contribution to the Church, if you wish, and of course we'll wish. Only right."

"What Church?"

"Companionship of Emanuel Swedenborg, Scientist and Seer."

"Golly!"

"It's a split-off from the real Swedenborgian Church. It claims to have gone farther into the thought and vision of Swedenborg."

"Never heard of him. Where did you get hold of this woman?"

"The police."

"The police! I don't want anything to do with the police!"

"Honey, you're talking to Ol' Rache! Would I plough up your heart and make it bleed all over again? But it's through the police I found her. You want a first-rate psychic, you ask the police. They use 'em a lot. You know – a child is lost, and when the cops can't find anything, you read in the papers that they've consulted a psychic. They only call on Mrs. Salenius in first- class crime."

"God! Does she use a crystal ball or what?"

"I don't know. But she's impressive, mostly because she isn't at all impressive. Baby, do you think I'd get you into anything we couldn't handle?"

So Esme agrees to go with Rache to visit Mrs. Salenius. Their purpose is to see if they can get in touch with my spirit, and find out what I have to say to my sorrowing wife. A few useful quotes for the book, with any luck. Comfort for the bereaved. After all, I was a journalist and ought to have a professional sense of the quotable. Rache sees it as a tremendous coup that will, in his phrase, "beef up" the book; what with this splendid bonus of the posthumous child, and me brought back from the tomb for a few classy quotes, it's going to be a knock-out. Esme is dubious, but has faith in Ol' Rache. I shall certainly be there. I never attended a seance in life, but I have no intention of missing this one in death. I hope to play an important role. Not perhaps for the benefit of Esme's book but in some form of revenge that I cannot foresee.

(6)

THE MEETING IS set up for the following Friday night. Esme now knows who Swedenborg was: not, as she had at first supposed, some American shaman big in the South and at Presidential prayer breakfasts, but an important eighteenth-century Swedish scientist, founder of crystallography, who foresaw nebular theory, magnetic theory, and such popular modern gadgets as the machine-gun and the aeroplane; also, as a physicist of unquestioned reputation, the propounder of a theory of the Universe as a fundamentally spiritual structure and a spiritual world populated exclusively by dead human beings, grouped in coherent societies. An embarrassing figure indeed, in a scientific world that wanted no truck or trade with spiritual matters. Esme, a good journalist, has made herself an instant authority on Swedenborg by an hour or two with the *Advocate*'s collection of encyclopaedias. Not that she is convinced. Not a bit of it. But she feels the agnostic's unwilling pull toward the gnostic, and she is curious to see Mrs. Salenius.

As Rache had said, Mrs. Salenius is not remarkable; she is a somewhat morose, stout woman, who speaks English in a quiet, regretful voice, the voice, as it were, of Garbo, speaking through a mouthful of chocolate.

She lives in an unfashionable old quarter of Toronto, west of Spadina Avenue, in one of those high-gabled, red-faced houses that Esme recognizes as the frequent subject of the unfashionable, but evocative, painter Franck.

"Not a seance, dear. We don't use that word. Just a special sort of stillness. An intent listening, you might call it. But I can't lead you until I know a few more facts than Mr. Hornel has told me. Your husband's full name, and what he did in the world, and when he died. The way he died isn't clear to me. Take your time. We're not going to do anything distressing."

Mrs. Salenius does not spend much on electric light, and she turns off what little there is in her dingy living-room, leaving two candles burning on a table.

The preliminaries over – and I am somewhat surprised by Esme's brief, factual but selective description of me and my murder by an unknown assailant – Mrs. Salenius' composes herself as if to sleep, in a large armchair.

"Be perfectly at ease, friends. Don't try hard to *do* anything. Just be very quiet and think about Connor Gilmartin. Think of him kindly, and with love."

Esme and Rache do their best. He never knew me, and he cannot keep his hopes in abeyance. Rache wants me to say something for the book, and it is about the book that he is really thinking. A block-buster. Something as long on the best-seller list as – he cannot contain his hopes – as long as Stephen Hawking's *Brief History of Time*. He sees the words on the compelling jacket: "Did my dead husband speak to me? I am a rational being, and I swear that it was so. But the message was for our unborn child."

Esme is honestly trying to relax. She is not bad at physical relaxation. Has studied it in books, and can ease her bodily tensions quite satisfactorily. But she has never given a thought to anything resembling mental relaxation; her mind is jumping between doubt and credulity and – she cannot deny it – fear. Am I going to spill the beans?

Most certainly I am. If I can. But how? Like the dead

lover in that song my grandmother loved, as sung by Emilio De Gogorza?

> *And like an angel bending down above you,*
>   *To breathe into your ear –*

Whose ear? Esme's ear? Mrs. Salenius's furry ear hidden under a fruzz of grey hair? For the first time since my death, I find that I am wholly at a loss. I decide on Mrs. Salenius. I get as near to her as I can – and that is very near indeed, in my present state – and do my best.

The murderer, I say – but unheard – the murderer was my wife's lover.

Mrs. Salenius gives no sign that she has heard anything. I realize that Mrs. Salenius does not pay much attention to crime news, and my name means nothing to her. All she knows is what Rache Hornel has told her. Rache does not know who killed me. She is in a trance, or asleep. Now and then she whimpers, quietly.

Am I not trying hard enough? As a spirit, communicating with the living, ought I to use a heightened language? Something along the lines of Hamlet's Father?

"List, list, O list – " I say, and immediately feel like a fool. I am not cut out for this sort of thing. But I am not a quitter. I try again. "I am Gilmartin's spirit/Doomed for a certain time to walk the night,/And for the day confined to fast in fires" – (a lie, but what am I to do?) – "Till the foul crimes done in my days of nature/Are burnt and purged away – "

Oh, the hell with it! This debases Shakespeare, and debases me, and is far above the level of this front-parlour mummery, and infinitely beyond the hysterical response of the Sniffer when I caught him in bed with my wife. Death does *not* cast a mantle of importance over folly. For the first time since my death I feel abjection and defeat.

But Mrs. Salenius is speaking, in a strange voice, unlike her own, and certainly not like mine.

"Dear heart, I pray thee, be not fearful," she says. "Grieve not for me. I am beyond pain, beyond care, but not beyond love. Love me now, as you loved me before our parting. Peace. Peeeeace!" Mrs. Salenius extends the word astonishingly.

Rache is wide-eyed, swallowing his spit. "Ask him who it was," he hisses.

Esme starts forward in her chair, as if to forbid any such question, but she is too late for Mrs. Salenius; she speaks now with greater determination, and in a stronger voice.

"Do not seek vengeance," she says. "Vengeance is of the world that I have left behind, for the world of the spirit. The man must live with his own soul. Do not rejoice in the burden of another's soul."

"Is that supposed to be my husband's voice?" says Esme. "Not a bit like him. He never carried on like that."

"I am only a humble instrument, dear," Mrs. Salenius says, without opening her eyes. "I am not an impersonator. I speak only as the message comes to me. Be quiet please. Connor Gilmartin may have more to say to us."

Connor Gilmartin certainly has much to say and I am boiling to say it. Who or what is putting this stuff into Mrs. Salenius's head? She is not making it up, that I know for a certainty. It is some sort of party line, some established opinion, arising from the Swedenborgian teaching, undoubtedly. But it seems to me that in addition somebody else is getting to Mrs. Salenius as I cannot do. I am as near as I can crowd to her waxy left ear, and I am hissing the name of Randal Allard Going with all the intensity I can muster, but so far as Mrs. Salenius is concerned I am utterly unavailing. She speaks again.

"Do not grieve for me. Grieve only for the unhappy man who brought about my death. I am secure in a world where we shall most certainly meet, in due season. It is a world of ineffable joy."

What do such people mean by "ineffable joy," I wonder? I could tell Mrs. Salenius a thing or two about life after death.

My observation and involvement with my forebears, as they have appeared in a series of films, has not been ineffable joy; I have lived with them through every vicissitude, felt every reverse of fortune, swung in the remorseless enantiodromia between good luck and bad, modest virtue and moderate vice; I have endured with Anna's resolute courage, known the simplicity of Janet's faith and the dark irony with which Malvina met the world; shrunk from the witch-like denial of physical love that gave Virginia domination over an artist-artisan; sensed the profundity of Thomas's belief and the debilitated philosophy of my own father; shared in the submission to duty of Walter and the triumphant victory over destiny of Rhodri: these things do not constitute "ineffable joy" but a sense of life more poignant and more powerful than anything I ever knew when I was a living man. "The stuff of life to knit me/Blew hither . . ." Yes; the poet knew.

But is there to be no vengeance? I cannot swallow that. I know a thing or two about ghosts, because I grew up with all the best ghosts in English Literature; my father used to tell me about them, when I was a small boy, and I loved the uncanniness and fear, as happy, well-protected children do. Ghosts come back to the living because they seek vengeance, which is another name for justice. Mrs. Salenius and her Swedenborgian congeries of bland spooks is not for me. Vengeance I shall have, and I shall bring it about myself.

How Esme and Rache Hornel take leave of Mrs. Salenius I do not know, but I suspect that they bought a good many copies of dense works by Swedenborg, in addition to leaving a money gift. What, I wonder, will Ol' Rache make of *Arcana Coelestia*, if he deigns even to look inside it?

I am off in search of Randal Allard Going, and I burn with the fury of my defeat in Mrs. Salenius's front parlour. I find him in the *Advocate* offices, where he sits at his desk, pecking rather ineptly at the word-processor he has not fully mastered.

Al is miserable. I know that, and so does everyone who comes near him. His managing editor thinks it is because he has not yet found a way of ousting McWearie from his office. His colleagues – Fine Art, Literature, Music, in the fleshy manifestations of the critics who share an office with him – think it is because he is wondering if he can handle his new job; in their dark hearts they are rather hoping that he can't. The secretaries think he is grieving for Connor Gilmartin, whom he never seemed to care for greatly while he lived, but whose death had affected him so painfully at the funeral.

I know that what ails him is guilt.

He has no religion. Brought up in a home of solid financial substance, he was sent to a boys' school famous for its progressive ideas and the open-mindedness of its headmaster and staff. Boys from all sorts of well-to-do families went to that school, and to the headmaster it was obvious that such a complex of rich reputed Christians, Muslims, Hindus, Jews, and Reformed Confucians could not be instructed in any sort of belief that would not step on somebody's well-shod toes and provoke crusty letters from disaffected parents. But some Preparation for Life, as the headmaster called it, was necessary, and so there was instruction in Ethics. The beauty of ethics is that nobody can be perfectly certain about what it includes or even what it means. But the headmaster talked about "tacit assumptions," the first of which was Sexual Purity – though in a world expanding as fast as our own, that should not be confused with monogamy, or heterosexuality or any of those outworn notions, and doubtless it was best in such a confusing area to "play it by ear" and try not to hurt anybody, even though that was not always possible if you were to realize yourself to the full. Then there was Charity, which meant giving away the surplus of one's income that was not required for one's own genuine needs; the sticker here was the decision as to how much of one's income should be regarded as surplus, but the headmaster knew that there were charitable agencies everywhere who would be eager to inform you on that point, and grab all they could. Finally, there was Commitment to Intellectual Development, which need not involve any tedious personal effort but which certainly meant giving generously to – well, for instance, to one's Old School, and if anything was left, to one's university for scientific research. Apart from these things, a general benevolence and sensitivity was advocated as becoming to – no, no, not a gentleman, for that word belonged to a shady past of snobbery and privilege – but to a person of education occupying a favoured position in society.

Before our present openness about sex, it was often said that boys picked up their knowledge of sex from the gutter; favoured children like Randal Allard Going found their morality in the gutter, where the out-of-favour ideas are thrown, and one of the things in his gutter morality (which looked very much like the Ten Commandments, ragged, drunk and disorderly) was that murder was a very bad thing. Murder, as his headmaster would have put it in his jocular, friend-of-boys way, was a No-No, because, even if it was part of your need to realize yourself to the full, it hurt some- one else very badly, and indeed irrevocably.

The Sniffer was suffering from a terrible onset of bad conscience, though the headmaster had once said that con- science was probably just the voice of parents or grandpar- ents, who might be dubious guides in a truly modern life. Was it something from the spirit of his revered ancestor, Sir Alured Going, that man who had been Humble without Affectation, Grave without Moroseness, and Cheerfull with- out Levity, that told him now that murder was a crime – except, of course, in a just war? A crime that irrevocably damaged the soul (an entity that the headmaster was careful never to mention by that name).

Though he was trying to write a pithy and well- considered piece about modern film, this was what was surg- ing and seething in a kind of acid indigestion of the mind in Al, when I came to him in the critics' room, where he was working alone; Fine Art, Literature and Music were all else- where doing highly responsible things in their own line.

There he sat, peering miserably at the white print on the green screen, seemingly trying to remember how to spell "indefeasible," but in fact brooding on his guilt. Heartburn of the soul possessed him utterly.

What was I to do? I was no better prepared than Al for the situation in which I found myself. A ghost in search of vengeance – what is it to do in such a world as ours? If only he drove a car – I'm sure I could manage one of those accidents where the car is said to "go out of control." But he is a taxi man.

Like a fool, I did what I have so often done in crises in my experience. Did what I had done when I found Al in bed with my wife, and called him "The Sniffer." I allowed my sense of humour to take charge.

A sense of humour, like every good gift, has a positive and a negative side. As Heraclitus would no doubt have told me, if I had been able to put it to him, its Apollonian scintillant perspicuity, if taken too far, is apt to turn to a Dionysian grossness of folly, as it did now.

I sang. I came as close to the ear of Randal Allard Going as I had come to the ear of the unheeding Mrs. Salenius, and I sang a song which, in my foolishness, seemed to me to fit the case. I sang –

> *The bells of Hell go ting-a-ling-a-ling*
> *For you and not for me;*
> *For me the angels sing-a-ling-a-ling*
> *They've got the goods for me.*
> *O Death where is thy sting-a-ling-a-ling*
> *O grave thy victory?*
> *The bells of Hell go ting-a-ling-a-ling*
> *For you and not for me!*

Was not this pitifully inept, undignified, absurd, vulgar and indefensible? Unworthy of a ghost with any sense of the nobility of death? Guilty on every count. But was it ineffective? Something in Al's posture told me that it was not entirely so. He drooped a little. I sang again, increasing the power.

He drooped a little more.

Overjoyed and hilarious at my success, I sang the song a third time and, so far as I could dance, I danced, derisively, with my thumb to my non-existent nose and my fingers extended, in an ecstasy of contumelious mirth. Rapture! I was getting through to Al, or so it seemed, for he suddenly dropped his head upon the keyboard of his word-processor and wept like – no, not like a child, but like a fool trapped in the web of his folly. A snotty boo-hooing.

He did not weep long. He went to the washroom, bathed his face, put on his hat and coat, took up his loathly walking-stick and left the offices of the *Advocate*.

(7)

WHERE IS THE Sniffer going? It is perhaps two miles from the *Advocate* offices to the University and, as a usual thing, the Sniffer is a taxi man. But he seems to feel that he must walk on this journey, which I sense he regards rather as a penitential pilgrimage. He trudges through the chill of the autumn night, carrying the walking-stick which he now hates, and from time to time, when he passes a street lamp, I notice that he glances apprehensively behind him. Why?

The University of Toronto has a large campus, upon which its constituent colleges and the buildings that house the science faculties are spread in a somewhat inconsistent manner. The Sniffer bears toward the eastern side of the parkland, passes the Pontifical Institute and makes his way to St. Michael's College. Why, I wonder? Why the Catholic part of the university? He does not know precisely where he is going and it is only after some false clues and many enquiries that he finds himself at the door of the private quarters of the redoubtable Father Martin Boyle, the Principal, under the Basilian Order.

The Sniffer expects austerity, priestly reserve. But Father Boyle comes to his door in a track suit, rubbing his head and face vigorously with a towel.

"Come in. You're lucky to catch me. I've been out on my evening run. Have to, you know. Drudge all day at the desk and the classroom, and you must have air or die. Without the run I'd be a dead man in a month. Now, what can I do for you? Mr. Going, is it? Oh yes, I read your stuff. I like to keep up with the movies. Theatre, too. I don't get to the theatre as often as I'd like, but I squeeze in a movie, when I can. Can't bear television. Rubbish, and they all mumble. Now, to what do I owe the honour, as they say?"

"Father, I want to make a confession."

"Ah? Well, let's take it gently. Talk a little first. May I offer you a drink? Rye's all I have, I'm afraid. Soda or the old tap?"

Father Boyle is cool, though genial, and I sense that he has met with strange penitents before. Indeed, Father Boyle is quite famous for his association, nearly twenty years ago, with three villains who had shot four policemen dead in the course of a bank robbery. Father Boyle visited them in prison, discovered that they were all Catholics, and had brought them into a thoroughly penitent frame of mind before he finally accompanied them to the foot of the gallows – for in those days the gallows was still the fate of such people. He was widely admired as a friend of the friendless and I knew that it was the Sniffer's keen sense of drama that had led him to this man. The fine face, the abundant grey hair, the thick black brows, satisfy his drama critic's notion of what a great priest should be.

Talking a little, as Father Boyle understands it, goes on for at least half an hour, during which he has more than one drink, and smokes cigarettes without cease as he listens. But at last he sums up.

"Mr. Going, I am truly sorry for you, and I'll pray for you. But I'm sure you can see that I can't accept what you've told me as a confession. Not as I understand that word. Not something I can hear as a priest listening on God's behalf, and forgiving on His behalf. That's a very special relationship, clearly defined by the Church and undertaken only within the Church. Now you – you've told me you're not even baptized and, although in ordinary circumstances I mightn't take that with desperate seriousness, it does mean that you've never given much thought to things of the spirit, nor has anybody ever done it for you. I don't want to be starchy, but you must understand that the Church has rules, and God has rules, too. So, as I say, I've heard you, and I'm deeply sorry for you, and I'll pray for you. But I can't, in God's name, offer you absolution. Just can't be done."

"Then what am I do to? I'm desperate! My God, I'll kill myself."

"Now, now, now; none o' that. That's piling Pelion on Ossa and heaping sin on sin. You're in sin good and deep right now, so don't add to it. You've got to be serious. Suicide, for all its horror, is, in the last consideration, a frivolity, an attempt to be an exception in the proper order of life. Jumping the queue, so to speak. No, no; you must find something better than that."

"But what? You're rejecting me. I'd hoped for understanding and sympathy."

"All the sympathy and understanding I have, my dear man, is yours, so forget all that foolish talk about rejection; that's newspaper psychology. I'm raking in my mind for something to help you. . . . Wait – there's a thing that's sometimes done in the Orthodox Church that we don't use ourselves, but as you're not of any church or any fixed belief, so far as I can tell, it might work for you."

"Yes – ?"

"Come to think of it, it might be the very thing. Dramatic. It'd appeal to the theatre man inside you."

"I'm asking, as humbly as I can, for help."

"Very well, then. Here it is. Have you an enemy?"

"An enemy? You mean somebody who hates me? Wants to do me down?"

"Somebody who'd break you, if he could get away with it."

"Well – of course there are professional rivals. There's always jealousy. You probably know how literary people are. But as for breaking me – I really can't think of anybody."

"Well, try it from the other side. Is there somebody you hate? Somebody you really detest and loathe and spit on in your heart. Somebody who stands in your way?"

"Ah! Oh well, if you put it like that, I think there is somebody."

"Good. Or rather – bad. Now here's what I'd do if I were an Orthodox priest – which I'm not, of course. I'd tell you to go to that person and bring yourself right down to the very rock bottom of humility, and tell him what you've told me tonight."

"But – but he'd probably turn me over to the police!"

"And you knew I wouldn't! Isn't that it? You wanted forgiveness. You wanted absolution for your crime – because it is a crime and the first crime God ever put his mark on. You've killed a man! You didn't mean it – murderers often don't – but nevertheless you robbed a fellow-creature of the life God gave him, and in doing that you've frustrated God's purpose. Think of that! Cain raised! The worst crime in the book! And you wanted me to keep it under the seal of confession! Now Mr. Going, that's very stupid thinking, and that's trifling with my sacred office. You just wanted me to get you off the hook. I can't. Man, you have no sense of the seriousness of your position. You're just fussing about your reputation, and your freedom, though in these days you don't have to fuss any longer about your neck. Stop fussing, and think about your immortal soul. It's your burden, not mine, and I can't lift it from you."

(8)

"**S**O IT WAS YOU who killed poor old Gil? All things considered, I'm not surprised."

"You think I look like a murderer?"

"I think you look like a jackass. I'm not surprised, because people who carry nasty things like that concealed weapon of yours usually end up by using them, and that's what you've done, and that's why you're in this mess. Your murder, my wee man, had its beginning the day you laid down good money for that tomfool bit of macho vanity. Oh dear, dear, dear; poor old Gil!"

It is late. Going has walked back from Father Boyle to the *Advocate* office, muttering to himself, now and then bumping into people, because more and more frequently he glances behind him. His state is pitiable, but I do not feel that I am quite the person to pity him. If he had not seen the light on in Hugh McWearie's room, would he ever have found himself in Hugh's visitor's chair? Perhaps not, but Hugh was working late, or musing and smoking late, and the Sniffer acted on impulse, just as he acted on impulse when he struck me down. Already he regrets his impulse, but it is too late to retract his confession.

"So what are you going to do?"

"Going to do? I don't follow you."

"Aren't you going to denounce me? Turn me over to the police?"

"I hadn't thought about that."

"Well – think about it now!"

"You're very hasty, Mr. Going. That's been your trouble. Haste. You were hasty when you struck poor Gil."

"I've told you – it was a wholly unpremeditated act, brought on because he called me by an opprobrious name."

"Now, now – not wholly unpremeditated. As I've tried

to explain, it was premeditated, or at least it became a possibility, when you bought that walking-stick with the bludgeon hidden in it. And as for an opprobrious name, what did you expect? Think, man. He found you in bed screwing his wife."

"No! We weren't – . We hadn't – ."

"Then you were working up to it, I suppose. What is called the foreplay, if I am not mistaken. But you didn't need any foreplay to get that cosh of yours into full working order. What the hell were you doing with it in bed – if it's not indelicate to ask?"

"It wasn't in bed. It was beside the bed. With my clothes."

"I see. That's your reputation, of course. Never seen without your fine stick. Not even when you are in an act of adultery – "

"Oh, for God's sake, McWearie, let's get into the twentieth century!"

"Just where I'm heading, Mr. Going. Just where I'm heading. Was it irresistible passion, or just whiling away the time? Tell me, now – were you and the beauteous Esme in love?"

"I've never been perfectly sure what people mean by that expression."

"I can well believe that. But let's explore it for a few moments. Had you exchanged words of warm admiration? Had she ever, for instance, told you that she preferred you to Gil?"

"I don't know what right you have to ask about that."

"Possibly I presume too far, but I rather thought that what you have just been telling me gave me certain rights that another person wouldn't have. Am I mistaken?"

"Why do you want to know?"

"Because I have a decision to make. The seriousness of your involvement with Mrs. Gilmartin would have a strong bearing on what I do."

"We had become lovers."

"But you weren't in love, is that it? The word lover has taken on a rather technical significance in our time."

"We were exploring the parameters of our relationship."

"Oh, that lovely word! You were measuring and quantifying what you felt for each other before declaring the fact. And that demanded lots of sport in bed, eh?"

"McWearie, you're being very nasty and very puritanical and I am convinced that you are very jealous. Esme is a lovely woman."

"And an ambitious woman. The buzz around the office is that she thinks her beauty and talent would work very well on television, and that you could give her a leg up – if you'll pardon the indelicacy of my expression – in that strange world."

"So what?"

"So this: was her complicity with you what could be called a *quid pro quo*? Or perhaps – pardon me again – a down payment?"

"McWearie, you – you shit!"

"No, not at all, my wee man. Not ever so faintly faecal. But if I am to decide what to do with you, I have to know some things, and my method of investigation is the one I grew up with. My father, you know, was a policeman. Not just your ordinary cop, though he began walking a beat in Edinburgh. But he ended his career as a well-respected Chief Constable of a large Scottish county. He was a good detective – the real thing, you know, not like those fellows in novels. And he was a pragmatist, which he said meant that you had to attribute the lowest motives to everybody, hoping you'd be wrong, of course. So you see I must suppose, just to get to the bottom of things, that Esme was using you, and you were muggins enough to fall for it."

"Could she be so vile?"

"Certainly she could, and what's so vile about it? She's an ambitious woman, and maybe she counted the cost and decided to pay, in a traditional coin. That's a pun, if you missed it. You're not as repulsive as many a ladder an ambitious woman has had to use. Now I understand she has found another ladder, and this one she pays in another kind of coin. An agent, who gets her what she wants and takes his ten per cent."

"That clown Hornel?"

"If she's changed her Harlequin – you, my lad – for a Clown, I suppose it's because he can deliver the goods and you can't. Clowns are very clever fellows."

"My God – *women!*"

"And men. Ambitious people play the game the same way, regardless of sex, and these are liberated times, as I've noticed you say pretty often in your reviews."

"One expects better of women."

"My father never did. *Varium et mutabile semper*, he used to say. He'd had a good Scots education, you see. He'd put it in the vernacular –

> *A windvane changeable – huff puff*
> *Always is a wooman.*

I suppose you've never been the least bit *huff puff* yourself, Mr. Going?"

"She was using me!"

"Had you no suspicion of that?"

The Sniffer is looking very down in the mouth. "That's what we were talking about," he says, at last.

"On the fatal night? You had quarrelled?"

"Not quite, but a quarrel was coming up fast. That was when Gil burst in."

"After you'd been what you call lovers, you were dis-agreeing?"

"We hadn't been lovers – not that time – in the way you mean. She told me she thought the time had come to break it off between us."

"And you didn't want that?"

"I'd better be frank."

"Yes, I think so."

"I'd meant to say that myself. In such situations, I'd always been the one who said it. After a lot of – well, tenderness and protestations of this, that and the other."

"And you were angry because she got in ahead of you? Liberated times, Mr. Going. Liberated times."

"That was when Gil came charging in and laughed at me."

"And you conked him?"

"Yes."

"Killed him?"

"I suppose so."

"No, you don't *suppose* so. You bloody well know you did. Now look here at my picture, there on the wall. *Degrés des Âges.* Belonged to my father, the Edinburgh policeman; he valued it as a guide in crimes like yours. Mankind, male and female, walking over the great Bridge of Life. Which of those men is Gil, would you say?"

"Need we go into this?"

"Yes, or I wouldn't be doing it. Look at the picture, man. Where's Gil?"

"That one, I suppose."

"Stop your silly supposing. Of course it's Gil. *L'Âge de maturité.* And it was just when he'd reached his maturity that you killed him. What did you kill? What possibilities? Gil was an able fellow, let me tell you. He might have done some very good things, as a journalist or whatever. But you put a stop to that, didn't you? Not really meaning it, which is a fool's excuse, when the fool's bloody well gone and done it. Poor Gil! To be murdered is bad enough, but to be murdered by a posturing ninny – ! He'd have laughed, I expect. May be laughing now, for whatever I know. He had a powerful sense of irony. So – ?"

"So what?"

"So what comes next? I know what my father would have done, of course. He'd have booked you."

"You'd better get on with it and book me yourself. Phone the police. I'm ready."

"Oh, but I'm not. Not yet. You're not alone in this. There's Esme, isn't there?"

"You seem to know a lot about Esme. Have you been talking to her?"

"I'd say she's been talking to me. Came to see me earlier this evening. Sat right where you're sitting now."

"She told you about the whole thing?"

"No. She wanted to ask me about Gil's interest in the occult, as she called it."

"The occult?"

"A foolish term. Gil used to come to talk with me about metaphysics. He tried to play the hard-headed newspaper man, but he had quite a turn for metaphysics."

"Religion, you mean?"

"Don't try to tell me what I mean, Mr. Going. When I say metaphysics, I mean metaphysics. The Queen of Pastimes, the sport of the intellect, the high romance of speculative thought; infinite in scope, relying on the treacherous subtlety and learning of the player; and yet, in its daring and refusal to heed mundane considerations, capable of splendid flights into the darkness that surrounds our visible world. Metaphysics, the mother of psychology and the laughing father of psychoanalysis. A wondrous game, Mr. Going, in which the players cannot decide what the relative values of the pieces are, or how big a board they are playing on. A wondrous, wondrous diversion for a really adventurous mind."

"Gil was into that?"

"He's into it now. You put him there yourself. With your pretty magic wand, that you are playing with. I wish you'd put it down."

"Listen – don't imagine I put any belief in this moonshine you are talking about – but just tell me where you, as a metaphysician, might suppose that Gil was now?"

"That's a very big question and, as a metaphysician, I can't give you a straight reply. But suppose, for instance, that those *kundalini* fellows have the right of it. At the moment,

Gil may be having a bad time with the Lord of Death. He's a
very bad character, you know. He would put a rope around
Gil's neck and drag him about, and cut off his head, tear out
his heart, pull out his guts, lick up his brains, eat his flesh and
gnaw on his bones – and yet Gil wouldn't be able to die; he'd
feel every outrage, and revive again, and go through the same
anguish, until the Furious Lord of Death thought he needed a
wee respite, to get ready to be reborn."

"Reborn?"

"Yes. And who might it be? Esme is going to have a
child, she tells me, with a maternal satisfaction that surprised
me in her. Maybe it'll be a wee Gil. More likely not. But
there's always the outside chance. Metaphysics is a world of
chances."

"How absolutely frightful! This is preposterous!"

"I'm teasing you, Mr. Going. It's irresistible."

"Why not just say Gil's gone, and done with, and
nowhere?"

"That's what you'd like me to say, is it?"

"It's the general opinion."

"You're a drama critic. Surely you remember Ibsen? 'The
solid majority is always wrong.'"

"Oh God – my nerves are absolutely shot to hell. Listen,
McWearie, I'm sorry I called you a shit."

"Not the first and won't be the last, I'm sure."

"This whole thing is killing me. Esme – I trusted her. Of
course I knew we were coming to the end, but I trusted her.
And – I can hardly tell you – but I'm beginning to have delu-
sions. Would you believe it? This evening, as I walked
through the streets, I'd swear I had two shadows!"

"Oh? That's because you're beside yourself."

The Sniffer leaps up and grabs his stick, but Hugh is too
quick for him, and snatches it out of his hand. "You're better
off without that thing. I'll just put it up here on top of the
bookcase, along with my skull – I call him Poor Yorick, and
that's a joke a drama critic ought to understand – and I'll give
you a drink. Rye? You'd better like it because it's all I have.

Now look here. It's not at all unusual for a man in your situation to think he has two shadows. I'll give you a metaphysical tip; there are a lot of mischievous things that are likely to happen when we step a little aside from the straight path of life. Nobody really knows who is talking, or why, or casting the shadow, or making the racket in the cupboard, or breaking the bread knife or getting up to all sorts of pranks. Even Freud was at a loss to explain them, and he was a ready man with an explanation, as you know. Maybe it's the Devil. He's a very handy explanation for anything we can't figure out. Drink your drink and get a grip on yourself."

"Yes. Let's get it over."

"Get what over?"

"Phoning the police."

"I haven't the slightest intention of phoning the police."

"You're not going to turn me in?"

"Why should I do your dirty work?"

"My dirty work?"

"Yes. You wanted Father Boyle to wipe your soul clean for you, and he wouldn't. Now you want me to turn you in, and I won't. Vengeance? I don't want vengeance. Turn yourself in, man."

"Yes, but that would be doing the dirty on Esme. She'd be dragged in."

"And her fine book on bereavement would have to take a different tack. There isn't a huge public for books about how to deal with life after your lover has murdered your husband, and it would be hard for that baby, when he – or she, we must say – was twelve or so. Ah, you're very gallant, Mr. Going. But you wouldn't mind if *I* did the dirty on Esme. You'd rather be dragged away to prison than just walk there on your own two feet."

"You're not going to say anything?"

"Not a word."

"Never?"

"I never say *Never*, but in so far as in me lies – and that's a lot farther than you probably suppose – Never."

"I suppose I have to thank you."

"You won't when you've given it a little thought. Suppose I turn you in: you'd probably be charged with manslaughter, because your act was not premeditated; you'd get something like three years, and you'd be out long before that, because these days the dice are heavily loaded in favour of the murderer. It's a hot dinner for the wrongdoer, and cold potatoes for the wronged person. And after prison I suppose you'd think of yourself as a man who'd paid his debt. So I'm not doing you a great favour in letting you walk out of this room a free man, because a free man is precisely what you'll never be. You must carry that stick, or who will know you're the celebrated Mr. Going. You must live with Gil's ghost – "

"Rubbish!"

"Just hold on a minute. Do you know what a ghost is? Trace it back far enough into the old languages where it began, and it means fury, or anger. You must make peace with Gil's ghost as best you can. And now, Mr. Going, I'm sure you won't want to thank me, so I suppose that is all we have to say to one another. Don't forget your stick. Don't ever forget your stick. A good-night to you."

(9)

– WHAT A MESS of mixed motives!
– *Were yours simpler?*
– I see it differently now.
– *Of course.*
– All those people in the films – how confused they were.
– *One feels for them.*
– Pity?
– *No. Pity implies a kind of superiority.*
– Compassion, then?
– *Compassion is still a thing of high-to-low.*

– What, then?

– *Love, perhaps?*

– I think I'm coming to that, but I've always shied off from that sort of love. So often it means something limp and greasy, like an old dollar bill.

– *People do shy off from strong feeling. It's one of the dangers of civilized life.*

– I'd never thought about those earlier ones. Didn't know them, for the most part.

– *You know them now.*

– Sad. Funny. Often trivial.

– *I don't think you should say trivial.*

– Sorry. No. They fought the hero-fight with whatever they had. That can't be trivial.

– *Not when you look at the whole life.*

– I wish I'd fought the hero-fight more consciously.

– *Of course. And you wouldn't say you'd been trivial, would you?*

– Is it for me to say?

– *Who else?*

– Self-judgement, you mean?

– *What else?*

– You're very sententious. Who are you?

– *Oh, Gil – you know me.*

– My mother. You must be my mother.

– *Must? Why must I?*

– Those films. All on the father's side. Had my mother nothing to do with the making of me? Where was she?

– *You might better ask, where wasn't she?*

– Nowhere to be seen. Not a shadow of her.

– *Everywhere to be felt. The way you observed. The irony you brought to what you saw. All hers. Inescapably.*

– Then who are *you*? You say I know you. Have I forgotten?

– *Remember what McWearie said about the woman in the man?*

– So that's who you are!

– *None other.*

– Like in the old morality plays my father used to teach? Are you my Good Deeds? No? Well then, should I call you

Lady Soul? Don't laugh. Must I be more up-to-date? Are you my Anima?

– *Oh, Gil, when will you stop* naming *everything? That is just a way of pushing it aside, of putting it in a prison. Just accept what I am. Don't label me. Am I a stranger?*

– Not now that I see you. A dear companion.

– *Of course. Always a companion. Thank you for "dear."*

– And you've come to take me away?

– *Where should I take you? I'm no cleverer than you are. What do you mean by "away"?*

– I don't know.

– *And I don't know, either. We'll find out.*

– Is this part of the hero-fight?

– *Perhaps.*

– And you'll fight with me?

– *Yes, my dear, but need it be a struggle?*

– It always was.

– *Perhaps not now. Shall we begin with acceptance?*

– But for the moment –

– *No moments here. Only Now.*